KATY FAMILY

KATY FAMILY

Gemini Wahhaj

JackLeg Press
www.jacklegpress.org

ISBN: 978-1956907131

Library of Congress Control Number: 2023945703

Also by Gemini Wahhaj

The Children of This Madness

Praise for Katy Family

Katy Family is a story collection with an expansive array of voices—the lives of Bangladeshis are told through the prismatic and astute lens of remarkable storytelling. With keen craftsmanship and imagination, Gemini Wahhaj creates characters who take journeys to unknown territories, both geographically and personally. Her stories investigate how one can be familiar with many places but never at home. Her characters live between hope and grace and work to find connection in everything around them. A beautiful, vivid collection, these stories are lucid and wise, and Wahhaj is a remarkable writer."
—Nina McConigley, *Cowboys and East Indians*

Wahhaj's stories are addictive—richly observed, thrumming with sly depictions of ambition and hypocrisy, painting a luminous panorama of an American subculture in all its comic and tender complexity.
—Elizabeth McKenzie, *MacGregor Tells the World*

In *Katy Family,* Gemini Wahhaj turns her intellect, humor, and a sharp eye toward affluent, professional Bangladeshi immigrants on the outskirts of Houston, examining their fraught, ostentatious, and sometimes absurd social lives. These stories are as funny as they are poignant and as sharp as they are tender. Full of surprise and delight, without a hint of exoticism or nostalgia, these American lives are reflected back to us in ways you would never expect. You will love this collection.
—Chaitali Sen, *A New Race of Men from Heaven*

Gemini Wahhaj's *Katy Family* is an exceptionally accomplished and perceptive short-story collection. At times, it's also very funny. Wahhaj's insights into the contradictory forces of nostalgia and attachment; ambition, competition, and scorn that her characters, many of them émigrés to the U.S., experience in regard to their homeland, brought to mind Jhumpa Lahiri's *Interpreter of Maladies*. Above all, however, Wahhaj understands the contrariness of the human heart. *Katy Family* is a terrific book.
—Christine Marie Sneed, *Please Be Advised: A Novel in Memos, Little Known Facts*, and *Paris*

For Maha and Luka and Arif

Contents

Gracious   1

Patent   16

The Lady Doctor   24

Katy Family   36

The American Cousin   50

Nature   63

Confetti   73

Dreams and Memories   80

The Frame   89

Meghalaya   101

Next Door   110

Urgency   123

The English Teacher   135

Cigarette   149

The Wheels of Progress   157

Two Mothers   170

Marker   189

The Limits of Speech   208

Three Sisters   235

Camping   258

Borders   278

Acknowledgments   306

Gracious

I first started to look for a nanny when my son turned six months old, and I had to return to work at the oil company where I'm a senior executive. My friend Ella suggested several women she had used for Brianna (Her lovely daughter Brianna is now eighteen and a freshman at Harvard, can you believe it?), but I was concerned about the immigration status of these women.

"Do they have papers, Ella?" I asked. "I don't want to get in trouble for hiring someone without proper documents!"

We were talking on the phone. Ella giggled sheepishly. Little bubbles of laughter sounded at the other end, as if cascading from her mouth. "They don't have papers, Nadiya. That was always our little secret, between the women and me. But, Nadiya, if they don't have papers, they charge less anyway."

"Hmm." I demurred, but I knew, and Ella knew, that I would have to return to work in a week.

"With a Spanish-speaking nanny, Rubaiyat will be able to learn Spanish," I could hear Ella's voice knocking on the other end, punching in the air confidently. "Learning a foreign language when young is so good for cognitive development! Besides, knowing Spanish is a huge asset anywhere in America, especially in Texas."

"That's it, Ella, I'm sold!" I said. "Find me a nanny with papers, and we have a deal."

Ella and I worked in the same division of our company, downstream, and we lived two blocks from each other. What I like about our subdivision, about the whole township of Fulshear, really, is that all our neighbors are of a certain caliber. Everyone is a professional–an engineer or lawyer or accountant. You couldn't afford a house in this neighborhood otherwise!

The day before I was supposed to return to work, I was still without a nanny. I was stressed out and panicking about what I would do about the baby, when I received a call on my cellphone from an unknown number. I almost didn't pick it up. But then I did.

"*Ha—llo*," a timid voice said.

"Yes? Who is it?" I demanded in an irritated voice, cradling my son Rubaiyat in one arm. I'd just picked him up from the highchair. His face and onesie were covered in banana mush.

"Sorry, is Mrs. Nadiya? My name is Grace. Mrs. Ella give me your number."

"Oh. Oh!" I said. "Are you calling about the nanny position?"

She confirmed this in a shaky, cracked voice belonging to an older person.

"Do you have references? How long have you worked as a nanny? If you don't mind, I'll have to do a background check on you. Can you bring your driver's license?" I fired away the questions as I wiped Rubaiyat's face and tray.

She took some time to understand and answer each question.

Normally, I would set up an interview. But there was so little time that I just called Ella again to find out more about the woman. Ella came right over to our house, bracelets jangling on her wrists, strands of dry, blonde hair stylishly piled on top of her neck. Ella was older than my husband Halim and me, with spots on her skin, all over her cheeks and arms. The corners of her mouth had started to gather like crows' feet. She had just had surgery done to fix the skin around her eyes. She intended to tackle her mouth next. Thinking that I would get the same procedure when it was my time, I'd already taken the name of the dermatologist from her, in case she retired and moved away before I got to her age.

Ella and I sat down at the kitchen table, bought at Pier One Imports, to have tea. Rubaiyat was asleep in his room for an afternoon nap, thank God!

"Listen, my friend Jody used her, used Grace. Jody says she is just the loveliest human being. Jody's two children speak perfect Spanish, thanks to Grace. One is settled in Venezuela as a missionary, and another is a big-time lawyer in New York."

"Okay. I guess I have no choice," I said, making a face and parting my bangs with my hands. "I have to go back to work tomorrow. And Halim is just not cooperating. He won't take the day off."

Ella stayed for an hour, reassuring me. In the end, I agreed to let Grace look after Rubaiyat for the day. I just asked her to bring her driver's license on her first day of work. I would stay for an hour to make sure everything was all right and Halim would come back early from his office.

Grace arrived the next morning. She was a skeleton of a person, a little stooped, with thin hair and colorless lips that almost disappeared into her gums. Honestly, she didn't look like she had much to eat. Halim and I talked hurriedly in Bangla, in sharp whispers, in our bedroom upstairs.

"I'm nervous. She looks old and feeble," I hissed, pulling on my pre-pregnancy black dress pants, too tight, and my old georgette top, also tight.

"She's not as old as she looks," Halim said. "She just looks like a woman who's had a hard life." He was standing with his arms folded, speaking to me in a patient, reassuring voice.

Who was he reassuring? I knew he didn't want to be saddled with the baby any more than I did. We emerged from the bedroom together and climbed downstairs. Grace handed me her driver's license and Halim made a copy of it on our scanner. Indeed, the woman's ID showed that Halim was right–she was just forty, younger than Ella! I took Grace up the grand staircase to the fourth bedroom on the landing, which we had painted a light blue color with a wall panel of elephants by the famous interior designer Jordie Thomas. Do you know her? She's really good! We paid ten thousand dollars for the design.

As soon as Grace and I entered Rubaiyat's room, he started wailing, throwing his fat arms in the air.

"Oh, he's beautiful!" Grace lifted him in her thin arms.

I watched them carefully.

"Oh, I will love him, Mrs. Nadiya," she said, a smile breaking over her pale lips.

I noticed that little wrinkles appeared all around her eyes as she spoke.

"Okay. Here is my number and here is my husband's number. Anything you need, anything, you can call us." I spoke kindly, making my voice gentle, so as not to alarm her. She seemed like such a frail person.

"Thank you, Mrs. Nadiya."

The fat baby, my fat Rubaiyat, who looked so big that most people mistook him for eight months old, squirmed in her arms. She seemed barely able to hold him. She must have noticed my trembling mouth because she said, "I can manage."

"Right. Let me show you the refrigerator, and what he eats. I make a rice dish for him with lots of vegetables. It's called khichuri. I store it in a Tupperware container on the top shelf of the refrigerator. And I'll show you where his clothes are…"

She followed me around, carrying the baby, as I showed her the clothes, the diapers, the diaper rash cream, all the things. Then, for the first time in six months, I left the house on my own, climbed into my black Mercedes all by myself, with a destination ahead, dreaming of my little cubicle. I drove eighty miles per hour all the way downtown, with nineties music blasting on my radio, singing along to the songs.

The background check on Grace came back in a few days. Everything was fine. Grace turned out to be great all around. Rubaiyat ate well, gained weight, slept soundly, and seemed to like his nanny. Grace did extra work around the house in addition to looking after Rubaiyat, a perk that Ella had promised with a wink. If Rubaiyat took a nap, Grace did the laundry, vacuumed his room, and even cooked khichuri for him, the way I had taught her. Soon, I got lazy. After dinner in the evening, I'd leave dishes in the sink instead of trying to cram them in the dishwasher. I had a lot on my plate at work. Even after returning from work, my eyes heavy, I had to cook dinner, feed Rubaiyat, and give Rubaiyat a bath, so it was nice that someone else could take over these little things for me. I would put the laundry in the washing machine and Grace would turn it on the next day, transfer the clothes to the dryer, and then fold them if she had time. Every morning, I would hand over a squirming Rubaiyat to Grace, apply lipstick and face powder and my tea perfume, and be off. It was nice.

It was also nice to be back at work. My friends plied me with gifts. My junior colleagues took me out to lunch. The first few years at the company, I'd had to work really hard to prove my worth. People don't expect an engineer from Bangladesh to amount to much. My colleagues had no idea about my university or my qualifications. I had to work really hard, and I also had to be confident and answer people who made snide remarks about my output, trying to put me down.

Five months went by smoothly. One day, Halim and I were sitting at the table, eating dinner. Rubaiyat, whom we'd started to call Ruby, same as Ella did, was perched on a highchair eating avocado, when he started crying, *Mas. Mas.*

"What's going on?" I cried in a panic, patting my cheeks with my hands. No matter what I did, I couldn't console him.

At last, Halim rose from his chair and lifted Ruby out of his seat. Avocado spattered the floor. Thank goodness we'd had the carpets removed and wood floors installed the year before. Even in Halim's arms, Ruby wouldn't stop crying.

"*Mas. Mas!*" he cried, his face red.

I called Ella in tears. "I don't know what's wrong with him. He was with Grace all day yesterday. Do you think she *did* something?"

"Oh, Nadiya! He's asking for more of whatever you were giving him," Ella said. "Spanish, baby. What did I say?"

I got off the phone, ran to the fridge, and brought out an avocado. I cut it in such a rush that the knife slipped off the seed and almost slit my thumb. Ruby was flailing in Halim's arms and Halim had his eyes shut from the tension, but as soon as I put a piece of the pasty green fruit in my baby's mouth, he stopped screaming and started swallowing, lips champing together.

"Well, well," I said, so proud.

After that, we learned more Spanish words from Ruby. Agua. Gracias. Hola. In fact, after Ma and Baba, the names he called Halim and me, most of the words Ruby picked up were Spanish. Foreign language, check.

Of course, with time, there were some problems. One day, Grace's beat-up old Toyota got hit by another car, so she had to take the day off to chase after that driver's insurance and get her car repaired. I had to take two days off to look after the baby. Unfortunately, the day Grace returned to work, I was backing my car out of the driveway, in a hurry to get to the office, and I backed into *her* car, making a hand-sized dent on the passenger side. She had parked with the nose of the car blocking the driveway. Anyone would have made the same mistake in my place! I ran inside the house, saying I was sorry and that I would pay for it. She came out with me to the street to look at the damage. She said it was okay since she had to get much bigger repairs done anyway.

Another day, while I was crunching numbers at my desk at the office, Grace called me on my cellphone. The phone rang loudly. I fished it out of my Coach handbag, looking around shamefacedly at my colleagues in the other cubicles.

"Hello? Is everything okay?" I hissed in a low voice.

"Mrs. Nadiya. My friend is here with me at the park. She wants to take me and Ruby to her house. Is okay with you we go?"

"No, no, no!" I shouted in a panic, forgetting that I was in the office. "Please, no! I have no idea who she is or if she has a valid license, and…sorry, but no."

"Of course. Yes. I did not think. She is my friend, but you don't know her."

"Yes. Yes, exactly."

Oddly, another incident took place about a week after this exchange. I used to be the first one to leave the office, at the earliest I could. Halim always came back at least two hours later. He was more ambitious, and climbing faster at the company, and put in more hours than me. One day, I came home, fighting rush hour traffic to find Ruby in the living room holding a large plastic cup from McDonald's full of a bright blue sugary drink. He was half crawling, half walking on the wood floor of the double-height living room, also designed by Jordie Thomas, in an off-white scheme, with off-white leather couches and white shelves lined with white-cover books only, and large white paintings (It had been really fun picking out the white paintings with Jordie). Rubaiyat reached me, giggling, extending his arms with that awful plastic thing still dangling from his fat fingers. I stooped and picked him up, sniffing him.

"He smells…sticky," I said, coiling my mouth.

Behind Ruby, standing straight with her hands clasped in front of her faded dress, Grace smiled nervously, showing the wrinkles around her mouth. Her hair was dry and loose, spilling out of her bun in strands. "He was drinking that," she said, pointing to the McDonald's cup with a dome lid and straw.

"It's a sugary drink?" I said. I was too upset to say more. I couldn't believe my son was out in the world without me, at a cheap, fast-food restaurant, God knows in what neighborhood, drinking a McDonald's drink. What if there had been a shooting at this place? What if something had happened to him? I kept my face averted from Grace. My heart thumped and my hands around Ruby's neck were icy cold.

After some minutes, as Grace was packing to leave, putting Ruby's toys away in slow motion, then picking up her torn, black handbag from the white couch, I asked her calmly, "Where is this McDonald's?"

"Oh. Mrs. Nadiya, is the one at the mall. I walked there. I took the stroller. I didn't take him in the car. My friend looks after another baby, so we met there."

I didn't say anything else, but really, what was she thinking? I was very alarmed. Had she not understood me when I had spoken to her the last time about meeting with this unknown friend?

Another time, perhaps that very week, I came home early from work one day. I'd been feeling a little sick and, also, missing Ruby too much. It was nearly his one-year birthday, and my mind was occupied with plans for his birthday party. I had organized a grand party at the Maharaja Restaurant on Highway 6 with one hundred invited guests. I found Ruby asleep on our white leather couch, alone and naked, his mouth sticky with some yellow food. Granted, it was May and steamy in Houston, but I was taken aback by his state of undress. It was cool enough inside the house? I mean, after all, we had central air-conditioning! I went to find Grace. I ran up the stairs and then back down. Then I climbed up a second time, looking in every room on the second floor. For a few minutes, my pressure climbed and climbed. When I was running back down, my bare feet almost slipped on the carpeted steps, I was going so fast. Standing in the living room, I got on the phone to call Grace, trying to locate exactly where she was in the house, when she appeared in the kitchen directly across from the living room. She wore a faded pink dress down to her knees with pantyhose and a cardigan, in this stuffy weather.

"Where were you?" I asked breathlessly, whipping my head.

She took some time to reply. "I was just in the garden. I was making a vegetable bed for you."

"Oh." I was still panting.

"The baby was sleeping. So I thought I would do some gardening." She bowed her head politely as she spoke to me, and yet, she seemed to do whatever she wished!

I glanced at the clock perched high on the kitchen wall, shaped like Dali's clock in that famous painting. I bought it at the Museum of Modern Art in New York for three hundred dollars. Going by that time, she still had two hours to work. Hurriedly, I did the math in my head. Two times twenty equals forty dollars.

"Listen, since I'm back, you can have the rest of the day off?" I suggested.

Grace raised her head in surprise, then nodded. "Yes. Sure."

Turning on the faucet above the kitchen sink, she began to scrub her knobby fingers. She worked slowly, drying her hands with the towel hanging from the holder (I planned to throw the towel in the wash immediately after she left), and then finally locating her handbag with cheap, chipped, painted leather, lying on top of my white sofa. I walked to my own purse sitting on the hall table and began to count out seven times twenty, one hundred forty dollars, minus the forty dollars for the two hours. The little mathematician in me felt triumphant. I'd saved forty dollars!

"Thank you so much," I said, handing her the cash.

By the time I saw Grace again, on Monday, I had collected myself a little after her strange behavior. I'd told Ella about it. The nanny had left my precious baby alone and disappeared to the backyard, as if she didn't understand her job description or something. She had left the baby alone inside the house for God knows how long while she had been gardening outside! I'd also talked to Halim, who talked about installing a camera (only talked about it. Why *hadn't* we done this already?).

But on Monday morning, I smiled sweetly at Grace as I piled on frosted pink lipstick.

"There's some cake for you in the refrigerator. From the birthday party. Feel free to help yourself," I said.

Grace was carrying a sleepy Ruby in her arms, his snug, milky body burrowed into the folds of her neck, next to her skin.

"Thank you, Mrs. Nadiya. You are very kind."

"Okay, then. I'll see you in a few hours?" I had an important meeting that day. I was wearing a blue blazer I'd bought for the meeting especially and matching blue high heels.

"Mrs. Nadiya, I wanted to talk to you about something."

"Really?" I frowned, my mind on the meeting and the traffic that would build up on I-10 in another five minutes.

"Yes, I…"

"Can you follow me downstairs if you want to say something? I'm late for work."

"Okay."

We'd been standing in Ruby's room. I took the stairs two at a time, and she followed behind slowly with the baby.

At the foot of the stairs, she came to a stop again. "Mrs. Nadiya. I have decided something. I have a friend in Atlanta. Her husband got deported…"

My eyes shot out in alarm. "Oh, no."

"Yes, is very sad…"

"Uh." I began to look around in panic. Now it was really getting late. If I missed the moment, I would be stewing in traffic for an hour.

"She has five children, aged ten to infant."

"I can call you from work later? We can talk on the phone. At lunchtime? I have an important meeting."

I walked to the front door and opened it. Grace followed behind, holding Ruby upright in her arms, his dark head of bushy hair nestled next to her hair.

"My friend's two youngest children, after the new baby, they are one and three. I want to adopt them."

"Oh." I was now standing outside the house, dangling my car key in my hand.

Did I tell you about our house? It is one of the famous architectural pieces of Houston, a unique build by an architect, not a standard build by a developer. It's three stories high with turrets and Roman columns, a swimming pool on the roof, and deep woods adjacent to our backyard.

Behind me on the street, other neighbors were backing their cars out of their driveways, in a rush to get on the highway before the traffic hit, but Grace was still talking.

"Yes. That's why…I'm afraid is not going to be possible for me to look after Ruby anymore."

"What?"

"I wanted to tell you on Friday…I only found out on Friday."

"Can we talk later?" I squealed in a panic.

Can you believe it? That was the last day she worked for us. Not even two weeks' notice. Even Ella agreed that it was very bad manners. As a matter of fact, Ella's daughter Breanna called her from Harvard and when Ella told her daughter about how Grace had left, even Breanna was shocked. Ella told her friend Josie too, the one who had originally recommended Grace to us, and Josie said she was so sorry, she would never recommend Grace to anyone else again.

But the thing was, I was desperate now for another person, any person. Ella couldn't come up with anyone. I tried a few agencies, calling numbers Ella gave me. It was such a long process! And honestly, I didn't like any of the four women I interviewed. One was too young, and another woman kept looking around the house with shifty eyes, as if she might steal something. While Grace had worked for us, I'd taken care to lock away my jewelry in a safe at the bank, but now I was even more panicky than when we had hired Grace. In the end, I called Grace again, begging her to come back.

"Are you sure you can't look after Ruby also, in addition to those two kids? Perhaps those kids can come with you? Some company would be good for him anyway. All the daycare centers are booked a year in advance. We're still on the waitlist everywhere. Please! Until I figure something else out."

"Mrs. Nadiya. I have a daughter who can help you."

"A daughter? How old?"

"Twenty-six."

How could this woman, whose driver's license said she was forty years old, have a twenty-six-year-old daughter?

"She has twins, ten years old, but she can leave them with a friend," Grace said.

"Okay," I said out of desperation.

I called the daughter, Joy, and told her to bring her driver's license. While waiting for Joy's background check, I had to take two days off work, unpaid. I felt really abandoned by Grace. How could she leave me in a lurch like this? Had she no care for the child in her charge, Ruby? I said as much to Halim over dinner.

As soon as the background check came in, I called Joy and asked her to start work the next day, breathing a sigh of relief when I got off the phone.

But the next day, Joy never showed up. I called her. She didn't pick up my calls either, so then I called Grace. I could hear babbling in the background–the kids she had picked up from Atlanta.

"Joy's phone got cut off," Grace explained calmly. "She didn't pay her bill." She didn't seem the least bit perturbed about the mess in which she and her daughter had placed me. Her voice cracked like the first time I had heard it, old, feeble, and distant, and wholly unreliable.

"What do I do now?" I wailed.

"Sorry. She is not being responsible."

"Well, could *you* come in? Just for today? I'm in a lurch here."

"Sorry, Mrs. Nadiya. I can't. I have the two children. My friend's children I told you about. I bring them from Atlanta to raise them."

In the end, I persuaded her to come anyway. Just for a day. To try it, I said, to see if the arrangement would work. She arrived with the two kids she had adopted, one thin little boy half of Ruby's size, who was supposed to be a year old. The sister, two years older, was shorter than Ruby. She stood by the wall, her face shy and vacant, trembling. I left the four of them behind, trembling at what might happen in the ten hours I would be gone. But I must say, I am an extremely lucky person! While I was at work, I got a call from a daycare center that had had our name for a year on their waitlist. They said that they had an opening for Ruby. It was a very prestigious school, too, a Montessori school, with gardening and foreign languages. Ella's daughter Breanna used to go there.

I spent the rest of the day happy and elated, full of gratitude to Grace, and forgiveness too, even though she had left our service and Ruby without notice like that and put us in such a bad place. When I returned from work, it was still light outside, a summer evening, with the sun blazing in the kitchen window.

The three kids played together in the living room, speaking in a mixture of Spanish and English.

"My husband and I drove to Atlanta and picked them up," Grace said.

We were standing in the doorway of the living room, gazing at the children together. Her face looked brighter than I had ever seen it, younger almost, although the skin was still loose, and the folds were still there.

"Grace, that was nice of you to help your friends by taking her kids," I said.

At these words, she started to cry. Great, big sobs fell from her mouth, and her thin shoulders began to heave as she put her face in her hands. I could see the top of her head with its untidy grey hairs.

"Is everything okay?" I said. I had never seen her express much emotion at all.

"Thank you, Mrs. Nadiya. Thank you for saying that. Only you understand! All my friends said that I did a very foolish thing, taking such a big responsibility, when my husband and I do not have much money." She wiped her eyelids with all her fingers and opened her eyes again. "Is a big responsibility. But I had to do it. Otherwise, who will look after the children? My friend, their mother, is not well. She just sits there. She too depressed."

I looked at the kids again. The boy was playing with Ruby, bubbling with giggles. His sister was standing quietly in a corner with big eyes, observing the two boys.

"She has some problems. I took her to a doctor. She needs speech therapy," Grace said, indicating the little girl. "The doctor thinks it was caused by the trauma she went through at home."

Grace began to prepare to leave, calling to the boy and the girl, the children she cared for now, to pack up.

"Wait a minute!" I spluttered in a burst of generosity.

I rushed about the living room and gathered up some of the toys Ruby no longer used. I had meant to donate them anyway. After all, I had to make space for the hundred birthday presents he had received at his one-year birthday party. While Grace stood with her chipped handbag over her shoulder, I cried *"Wait!"* again, ran upstairs to the nursery and picked up some of the clothes Ruby had gotten too big for, and stuffed them in tall trash bags from the kitchen cabinet. For the next several minutes, I moved maniacally around the house in a great burst of activity, picking up board books and baby toys, expensive things too, big toys that had cost thirty, forty dollars apiece, like the clunky Fisher-Price contraptions with buttons and sounds.

Then I returned to Grace, who was still standing between the kitchen and the living room, her hands gathered in front of her. She had on a smart white dress today, with little embroidered flowers.

"Here! These are for the children!" I gasped, holding out the trash bags.

"Thank you," she said with red eyes. "You are very kind."

"And here." I counted out the hundred and forty dollars I owed her for the day, fishing the notes from the purse still hanging from my shoulder (I had not taken off my shoes either). My eyes fell on the two twenty-dollar bills I had saved on that earlier occasion, when I had let her off because Ruby was sleeping. On a whim, I produced the two bills, crisp and flat, and handed them to her. "For the children."

Grace began to cry again, the second time that day. She pulled me to her chest and embraced me hard. Our necks nestled, head against head, my moisturized cheeks against the rasp of her sandpaper skin. She smelled of cinnamon and cloves and something faintly floral.

"You are so kind. Thank you," she said.

"Of course. No problem," I said. "I'll look after the children while you put the bags in the car."

She nodded and walked outside with a trash bag in each hand to her bent-up Toyota parked on the street while I watched the children playing together for the last time. My heart expanded, as our hearts do sometimes, filled by our little acts of kindness. I watched the children shout and laugh, and I beamed and beamed and beamed at my own grace.

Patent

Mirza was a brilliant scientist. While pursuing his PhD in mechanical engineering at the University of Texas at Austin, he made an important discovery in his field and published a paper with his supervisor that had been cited no less than fifteen thousand times and earned him a patent.

Among his classmates from his alma mater, the Bangladesh University of Engineering and Technology, he was a legend, the guy who had made it. At forty, Mirza was head of his division at a multinational engineering company in Houston, with fifty engineers working under him. His salary was half a million dollars. He lived in a one-point-two-million-dollar home in The Woodlands, built on a two-acre lot that backed onto woods. The whole property was meticulously landscaped, with trimmed edges, stone patios, trellises, a circular gravel driveway long enough to park ten cars, and a rose garden tended by gardeners. The house itself was massive, with six bedrooms, two staircases, and three garages, and filled with guests the year around.

In person, Mirza was as spectacular as his many public images, published on websites and in glossy magazine articles about him, a smooth, rich complexion, a head full of black hair, pink lips and even, white teeth. At six feet one inch, he towered above all his friends. Only the people in his inner circle, the Bangladeshi engineers who lived in Houston whom Mirza and his wife Sumona considered their friends, knew about a darker side to his character. In casual conversation among friends, Mirza tended to shout and curse. He got angry if anyone contradicted him, especially on a point of science, no matter how small the point of difference. His peers, who had not been so successful and had resigned themselves to mid-level jobs simply to earn money to support their families, felt the sting of his sharp tongue especially. The thriving, handsome, rosy Mirza reminded them of all the gall of their disappointments.

On that particular day in December, Mirza and Sumona had invited about ten families, their close friends belonging to an elite group who had nicknamed themselves the double "BUETicians," meaning that both husband and wife of each family had graduated from their prestigious alma mater in Bangladesh. They often referred to themselves as the cream of the cream, as only a small, select group of students got admitted to BUET out of the tens of thousands of people who passed their higher secondary exams all over the country.

For the occasion, Sumona had catered food from a famous restaurant in Houston, choosing their most expensive menu items. The housekeeper and gardeners had been preparing the house and grounds for a week. On the day of the party, Sumona retained two servers to help her. Everything in her house shone with an extra brilliance, including Sumona, decked out in a peacock blue silk sari and gold earrings that Mirza had bought her for their sixteenth wedding anniversary.

Mirza and the other men were lounging in the massive living room, a thirty-feet long, split-level hall with a baby grand piano and glass-fronted showcase placed on the upper level and a set of white leather sectionals arranged on a sunken lower level around an expensive white carpet. A flatscreen TV of the newest model was mounted on a wall, and directional lights flooded the room. Mirza sat in a relaxed posture on one of the white armchairs, his arms draped over the arms of the chair, dressed in an expensive, brand-name silk shirt that Sumona had bought him, with the sleeves rolled up a little, laughing frankly as his friends congratulated him on his latest project, which he had just told them about.

One of his friends Javed started to talk about a pair of engineers in Bangladesh who had built a cheap, low-tech device to clean polluted water using very mundane science. According to Javed, this pair were giving away their technology for free in all the villages and urban slums in Bangladesh.

"You see, the villagers were suffering from diarrhea because of unclean water on the one hand and arsenic poisoning from tube wells on the other. Already, lots of villagers are using this device and getting relief. Everybody is praising their invention!" Javed said excitedly.

He spoke in a long-winded, rambling way. His friends often had trouble understanding him. He was a disorderly person, with dirty fingernails and receding hair, with flecks of dandruff visible on his scalp. He had had to change jobs five times in the past ten years, not out of choice but because he had been laid off. Several times, he had had to ask for help from his friends, Mirza among them, for a loan or for employment. Now he was speaking in a high, nasal voice that annoyed Mirza.

"What stupid mundane science are you talking about? How can they ever hope to scale up their project?" Mirza challenged Javed with flashing eyes. He was still sitting in a relaxed posture, with his legs apart, and he had not raised his voice, but something in his tone hurt Javed's ego.

"Listen! They are helping their country!" Javed cried out in a high, childish voice. "That's what's important. They stayed in Bangladesh, and now they are doing something that is meaningful for Bangladesh. Our country gave us practically a free education. And what are we doing with that education, just working for money?"

"Speak for yourself," Mirza said, smiling coolly, showing his perfect white teeth. "You may have self-doubt about what you have accomplished. I'm doing very well for myself."

"That's not what I meant!" Javed cried with frustration, shaking his head. "I'm not talking about whether you are successful or not," he continued in the same shouting voice. "You can be as successful as you want. You can achieve personal excellence working for a private multinational company. But—so what? All your achievements are individual at best. They are only for yourself, to boast about, and then what? Nothing you do extends beyond yourself! Our friends who stayed behind in

Bangladesh do things for their country, to make their country proud!"

Javed's eyes were red and puffy, and he looked a little mad, as if, their friends would gossip later, as if he were a little jealous of Mirza and trying to show him up!

"Javed," another friend who had also got his first job through Mirza cut in gently. "What are *you* doing for Bangladesh? You're living in Houston and working for a private company just like the rest of us."

"I'm not talking about myself!" Javed cried, shutting his eyes in frustration. "I mean, what I am trying to say is, all our friends in Bangladesh, anyone who stayed back, each one of them is doing a far better job of giving back to their country."

"If you feel that way," Mirza said, still smiling, "why don't you go back?"

"This isn't about me," Javed muttered, squirming and looking away. "I'm a failure. I admit it. I'm just talking about your idea of achievement. All of you sitting here who think you are so successful."

"Mirza is a genius!" another man piped up loyally. "He has a patent in his name! He, of all people, has made Bangladesh proud!"

"Ha!" Javed scoffed, rubbing his unshaved chin. He went on in a nasal, spiteful tone. "What will come of all his achievements? No one carries his achievements to his grave!"

Mirza stopped smiling. He stood up abruptly, walked to the thermostat, and turned down the temperature by a few degrees Fahrenheit. "I'll go check on the food," he said, exiting the massive, bright living room.

The shameless Javed stayed for dinner even after this altercation, although some of his friends avoided talking further with him. Later, the friends remarked that, as rude as Javed had been, it was weird that Mirza, ordinarily so loud and so forceful, had gone so quiet. Some argued that it was Mirza's coolness that betrayed how unnerved he had been by Javed's mad speech about the meaninglessness of all his achievements.

Six months later, Mirza called his intimate friends one by one to give them the bad news. "Friend, I have just been diagnosed with brain tumor. Yes, cancer. It's very aggressive. The doctors said I have hardly six months to live."

Mirza's illness was as elegant and as precise as the rest of his life. Within six months, he died quietly at a hospital. He left behind a brilliant and beautiful wife, Sumona, who was doing well professionally as a civil engineer, and two sons away at college, one at Berkeley and one at Stanford.

The children flew back for the funeral, which Sumona called "a memorial". A select group of close friends was invited, all respectable, high-achieving people. Sumona called some of Mirza's closest friends, asking them to say a few words about him, and told them exactly what to say. No sad words and no downers, she commanded. Just a memorial at Mirza's house celebrating his life and all that he had achieved. She even emailed them each a script, listing all the accolades they should mention in their speeches.

The memorial turned out to be another big party, just like the parties Mirza and Sumona used to throw for their friends when Mirza had been alive. For the occasion, Sumona got a new haircut, in layers that cascaded down her shoulders, and ordered a matted silk sari in a peacock blue shade, Mirza's favorite color, from an online shop. She looked dazzling in a gold choker at her slender, long neck and the big gold earrings that Mirza had given her at their last wedding anniversary, just over a year ago.

Many of the friends gathered had been frequent visitors at their house during the past six months while Mirza had been sick, smuggling him his favorite white milk chocolate and butter cookies, all the things that Sumona and his doctors had forbidden him to eat. On several occasions, Mirza had sneaked out of the house, lying to Sumona that he was going for a grocery run, and driven fifty minutes to Javed's house in Sugarland, to smoke a cigarette, a habit he had given up a long time ago at Sumona's advice during his rise to brilliance but missed terribly during his illness. The two friends would step out onto Javed's messy backyard and stand in the tall grass under the sun or the moon or a dark sky, smoking and chatting about their university days.

Sumona started the ceremony by playing a long reel of Mirza, showing him as a young student at the engineering university in Bangladesh, then at his PhD graduation, and other shots in which he was accepting an award or another. During the video, a voiceover recorded by Mirza and Sumona's eldest son, the one at Berkeley, related all his life's achievements in a rich, deep timbre–being accepted to BUET, as the cream of the cream, earning a full scholarship to pursue his PhD at the preeminent University of Texas in Austin, his academic papers, and the patent in his name.

All of Mirza's friends, decked out in dark suits, sat before the projector screen with teary eyes, deeply moved by the emotional combination of sound and image. Then it was their turn to speak. One friend stood up and talked about Mirza's groundbreaking paper in detail, as he had been directed by Sumona, explaining the science on a Powerpoint presentation. Another friend talked about the patent in Mirza's name. A classmate read aloud from his own article in memoriam published in a Bangladeshi newspaper about the great Mirza, the pride of their nation, who had put Bangladesh on the map! Finally, Javed took the stage. In a deeply emotional voice, Javed talked about how Mirza had helped him, and countless others, in their careers, but especially him, Javed. When he was at his lowest point, when he had just graduated from his master's program and was unable to find a job in America, it was Mirza who had given him a job and brought him to Houston, Javed revealed to his friends, his eyes brimming with tears. His speech was the most emotional, the most heartfelt, and the most moving of them all. Later, the friends would agree that the awful argument at Mirza's party last December had been just that, a heated, intellectual argument between two friends. Neither had meant anything by it. Javed had not meant it at all as a personal attack against Mirza, and Mirza, of course, had not taken his words to heart.

After the speeches, Mirza's friends and family drove in a procession of cars to the Forest Lawn cemetery in the south of the city. They huddled together in their shawls and caps on the cold Houston winter day as two workers sitting in their tractors dug up a deep grave, pulling away the mud and piling it in heaps around the grave with their machinery. Four of Mirza's friends, including Javed, lifted his wood coffin onto their shoulders and descended into the earth, trembling under the burden of his weight. After lowering Mirza's body into the soil, they climbed out of the hole, pulling up one another by grasping hands.

Sumona stepped away from the pavilion where the rest of the party had been gathered and approached the freshly dug grave where her husband had been lowered, flanked by her two sons. She had covered her head loosely with the edge of her blue sari. Her shoulders were adorned with a Pashmina shawl, a gift from Mirza from one of his business trips. Whether from the cold weather or from a deeper emotion, Sumona shivered slightly, jerking her chin in the air. Then, unzipping her large leather purse, she pulled out a tube of paper tied up with a red ribbon and dropped it into the freshly dug grave. It fell to the bottom with a thud.

"What is that?" Javed asked curiously, turning his head.

"A laminated copy of his patent," Sumona said. "He asked for it to be buried with him."

She moved back to the pavilion, accompanied by her sons. After a few minutes, the four men who had lowered the coffin rejoined the party at the pavilion. Together, they watched quietly as the small digger moved back and forth, picking up clumps of earth and dropping them into the hole. Mirza's friends were clothed in jackets, cardigans, and shawls, but they shrank and shivered in the cold as they stared at the earth that would seep into the coffin, surrounding Mirza's body, the body that would rot as it was eaten by insects and bacteria and become one with the earth, all except for the plastic patent certificate, which would remain forever as a testament to the greatness of the man buried there. When the scientists of the future dug up Mirza's grave,

they would know instantly, from his rolled-up certificate, what
kind of man he was and recognize him as a man of great stature.

The Lady Doctor

Dr. Hasina Rasheed had been excited to be invited to her first party in Houston, where she was visiting her daughter, but within minutes of entering the drawing room of the monstrous house in Sugarland, she was shepherded to a small alcove to the side by the hostess, with the words, "Aunty, sit here. I invited my other friends' mothers so you would have company." The hostess (what was her name? Dina? Mina?) was a frail, young thing, short and thin with a pale, slender face. Dr. Rasheed thought that her eyes were set too wide apart.

Hasina Rasheed herself towered above every other woman at the party, and even some of the men. When her husband, the *other* Dr. Rasheed, had been alive, she had carefully abstained from wearing high heels so she would not tower above him. At five foot eight, she cut a majestic figure, with broad shoulders, a long neck, and a large head. Now that she had grown stout in her middle age, she looked even more imperious.

"Here, Aunty, sit. This is Jharna Bhabi's mother," the hostess (Dina?) said, almost pushing Dr. Rasheed down on a high dining chair next to a fat woman shrouded in an ashy silk sari and an ugly gray shawl.

Hasina Rasheed took one look at the woman's garments and decided that they were very impractical. The poor woman seemed hobbled by all the loose, floating garments of her get-up. Since arriving in Houston, Dr. Rasheed had traded the starched, cotton saris she wore to her medical practice in Dhaka for shalwar kameez suits of a synthetic material that required no ironing or starch. She had had the three-piece outfits tailored hastily at a shop at Gawsia Market before flying to the US. As a matter of fact, she was dressed in one of these shalwar kameez now, a practical outfit that left her arms and legs free to move swiftly.

"I will bring you some appetizers here, Aunty...," Dina (or Mina?) said.

"My name is not Aunty!" Hasina Rasheed barked. This was the third time the hostess had addressed her in this manner. "Call me Dr. Rasheed. I am a lady doctor. A gynecologist."

"Oh!" The hostess smiled widely, wearing a simple, unintelligent expression on her face.

"What is *your* name?" Hasina Rasheed demanded of the girl.

"Pinky."

"Pinky, do you know what kind of doctor a gynecologist is? I have treated thousands of women like you in my career."

"Yes, Aunty," Pinky said, nodding readily and smiling with a toothy grin and a vacant look in her eyes.

Gay laughter exploded from the drawing room, where there was evidently much excitement afoot. Dr. Rasheed had been having a great time in that room, consorting with three smartly dressed young women. She had been sitting next to them on the deep sofas, asking them what they each did and expounding on the current political situation in Bangladesh, when she had been so rudely pulled away and exiled to this dead corner.

"Excuse me, Aunty," Pinky said, "I'm just coming." Pinky hurried off.

Dr. Rasheed crossed her arms, rubbing them in the chilled room, and glanced at her wordless companion. "Salam." She nodded curtly to the dowdy figure seated beside her. "What is your name?"

"I am Jharna's mother," the old lady mumbled.

"I don't know who Jharna is. I asked you what *your* name is. Speak up! You're not a little girl anymore. What do you do?"

"I don't do anything," Jharna's mother said, glancing up with a fearful look in her eye, before going back to spooning her appetizer (a grayish-brown mush of *chotpoti*) out of a Styrofoam bowl with a white, plastic spoon.

"Plastic is bad for you," Hasina Rasheed said, attempting to make conversation with Jharna's mother one more time.

Jharna's mother nodded her head up and down, smiling timidly. Her eyes glistened with moisture. Hasina Rasheed made a decision. Life was too short. She would not be deterred from seeking out the joy she could have while she still had time. Rising from her chair, she marched to the drawing room.

Several young women seated on the brown leather sofas cried out in delight at seeing her again. "There she is! Aunty, we were talking about you. What a grand time we had been having chatting with you!"

The three young women Dr. Rasheed had been chatting with earlier, Sonia, Lilly, and Bithi, were very smart looking, with red highlights in their hair (layered and puffed up in identical styles), dressed in silky caftans paired with tapered Western pants, and high-heeled, open-toed sandals. They all carried fashionable purses, which they pressed daintily against their laps as they sat.

"I was having fun, too, my dears!" Hasina Rasheed settled down beside the giggling women. "Imagine, Pinky put me in that room with that other woman, someone's mother, just because we're the same age. Does Pinky think I have to talk to an old woman just because I'm old also? No, I enjoy *your* company. We're like-minded. I enjoyed our conversation so much. You are all very intelligent. That's how young women should be, intelligent and interesting. Don't you think?"

"Oh, Aunty, you flatter me!" Sonia cried. She was taller than the other two, slim and upright with a thin face and hollow, rouged cheeks. "I will never forget this compliment. That you, being a great doctor, called *me* intelligent."

"I speak the truth!" Hasina Rasheed cried gaily, gesturing with her plump arms and flinging back her bobbed hair. "But do you know what? To help your brain, you must take B12 regularly. Do you take B12?"

"Oh. No, I didn't know. B12? I'll make sure to take it," Bithi said. She had a round, apple-shaped face, with pretty, dyed bangs covering her forehead.

The floor of the drawing room was depressed from the level of the dining room and kitchen. Big paintings hung on all the walls in the darkened room. The paintings had no pictures, just colors and shapes, the kind of art one would see at a bank in Bangladesh. The sofa was a brown leather sectional, with a holder for all the remote controls. A large television set, mounted on the wall above an electric fireplace, showed a song and dance sequence from a Hindi film, with the volume turned down low.

As she chatted with the young women, Dr. Rasheed watched her daughter Munia sitting quietly on one end of the sofa, staring at the TV screen with deep concentration. Munia's body had grown plump recently. Her kameez looked about to burst under her arms and at her sides. With a pang, Hasina Rasheed noticed that a few gray hairs had sprouted at the front of Munia's scalp, no doubt a consequence of the recent stresses in her life.

"Hallo." A reedy woman with a long chin plopped down beside Munia with a bounce. "We haven't met. I'm Shompa. Do you have kids? I heard you mention to someone that you have two kids?" Shompa asked in a breathy, singsong voice, dangling her long neck and casting Munia a blinding smile. She shifted her position and moved her arms, and the stones on her shalwar kameez sparkled and shone.

"They're on visit," poor Munia mumbled softly. She looked straight ahead, her eyes fixed on the television set. The light from the screen flickered over her ashy face in the dark room, throwing shadows.

"What?" Shompa craned her neck, gazing at Munia through protuberant eyes. "I don't understand."

"Visit. They're on visit," Munia repeated in a pained voice.

"What does that mean?" Shompa asked loudly.

A few heads turned to look at the two women.

"They're with their dad. He has visitation rights today," Munia said, sitting up stiffly.

"She's divorced!" Hasina Rasheed cried from across the room, to stop the tide of interrogation.

The color mounted Munia's face, rising from her chin to her forehead, flaming her features.

"Is that your daughter?" Sonia asked Dr. Rasheed. "I had no idea that Munia is your daughter, Aunty!"

"I'm so sorry about what happened, Aunty," Bithi said, lowering her head and speaking in a soft voice. "We heard a little bit about your daughter's misfortune. So many times, we saw her come to a party crying. If we only knew that her husband was mistreating her."

"What happened? I didn't hear anything?" Lilly leaned forward.

"Her husband abused her. He beat her. Not once, but several times," Dr. Hasina Rasheed confided in her young friends. "He threatened to beat the children also. They are small, you know. Two boys. Just one and three years old. I had to come to Houston to rescue my daughter."

The three women nodded rapidly, their eyes dancing.

"After coming here, I took one look at the situation, and I told my daughter to get a divorce. Now I am staying with her and taking care of her and the children."

"So sad, Aunty." Sonia shook her head sympathetically.

"It was so good of you to come and take care of her. She needed you, Aunty, and you came," Bithi said. Her cheeks dimpled with compassion.

"Do you know what? He is good for nothing," Hasina Rasheed said, warming to the young women's sympathetic looks. "So what if he is an engineer? My daughter is a doctor also!" As she spoke, she imagined that she would be great friends with these women. She would tell Munia to invite them, so that they could all have tea together.

Sonia bent her neck to examine Lilly's diamond ring. Her black caftan glistened in the dim light of the room, the fabric falling in shimmers across her arms. "How many karats is it, Lilly?" Sonia asked.

Lilly named a number. Bithi also began to examine the ring, taking Lilly's hand in hers. The three women became engrossed in a discussion about a jeweler in Hillcroft. Hasina Rasheed stared at them with a look of confusion. Her lips curled downward, and her eyes darted around the dark room.

The host Pinky entered the drawing room from the kitchen and picked up the remote control, cradling it among her blood-red nails. "Hey, do you all want to watch the latest Shahrukh Khan song?"

"Yes! Yes!" the room exploded with excited cries.

"Turn the volume up, Pinky," Sonia suggested.

A song and dance routine materialized on the TV screen. Shahrukh Khan was dancing with a smooth-faced, willowy young actress whom Dr. Rasheed did not recognize. The women watched the larger-than-life figures on the screen with flared nostrils and shining eyes. Dr. Rasheed sat upright, maintaining proper posture, staring blankly at the spectacle that everyone else seemed to be enjoying. Someone must have opened a window, because a cool draft blew over Dr. Rasheed's arms, making her shudder through the nylon sleeves of her kameez. She wished she had not handed her coat at the door.

After the song ended, the three young women seated beside Hasina Rasheed continued to talk among themselves. Hasina Rasheed listened to them intently, trying to follow their conversation, waiting for a good opportunity to jump in. They did not pay her any attention. A long time passed. Her face settled into heavy folds. Her body sank into the recesses of the overly soft sofa. She pulled herself up and sat up straight again, drawing her back tall. If there was one thing she feared, it was her body going soft.

Pinky reappeared in the dark room and announced that the men had taken their food. It was the women's turn to serve themselves. The women sprang up and headed to the kitchen, picking up the thin paper plates stacked on the kitchen island. Dr. Rasheed noticed that her poor daughter still sat on the sofa in the dark, her arms crossed across her tight bodice and her eyes fixed on the TV screen. Hasina Rasheed rose from her sofa with a struggle and walked across the room to her daughter.

"You won't eat?" she asked, bending low and bringing her lips close to Munia's face, ministering to her the way she used to when Munia had been little, and later, when Munia had been a medical student studying for her exams, her two pigtails framing her narrow, dusky face with those large black eyes.

Munia shook her head. Specks of tears glinted on top of her shiny face powder. Her hair was thinning and the skin on her forehead was dull and flaking. The tinsel figures on the screen gyrated to cheerful music, throwing bright lights on the walls and across the surfaces of the paintings. Dr. Rasheed remembered the moment of her daughter's birth. Despite being a doctor, she had been terrified, screaming for narcotics. Her doctor friends and her doctor husband had surrounded her. A few minutes after Munia was born and brought to her, as she suckled at her breast, Dr. Rasheed had fallen asleep, shutting her eyes from blissful exhaustion.

"All right." Hasina Rasheed made a decision. She marched to the kitchen. She found Pinky dishing *pulau* out of a gigantic pot on the stove using a saucer, her blood-red nails and the thin gold bracelet on her wrist covered with oily rice grains.

"Pinky! I need to leave!" Dr. Rasheed cried loudly, drawing herself tall and pulling up her chin.

"Oh, Aunty! Really?"

"Yes! We have to leave on my account. I have taken a job at CVS pharmacy, to relieve my boredom, you see. I have to show up at work this evening. I must take Munia with me also, since I don't drive."

"Aunty, you won't eat before you leave?" Pinky asked.

Dr. Rasheed was taken aback by the girl's sincerity. "No, no. Another time. Thank you for inviting us, Pinky. Beautiful house…"

Dr. Rasheed took her good-byes from all the women, including her three young friends, Sonia, Lilly, and Bithi, who avowed their disappointments in loud voices. Then she shepherded her poor, broken daughter out of the house, pulling her along by the arm. Outside, she pulled on the puffy pink jacket she had bought at Bongo Bazar in Bangladesh, where surplus and rejected export clothes from the garments industry were sold. Munia stood beside her, tugging her tight green velvet jacket around her wide girth.

"Good-bye!" Pinky cried from the door, waving.

Munia's car was parked in front of the house. They climbed inside the Toyota Camry. Munia blasted the heat and the fan.

"If you turn on the heat, take off your jacket," Dr. Rasheed said. "What? You won't take off your jacket? You will be too warm!"

Munia ignored her. Pinky was still waving. Dr. Rasheed waved back frantically, lowering the glass. Munia hit the indicator, swerved out of the parking space, and circled the cul-de-sac. When the car came around to the house again, Pinky was still standing at the front door, her silk sari and gold jewelry scintillating under the porch light.

"She's waving. Wave back," Dr. Rasheed said, raising her own hand. "Munia?"

Tears were flowing down Munia's cheeks. Dr. Rasheed stared at her daughter, then turned back to her window, pursing her mouth. All Munia ever did was cry! Much to Dr. Rasheed's disappointment, Munia had reduced herself to just being a housewife to her engineer husband. Even after the divorce, Munia had not bothered to look for a job. "You trained as a doctor in Bangladesh!" Dr. Rasheed kept reminding her daughter.

In no time, they reached Munia's house, in the same subdivision and only a few blocks away from Pinky's house. Munia parked the Toyota inside the garage, then opened her door and climbed out and slipped inside the house, without a word to Dr. Rasheed. Hasina Rasheed sat inside the car for a few minutes, enjoying the bright light and quiet hum of the warm garage. At last, she emerged, shutting the passenger-side door gently, and walked past the stacked plastic storage bins that had not been unpacked yet. She did, indeed, have work later that evening at the pharmacy, but not till ten. She would rest a little, perhaps drink a cup of tea and think about her pleasant conversation with her three new friends at the party, those sparkling young women, Sonia, Bithi, and Lilli, who laughed so gaily. Dr. Rasheed felt that laughter was very good for the health. It produced gamma brain waves. She wished that Munia would laugh more.

As soon as Dr. Rasheed entered the house, she could hear Munia sobbing. She tightened her sari about her waist and marched through the dark house to her daughter's room. Munia's ex-husband had kept their house in the Woodlands. Dr. Hasina Rasheed had bought this house for her daughter, with her own money. It was modest, with two bedrooms, one for Munia and the kids and one for Dr. Rasheed. Parking herself outside Munia's bedroom, Dr. Rasheed placed her ear against the door and heard piteous howls, rising and falling. Turning the knob with her gnarled fingers, she opened the door and found the room in darkness.

Munia sat on the bed, a dark mound, her cellphone pressed tightly to her ear. Her eyes were squeezed shut and she was speaking in a hushed, desperate voice. "I want to come back. Please!"

"What are you doing? Are you calling your husband again? That scoundrel?" Hasina Rasheed marched to the bed and yanked the cellphone away from her daughter and pressed the red button to end the call. Holding the phone behind her back, she stood in front of her daughter, panting. "Have you gone mad? Why do you want to go back to him?" she shouted.

"Who will want me now?" Munia wailed. "I'm thirty-four years old, an old woman! No one wants me." She sniffed loudly, rubbing her inflamed nose. Dirty tears lined her cheeks.

"You're not old!" Hasina Rasheed cried. "I'm still young, and you're my daughter!"

"I want him back!"

"No! You cannot go back to him!" Hasina Rasheed said. Her voice was deep and authoritative, the way it used to ring out in the corridor of the hospital. She felt reassured by it.

"*You* did this!" Munia cried, twisting her body violently to face Dr. Rasheed. "You ruined everything! *You* made me get a divorce. You should leave!" Her face contorted in an ugly way, elongating her mouth and puffing her cheeks, and enlarging the whites of her eyes.

"I only want to help," Dr. Rasheed said.

"You can't help me!" Munia sobbed. She bent her head and covered her face with her hands. Her shoulders heaved. She was still wearing her heavy jacket on top of the synthetic outfit, and she smelled slightly of sweat.

Dr. Rasheed hesitated, then cleared her throat and said softly, "You know, Munia, if you lose some weight, you will look pretty again."

When Munia did not answer, she said, "Will you drive me to CVS later?"

Hasina Rasheed retreated, closing her daughter's bedroom door softly behind her and taking the cellphone with her. She only had a little time to rest before her shift later that evening. Walking into the bathroom, she turned on the light, depositing the phone on the sink counter. Did Munia really mean that she had ruined her life? Did Munia want her to return to Bangladesh? Dr. Rasheed took short breaths, seized with panic. For years, she had been coming to America for a few months at a time to maintain her green card status, but this time she had assumed that she was coming to live here forever. She had retired from her position as a gynecologist at PG Hospital and sold her house in Dhaka, and all her furniture with it, and packed up to move to Houston permanently, for Munia's sake.

Every night, after she retired to bed after a long day of taking care of Munia and the two boys and put her head on her pillow, she missed her patients. She saw them in her dreams. She had been a tough doctor. Her massive frame had moved swiftly through the corridors, braced by a corset and safety pins, her voice echoing off the walls. Oh, how those patients had worshipped her, how they had gazed at her with eager, shining eyes and open mouths.

For the last few months, she had taken her grandchildren to the nearby park to play, holding the elder one by the hand and carrying the younger one on her back. If she tried to put the young one down on the ground, he cried, "But Nani, I am little. You have to carry me!" She had fed the babies and read to them and let them caress her face with their fluttering, feathery fingers.

"You have small ears," the three-year-old had said to Dr. Rasheed once. "Your skin is too loose."

"Yes! I'm a wolf!" she had teased the child. "I'm going to eat you!"

She liked to think that she had made their lives a little better. She had envisioned a life of sweet moments with Munia and the two boys, eating at the boys' favorite restaurant McDonald's, going grocery shopping together with her daughter, picking out the good okra, sitting together in the late afternoon, drinking tea.

Now that plan also included those young women, so attractive and smart, with whom she had talked so energetically at the party. Perhaps she could arrange to have a picnic with them sometimes at some nice park. Or they could go for a walk together, on the clean streets of Sugarland. But, Dr. Rasheed remembered, Sonia, Lilly, and Bithi had lost interest in her at the party. They had stopped listening when she had been her most animated self, telling an interesting story about her daughter's divorce. At first, they had appeared so interested in her. What changed? Why had they stopped speaking to her? She felt very hurt and confused by their behavior. Dr. Rasheed examined her face in the mirror. Then, lifting her cold hands to her cheeks, she removed her glasses and peered once more at her reflection, moving closer to the mirror, and she saw, at last, how they saw her, the young women at the party who had sparkled all evening, with bright rouge on their plump cheeks, and their glittering purses, highlighted hair, stiletto heels, and painted nails. Her cheeks were inflamed, and the sides of her mouth had lost their elasticity and settled in thick lines like craters. She opened her mouth. Her teeth were stained with black marks, and there were gaps between the upper teeth. She switched on one more light.

No wonder, she thought. She had grown old. When had she grown so old?

Katy Family

When Khaled and his Japanese wife Rika were divorced, he began to visit his Bangladeshi friends in the suburbs more often. Khaled and Rika had lived in downtown Houston. Khaled taught engineering at the University of Houston and Rika had made art, consorting with the local artists and art gallery owners in Houston. Their friends had been mostly white, mostly artists and academics who made their way around the circuit of Houston's interesting restaurants, cafés, and museums. It wasn't until after the divorce that Khaled realized just how uncomfortable he had felt around his white friends. He was tired of their fears, their suspicions of new customs and new foods, and tired of explaining himself. Once, he and Rika had met with a white couple, friends of Rika's, at an Indian restaurant. The other couple had studied the menu with suspicion, asking many questions in nervous voices before they ordered. When their food arrived, they had run their forks through it, placing the spicy curry gingerly on their tongues, their eyes open wide, as if they thought the food might poison them.

Another time while he had been married to Rika, Khaled had invited two colleagues from his department to dinner. He had cooked up a storm of Bengali fare: buttery, fluffed rice called *pulau*, rich, creamy chicken curry, and big medallions of fried eggplant. His lanky male colleagues and their thin spouses had barely touched the food. Their pupils had narrowed, and their movements slowed, betraying their heightened fear of the unfamiliar items. When Khaled and Rika had shown them around their home, a renovated craftsman house in the Heights that they had decorated with Bengali stitched *katha* wall hangings and Japanese screen paintings, and Japanese and Bengali literature arranged tightly on bookshelves in every room, rather than being interested or curious, they had looked stunned. His colleagues had spent most of the evening sitting on the edges of their chairs, avoiding looking at anything in their surroundings, sticking only to the wine and desserts they had brought themselves. Khaled still had a sinking feeling thinking of that ruined party.

When he had been married to Rika, Khaled hadn't realized how much their white friends' behavior bothered him. After Rika left for Japan with their five-year-old daughter Maya, saying that she could no longer stand to live in a strange, foreign country (the divorce had been an indictment of America as much as of their relationship), Khaled called up Munir, an old classmate from his engineering university in Bangladesh. Munir worked in oil and gas. He lived in Katy now, along with many other Bengali engineers. Khaled was glad to reconnect with his old friend, and through him, a large Bangladeshi community.

Soon, Khaled started to drive to Katy every weekend for social gatherings, sometimes on both Saturday and Sunday. They were big, lively parties with twenty, thirty families. The tables overflowed with Bengali food. The conversation flowed in Bengali. Khaled enjoyed the Bengali songs, Bengali jokes, references to Bengali movies, and the discussion of Bangladeshi politics. The women wore bright, beautiful saris. The men huddled together outside, smoking cigarettes. Khaled knew many of the people at these parties from Bangladesh. Some had been classmates at his university in Bangladesh, while others were the children of his parents' friends, distant relatives, or friends of relatives. He didn't have to explain anything to anyone. Everyone liked Khaled. He had a clean-shaven face, with handsome, slightly cold features, a straight and narrow nose, and thin lips. When he spoke, a shy smile accompanied his words, and when others spoke, he nodded intently.

He felt very much at home at these parties. His friends' houses were comfortable, big, sprawling, suburban structures with warm, insulated interiors. Khaled began to associate these houses, often sporting identical floor plans, with the Bangladeshi community.

As he settled into his new life, Khaled began to set down new roots. In the spring, he planted a vegetable garden and started a compost heap in his backyard. For his next project, he constructed a chicken coop and went out and bought two hens from the animal feedstore near his house. One day, he drove to a rescue shelter and got a dog, a Labrador puppy with pale yellow fur and a black snout, and named him Tommy.

His classmate Munir and Munir's wife Tania began to tease Khaled about having a party at Khaled's house. The three were sitting on couches set out on the back porch of Munir's house in Katy, under a moonlit sky, talking, when Munir again brought up the question of having a party at Khaled's house.

"Come on, Khaled, we want to visit your house in the city," Munir nagged, like a broken record. "You're the only one among us who lives in the city."

Munir resembled Khaled, with a clean-shaven face and a square jaw, dark, wavy hair. He wore the same button-down shirts with pleated dress pants as Khaled.

"Khaled Bhai, all the women are demanding to see your bachelor pad!" Munir's wife Tania said, shaking out her long, thick hair, the beauty of Bengali women.

Khaled tried to avert the topic. As a bachelor, he felt nervous about inviting his friends, accomplished homemakers, to his home. "I'm not as good a cook as you, Tania," he protested shyly.

"Nonsense, Khaled Bhai, we will eat whatever you cook," Tania said.

"Tania can help you. Perhaps she can cook a few dishes and bring them to the party," Munir suggested.

But Khaled kept making excuses. He really did feel shy entertaining on his own as a bachelor.

"All right, we'll wait till you marry and bring a wife to your home. Then you can throw a party," Tania said, giggling.

Khaled colored. When he spoke to his mother on the phone, she also mentioned getting him married again. She had been checking out various young women at Eden college, a women's college in Dhaka. She waited outside the gates watching the young women who stepped out after classes, dressed in saris or printed shalwar kameez, their thick, dark hair piled up in luxurious buns, their slender arms clutching books and notebooks. Tania's words now reminded Khaled of these sensuous descriptions from his mother, luring him to take a Bengali wife. When he expressed his fear of marrying again to his mother, she reassured him that a Bengali wife would be more compatible with him than his Japanese wife had been. It was her opinion that his marriage hadn't lasted because Rika had been too thin, too small, too delicate, and not wide hipped enough for childbearing.

"When you are from the same culture, you have more in common and less conflict," she consoled him.

Now, sitting with his friends in the moonlight, chatting idly and drinking milk tea while the night breeze hit their faces, Khaled thought that his mother had been right.

The following Friday night, Khaled attended a small dinner party thrown by Munir and Tania. Another of their batchmates Farid was there. Farid had made a successful career in oil and gas. Farid had grown rather stout, with a thick neck and broad chest. There was one other man whom Khaled only vaguely remembered from university and whose name he kept mixing up– Shahed or Shahid or Shahi. Someone had brought playing cards. The four men played contract bridge late into the night, sitting under a ceiling fan in the dining room. It was summer and getting very hot. The temperature rose into the hundreds during the day and hovered above ninety during the night. Tania served the men sweet milk tea. It was sheer joy to Khaled to be drinking tea with *samosas* late at night while holding a fanned hand of cards. The whirring fan overhead added to the effect of the feeling that he was back in Dhaka, among friends. He felt known among these people, bound together by common bonds and memories and customs, their shared pleasure in the same things. He felt that there was no greater comfort in life than being among his own people, around all that was familiar and beloved to him. His ex-wife Rika had been wrong. One *could* set down roots in America, simply by finding one's people.

Khaled and Munir won the game. The women began to clamor the winning team to throw the next dinner party.

"You are already attending a dinner party at my house!" Munir said. "I propose that we meet at *Khaled's* house the next time we get together."

"Yes, yes!" everyone cried.

Khaled's friends were obviously curious to see his house in the city, a bachelor's house no less.

When Khaled demurred, Tania said, "Khaled Bhai, you don't have to worry about anything. We will cook the food and bring it!"

Khaled looked at her. Her dark eyes creased at the corners and her lips parted in happiness. The other women added their voices to hers.

"Or we could wait till Mrs. Khaled gets here, but don't wait too long to get married and bring her over," Munir teased him, just as Tania had earlier.

"All right then," Khaled agreed sheepishly, shy but also happy that his friends really wanted to come to his house. He had not had guests at his home for six months, at least. In his mind, he also fantasized about bringing a new Mrs. Khaled home. Perhaps this time, if he married someone from his own culture, things would go more smoothly.

The week of the party, Khaled hired a company to clean his house. He drove to Whole Foods and bought the best grass-fed beef and lamb, planning to cook lamb curry and beef *biriyani*. He also bought organic tomatoes and cucumber for a salad, and eggplant for his favorite, fried eggplant with turmeric and salt. Lastly, he bought some excellent chicken drumsticks to barbecue. Every night, Khaled returned exhausted from the office and stumbled into the kitchen to heat up a canned soup for himself and open a canned dinner for his dog. Then he put on some Bengali music and cooked a dish for the party. One evening, he cooked *daal* and froze it. Another evening, he cooked the lamb, dicing onions and garlic expertly with a sharp knife, adding a generous dash of chili flakes to the curry. After he had cooked, he sat outside with his dog on the deck, looking out at his small vegetable plot, where he had planted tomatoes, peppers, and Bengali green beans. He brushed his dog's hair with a pink brush, and his dog purred with happiness.

At last, it was Friday, and Khaled's home was ready for the party. It was a one-story house and much smaller than his friends' mansions in the suburbs, but it was a carefully preserved historic craftsman home built in the 1900s, updated with modern appliances. Khaled and Rika had been very proud of their home. Farid and his family arrived first at eight, explaining that they could not come any earlier because they had to drive back home to Katy from the city first to change, then drive back to the city.

"My work is very close to your place," Farid said as he entered the house. "The traffic is a killer when I drive back."

"Your house is very far," Farid's wife said unhappily. She was a plump, heavy woman, and a great cook. "It was horrible driving through all that traffic on the highway to get here."

"You should all buy a house near me and move here!" Khaled cried, as he chanced upon the delightful idea. "It will be good for Farid to live nearer his work. That way, he wouldn't have to drive so much."

"We like Katy for the schools," Farid said, taking off his shoes.

"But there are good schools in the city," Khaled objected.

"No, no, the standard is very low at these city schools," Farid's wife said, pulling her small daughter by the arm. "Only poor people go to school in the city. I heard there are too many Mexicans. In Katy, you can be sure everybody who lives in the neighborhood has a certain standard."

Khaled glanced at her in surprise. His own daughter Maya had studied at the neighborhood school, but since he had forsaken his earlier life and begun anew, he didn't bring up his daughter's experience or try to argue with Farid and his wife's perspective of the schools inside the city.

"It's cold, Ma," the little girl complained. The child's mother had taken off her shoes. She was standing barefoot on the wooden floorboards.

"She can keep her shoes on," Khaled said. "Please, make her put her shoes back on." He had forgotten that his friends in the suburbs all had luxurious carpets.

Soon, another family arrived. The man's name was Shahi or Shahan or Shah. For the life of him, Khaled could not remember which, although they had been students together at the same university in Bangladesh. The husband and wife worked together at an oil company. They had two genius, bespectacled teenaged daughters who had won many academic awards at their high school. The teenagers had brought their phones and earphones. They asked Khaled for his Wi-Fi password, which Khaled had to retrieve by searching through various files on his desktop computer in his bedroom. Entering the dark room alone, he surveyed the space quickly and satisfied himself that he had already removed all the photographs of him with Rika and Maya. Only one photo remained, inside an eight-by-ten-inch-frame propped up on his bedside table, of Khaled standing alone, smiling at the camera.

When the last guests Munir and Tania arrived, Khaled heaved a sigh of relief. Now the party could begin.

"We'll move outside to the back porch," Khaled announced with a grin. "I've prepared the barbecue grill."

He didn't notice anyone's expression as he led the way, throwing the glass French doors wide open to step out into the yard, but behind him the two teenaged girls began to complain loudly.

"Can't we sit inside, Ma?" they hissed in their mother's ears. "It's hot outside. There are bugs outside."

Their mother nodded silently, and the girls went back inside the air-conditioned house. They settled on the sofa in the drawing room, putting in their earphones. Their mother smiled apologetically at Khaled. Khaled smiled back with empathy. He supposed that he, too, hadn't liked nature when he had been a young lad.

His guests were gathered on the back patio. Khaled's party was finally starting, and Khaled was grinning. His dog Tommy came bounding out from behind a pine tree. Tania gave a yelp.

Couldn't Khaled take the dog inside? Munir suggested gently.

Since the teenagers were sitting inside and they also were "dead scared of dogs," as they put it, Khaled had to lock up Tommy in Maya's old bedroom. Tommy whined pitifully, whimpering like a small, frightened child.

"All right," Khaled said, emerging on the patio again, rubbing his hands together, "let me get the grill started."

The men began to examine the grill—a free-standing, chrome-polished propane grill—asking if it was a good model. Munir said he was thinking of buying a barbecue grill himself. He had been looking at various models—there were grills with multiple burners, high-ignition and high-performance burners, and wireless meat probes; or he might install a permanent grill as part of an outdoor kitchen. From grills, the conversation drifted to the purchase of other household appliances, and cars, the latest SUV models. Khaled had expected his friends to help him cook, to participate in the tradition of barbecuing by passing him the chicken or tending the fire or passing plates. But when he explained how he had built the perfect pyramid with the coal to keep the heat going, their eyes glazed over. Munir began to discuss the scores of a cricket game. Everyone's ears wandered to the discussion of the game. As the fire heated up, the women, who wore soft silk saris, withdrew from the heat and went to sit on the plastic chairs on the deck. At some point, the women withdrew completely into the house.

Khaled concentrated on his juicy chicken legs, explaining the intricate chemistry of how to cook the outside skin to a crisp texture while keeping the inside meat tender and soft. Munir excused himself, saying that he had to go inside. He had severe allergies. Otherwise, he loved nature.

Khaled said, "Oh, I'm sorry, friend. You should have told me so before. You go inside, please."

Then he noticed the other men and said, "Please, you all accompany Munir. I won't be long here."

Finally, the chicken was cooked, and Khaled whisked the charred legs triumphantly into a metal pan with raised edges and two handles on either side, carrying in the hot, juicy food. Warm odors wafted in the air.

"Ah! That smells nice!" Tania said, coming forward to help Khaled.

Tania and the other women helped Khaled to heat up the food they had brought in the oven and set the table. During the week, Khaled had gone to a thrift store and bought lots of used china for the party. He told Tania the story as he brought these down from a top shelf, placing them in the sink to rewash them. They were bone china, painted with little delicate white flowers and golden stems. The woman at the thrift store had told Khaled that they had come from someone's estate sale, a wedding set perhaps. He was proud of his purchase, and he told Tania the story in detail.

But when he turned around, there was a wild expression on Tania's face. Her eyes were wide open, and her thin nose was quivering. "Khaled Bhai, why go to all the trouble with real plates? Don't you have paper plates?"

"No, no, it's no trouble. I bought these specifically for the party since I have not had so many guests before."

"But didn't these belong to dead people?" Tania said.

Khaled laughed heartily. "Dead people! That is very funny. Yes, and that is why they are very precious, because they are a rare china that is not even available anymore. Besides, when I wash them, they will be as good as new."

"Really, we can eat out of paper plates," Tania insisted in a tense voice. "*Do* you have paper plates? If not, shall I send Munir to buy some?"

There was real tension between them now. Tania stood barring the sink to prevent him from getting to the used china. But Khaled reached around her and turned on the tap and began to wash the plates with soap and water.

"Khaled Bhai! Give us a tour!" Tania called.

"It's so small. There's not much to see," Khaled protested sheepishly, blushing and happy at the same time to have so many people in his home.

Nevertheless, he obliged, taking his fellow countrymen and women on a tour of his home away from home. He showed off his books and records, and the twin speakers he had built himself. His Bengali friends moved around the small house, a ten-foot-by-ten-foot drawing room, a small dining room facing the backyard, and two rooms on the side of the drawing room, with a single bathroom in between. One of the bedrooms used to be Maya's room and the other had been Khaled's shared bedroom with Rika. When he brushed past Maya's door, he did not open it, explaining that the dog was locked inside. He heard Tommy let out a cry inside, a howl of deep anguish, and laughed sheepishly at his guests. At last, he showed off his bedroom, feeling a bit self-conscious, a bit nervous. His eyes fell on Rika's screen painting–tiny white flowers etched on a gold background, an homage to the screens from the Muromachi period. The screen hung on the wall behind their bed, massive and unavoidable, reaching from the floor to the ceiling. Thankfully, no one commented on the painting.

"Is that a picture of you, Khaled? You look so young and handsome, my friend." Munir slapped Khaled playfully on the shoulder.

"Yes." Khaled blushed.

His eyes fell on the photo. He realized that it had been taken by Rika, soon after he had arrived from Bangladesh, as a PhD student at the University of Houston. Rika had been studying art at the university and they had met at the library one day and fallen in love. At the time the picture was taken, they had just met, probably. In the photo, he was posing in front of the library building. Rita had framed it and placed it on the bedside table.

"You've changed a lot, man," Farid said.

"What do you mean? Our Khaled Bhai is just as handsome as ever," Tania retorted.

"No, that's not what I meant," Farid said, blushing. "I just meant that he looks changed from that picture. He has changed inwardly, probably."

"Farid is just jealous of Khaled Bhai's good looks," Farid's own wife teased him. "You should be talking. Look how stout you've become."

"Don't you see it?" Farid insisted, pointing out the features that had changed, the face, the hair, the build.

The women protested even more loudly that Khaled had all his hair from the photograph, and he looked just as slim, and, if anything, he had gained some gloss and sheen on his face, eating American food.

"Never mind, I give up!" Farid protested.

Khaled stared extra hard at his own image, trying to find some resemblance between the young man in the picture and himself. The man appeared to be a stranger to him. Seeing that the photo had caused so much trouble, Khaled wished that he had hidden that picture also, along with the others.

Khaled felt a bit muddled giving his friends a tour of his house. He thought it was from being so unused to receiving company and showing off his home. The oven and stoves had heated up the house, and the warmth flushed his skin. Everything felt a bit rushed and blurry. The party had been surprisingly overwhelming so far (indeed, it was not easy to throw a party as a bachelor), not at all along the lines of how Khaled had imagined it, planning it for so many nights. No one had commented on his Bengali book titles, even though they were novels they must have all read in their youth. No one was interested in his father's gramophone either. Khaled had carried the gramophone on a plane from Bangladesh, along with his father's extensive gramophone record collection, paying heavily for the extra baggage weight. He supposed the songs must be a little ancient by now, and people had moved on to modern songs.

As he was concluding the tour, he had a tremendous idea.

"Friends, I have the nicest surprise for you!" he squealed. "Follow me outside again, just for a bit. Even you, Munir, yes, even those with allergies, and, teens, you too."

He thought that he had the best thing to show them, one aspect in which his house rivaled all his friends' houses. He was sure that they would marvel at what they were about to see. He insisted, and the three men and their wives and even the three children followed him outside. Khaled led them around the pine tree to the very edge of the fence, where, beside the compost heap, he had built a chicken coop with steps leading up to a stoop. He had painted the whole thing red. Two speckled hens with red tufts walked around the upper level of the house. The whole structure was surrounded by wiring.

Farid's small daughter clapped her hands. "Wow. Are those chickens real?" she asked.

"Cool!" the teenagers cried, showing some expression at last in their eyes behind their glasses.

"You built this yourself?" the engineers asked with admiration.

Khaled smiled. At last, his party was going according to plan. The evening had cooled a bit. Even though sweat pooled on their necks and upper lips, they felt a refreshing breeze.

"See?" Khaled said. "Wasn't this worthwhile?"

Tania slapped her arms. "There are mosquitos, Khaled Bhai," she said.

The others began to slap their arms too.

Farid's wife let out a piercing scream.

"What is it?" Khaled asked with alarm.

"My daughter stepped in chicken droppings!" she cried hysterically, lifting the child and throwing her shoes off. She began to scream to Farid to wash her daughter's shoes.

"What will *I* do?" Farid yelled back. "I can't touch those soiled shoes."

"No matter." Khaled went to fetch the hose lying coiled by the gate. He returned and washed down the black shoes, holding them by the heels. Some of Khaled's spirits had dampened, as if someone had thrown water over the party as he was pouring water over the shoes.

They walked back single file to the safety of the air-conditioned house.

"Let's eat," Khaled suggested once they were all inside, eager to hurry the whole thing along, to get to the smooth part, the food.

The women set the table efficiently, and the men helped themselves first, carrying their plates back to the living room. The women stood around the kitchen feeding the children, including the teenagers, who played on their phones as they were being fed.

"It's so good, Khaled Bhai, very tasty," the women said periodically, as they tasted a stray morsel of meat from their children's plates while feeding them.

"Eat, eat. Serve yourselves," Khaled said to the women again and again.

"You eat, Khaled Bhai. We'll feed the children first."

The women didn't start till the food grew cold. At last, when the women had served themselves and seated themselves at the table, Khaled went to sit by the men on the sofa with a plate of food.

"Where did you buy the chicken? Hamza farm?" Farid asked.

"I bought all the meat at Whole Foods. Pasture raised, grass fed, and organic."

His Bengali friends stared at him. The dining table, where the women sat, went quiet as well. All conversation died down. All the laughter and the music and the jokes of the past few months stopped.

First Munir put down his plate, then Farid, and then the other person whose name Khaled could not remember.

"We can't eat this food," Munir said. "It's not halal." He looked at Khaled through small, narrowed eyes, with a nervous expression.

Khaled stared at his guests, looking from one to the other. He had no words to explain himself. He breathed in the fear of the room, odorous like the raw onions and garlic and turmeric with which he had cooked all week. He was flushed from the heat, and bleary eyed, as he observed his guests across a great distance. For a long time, no one spoke. Only Tommy mewled from Maya's bedroom, wondering what was going on outside.

The American Cousin

It was the beginning of summer holidays, and the two sisters idled their days away. They could be said to be very lazy, not consisting of much substance, just idle daydreams and faint fancies, except that they were given many chores by their mother, grandmother, and their two elder sisters throughout the day.

Ruma was fourteen and a student at the Dhanmondi Girls' School in class nine, a time when things were getting serious with the matriculation exams ahead. She had spent the year studying till late night, sitting at the short, rectangular dining table under a dim tube light, her books stacked in front of her, a small hill on the plastic cloth covering, rocking back and forth as she memorized the facts of chemistry, physics, and biology. She was tall and lean, with stick legs and arms, two tight oily braids on either side of her narrow head, a long, almost sour face, and a long nose, sharp features in a dusky complexion. Overall, her appearance tended toward the morose, the most attractive feature of her person being her slender, jointed fingers. Now that summer had started, Ruma was relieved to be taking a little break from her studies before the start of the next school year, when the litany of hired tutors would start again, and she would have to double down and start studying for the national matriculation exam.

Jhumu, at thirteen, was only a year behind her sister but appeared younger because of her childishness. She liked to barge into the kitchen and make a paste of tamarind, sugar, and salt to lick or steal a large rock of jaggery from the glass jar in the meat safe and masticate noisily. She was short and squat, with tiny features, chocolate-brown plump arms and legs spilling out of frilled and laced cotton dresses. People often mistook her for a much younger child.

Their family had been made poor by the sudden death of their father, whom the youngest two, Ruma and Jhumu, did not remember. He had been killed in a car accident. Ruma had been two at the time, and Jhumu had just been born. Since their father's death, their numerous uncles and aunts (five uncles and four aunts on their mother's side and two uncles and six aunts on their father's side) had supported their widowed mother, building the house that they lived in, buying the children gifts on their birthdays and on Eid Day, and stuffing money into their mother's fisted hands for household expenses whenever they dropped in. Their grandmother–their mother's mother–had moved in with them as a guardian. All these relatives were a constant presence in the sisters' lives.

Their grandmother kept an album in her black, rectangular trunk. The two sisters used to like to take out the album and turn the pages, remarking on their glamorous relatives who lived far away, some of whom they had met just once and others they had never seen. The cover of the album was a thick, padded material, with a red and white wavy pattern. Inside, the photos had been pasted under cellulite film, arranged by year and family on each page. The sisters spread the album over their grandmother's bed in the bedroom that she shared with their mother. They sat on the floor, turning one heavy page after another while the fan whirred overhead, studying the minute details in each photograph of their relatives in foreign lands, the bare limbs of trees like glass and snow icicles of a winter in Canada, a red Pontiac Sunbird in the background behind an American cousin and a can imprinted with the letters Coca Cola in bright paint in the cousin's plump hand.

"Hey, give back the album! You'll break it!" their grandmother scolded, coming up from behind. She wore a starched white sari, her braless white blouse hanging low with their weight.

Ruma and Jhumu sprang from the floor, snatching the red album, and ran away from their grandmother to their own bedroom, where they locked themselves so that they could look at the album in leisure.

"Give it back!" Their grandmother shouted from the other side of the door, beating at it ineffectually.

Much as they hated her, the sisters could appreciate that their grandmother was a beautiful woman, slim and of medium build, with a head of black hair which she tied in a braid at the back. Having been widowed at the age of forty, she wore white saris, white blouses, and white petticoats that were washed every Friday and hung out to dry with clothes clips on a line in the backyard (this was one of the sisters' tasks). She was mean to the girls, telling them to turn off the ceiling fan in their bedroom because the motor would burn out. The fan had been donated to them by a rich aunt, and the grandmother acted as if she were guarding the aunt's property, as if they were beggars receiving its air like alms. One time, an aunt who lived in America brought them some biscuits in a pretty, painted round tin as a present. Their grandmother snatched the tin from their hands and hid it, complaining that Ruma and Jhumu were eating the biscuits too quickly.

But their grandmother also prepared delicious snacks for them and taught them how to cook sweetmeats with milk and molasses and fry *singara*, standing huddled together in front of the stove in the small, hot, oil-splattered kitchen. For all her faults, she was more present than their mother, a woman who had been cheated of life by early widowhood and reduced to a state of non-existence. While their mother lay in bed for hours or watched television sitting hunched forward in the stuffed, dark drawing room, wearing the same wrinkled sari day after day, eating her food by slurping and swallowing rather than taking the pain to bite, having lost two front teeth prematurely, almost relishing this fact, the loss of her teeth and youthful skin and her hair, inviting the onset of disease and early death, their grandmother moved around the house with energy and purpose, dusting furniture and fluffing up pillows, folding clothes, and ordering them about. The sisters couldn't deny that their grandmother brought glamour to their lives through her stories about their relatives, the fancy food she had eaten at an uncle's or aunt's house, and the grand things she had seen while visiting her other children in foreign countries.

It was their grandmother's family album that made the most vivid impression on the sisters. Among their five uncles and four aunts on their mother's side, prominently displayed on the pages of the album, three aunts lived in Bangladesh, and one lived in America. The uncles all lived abroad at present, in Canada, America, Australia, and England. Two of the uncles were diplomats who relocated to a different country every few years. Their grandmother often went on short visits of six months to a year to live with her other children and returned bragging of the things she had seen, the snowy alps of Switzerland or the scones that she used to eat with jam and butter every afternoon for high tea in London. She spoke highly about her other grandchildren, dearest to her heart, whom, she said, she had been forced to abandon because she was taking care of Ruma and Jhumu's family.

"Oh, my Fahim misses me so much. He kissed me and kissed me, and he held me tight at the airport. He would not let me go when I was leaving Texas. That was so many years ago," their grandmother would moan, making herself a betel leaf, packing the green leaf with nuts and powders and white lime paste, staining her lips and tongue a deep red (the betel leaf and the *jorda* were her one vice, which gave her ulcer of the mouth and made her hack and cough, which thrilled the sisters).

Stooping over the red book in the dark bedroom where all the sisters slept, Ruma and Jhumu peered at their older cousin Fahim's photo (they called him Fahim Bhai out of respect). There were three sets of doors to their bedroom, one connecting to the room where their mother and grandmother slept, a second leading to the dining room and the front of the house, and another leading to the back balcony and the backyard where they hung their clothes to dry. The windows of the bedroom were heavily draped with long, thick curtains for privacy. Still, sunlight cracked between the gaps in the curtains through the dirty glass, throwing shadows over Fahim Bhai's smiling dimple in the photographs. There were many photos of Fahim, chubby in a red sweater at ten, suddenly tall and handsome and sporting long hair at fifteen, and then older, less smiling, muscled or plump, wearing a T-shirt with a graphic design and blue jeans, thighs bursting at the seams of the pants, a college student posing in front of a red sports car, the magnificent Pontiac Sunbird.

"So handsome," Ruma whispered, running her fingers over Fahim Bhai's celluloid image.

"What do you think he is doing now?" Jhumu whispered, sucking a thumb.

"Mmm. I don't know. It's ten in the morning here, so in America it must be night. Do you think he's in bed now?"

"Maybe." Jhumu giggled and clapped her hands.

They were quiet for a moment, imagining their American cousin Fahim going to bed. From their grandmother, they had heard what kind of bed he slept in.

"He has a waterbed," their grandmother had told them over dinner the night before.

"What is a waterbed, Nani?" Ruma had asked. She spoke in a deep baritone voice that had a tragic ring to it. It should have been apparent to anyone who cared to look, from the slight tremor in her cheeks or the twitch at the edges of her eyes, that she worried too much, that her heart was heavy with the problems of her mother and older, unmarried sisters and the cruel words her grandmother spoke.

"It is a modern invention," their grandmother had explained. "It's filled with water."

"Ha ha! How does it keep its shape?" the childish Jhumu had started to laugh without control, holding her belly and bouncing in her chair, knocking over the salt dish.

"Hush. Don't be foolish. You won't understand," their grandmother had barked, annoyed. She had served each piece of beef carefully measured out. The beef stew, cooked by a maid who came to the house in the morning, was thin and watery, the finite pieces of meat floating on top. The meat had been sent from their aunt's house in Gulshan as a present that day, or else they would have eaten an egg curry instead, fried in a soup of thickly cut onions.

Their two elder sisters had been at the table also. They were both attending university, caught in session jots amid student strikes and university closures that had prolonged their studies by several years. They were also stuck in another way. Since the eldest, Alia, couldn't get married, at twenty-two (no one wanted to marry a girl without a father and three younger sisters to take care of), the second sister Jamila could not marry before her sister either.

"Nani, you love your American grandsons more than us," Alia had accused their grandmother at the table.

"Why, that is a lie!" the old woman protested, her eyes throwing red flames.

"No, it isn't," Jamila said. "When Fahim Bhai came to Bangladesh last year, you cut white bread into little triangles to make him cucumber and chicken sandwiches. You plastered butter on the white bread. And you wouldn't let us have a single sandwich. Think how Ruma and Jhumu felt being treated like that, like our cousin is royalty and we are nothing?"

At this reminder of their position in the family, their mother had started to cry, and the dinner had ended in a chaos of angry words.

"Do you remember what he looked like when he came?" Ruma asked her younger sister now. They were lying on their backs on the hard, narrow spring bed, the heavy album balanced across their chests. Ruma had started to wear three-piece shalwar kameez suits, even at home, covering herself, as her grandmother warned her against immodesty.

"He was very tall, and he wore an earring in one ear!" Jhumu said. "He told us he rode a motorcycle!"

"Go switch on the fan," Ruma ordered her.

Jhumu jumped up on her squat legs and sprinted to the panel of fat, round, black switches.

The room was packed with three beds, laid side by side. There was just enough room for two pieces of furniture pushed against the wall, a small dressing table with an attached swiveling mirror and a steel almirah in which their mother stored bank cheque books, gold jewelry, land deeds, and other important documents. Without the fan, the room was stuffed with still air. The sisters often awoke in the middle of the night with beads of sweat on their upper lips and ran to the bathroom sink to throw water over their faces and on the napes of their necks, so that they might fall asleep again. It was a wondrous room full of feminine mystery. The dressing table had tiny, narrow drawers that held glass bangles of translucent colors, some with gold specks on them, tied together with a satin ribbon, face powders and perfumes, cheap lipstick, dried up nail polish, and oxidized silver jewelry. Adjoining the bedroom lay a dark closet area piled with sheet-covered hard suitcases, which the elder sisters called their wedding suitcases. These were already filled with the wedding trousseau that their aunts had bought them for the day they would get married—woven silk saris, two-story makeup boxes, and a hairbrush set each, packed away safely for a future day, plastic brushes with different patterns on the back, one with little heart shapes, one of yellow stars in a blue sky, one of red, plump cherries, and one of little strawberries.

"Turn off the fan!" their grandmother yelled from the other side of the door. "I can hear it running."

"Oh, the witch! She hates us!" Jhumu cried, mirroring her mother's expression.

"Let's go to the roof," Ruma suggested. She never spoke ill of anyone, but her grandmother's attitude hurt her. She shoved the album under her arm, not caring if she broke her grandmother's precious possession.

The sisters exited the room via the back door to the back balcony and ran across the yard to the outside staircase that led to the roof before the old woman could catch them. Under the staircase, a small motor rumbled throughout the day, sending water slowly up to the water tank on the roof so that they might get water at the taps. Before one of their uncles had sent money for the motor, they had run out of water frequently and had to store water in steel buckets and pots in anticipation. The staircase had no rail guard, and the steps were covered in green moss, which made them slippery, but the two girls took the slime-covered stairs at great speed, carefree and fearless. The flat roof was bounded by a low parapet. The floor and walls were covered with greenish-blue damp mildew and moss. A *boroi* tree reached up one side, close enough to the parapet that they could pull the branches near their chests and pluck the sour fruits with fat fingers, popping the *boroi* in their mouths one by one like candy balls and spitting the seeds over the parapet to the grass below.

Ruma and Jhumu ambled over to the side with the *boroi* tree now and sat down on the ground near the parapet, impatient to get back to their fantasy about their cousin.

"Do you think Fahim Bhai eats burgers for lunch? Remember how he talked about McDonald's when he came here?" Ruma said.

"Hmm." Jhumu nodded, making sufficient sounds to keep their fantasy going. She plopped a smooth, orange *boroi* into her mouth. It had just started to ripen and had a tart, sharp bite.

Their cousin Fahim had come to their house by car from Gulshan, where their aunt lived, to eat the finger sandwiches prepared for him by their grandmother. They had watched him as he inserted the dainty white triangles in his mouth, where they melted away.

"What grade are you in?" he had asked Ruma politely.

Ruma had been so embarrassed that she had been unable to speak. Her cheeks burned red and her whole body trembled. She understood then how her eldest sister felt when she was shown to suitors in drawing rooms or at restaurants, why she froze, and why their aunts scolded her later when the suitors turned her down. She had once heard an aunt saying that nobody wanted to marry a fatherless young woman with three younger siblings.

What young man wanted to be stuck with being financially responsible for a whole family? Men wanted to marry the daughters of rich people, prominent people.

"Fahim Bhai was so funny. His cheeks dimpled when he ate," Jhumu said, giggling.

Ruma remembered this too, how beautifully Fahim Bhai's cheeks dimpled and how his lips were pink. He had slicked back his hair with gel and readily admitted it when the girls' mother had asked him about it. His large eyes were lined with thick, long eyelashes.

"His eyelashes are like a girl's," the sisters said now, hooting with laughter.

They sat together with their legs dangling over the parapet, eating one fruit after another, remembering their cousin's long eyelashes with tenderness.

"How big do you think Texas is?" Jhumu asked.

"Much bigger than Bangladesh."

"What sort of girl do you think he dated?"

They had heard from hushed telephone conversations between their grandmother and their aunt that Fahim had been engaged to a young woman, but she had broken off the engagement. He was heartbroken. One day, their aunt had taken Ruma along with her to a religious man, with a long, white fluffy beard. They had stood in a long line of women to see the bearded man, who said a prayer for whichever relative the women were worried about. When it was their turn, Ruma's aunt had whispered, "Please pray for my son Fahim. He is hurting very much." Her dainty, elegant face looked small and soft, circled by the wound edge of her silk sari

A week later, Fahim was in a motorcycle accident. He had been driving to a beach in a town called Galveston and two trucks had hit him, one from either side. His motorcycle had been crushed between the two heavy vehicles and he had ended up in the hospital for months. The two girls knew every detail of the accident by heart. Ruma had prayed for him, sitting down for every prayer at the right time, elaborately washing her face and hands and feet and ears and donning a long cotton scarf over her head. Jhumu had sworn to go without stealing mango pickles from the kitchen for a whole week. Then Fahim Bhai got better, and he came home to Bangladesh to visit his mother, and their grandmother cried; happy tears sprang from the corners of her eyes and rolled down her cheeks.

"Fahim Bhai is magnificent," Ruma said now. "We are nothing to him." She spat out the seed of her *boroi* onto her sticky palm and threw it over the edge.

Jhumu lay down on her back on the concrete ground of the roof and peered up into the endless blue sky. "Do you mean that we mean nothing to him or that we are nothing compared to him?" she asked in a philosophical tone of voice.

"Both, I guess," Ruma said, sighing like a mature woman ravaged by life's vagaries.

The walls of their house were damp and became electrified during a thunderstorm, giving off shocks, drawing her mother's face down in alarm. Every visit to the bank, every opening of the armoire door to pay for the day's groceries, set their mother off in a panic, which she drowned by folding fat pieces of *ruti* and stuffing them in her mouth, chasing the dry bread with sugar tea. Their mother went to the bank simply to take out one hundred Taka to buy groceries for ten more days. Sometimes, they ate no meat or fish, just eggs for lunch and dinner. In the morning, Aliya cooked breakfast for the entire family, kneeling on the kitchen floor beside the stained walls with peeling plaster, stirring the egg with a pointed metal spoon on the gas stove and rolling dough with her hands into round *ruti*, before catching the bus to her university. Once, while the sisters lay in their beds gossiping late at night, a piece of plaster had chipped off the roof and fallen on top of Aliya's bed, just missing her head by an inch.

And then, there was the future, all four of them girls. Their only hope was to get married, and yet, they were unmarriageable! They all looked like their mother already, with the same high-pitched alarm in their throats and the same, thick line drawn across their foreheads and at the corners of their mouths. Yet for all their troubles, their lives were inferior and insignificant compared to their cousin's splendored life. Almost every day, one of their elder sisters cried from fright at the prospect of never getting married. At times, Ruma felt adrift herself, as if she were floating in the air, somewhere above everyone's heads as they fought and hurled out accusations or wailed in pain. Now, sitting so close to the edge on the roof, she wanted to be so light that she could hover in the air, slowly rise in the atmosphere, and drift away.

Lying on her back, Jhumu folded her knees to her chest, and rested her hands on her belly, staring into the universe. She had the sensation of lying on the surface of Earth as it spun through space. It was a dangerous sensation. She could be flung off the surface of the planet at any moment. What was to prevent her from falling off and shuttling into space?

"What do you think Fahim Bhai is doing now?" Ruma asked, picking up their fantasy again.

"Perhaps he is lying in bed dreaming. Perhaps he is sleeping with a heavy comforter and there is a heater in his room. Do you think Texas is cold in the winter?"

They discussed his smiling, dimpled face as it must look in sleep and the kind of apartment he lived in, imagining the faucets in the bathroom and the kitchen. Their aunt had said that in America it was possible to get hot water directly from the tap, to turn the faucet this way or that so that you could get just the desired temperature of water. They knew that Fahim Bhai drank bottled mineral water, pure and natural, from the springs. He must be wearing pajamas now in his bed in Texas, with little reindeer printed on them perhaps, his hair slicked back even in sleep.

"Do you think he has an automatic washer and dryer in his apartment?" Jhumu asked.

"How should I know?" Ruma said, but then she asked herself, "Does he know how to cook?"

"He cooks in a microwave oven," Jhumu said.

"Do you think he bought a new motorcycle?"

"Yes, definitely," Jhumu confirmed.

The sun rose in sky, beating down on their heads, the moisture in the air settling on the skins of their arms and necks. Whether speaking or silent, they continued to think and think and think about their American cousin, turning over every aspect of his life, biding time with him as he slept, waiting for him to wake. The sun circled them, heating up their heads, sticking their cotton clothes to their thin bodies, and sweating their hands damp as they reached for the hot, juicy fruits. Summer extended in their minds for months and months, an eternity, during which, every moment of every day, they would talk for endless hours about their cousin, about what he ate and where he went and how he walked and how he dressed, spinning out a delicious fantasy till it felt more real to them than their own tiny lives. Time seemed to move fast, propelling the day forward even before they had done anything but also standing still at the same time, stuck, as they put their lives on hold to consider their cousin's life.

"He must use an aftershave lotion when he shaves," Jhumu said, simply to add another element to their imagination. She looked to her sister for approval.

"How should I know?" Ruma spat out a *boroi* seed in disgust. She was frowning, her lips curled downward in a horrible, twisted expression. "Do you think Fahim Bhai sits around thinking about *us*?" she demanded in a harsh voice.

Jhumu frowned, hurt, not sure what she had said wrong. She sat up, hugging her knees, her body jerked into position. The sensation of falling off the surface of the planet ended abruptly. "No, he doesn't think about us," she answered honestly.

Below them, they could see the street with its usual traffic of rickshaws and an occasional car, and the fruit trees in their front yard, two mango trees bearing two different kinds of mango, the *boroi* tree, and a line of papaya trees with the sweetest fruit. Across the street, they could see into other people's houses, a child playing with a kitten, someone hanging the wash to dry, a mother plaiting a child's hair sitting on the verandah. The two sisters looked at each other.

"Forget this!" Ruma said savagely, standing up and brushing the dust off her cotton shalwar and kameez.

"Yes, let's go," Jhumu said, rising with her, leaving the album behind.

Ruma raced down the treacherous, unbounded stairs without a guardrail, Jhumu following behind loyally, to the tiny courtyard, the broken gate, and the high boundary wall with glass shards on top to hold off any ambitious thieves, past the loud motor that groaned and pumped water with all its might, and back inside their house, which was cool and dark behind heavy curtains at all times of the day. They marched through their bedroom and the stuffy dining room that smelled of old food on the dining cloth and oils from bottled pickles to the kitchen, where a wood meat safe with net doors always held snacks to fill an empty stomach—preserved lemons and chili peppers, and a tart tamarind that could be mixed with salt.

Nature

The two brothers had been close in childhood, both in age and temperament, but after they graduated from the Bangladesh University of Engineering and Technology, Asif left for higher studies in Texas while his older brother Zahid remained behind in Bangladesh.

After Zahid married, he and his wife continued to live with his parents in their flat in Muhammadpur. Zahid was also an engineer like his brother, but the only lucrative job he could get in Dhaka was at a bank. Zahid rode an autorickshaw to his work in the commercial district of Motijheel and his wife rode a bus to her job at another bank in Uttara, at the north end of the city. When they had children, the two boys and one girl had to share a bedroom, into their teens. Zahid didn't blame his brother for being absent from their lives, but he missed his only sibling very much. He often wrote emotional emails to his brother, asking Asif to return to Bangladesh after his master's degree.

What meaning can you find working in America? If you work in Bangladesh, the whole country will smile with pride at everything you accomplish, as you are a son of this land.

He even cut out job advertisements from the daily newspaper and mailed them to his brother.

However, after earning his master's degree in chemical engineering, Asif was immediately hired by an oil and gas company in Austin. A few years later, when Asif wrote to Zahid that he was getting bored at his job, Zahid wrote to his brother again, urging him to return home.

There are so many jobs in Bangladesh. The private universities, the drug companies here, they will all scoop you up, like anything!

After three years, Asif landed another job, this time in Houston, at a higher position with higher pay. Soon afterward, Asif married a young Bangladeshi woman living in America whom he had met through the Internet. He and his wife came home for a short visit to attend a hurried wedding, at the insistence of their parents. A year later, they had twins, whom Zahid and his parents never saw. In the next fifteen years, Asif changed jobs three more times, each time landing a promotion, at a higher pay scale. He explained to his elder brother once that the moment he landed a new job, he started looking for another job.

When their ageing parents became critically ill, Zahid began to nag Asif to return home, to spend the last few years of their parents' lives with them. Asif was thinking about it, but before Asif could consider a career change, their parents perished quickly, one after the other. Their father, a chain smoker, had been the first to die, of lung cancer, deservedly, but their mother, who followed him just a year later, had probably been the victim of second-hand smoke. At his brother's insistence, Asif showed up for both funerals, each time on a three-day grief leave.

The last time he visited Bangladesh, when their mother died, Asif wore a stylish Polo Ralph Lauren Shirt in a neon pink color, pulling a purple carry-on suitcase on wheels behind him. Zahid was struck by Asif's handsome, rosy looks– the sharp French beard that accentuated his pink lips and the Ray-Ban titanium sunglasses that blocked his eyes. A musky, foreign perfume wafted off his shoulders and neck. At one time, the two brothers used to look alike, but now Zahid was fat, his skin spattered with the dust of bricks and particulate matter that hung in the air of Dhaka City.

Zahid's heart ballooned at the sight of his younger brother. Childhood memories engulfed him. As boys, they had looked so alike that relatives couldn't tell them apart—the same skinny legs, impish smiles, tufted hair, and big eyes. It hadn't helped that their mother had dressed them in matching clothes or that their names were so similar. But what bound them together now, more than their looks, Zahid thought, were their memories of the place where they had been born and grown up together.

After their mother's funeral, Zahid began to poison Asif's mind with their childhood memories, to persuade his brother to return home. "Don't you remember how we used to catch fish by the gutter on our road? We had these glass jars that our mother gave us!"

They were eating dinner at their childhood home—rice and daal and fish floating in an oil curry, with the ceiling fan rotating overhead, their feet planted on the cool mosaic floor of their childhood days.

Asif nodded. His eyes seemed to light up. His lips, surrounded by his mustache and beard, broke into a childish smile.

"Why don't you move back to Bangladesh?" Zahid coaxed him.

The mango wood dining table from their mother's wedding furniture was covered with a plastic cover, as it had always been. It was laden with dishes in bowls familiar to them, a big porcelain bowl with flowers printed on it, a flat porcelain dish painted with blue raindrops, and a fitted container with a lid to keep the rice hot. Everything was like old times, *could* be like old times, Zahid persuaded his brother, if only Asif willed it.

"What do you say, brother?"

Asif smiled and grunted. Encouraged, Zahid leaned forward energetically. He began to speak rapidly, rocking his head back and forth, listing all the jobs that Asif could have. Carefully, he enumerated to Asif the many advantages of living in Bangladesh, near relatives, friends who knew him, and a niece and two nephews who adored him (Zahid's children). He listed all the facts (he had made an actual list once on the back of the morning paper, using his son's pencil). Asif only smiled politely, his white teeth in a straight line, his bottom lip pushed down.

"You're not going to come back, are you?" Zahid accused his brother in a frustrated tone. "Why not?"

Asif chewed on his fish, picked out a bone, then licked his fingers. He lifted the crystal glass and swigged ice-cold water, rolling the liquid in his mouth.

"What's the problem? Is it the traffic? Is it corruption you fear? Pollution?"

Asif made a helpless face. His youthful cheeks dimpled. "You'll get angry if I speak my mind."

"No. No, tell me." Zahid jerked his head. Dust flaked off his skin and flew off into the air. "Please, just tell. I'm listening."

Asif rubbed his jet-black beard, darted a nervous glance at his brother and spoke earnestly. "I just can't stand the traffic and pollution. The dust! The crowd! The lack of trees. It's all…just concrete."

Zahid nodded, trying to understand, tapping his feet under the table.

"Where I live,' Asif continued, "I'm surrounded by nature. Just next to my house, there is a jogging trail, and a lake lined with trees. I like being close to nature." Asif looked at his brother helplessly. "Are you angry? You asked me to speak my truth."

"I know, I know. Thank you." Zahid sat with what his brother had told him, trying to imagine the pristine, idyllic place where his brother lived.

After Asif left Bangladesh, his words began to sink in for Zahid. Zahid still missed his brother, but he began to appreciate that Asif was happy where he was. He began to especially appreciate Asif's comment about wanting to be close to nature. But he still broke out in dreams about his brother at night, sobbing, his heart beating loudly. Out of longing for his sibling, Zahid Googled Texas on his phone or on his desktop at work, trying to look up articles about nature there. He read about Big Bend, a national park in the Rio Grande River, encompassing the

Chihuahuan Desert, several canyons, and the Chisos Mountains in the skies. Texas had so much open land, just acres and acres of green! There were ranches, rivers, canyons, and meadows dotted with live oak trees. Cattle grazed on golden grass dried out in the winter sun. Whenever someone visited from America—say, someone from Houston who had come bearing gifts from Asif—Zahid made a point to ask about Texas. What was their national bird? Was it true that Texas had big national forests and parks where families went camping?

From his online research and his conversations with people who knew, Zahid formed a picture in his head of the natural scenery of Texas. He began to understand why Asif was so happy in the expansive, land-rich state, so full of green pastures and wooded forests, in sharp contrast to Zahid's own reality in Dhaka.

Zahid's three teenaged children each rode a rickshaw to school (they attended separate schools, in three different areas of the capital city). Every day, Zahid and his wife worried until all their children returned home, each on a separate treacherous journey, winding through traffic and pollution. On his own journey to his office, Zahid began to notice how the buses and trucks in front of him on the road pumped out black, murderous exhaust gases that rose in the air and coiled around him. He was forced to inhale the smoke as he sat trapped in his auto-rickshaw, at a lower height than the other vehicles on Mirpur Road. He also started to see the dust, invisible to him before, that now materialized everywhere—on his wife's ashen face and dirty clothes when she returned from work, on their furniture, which had to be wiped twice a day by the servants who worked tirelessly, on the outside walls of their residential building, on all the windows of all the buildings in Dhaka, and the dust rising off the streets, not to mention the dust of dead skin and detritus of all the crowded population of Dhaka flying in the air.

At last, after so many years, Zahid began to understand what his brother had been trying to tell him. Like their parents, Dhaka city was composting, stepping closer to death every day. All the crowds, gaiety, shop signs, neon lights, and honking of horns could not stop that coming of death. Who could blame Asif for wanting to escape this great trap, the hell hole of concrete and dust and traffic jam, to live somewhere closer to nature?

Three months after their mothers' death, Zahid made up his mind. All these years, he had been asking his brother Asif to give up everything he had built in his life in America and return to Bangladesh. Now, as Asif's only surviving relative, Zahid felt that he had a responsibility to witness how Asif lived, what Asif cared about, and the nature that his little brother admired so much. Zahid confided in his wife that he was missing his brother after their parents' death and that he felt a great need to see his brother.

Then he wrote to Asif.

I want to come visit you. Tell me when is convenient.

Although Asif was always busy, flying to conferences and business trips abroad, he said to come right away, in December. Asif would take a week off, plus there were days off for Christmas and New Year. The winter was wonderful in Houston. The weather was mild, yet cool. They might not be able to go away too much, as Asif's wife, who was a doctor, would still be working, and their twins had college applications due. But they would hang out in Houston.

Zahid was ecstatic. He packed his clothes and gifts for his brother and brother's wife and the boys. As the day of his flight approached, he read more about Houston. There were parks everywhere–the Sam Houston National Forest to the north, the Stephen F. Austin Park where vultures and owls lived, Brazos Bayou for crocodile sightings, and, most wonderful of all, the Katy Prairie. Since his brother lived in Katy, in a new suburb called Fullshear, Zahid read more about this area. He found out that the prairie was home to thousands of migratory birds that flew south every winter. There was even a conservancy that preserved coastal prairies and wildlife. While he was reading article after article, Zahid came across a rather negative one, claiming that the new highway–the Grand Parkway, also known as State Highway 99–and the new suburbs that came with it were destroying the prairie lands, encroaching on wild rice fields that had been home to mice and other wildlife. The article said that the new construction over prairie lands had even caused the recent floods in the city! Zahid frowned at such nasty writing and went on to find another one.

At the George Bush International Airport, Asif looked more handsome than ever, clean shaved and smooth, tiptop in a sharp-looking business suit. The brothers embraced.

Asif lifted Zahid's two heavy suitcases and carry-on bag into the back of his BMW, joking, "What did you pack in these? All the bricks of Dhaka?"

As they flew over the freeway, Zahid looked around him with wonder, admiring the number of lanes, the speed at which they moved, and the billboards in the sky.

"I was reading about Texas. So much land," he said knowledgeably to his brother.

The BMW entered his brother's subdivision, Zahid drew his breath appreciatively. Fullshear was an expensive suburb of Katy with custom-built houses over five thousand square feet and massive oak trees. When they arrived at Asif's house, Zahid could scarcely contain his excitement. He bounded out of the car and stood frozen in front of Asif's house, dumb with emotion at his first sight of his brother's home.

The elegant, white mansion stood two stories high, with arches and turrets and a fountain at the front, water slowly dripping over stones. Two chimneys rose from a majestic grey roof, shooting off into the picturesque blue sky, colonial balconies girded French doors upstairs and downstairs, and a row of coy, curtained windows guarded the rest of the front façade. There were three garages for three cars. But that was not all. There was a landscaped garden at the front and a garden at the back, with little, cheerful flower beds, and a wild section with trees in the back that melted into the forest beyond. Asif's wife and twin boys, both seventeen, stood smiling on the driveway to greet him.

Zahid turned to his brother and patted him softly on the shoulder. "I wish our parents had seen this, brother. Truly, you have created a paradise."

"Why don't you eat and take a nap?" Asif said when they were inside the house. He had hauled Zahid's two suitcases and one lumpy black bag out of the car and across the driveway, depositing them in the guest bedroom downstairs that would be Zahid' room.

Zahid nodded eagerly, looking around the dazzling white foyer with its glass vases placed on a long console table, a white chaise lounge lying lazily in the way, and the tall ceiling overhead, from which hung an opulent, golden chandelier. The house was immaculate. Zahid could scarcely wait to see the nature outside, surrounding the house.

"We're in the Katy Prairie, yes?" Zahid asked his younger brother reverently, his voice a hoarse whisper. "It's home to many migratory birds in the winter, I read."

"Yes, yes, it is. I will show you everything. I'm so glad you're here."

Zahid enjoyed the light lunch, of grilled chicken breast and Caesar salad, sitting at the majestic dining table facing a line of windows overlooking the backyard with a magnolia tree and a crepe myrtle, so familiar to him from his extensive reading. He appreciated the little, triangular paper napkins and the big, square-shaped modern plates placed in front of him.

"When you take your daily walk today, brother, I would like to go with you," he said to Asif.

"Today? But you must be tired! And jetlagged." Asif cried in surprise. "It is the middle of the night in Bangladesh!"

"No, please, I would like to accompany you. I am dying to see the beautiful nature near your house."

Finally, at four in the afternoon, Asif knocked on the door of the guest bedroom to call Zahid for a walk. Asif had changed into jogging pants and a white T-shirt. In the foyer, Asif sat down on a bench and pulled on Nike shoes that he said were good for walking. He had another pair for running.

"Running shoes are not the same as walking shoes," Asif explained.

Zahid was mesmerized by each new piece of information. A different pair of shoes for running and walking! Such careful homage to nature!

The two brothers emerged from the tall front door and started to walk on the sidewalk, passing neighbors who were also walking. Asif waved energetically to some people as they passed them. The sidewalk veered off into a concrete path over a water body. Little shrubs lined either side. Asif walked confidently, his body lean and upright, using long strides, lifting his foot clear off the concrete. Zahid tried to keep up with his brother. The path extended for several miles, winding up and down. Zahid stared around him, observing the sky above and the water flowing gently below them.

"What is that?" Zahid asked his brother. "Is that…is that a lake?"

"It's a retention pond to hold the rainwater," Asif said proudly. "The wonders of modern planning and technology."

Zahid stared a little distractedly at the water, the manicured banks with uniform grass and evenly spaced trees. What he was looking at was not a river or a bayou or even a lake, but an artificially constructed reservoir to hold the rainwater. In front of them, for miles and miles, stretched the concrete footpath where his brother purported to walk every morning and evening. The sky above them colored and darkened, from a deep blush to a purple wound.

"Where is the prairie?" Zahid cried. "Where are the meadows? Where are the birds?"

"What?" Asif was far off ahead. "I can't hear you. You better walk a little faster. This is too slow to even call a walk. Pick up your pace, brother."

Zahid stepped up his pace, still swiveling his head around, trying to look further into the distance, searching for the things that he had read about, the forests, the coyote, the armadillo, the migratory birds, the eagles, the vultures, the owls, the field mice, the prairie, and the tall grass. He kept falling behind his brother, because he kept stopping to look, searching for nature.

Confetti

Nadia Bianchi was Syrian American. Her husband Rusty was the son of a Bengali mother and an Italian American father. Thus, the last name Bianchi. At their wedding, Nadia and Rusty had tossed sweetmeat at the crowd–honey, dried fruit, seeds, and nuts. Children were handed cascarones to break over one another's heads, spilling confetti all over the wedding hall–a rented space at a Bengali restaurant. Before the ceremony, Nadia had accompanied her parents to each guest's house in Detroit, Michigan, delivering white Jordanian candy along with a wedding invitation printed on embossed cardstock.

Rusty worked in IT, and Nadia was a schoolteacher. Soon after they were married, in Michigan, Rusty found a job with an IT company in Houston, and they moved together to the new city. Nadia interviewed for a job at a public school in Houston, R-Elementary in the Heights, and got the job. They rented a garage apartment at the edge of the Heights, a painted blue cottage on top of a steep flight of stairs in someone's backyard that fit their aesthetics and budget.

The fifth-grade class at R-Elementary adored Nadia. They called her Miss B. Nadia had the classic looks of an old-school teacher–a heart-shaped, sweet face, olive skin, dark brown hair that she wore in a bun or plaited at the back, and bright, brown smiling eyes. She wore long, printed dresses with ruffled collars and pleated sleeves, prairie skirts, peasant tops, ribbed cardigans on top in bright colors, field green and orange and peacock blue, and black pumps, with knee-length stockings, striped or candy red or pale yellow. The children loved to comment on Miss B's hair, the different shades of eye shadow she wore each day, her painted nails, and her earrings–dangled stars, golden globes, or, their favorite, a pair of delicate butterfly wings.

Throughout the year, Miss B read them books, *Holes* by Louis Sachar and *Harry Potter* by J.K. Rowling. She taught them how to write essays, starting with a big idea–a memory they wanted to share or a dream. She read their essays laboriously, drawing smiley faces in the margins, and writing out comments in purple ink that brought smiles to their faces.

Julia, I loved this story about your first stuffed animal.
It brought tears to my eyes. I loved how the Teddy bear
protected you and gave you good dreams, and I shivered when
I read that when you lost it you felt alone.

Only Rusty didn't like the parents at the school. Whenever he dropped Nadia off in front of the orange brick building (a beautiful building, of contemporary design, with lots of glass and metal, sunlight pouring through all the spaces inside), Rusty took one look at the parents, their French beards and designer clothes, and cried out in disgust.

"There go the PMC! Look at them. Look at their cars. Their BMWs and Mercedes. And their ideas of their own moral superiority."

"Darling, what is the PMC?" Nadia asked, getting out of their beaten-up Volkswagen Beatle in the teacher's parking lot next to the school garden.

"The professional managerial class," Rusty said with a grin. He had *wanted* to be asked.

Rusty was a big bear, all jokes and hugs, a burly guy with a red beard. He liked to march and protest and join in worker strikes. Both their fathers had worked in the automobile industry in Michigan and faced the worst of the depression after the car companies left. Both had been raised in the working class. But Nadia saw nothing wrong with the decent, smiling parents at R-Elementary who dropped off their sweet angels in her care every morning.

Nadia shook her head, laughing at her husband, waved cheerfully, and took off, swinging her tote bag jauntily, stepping over stones as she walked between the vegetable plots planted by the different grade levels. The garden was beautiful, one of the best aspects of the school–it brightened her morning as she made her way to her classroom. There was a painted woodshed in the middle, with a shovel, spades, and garden rakes. A pond held turtles and koi fish. All around the boundary, fruit trees swung in the wind, dwarf apple trees and orange trees. A clump of flower bushes stood in one corner, tall stalks of sunflower swaying gently, tulips, irises, lilies, whatever the season sprang. Parent volunteers could often be seen kneeling on the earth, planting bulbs or saplings.

The parents at the school were very involved. The parent teacher association was strong. There was a foundation, a grant writing committee, an annual auction, and swift giving campaigns organized for anything a classroom or teacher might need. Nadia had asked for help once to construct a café where students could sip coffee and read. Parents had shown up, built the café overnight from plywood, donated wood benches and chairs from their own houses, and supplied pizza and coffee and cookies. At another teacher's suggestion, Nadia joined the Facebook community group for the school, where she posted pictures of her class working on projects outside in the sun or reading aloud poetry in the café that the parents had helped her create.

In October, Nadia discovered that she was pregnant. Rusty and Nadia were ecstatic. They walked in the city parks, imagining their child riding the train at Hermann Park and feeding the ducks, watching the bats soar into the sky at sunset over the bat bridge near Buffalo Bayou, or exploring the myriad shaded paths in the wooded arboretum of Memorial Park. They were very happy in Houston, each of them doing what they had always wanted to do. Rusty took the bus to Austin to protest various bills. He became involved with a local socialist organization, organizing to fight for contractors' rights, amend the city charter to take power from the mayor and give it to city council members, rebuild a low-income neighborhood that still lay ravaged years after Hurricane Harvey, and stop the city from hiring a private contractor to police black neighborhoods. He still made fun of the parents at Nadia's school, calling them the professional managerial class, stooges for corporations–oil companies, pharmaceutical companies, big insurance companies, and the law firms that represented these corporations–filled with self-importance. Nadia just shook her head, saying, "Stop it. They're very nice."

In March, Nadia and Rusty went to Nadia's obstetrician-gynecologist appointment for her five-month ultrasound and found out that they were going to have a boy. Nadia decided to share the news with her class. That weekend, she bought a set of gender reveal confetti canons from a local store. She had never seen one of these contraptions before, but another teacher had told her about them. There were four canons, two blue and two pink, filled with biodegradable confetti. She practiced on the pink canons with Rusty. You had to rotate the upper part of the contraption clockwise, while twisting the lower portion counterclockwise at the same time to release the confetti.

On Monday, Nadia led her class outside and told the students that she was going to have a baby.

"I'm so happy! I wanted to share my special news with you," she said.

The kids cheered, especially the girls.

"Miss. Perhaps your kid will study at R-Elementary one day."

"Perhaps," Nadia said.

Some of the girls came up to her and hugged her around her belly. One girl wanted to hear the baby's pulse. The kids were good, bright, interested in the books they read, whether fiction or nonfiction. They were smart and concerned, whatever their professional managerial class parents might be.

"All right, so. We're going to find out if I'm going to have a boy or a girl by using these confetti things. If the confetti is blue, I'm having a boy. And if it's pink, I'm having a girl. Right?"

The children nodded. Nadia marveled at how quiet they could be, how still, how they listened with small, tense faces and clear, cool eyes.

"I need two groups because I have two cannons here. I'll show you how to set them off."

The children gathered in two groups, on opposite ends of the garden. It was a beautiful day; cotton-soft clouds floated in a powder-blue sky. The grass was lush and green. Even in the winter, stalks of kale and chives sprouted in thick bunches in the vegetable plots. Nadia wore a yellow dress with a white cardigan, with leggings underneath, and Texas cowboy boots. The children wore jackets and sweaters.

A quiet girl named Julia, tall for her age, held one of the rockets, with a serious expression on her triangular face and clamped mouth. Robert, a small, frowning, bespectacled boy, held the other one, standing at the opposite side of the garden.

"Ready. Set. Go!"

With an enormous crack, both cannons shot off into the air, raining confetti on the grass, covering the green with a carpet of blue. The rockets worked. They were loud!

"It's a boy! It's a boy!" The children yelled.

That night, Nadia logged into Facebook from her home, a mug of hot chamomile tea by her side, and checked the community page for R-Elementary School, intending to post a photo she had taken of the confetti launch. Her eyes fell on an irate post from a mom, Facebook name Mel S, complaining about pollution in the garden. For a few moments, Nadia's eyes blurred, and her brain whirred, as she tried to make sense of the post, trying to understand what the mom was referring to. Mel S wrote that she had walked into the garden at school for pickup and was shocked to see paper littering their beautiful school garden that they had worked *so* hard to build, donating so much money, and hiring a gardener for maintenance. As an active member of the PTA, the auction committee, the grant committee, and the foundation, she had never seen anything more concerning. She was disgusted, she wrote.

> *Who did this? How dare they? Who would have the audacity to pollute our beautiful garden, so carefully built by so many donors? Whoever did this, I don't care, parent or student or staff, doesn't belong in our wonderful school community. We are about building, about coming together, creating something beautiful, NOT destroying.*

Her fingers shaking, Nadia typed out a reply in the comments section.

> *I'm sorry, it was me, I teach 5th grade. My husband and I recently found out that I am pregnant with our first child. We have no family here, and I wanted to share this wonderful news with my students. We set off two confetti cannons in the garden. They are biodegradable. I had cleared it with the principal first. The kids were very happy. I am sorry that my actions have caused so much trouble.*

Two weeks later, the pandemic hit Houston. Classes went online. Nadia had to work harder, creating an online environment from scratch. In the summer, Nadia had her baby, cocooning him from the harsh heat of Houston, which Rusty said was made worse by climate crisis, caused by the oil and gas companies all around them, the smokestacks they saw from the highways each time they drove out of the city for some air. Perhaps because Rusty showed them to her, Nadia saw pollution all around her, borderline communities surviving on the edges, just outside of Houston, adults and children suffering from lung disease and cancer and asthma.

Toward the end of the summer, Rusty was laid off from his job at the IT company. Everybody was getting laid off. Nadia and Rusty packed up, Nadia resigned from her position at the school, and they moved back to Detroit with their son.

The incoming fifth grade class was sorely disappointed that they would not have her as a teacher. The graduating fifth graders told them all about Miss B. How she made puppets to act out stories. How she printed out the stories the kids wrote, laminated and bound them, and put them up in the reading section of the class as real books to check out and read. *She was awesome,* they said.

The graduation ceremony of the fifth grade class was sponsored by a big accounting firm (the name of the sponsor displayed on a large banner hung over the auditorium). In their graduation speeches, all the fifth graders said that their favorite teacher was Miss B.

The next fall, at home, over dinner, Miss B's former students still talked about her class, telling their favorite stories and sharing fond memories of their last year at R-Elementary school, while their parents smiled and nodded indulgently. But perhaps when they talked about Miss B, the children and the parents were filled with nostalgia and longing for their own lives, with not a care for what had happened to their teacher who had served them, then scattered into thin air with her husband and child, like a handful of confetti.

Dreams and Memories

Three friends met at a house in Katy, Houston. They had been classmates at the Bangladesh University of Engineering and Technology. One of them, Bappi, was a businessman in Bangladesh who had come to America to attend his nephew's wedding in Texas. He had called up his friends, wanting to meet them before he returned home. The other two were successful engineers in oil and gas. The house in Cinco Ranch belonged to one of the successful engineers, Murad, who was slight of build, lithe, with a full head of jet-black hair. He dressed crisply in the most respected name-brand clothes, a Polo Ralph Lauren shirt paired with woolen black pants and cashmere socks. His wife had worked at various upscale department stores at the mall, where she had earned excellent knowledge of how men should dress. He was shrewd and well-spoken, and he knew how to smoothly network at work and speak back aggressively when colleagues challenged him. Without these skills, an engineer from Bangladesh could not make it in the industry. The third friend Javed was even more successful than Murad. He had recently moved to Fullshear, where the lots and houses were bigger than in Cinco Ranch.

The three friends had just collected their food laid out in the dining room by Murad's wife and carried their heaped plates back to the drawing room.

"So, Bappi, how is business in Bangladesh?" Murad asked, settling on the expensive, white leather couch and digging into the delicious goat *biriyani* that his wife had cooked.

"It's going well, it's going well," Bappi chirped, but to the other two it did not appear that things were going well for their Bangladeshi friend.

Bappi's face was bloated and punched up, sitting atop a thickened neck. His hairline had receded to the very back of his skull, his eyes were sunken, and his skin was dry and scaly, like the skin of a man on his deathbed, poisoned from the car exhaust and particulate matter he inhaled daily on the streets of Dhaka. Murad and Javed often gossiped about how their friends in Bangladesh looked so much older than them, like corpses almost, and here was Bappi as living proof of their words. Bappi looked like he was on the brink of a heart attack or a stroke.

"I've heard that it's difficult to do business in Bangladesh with all the corruption going on," Javed remarked. "I could never work in a corrupt environment like that." He shook his head to emphasize his disgust of people who did business in Bangladesh.

"It's not so bad," Bappi mumbled between bites. Swiveling his thick neck, he admired the palatial high ceiling of the living room and the grand staircase in front leading to a theatrical balcony upstairs. The square, glass-top center table looked like it had cost a fortune. Massive art pieces rested on shelves set into the recesses of the walls and on tops of various tables, their sizes alone declaring their value.

"Do you have to pay bribes to get things done over there?" Murad pressed the issue, looking Bappi in the eye. He was a talkative fellow who liked to have things out in the open.

"Yes, you have to, a little bit, but it's okay," Bappi said, shifting his gaze and changing his position on the sofa. His drooping eyelids, which gave his eyes the appearance of being hooded, dropped a little lower, making him look helpless and slightly frightened as if he felt trapped by the questions.

"Apparently, you can't move an inch in that place without bribing." Javed laughed. "Anyone who lives like that, engaging in that kind of corruption every day, can have no soul left."

Bappi nodded, having no answer to these accusations. As the owner of two garment factories, his days involved as much technical work—getting new work orders, visiting factories, and looking over financial statements—as sending gifts to ministers' houses or making calls for a government official's daughter to be admitted to a prestigious high school. It was all about doing favors and oiling the machine to keep the machinery in his factories running.

Murad's wife appeared in the doorway. She had a small, delicate face, like a young teenager. She was dressed in slim slacks and a peasant top. "Bappi *Bhai*, is the food okay?" she asked in a sweet voice. "Cooking for a person from Bangladesh, I'm nervous."

"It's good, very good," Bappi replied, smiling nervously, intimidated by his friend's modern wife. His wife was twice his size and could hardly move because of complications from gout. She had to use a step tool to climb into their car on the few occasions she ventured out of their flat.

"We can't compete with food from Bangladesh, *Bhabi*," Javed said with a derisive laugh, addressing Murad's wife. "Without all the contaminants they put in the food in Bangladesh, food is not tasty."

"Ha ha, that is true." Murad's wife laughed heartily, throwing back her head, white teeth gleaming against painted lips. "But I tried my best. Murad bought fresh goat meat from the farm we have here. I made the ghee myself at home from organic milk. Bappi *Bhai*, all the ingredients in the food are fresh and organic."

"It's very good, very good," Bappi said again self-consciously.

When Murad's wife left, the three friends talked about common friends–who was doing what, their old days at university, and the trips Murad and Javed had taken to Bangladesh.

"You understand, friend, the traffic in Bangladesh drove me crazy," Murad confided in Bappi.

"It's better now. How long ago did you visit?" Bappi asked sheepishly, chewing on the organic goat meat. He had to admit that it tasted better than the food he usually ate, even at the most expensive restaurants in Dhaka, where the curry was cooked in old oil. He always suffered from a stomachache after eating out, and sometimes he even had food poisoning.

"About five years–" Murad said.

"It's better now," Bappi said. "They put that over-bridge in, and now the traffic goes faster."

At these words, Javed shook his head in disgust.

"Where, *bhai*, I didn't see the traffic move any faster," he challenged, twisting his thin lips. He was taller than the other two, and he had a handsome, chiseled face and a body rippling with muscles. Unlike Murad, who had risen in his profession through his friendliness and his ability to socialize, Javed had made it through sheer smarts and his refusal to take any nonsense from anyone. "I was in Dhaka this summer. From what I saw, now there is a traffic jam on the bridge *and* on the road too. It took me three hours to go from Baridhara to Gulshan. Unbelievable!"

Bappi jumped a little at his friend's statement of the harsh facts. He had no defense in response. He bent his head and ate in silence, studying Javed's tight, angry face. In Bangladesh, Bappi remembered, Javed used to wear thick, dusty glasses. But now, there were no glasses to be seen. Bappi wanted to ask if Javed wore contact lenses now.

"How long does it take you to drive to work, Bappi?" Murad asked.

"Uh, if I leave at nine in the morning, about two hours," Bappi answered.

"Two hours! Two hours! And your factory is just in Mirpur, isn't it?" Murad said, leaning forward with sympathy. "And your home is in Dhanmondi? It shouldn't take more than twenty minutes, tops. Unbelievable. This is unconscionable. These leaders of Bangladesh couldn't even solve a simple problem like fixing the traffic."

"None of that for me, no sir," Javed said. "Do you know how far I drive to work every day? Thirty-five miles exactly. And it just takes me over half an hour to get home. Then I go out and play squash at the gym."

Bappi nodded in self-defeat, looking down dully at his misshaped body, which he had let go to waste in the race to make money and be successful. In contrast to the idyllic picture his

American friend had painted, Bappi's every day consisted of hours spent sitting in traffic and running around government offices to bribe so-and-so to get a simple piece of work done. When he returned home, there was nothing to do but sit in front of the TV and eat oily snacks.

Taking advantage of a lull in the conversation, Bappi looked around the dimly lit drawing room at the surround-sound speakers and the plasma TV mounted on the wall, all things he admired and envied. Putting down his plate, he sucked his finger. Murad quickly fished out a napkin from under a paperweight shaped like a swan trapped inside a glass vessel and handed it to Bappi before he could wipe his hand on the sofa.

"Thank you," Bappi said, taking the napkin.

"Imagine kids having to sit in traffic that long just to go to school," Murad said, sitting back down. "My kids just go to the school next door. Their mother walks them there. Best school in the country."

Bappi had paid Taka One Lakh to get his only son admitted to a good private school in Dhaka. He could brag about that, but then he remembered that his son had developed asthma from sitting in traffic every day.

"Honestly, friend, I settled in America for the children," Murad said philosophically, locking his arms behind his head. He sat with his legs planted apart and stretched out in front, in a mood of deep relaxation. "Education is free and good in this country. The children learn so much. The math they do would shame us."

"The education system in Bangladesh is totally messed up!" Javed agreed. "Even the wealthy people in Bangladesh are sending their children to study abroad. Hey, Bappi, is it true that the well-to-do don't even vacation in Bangladesh? They just fly to Malaysia, Singapore, or Thailand at the slightest opportunity? It's like they can't stand to be in the country any longer than necessary! Do you go to vacation abroad as well, Bappi?" Javed smiled, his lips curling, showing his pink gums.

"Actually, my father just passed away recently," Bappi said.

"Oh, I'm sorry to hear that," Murad said warmly.

"Thank you, friend. My father had some lands in his village, in Sylhet, and a house," Bappi continued. "A caretaker used to live in the house and send us crops from the agricultural lands. After my father died, I tore down the old structure and built a brick house," Bappi said.

"Then your engineering degree came in use after all!" Javed said in a mocking voice, making a dig at the fact that Bappi was just a businessman, whereas Murad and Javed were working as professional engineers at the world's preeminent multinational companies.

Bappi had been a better student than the other two at the engineering university, but *they* had had big dreams. They had dreamed of coming to America for their graduate studies and settling abroad, working for big companies, and living in grand houses. By the time of the graduation ceremony, about half the engineering class at their university had already left for higher studies in America, following their dreams. When they called the roll for people to receive their degree certificates at the ceremony, half the auditorium was empty! One night, Javed and Murad sat in this very living room talking about the difference between successful engineering graduates like themselves and those of their classmates who hadn't made it. They had specifically mentioned Bappi as an example of a good student who had fallen by the wayside. The problem, they had decided, was that these people who had not made anything of themselves had not dreamed of big things. They had no vision, no ambition.

"Yes, my degree did come in handy!" Bappi laughed sheepishly along with his friends at this dig at himself. He continued, "After fixing up the house, I've started to visit my father's village house on most weekends. On Friday, after work, I pack up the family, and we drive out to Sylhet. My father's home was in Taherpur in Sunamganj, near the border with India. It's low *haor* land. The fields are submerged in water and so fertile. During the floods, I take out fishing nets to the waterbody that stretches from end to end like a great, big river, and my son and I sit for hours fishing. Sometimes, we fish in the dark. The evening *azaan* from the nearby mosque sounds over the waters and moonlight plays on its surface. You can smell the salt of the water. There are other fishermen standing on the bank or in boats in the water, crying out as they haul their fish. Sometimes, we take out a boat on the water ourselves. We can see the Khasiya mountains far away. Over our heads, there are so many multicolored migratory birds flying. At times like this, I feel connected to my father and his father and all of my history."

Bappi's two friends frowned, shutting their eyes slightly. Something seemed to pass over them. As their friend talked, they could taste the salty morning air and hear the rustle of birds and bird calls from their childhoods. Old memories stirred inside them, things they had not thought about in decades while driving inside their solid, metal cars on the highway between Katy and downtown. They shook their heads to clear the memories.

Perhaps they were comparing themselves to Bappi, trying to prove to themselves that their lives were better. At the mention of the prayer from the mosque, they told themselves that they attended prayers at their grand neighborhood mosque, which had been built by donations from wealthy immigrant doctors and engineers. At the mention of fish, they comforted themselves that the fish in Bangladesh were polluted, and that they could buy the biggest ocean fish in Houston. In all aspects, they had fared better than their friend by coming to America.

"Sometimes, we catch so many small, silver *puti* fish," Bappi continued in a far-off, dreamy voice. "My son and I sit on top of the muddy water and disentangle the fish from the net, one by one. All around us, there are lily pads and water hyacinth, and the simple slop-slop sounds of water. Then we walk with our treasures stashed in a tin pot through the morning fog, stepping through the mud and rice paddy. I tell you, my friend, a few hours spent in my father's village, and I feel like I'm in heaven!"

Bappi had an expression of unearthly delight on his face now, as if he were dreaming a dream rather than sitting in an elegant drawing room in the oil-rich city of Houston.

"Well, well." Murad laughed a little shakily. "Look, my wife has returned with sweets. Her homemade *rosgollas* are the talk of Houston."

"Eat, Bappi *Bhai*," Murad's wife said, bending down to place a heavy bowl of white sweets swimming in syrup, three smaller bowls, and some dessert spoons on the glass table.

"Thank you," Bappi said, acknowledging the sweets she served him, but his eyes were glazed and far away.

"Be careful with the sweets. You're getting fat, my friend," Javed said with sudden viciousness. "And your hairline is receding too!" he cried more fiercely. "Perhaps eating all those fish did something to your hair!" Something in Bappi's words had shaken Javed, destroyed his tranquility, and distorted his reality. He blinked his eyes rapidly, again and again, trying to clear them.

Murad gulped down his wife's famous sweets, then stood up and turned the lights up to full brightness as if to announce that the party was over. "It's getting late, friends. I have work tomorrow," he said abruptly.

"Me too, me too," Javed said, jumping up from the sofa. "I have a long drive home. Idle chat is nice, but one has work to do. It's not like in Bangladesh, where no one shows up to work on time, and everyone leaves for lunch halfway through the day. I bet in Bangladesh, you guys have so much time that everyone is always going fishing!"

Bappi stood up too. "Thank you for seeing me. It was good to see you both. Thank you for the lovely dinner…"

"No problem, no problem," his two friends said, hurrying him toward the door, trying to get away from him and what he had aroused in them. He was a danger to their happiness.

"Come visit me in Bangladesh," Bappi said at the door.

"Sure, sure," his friends said, averting their eyes as they encouraged him out.

Bappi said goodbye again, standing under the night sky outside, then walked to his rental car, lowering his torso slowly into the driver's seat as the space was too tight for his corpulent frame. Javed marched past him to his new Lexus SUV, striding easily in his long legs. He whistled jauntily, swinging his key, but his sleek, black car only reminded him of the long drive to work the next day and the next and the day after that. The third friend Murad shut the door of his house, going back inside to the dark cocoon of his carefully constructed life abroad.

The Frame

I hate these Bangladeshi parties, don't you?

For Munia Auntie's party on Bengali New Year's Day, my mom made me wear a sari. I was suffocating in it. Saris give me anxiety because I can't walk properly in them. It doesn't help that they make you take off your shoes at the door. You've sunk two feet, and the sari is under your feet! I had to hold the skirt of my sari on either side in my hands to lift it off the floor, like a lady, so I wouldn't trip on it, especially going upstairs. Why do they send all the kids upstairs at these parties. Right? As soon as you walk in the door, you're marched straight up the stairs and locked up in a bedroom with screaming kids. By kid, I mean anyone between the ages of one and twenty.

What? Do you like saris? *Really?* I *guess* they're gorgeous. Sexy? I guess. But that's what gives me anxiety: showing off my midriff and belly. I wonder why my parents get mad when I wear crop tops, when a crop top is basically a sari-blouse? I have horrible anxiety. Wearing something that hobbles me really pushes on that. *Yeah, I know, cool SAT vocabulary word, baby. Hobble.* Actually, sari or no sari, going to these Bengali parties gives me anxiety.

Anyway, I didn't mean to talk about saris. It's cool that you like them. I love shalwar kameez. But this is what happened at Munia Auntie's party. As soon as I got upstairs to my friend Rosie's room, I took off the sari and she gave me one of her shalwar kameez outfits to wear. Rosie and I have been protecting each other from our moms' wraths since we were little.

Two minutes later, my mom came upstairs to find me, to take a photo with me. When she sees that I've taken off the sari she forced me to wear, she's really upset, like, tears running down her face!

Anyway, seeing my mom mad at me, I started to cry. She left, muttering self-pitying words. I had to lie down in Rosie's bed. I had a headache.

I must have slept for half the party. It was during the day, and the sun was shining hard through the window, into my eyes. When I woke up, all the girls were still sitting in Rosie's room, wearing their red saris, with red lipstick and painted faces, browsing videos on their phones and chatting. They'd let me have the whole of Rosie's bed, so they were huddled together on the white shag rug on the floor.

I struggled to sit up, rubbing my head, which still hurt from dehydration, maybe, or from the bright pink paint on the walls and the pink comforter and pink bedsheets. "Sorry, Rosie."

"It's okay," she said.

Rosie is petite, with short hair, and large eyes in a dusky, triangular face. She looks younger than her age, like a ten-year-old, a little lost, with large eyes, eager to please. Rosie's quiet, like *really* shy. She would never act that way with her mom, the way I act out with my parents. Whatever Munia Auntie wants, Rosie obliges. Munia Auntie still buys her clothes, with frills and laces, girly and childish, even though Rosie is now in high school, like me.

Rosie was looking after the younger girls, putting henna on their palms, drawing intricate patterns with a cone. I'm an artist, but I would never have the patience to do everyone's henna at a party.

"I better go say sorry to my mom," I said. "I think I've upset her."

Rosie nodded. I stepped down from the bed and noticed that several of the girls were on apps where you go to hook up with people. They were talking about people they had met online. That's the other thing about these parties that makes me want to scream, or laugh, how these parents are sitting downstairs bragging about how modest their kids are and meanwhile they've thrown their kids into this room where they are doing dangerous stuff, connecting with strangers online on sites like Omegle,

Yubo, and Tumblr, sending them photos, and agreeing to meet them at some random place. Right?

I found my mom downstairs, and we hugged, teary-eyed. Munia Auntie suggests that my mom and I get our photo taken together, although, note, I'm no longer in a sari, or even wearing the right colors, red and white. My kameez is a bright electric blue.

"Sure, let's do it," I say. I reach up to my mom's cheeks and kiss her, making big, squelching noises. "Mmm. I love you." I mean it.

Munia Auntie is short and fat, with big, curly hair and glasses. She spoils me with gifts and candy all the time. I love her. Munia Auntie leads us to the staging area, where the guests are supposed to have their photographs taken in front of a cardboard poster, painted in gaudy colors, with the words *Happy Bengali New Year* written in Bengali alphabet, *Shuvo Noboborsho.*

An uncle arrives carrying a professional camera and snaps a photo of me and my mom. I rush over and grab the camera from the uncle's hands to check that I look okay. The photo shows my mom and me turned at forty-five degrees toward each other, misty-eyed and smiling. You can tell how out of place I am, wearing a bright blue outfit when everyone is supposed to be wearing red and white, the women in red and white saris and the men in red flowing shirts (what are they called? Punjabi! Yes!) and white shalwar pants. My mom is beautiful in the photo, plump and happy, wearing an embroidered white cotton sari with little red flower appliqué, very artistic. Her face is round and adorable, her hair up in a loose bun, soft tendrils falling over her ears. I sigh and hand back the camera to the uncle and demand a second photo.

"It's not good?" he asks.

I shake my head. "My mom looks good, but I don't look good."

After taking a second shot, the photographer uncle puts up a hand to indicate that we should not move. He is a puny man, balding at the front, long hair at the back. His big SLR camera earns him heft at these parties.

"Wait, don't move. Where is the frame?" he asks.

I look around in confusion. "What frame?" I squawk.

Then I see *the frame*, a cheap contraption made of four pieces of cardboard stuck together, like something kids make in kindergarten. On the bottom edge of the frame, someone has painted the same letters in Bengali, *Shuvo Noboborsho*. The photographer uncle holds up the contraption and indicates that my mom and I should stand inside this frame and grin at the camera.

"No!" I say rudely. "I think we've taken enough photos."

My mom's mouth starts to droop. I don't want to upset her again, so I kiss her and say okay, and I get my photo taken in this super embarrassing pose, standing inside a frame and holding it up, grinning, showing all my teeth.

So, what's up with this frame thing? Do you understand it? Suddenly this year, there's a photo frame. Every family is photographed standing inside the frame. What, you know what the frame's supposed to represent? What is it? I don't know, but it's nuts, like suddenly there's a frame at every party, or people are asking, where's the frame? It was already weird that there was a dress code at every Bangladeshi party. All the aunties wear the same color sari, decided by the host. The color code is included in the invitation. Now even the men wear the same color shirt, matching with their wives.

After my mom and I have our photo taken, an uncle and auntie pose together. Someone says to the uncle to hold on to the auntie's waist. Then, they get the kids in the frame. The auntie has paint on her face. Her hair is tied with artificial extensions. Mascara curls on her eyelashes. Seeing that her curly hair is sticking out of the frame, another auntie shouts at her to tie it back. The uncle, with fat under the skin on his face, is grinning with big, white teeth. A husband and wife with two children, one boy and one girl. The picture of an ideal family. Another family is waiting patiently to have their photo taken inside the frame.

This auntie is taller than the uncle, so someone pulls a chair for her to sit on because she's not supposed to be taller than her husband. Ha, ha! Another auntie's mother-in-law is visiting, so she lets her mother-in-law pose next to her husband, and she stands on the end, but she looks a bit miffed about it. Wow, I love that explanation you just gave me about what the frame is supposed to represent. Everyone is being made to perform and give a salute to patriarchy. Yeah, what are they even doing? It's like they're all brainwashed.

I'm fascinated by the photography session, so I stay downstairs, cradling a glass of cold water I've poured myself from the refrigerator door, watching the scene. The men are in the front room. Why do men and women have to sit separately? I've visited Bangladesh every year since I was born. My mom has this fear that her parents are going to die, so in the summer, right after school ends in Houston, off we go. In Bangladesh, when we go to someone's home, men and women sit together and talk together and laugh together, drinking sweet milk tea and eating sweets. When I see the men and women sitting separately at these parties in Houston, I want to challenge them and ask them, what custom is this that you follow? Because it's certainly not Bangladeshi custom. Ha!

Usually, the aunties give me so much anxiety that at any party, I go straight to the room they direct me to, wherever they want to lock me up, and fall asleep promptly. But now I watch, fascinated, as a group of forty-year-old women pose in formation with simpering smiles, getting their group picture taken by the professional cameraman uncle. The uncle says that the aunties should turn sideways, so all their figures show better. After taking a few pictures, he says he wants to get a photo of the aunties holding their hands out in front, showing off their glass bangles.

Do you know why I get angry, watching the women acting this way? It's not because I'm judging them, but because *they're* so judgmental. Once, when I was in seventh grade, I won first prize at debate. It ran late, right, because I qualified for the finals, and my parents picked me up and drove me straight to the party.

I was wearing a skirt and blazer for debate. As soon as I entered the house, I ran to the bathroom to change into my shalwar kameez. When I come out, I see all these aunties whispering about me, pointing at me, saying things about me, how I'm not dressed properly, that I haven't been brought up right. That's why whenever I see aunties with painted faces and saris, I just think what are they even doing? It's funny how they judge a child for wearing a debate skirt, but this same community has nothing to say about a man who beats his wife. They'll laugh and joke with a guy like that and support him, but they're super concerned about how a woman should dress. Right?

The next time I come downstairs, it's with the other girls. We've been called to eat. The food is traditional for Bengali New Year, white rice with various mashed vegetables in little clay pots, and dried fish. It's all very spicy, so you need a lot of rice. I love the food. I pile it on my plate. An auntie pushes me out of the way to get food for her daughter.

I move aside. I hear her saying to her friend, "*Chi Chi,* the younger kids were watching some homosexual music video? I went and scolded them. Do the parents not teach the kid? It is something Allah dislikes very much…We should not accept it…" Her face crumples with disgust.

I scowl, making sure the auntie sees me. I cross my eyes and wrinkle my nose. I want her to see how rude I can be.

"Which one, Bhabi?" Her friend asks. "But that's a famous music video! Did anyone complain about it?"

"No, I'm just saying," the furious auntie says.

It's Bilquis Auntie. Do you know her? She's short and thin, and she wears these big diamond rings on her fingers. She has two pudgy little kids. It's weird how she's constantly talking about all the things she is furious about like she's burning up inside.

What did you hear her say? Really, she said that about Bengali New Year? So, some young women were celebrating Bengali New Year on the streets in Dhaka and they were molested by some men, and Bilquis Auntie said that it was the women's fault, for going out? Typical. Victim blaming!

I love Bengali New Year in Dhaka. I went one year with my mom, in April. I had to miss school for a few days. We took a rickshaw to Ramna Park early in the morning. Thousands of people were gathered in the park and a stage had been constructed under a huge banyan tree where these famous singers sat. At daybreak, when the sky was still dark, a song started up, rising in the air. Later, we walked to Art College and watched the art students marching. They wore painted masks. They had painted the road in colorful patterns called *alpana*.

But anyway, back to the party. You won't believe what I have to tell you.

Rosie is standing next to me, getting food and soda in a cheap, red plastic cup.

I make a face at her. "Did you hear what Bilquis Auntie said?" I hiss loudly, on purpose, so that Bilquis Auntie can hear me.

"No, what did she say?" Rosie asks.

I push her sweet, angelic buttons. "That auntie is very rude!" I say. "She said *homosexuals will go to hell.* Who made her God?"

Rosie just smiles a liquid smile and looks away. She would never be rude to the aunties. This is the difference between Rosie and me. She's two years younger than me and still under her mom's thumb. She fits in with the community, and I don't. I think, she'll probably marry a Muslim Bangladeshi man one day, picked out by her parents, and settle in the suburbs, raise kids in a big, bland house like this.

"Doesn't that bother you, the way she's so prejudiced?" I hiss in Rosie's ear as we walk back up the carpeted stairs, balancing our food precariously on thin paper plates. At least I'm not wearing a sari that falls under my feet.

"Maybe that's not what she meant. Maybe you misheard," Rosie says. She gives me a thin, watery smile.

"Oh, okay." I roll my eyes.

We finish eating, crowded together in Rosie's room. Then, the "kids" are being called downstairs to participate in a cultural program. A makeshift stage has been set up in front of the fake, electric fireplace in the living room. The aunties sing tunelessly, with shut eyes, painted mouths open in ecstasy. Some recite self-authored poems. Their friends tell them how talented they are. The uncles stand in the background of the crowded living room with bored, long faces, except for the cameraman uncle, who is now busy shooting videos. All these photographs and videos will be posted the next day on everyone's Facebook page, photo-edited by whoever is posting so that everyone else in the photo looks bad, but the auntie posting the photo is air-brushed and polished, with an aura above her head.

It's the kids' turn to perform. No way! I turn to leave, to retire to Rosie's room with my cellphone and catch up on texts from my classmates. But Rosie's being called to the stage, and I feel bad leaving when it's her turn to perform. I feel obliged to support her, so I stay, standing in a corner under the stairs. Rosie and all the other children are supposed to speak a few words expressing their gratitude to their parents and culture.

Rosie takes the microphone and says, "I love you, Mom. I love you, Dad. I love that you bought me a sari. I feel proud to be a Bangladeshi." She breathes into the microphone, her voice shaking. The microphone booms, trembling the air. Rosie sounds childish, like she's changed her voice to sound like what the aunties want to hear. She squirms, looking out of the sides of her eyes.

Everyone claps. Unlike me, Rosie knows what the community wants, and she has the composure and grace to act in the way she's expected to.

"That's so sweet," Bilquis Auntie says. "Keep well, child. Be obedient. Pray and stay on the right path…you know what the right path is in our religion, right?"

Rosie stares at Bilquis Auntie, smiling and simpering, nodding her head rapidly as if she has a nervous tick. Someone calls the next child to the front of the room. I try to catch Rosie's eye so that we can escape upstairs together, but Rosie is very much part of the program. She sits back down among the other children, with her knees pulled up to her chest, facing the stage. I guess it's her house, so she has an obligation to host. I leave. My mom tries to catch my eye, but I ignore her and climb the steps, carefree and happy in my flowing shalwar kameez that I borrowed from Rosie.

From my vantage point on the stairs, I can see Bilquis Auntie approaching Rosie, where she is sitting on the floor, maybe to offer more congratulations.

"Rosie, I wanted to say something to you, if you don't mind. You look a bit horsey with your short hairstyle, like a boy. You should grow out your hair. In our religion, girls should have long hair." She's speaking very loudly because I can hear her from the stairs. She sounds passionate and sincere, bending her small face with small eyes and small mouth close to Rosie as she speaks.

Rosie listens with an upturned face. For a moment, I think that I am the only one who has a problem with these words, that people like Munia Auntie and Rosie will always receive Bilquis Auntie's ill-mannered words gratefully, even defend her intentions. Then Rosie's face crumples. She rises to her feet in one motion and leaves the living room, meeting me on the stairs. I take her arm, pulling her close, and we go up to her room together.

I close the door, and Rosie starts to cry.

"That was so rude. I'm so sorry," I say, holding her. We're sitting on her pink bed. "You're not horsey looking at all. You're very pretty."

"I have to tell you something." Rosie stammers through her sobs. She's taking it really hard.

"What is it? What's the tea?" I say, trying to cheer her up.

Instead of speaking, Rosie pulls her blood-red sari up to her knees and shows me her legs.

"Oh, Rosie!" I gasp.

Her legs are gashed, as inflamed as the red sari on her. All I can see is pain, so much pain, etched like ladders up both legs. "Rosie, what is it? What's wrong?"

"I'm gay. I keep telling my parents, and they say I'll get over it. They say that I don't know what I'm talking about. No matter what I say, they think I'm a baby."

"I'll murder that Bilquis Auntie," I mutter. Then I collect myself and try to act mature. "I'm glad you told me, Rosie. You can always tell me anything. I have your back."

A part of me is jubilant that, finally, Rosie and I are on the same side. At last, someone at these parties agrees with me, sees things the way I do.

"I can't imagine what it must be like to have to pretend, to let these people constantly say these rude words to you!" I cry. "Rosie, I feel guilty that I didn't know. You had to face all this bigotry alone!"

"It's okay," she says. She wipes her eyes and smiles through her tears.

"You should smoke," I say, bringing out a cigarette from my purse (that's the only reason I carry a purse, to bring along these contraband items). "It'll help you ignore them. Want one?"

Rosie shakes her head.

"Rosie," I say. "You have to reject them. You have to throw back their narrative in their faces. Fight back. Think! How to reject them and their ideas?" I blow smoke in her face and fill up her room with foul odor.

"Children! Dessert is served!" We can hear Munia Auntie downstairs.

This is the last stage of the party. Then, hopefully, we will leave, and I get to lock myself in my bedroom and smoke for the rest of the day to recover from the party.

"Rosie! Come help serve the dessert!" Munia Auntie's voice again, coming up the stairs.

Rosie stands up and smooths her hair with her hands. She picks up a pink lip gloss and slathers it on her lips, covering her whole mouth. Then she adjusts her eyes and her mouth in a pretty, obliging smile. She opens the door and leaves. I run after her, putting out my cigarette and coughing all the way down the stairs.

Downstairs, the frame is out again. A beautiful auntie is pouting and posing with her husband for a photo, standing inside the frame. The husband and wife each hold up one end of the frame and smile. There is a line of couples waiting to have their pictures taken. Bilquis Auntie stands in a corner, whispering passionately to another auntie. She moves from group to group, hissing, her head moving up and down, and they're turning their heads, one by one, upwards, looking at us as we descend.

When Rosie reaches downstairs, Bilquis Auntie grabs her by the arm and pulls her into an unlit alcove, running her hands over Rosie's back.

"Rosie, we didn't finish our earlier conversation…I came to know from the other kids that…I think you were talking about homosexuality, and you might have said that you are of that type? This made me really worried…Did you really say that?"

Rosie stands, looking at Bilquis Auntie, the face that's usually arranged so eager to please slowly dissolving, the whites of her eyes growing larger, the pupils disappearing. I can hear snatches of her words.

"I think you might not want to talk about such things at social gatherings…I urge you to also learn about what Islam thinks about such things…how the people of Lut were destroyed due to this…"

"Rosie!" I cry loudly, emboldened by my smoke. "Come *out*, Rosie!" I dive into the dark alcove and pull her out of the embrace of the villainous auntie.

"Come on, let's take a picture together!" I shout. "Uncle, can you take a picture of Rosie and me?"

I push past a newly married couple, thin husband (the men grow progressively fatter and richer as they age) and his pretty, young wife bedecked in wedding jewelry. They look startled. Usually, these uncles and aunties are pushing us children out of the way, out of sight, shushing us, telling us to eat sitting on the floor, using those horrible paper plates that can buckle and break, making us spill our food. Now, all my anger is coming out.

"Take a picture, Uncle," I say, pulling Rosie next to me in front of the New Year poster. "Take a picture of us!"

The balding uncle turns to us slowly. I pick up the square frame lying on the carpet, propped up against the wall, and lift one end high in the air. Rosie grabs the other end. Together, we hold up the frame in front of us at a lopsided angle. The uncle snaps our picture, gesturing to us to straighten the frame.

"Another one!" I cry, grinning at the camera.

Rosie smiles, too. Her eyes and lips shine through her tears. Everyone is looking at us. The camera clicks again.

"One more!" I cry.

I pull at one end of the frame and Rosie at the other.

"Careful! It's breaking!" an auntie shouts.

"You damaged it," the camera uncle cries.

"It's okay! It'll do. It's fine," I reassure them.

It's a flimsy frame to begin with, as all things at these parties are, the cheap plastic cups and the thin paper plates, all disposable and, ultimately, breakable.

Meghalaya

The husband and wife both worked at a multinational oil company in Dhaka. After a year's employment, they earned a week's vacation and planned a getaway to Shilong in India. Saif worked in the explorations department as a geologist in training, and Raika worked in accounting. They liked to boast to friends about how they were helping to solve the energy crisis in Bangladesh and alleviate its poverty by developing the country's gas. But they were both tired and ready for a well-earned vacation, a chance to get out of the capital city and breathe some fresh air, see new sights that would bring a fresh view to their lives.

They hired a rental car to take them to Sylhet, where Raika's cousin and cousin's husband lived in a big house in a prestigious residential neighborhood, with an orchard full of fruit trees and a roof lined with potted flowers. The cousin's husband worked at a foreign cement company, where he earned a handsome salary. After a pleasant day at Raika's cousin's house, Saif and Raika set off for the Sylhet-Meghalaya border in one of the cousin's three cars, complete with chauffeur. The car dropped them at the border.

Some people Raika knew slightly, friends of her cousin, were already waiting at the border post, a group of three fat, middle-aged men and their wealthy-looking wives, with styled red hair, bleached, fair skin, and rings on their fingers. The men and women teased Saif and Raika, a newlywed couple on their honeymoon. Saif and Raika protested that they had been married two years. One of the women cupped Raika's chin, saying *she was so sweet and innocent*, with her bobbed hair, slender neck, and slim waist, and her whole future ahead of her. They also said nice things about Saif, how cute he was, what a cute husband Raika had caught. Most of all, they were impressed to hear where Saif and Raika worked. The party thanked Saif and Raika for leading Bangladesh on the path to prosperity and bringing Bangladesh to the world stage by developing its gas. When Saif told them that his former boss in explorations, an American who had returned to his home state Texas, hoped to hire Saif to the Texas office as a geologist, they were even more impressed.

"Well done! We need more Bangladeshi geologists on the global scene!" they congratulated him.

Soon afterward, the border office opened. They showed their passports with visas, and crossed the border to the other side, where the mountains were bigger, and the scenery was breathtaking. Saif and Raika hired a taxi to take them to a town near Barapani Lake, where they would stay in a hotel. The ride was harrowing. The taxi climbed higher and higher on the mountain, going perhaps eighty kilometers an hour on a narrow, winding road. They held their breaths and squealed by turn, holding each other, joking that they were about to be flung into the sky at any moment. Raika asked Saif to sing a song, and he obliged, singing tunelessly. As they climbed higher, Saif's lungs expanded. He opened the window and breathed the cold, clean air, crying out in surprise in the wind.

"Something is changing inside me! I can feel it." He felt like a man who had just been let out of jail and gulped his first breath of fresh air.

Raika dimpled her cheeks, blushing to see her husband so happy.

At their hotel in Barapani, they were informed that there was a curfew after dark because of the local insurgents. They had been unaware of any trouble in the region. Now they read on their phones about the rebel groups in Mizoram. They drank some tea and hurried to see Barapani Lake, which was a little distance from the hotel, so they could return before the curfew. It was an artificially constructed lake, created by an impressive dam, clear, blue water that stretched for miles. A soldier in uniform approached them. He was a short, slim man with a thin, long face and small eyes.

"Are you Bengali?" he asked them, looking lost and desperate.

"Yes," Raika said, a little surprised by his brazen approach, a stranger.

"I have been stationed here for months. I'm so lonely, away from my home in Calcutta. I hate it here!" the young man cried.

They chitchatted with the soldier for a while, then drifted off to be alone together and admire the beautiful view of the blue water.

In the evening, back at the hotel, Saif dressed in a blue shirt and dress pants, and Raika wore a pale pink shalwar kameez and an expensive imitation set with pink stones (a choker and two bracelets) that she had bought with her salary from the oil company. They walked out of their room together and sat down to eat at an outdoor restaurant near a sparkling swimming pool. The food was delicious, steaming white rice with fish curry, three different kinds of fried vegetables, and lentils.

"My work is hard," Raika complained. "I crunch numbers all day, sitting inside the four walls of a cubicle. It's not easy. But I'm proud of myself."

"It does feel exhausting sometimes to work inside all day, inside four walls," Saif said.

"They're not even walls!" Raika cried, a little forcefully. Her pretty face twisted, and her mouth turned down. "They are fake walls, cubicle walls!"

Saif nodded. He didn't say anything about how he felt about his own work. His eyes glazed as he stared at the bouncing waters of the swimming pool. He liked to look at the surface of things. On the surface, he had been a brilliant student and now he had been hired by a prestigious multinational company. Soon, he would be going abroad to work at the Houston office of the company. He made his family proud and earned a lot of money, which brought him all the things he desired, including this vacation.

The next day, they hired a taxi to take them to Shilong, where they checked into the Shilong Club Hotel. Then they boarded a tour bus that would take them to Cherrapunji, the highest point in the state of Meghalaya, literally the home of the clouds. As they started on a mountain road to the Khasi Hills, the bus drove even faster than their rickety taxi on the road to Shilong. Raika whispered to Saif that she felt safer on the bus because it was bigger. During the journey, Raika looked around her, observing the other passengers. Saif just stared out the window at the world outside.

As the bus climbed the mountain, the clouds that had been above them lurked below them. *They* were flying above the clouds, looking down at the fluffy, white balls. They passed a village with huts, with pigs outside. The houses were neatly stacked, stuck among the trees, with the dwellers' spades and brooms and little haystacks arranged in an orderly manner. Further ahead, Saif watched a little boy walking a black goat along the mountain road. The boy had brown sticks for arms and legs. He wore a pair of purple shorts hugging his hips. He looked about eight, with his big head, sticking up ears, and cropped hair, but perhaps he was small for his age. The boy and the goat walked together on the grass, in step, with the mountain and the sky behind them. Saif was struck by how close to the earth the two were, at one with the trees and the mud and everything around them. He was thinking how removed he himself was from all these things, stuck in his office doing calculations about where to find gas. Watching the boy and the goat, Saif's heart cried to be so close to the earth every day of his life, at every hour, not just while he was on vacation. It was difficult for him to gain respect at the company as a local, the label by which the expats referred to the Bengalis at the office. He tried to keep up on his science and push back at the expat geologists and engineers who tried to put him down, and he worked extra hard so that no one could ever find fault with him, but it was a lot.

Saif turned to Raika. "I really needed this vacation," he said.

Raika smiled sweetly and pressed his arm. "You deserved it, my *Jaan*," she said, addressing him by her favorite endearment.

Her face was heart-shaped and angelic, with small ears pressed back against her head, large eyes, and thin lips. He reminded himself how lucky they both were—young and in good health, working at a foreign company and now enjoying this beautiful scenery together.

The bus reached the top of the mountain and grunted to its designated stop. The passengers climbed out one by one, pulling on jackets and shawls. Raika piled on the embroidered wool shawl she had carried in her suitcase, and Saif put on his wedding-suit jacket. Perhaps for the sole pleasure of the tourists, a café had been constructed on top of the mountain, among the clouds.

"Welcome to Meghalaya, the home of the clouds," a dusky young man in an open-neck shirt and a blue blazer greeted them. The man wore a gold chain around his neck and pinkish-colored bell bottoms with white tennis shoes. His hair was cut in a longish style. He had good white teeth, which he flashed when he smiled. "If you put your hand out here, sometimes, you can touch the clouds, and your hand comes away wet. Yes, like that. You are in the clouds! Can you believe it?"

His English was broken and accented, but so was theirs. Saif and Raika both had trouble speaking English with the Europeans and Americans at their company, but they listened hard and were improving every day. Raika looked around and struck up a conversation with some of the other passengers from the bus. Saif, quieter, stood behind her and smiled appropriately when she mentioned him. One of the other tourists was a young man backpacking through India. He planned to go to Bangladesh next. Another couple was from the Andaman Islands, which was at the tip of India, in the middle of the Indian Ocean. Listening to the couple describing the islands, Saif's eyes lit up, and his heart widened. Again, he had that strange feeling that there were places he wanted to see and things he wanted to do, that he could feel happy in a way that he did not usually feel in his daily life.

The café was a small hut with wobbly tables and chairs and lit with tube lights. The inside smelled of fried oil and spices. The menu was limited, burgers and chips and egg rolls, with different kinds of soda to drink. Saif and Raika chewed on their burgers, drinking Coca Cola, and marveled at the mountainous region.

"It feels like heaven! This place must be heaven," Raika said.

"Yes, if there were a heaven, this would be it," Saif agreed. "The air is so crisp and fresh."

"I bet anyone who lives here is the happiest person in the world," Raika said.

Saif turned his head, looking around. He kept staring at the young man with the gold chain, probably only a few years younger than himself, who lived right here, in heaven. The young man went around from table to table, chatting with the tourists. When he reached Saif and Raika's table, he asked politely if he could sit with them.

"Yes, yes, of course," Raika said.

The young man sat down. He moved and talked like a mere boy, full of life, jumping onto the chair, moving nimbly. On his fingers, he wore fat rings with stones. He introduced himself as Dev.

"Do you manage this café?" Saif asked him.

"My uncle owns it. I help out," Dev said.

"Do you live here? It is so beautiful," Raika said.

"It's heaven," Saif supplied. Inside him, something was bubbling, bursting out of him. He had almost come to a decision. At any moment, when this young man left them, he would turn to Raika and tell her.

"Yes, yes, it is." Dev smiled.

"The air is so fresh, and the view is beautiful. And to be so close to the clouds. It's like a fairy tale," Raika continued.

"You know, legend says that the gods live in these clouds. Meghalaya is the temple of the gods," Dev said, in command of a never-ending array of superlatives to describe the place. He had a shining, triangular face with bright, intelligent eyes, thick eyebrows, and a slightly broken nose.

"What do you do?" Raika asked the young man.

"I just finished college," Dev said.

"And what will you do next? What are your plans?" Raika's voice was sweet and generous.

"I just hang around and help my uncle at the café. In the evening, I play guitar with my friends. That is all. I make music and help my uncle," Dev answered a little damply.

"Oh, no, I didn't at all mean that helping your uncle to run the café and playing the guitar was nothing. I think that your life is wonderful. You live in heaven," Raika said, beaming sweetly at the young man. "This is simply heaven! You must be very happy. I would trade my life any day for yours."

Dev frowned. "I don't play very well," he said.

"Oh, I'm sure you play very well. No matter how you play, you play for the gods, and the gods must be happy."

Raika had a way with words, which was why she had been so successful at the oil and gas company.

Dev grinned happily again, showing his strong, white teeth. "Can I tell you something?" he said. He cocked his head. "Just wait. My uncle is calling me. I'll come back."

After Dev left, Saif turned to Raika. "Listen, I've been thinking," he started. "I've never felt this way, like I am now, up here on top of the world. I feel so…alive. The air is fresh, and I feel so close to everything else that is alive."

"I know, I know," Raika said happily. It had been her decision to come to Meghalaya. She had booked the tickets and made all the arrangements.

Their guide and their bus driver appeared in view, telling the passengers that it was time to board the bus. People started getting up from their tables. Dev was nowhere in sight. Saif and Raika walked out of the cafe with the other tourists, emerging outside under a weak sun in a clear sky.

"What I mean to say is…," Saif said to Raika, "I want to feel this way every day of my life. I don't want to have to run away from my life when I am suffocating, and it's unbearable. I don't want to be alive only for a few days, only when I am on vacation." His voice was earnest, and his throat bobbed up and down.

He felt bold, close to a decision. He no longer wanted to live like that, trapped for eight hours a day in the office, feeling dead, fossilized, out of breath. And what if his former boss kept his promise, what if, and it was a big if, Saif did get to go to America? He was sure that he would continue to feel just as dead. His life would be meaningless as long as he was removed from the earth and the air.

All living things should breathe freely, he thought. That little boy walking his goat among the combed farmland had moved Saif to a tragic feeling. His heart had throbbed for what he could not touch, this view from a window, a life passing by. But now that he was standing on top of the mountain and looking at Dev, the man who lived his life in the clouds, Saif felt that he could be courageous, too. His lungs were full of the air on the top of the mountain.

"What are you saying?" Raika peered at him, shading her eyes and frowning.

"I want to quit my job," Saif started to say.

Dev reappeared beside the husband and wife. "Sorry, I was helping my uncle."

"We're leaving." Raika smiled apologetically at Dev.

"The story I wanted to tell you," Dev said energetically as if Raika hadn't spoken. "A few months back, I met an American man on this tour. He came on that bus, the same as you. And he said to me that when he got back to his home, in Texas, he would arrange for me to get a visa to America. So that's my plan. Soon, the American will make arrangements for me, and I will go away from this place. I will go to America!"

"But why?" Raika asked. "You live in the most beautiful place on earth."

"I'm bored here. It's so boring! I want to get away. I want to go to America." Dev grinned at Saif and Raika, his white teeth flashing, his gold chain glittering in the sun.

Saif studied Dev's face. His own face was twisted horribly, as if the young man had cut him deeply. He had been looking at Dev as a sign, as the source of courage and wisdom. And now, Dev, who was supposed to be a guide welcoming them to the abode of the clouds, was planning the same thing as everyone else. He was planning to emigrate to America. Saif turned away with a punctured heart. He avoided looking at Dev even while Raika chatted with the young man in a soft voice.

Soon, it was time for them to board the tourist bus. Raika shouted bye-bye to Dev, wishing him luck. Raika and Saif took their seats on the bus. The driver started the engine noisily, and the bus began to descend from the top of the mountain.

Raika turned to Saif. "What were you saying, my *Jaan?* Earlier?"

"Nothing. Forget it," Saif said. He shook his head, staring out the window at the deep ravines below, the pine-ravaged mountains, the play of sun and shadows, and the impossible majesty of the clouds so near. "Forget it."

Next Door

When Muna and her husband Mark moved into their new home in Oak Forest, she baked a big batch of cookies and carried them to her neighbors' doors. Her neighbor on her left side was a widow named Mrs. Smithers, a sweet old woman who lived in one of the last crumbling cottages in Oak Forest. On her right side, a young family of four had just moved into their newly renovated house, a husband and wife who worked in IT and their two-year-old twins. Muna had watched their house transform in front of her eyes—the old garage had been converted into a room, and the sidings and roof had been replaced recently.

"Oh, my gosh!" Muna gasped, seeing the blue-eyed toddlers. "I want to come over often and smoosh these guys!"

"You're welcome to come any time and take them off my hands," said the twins' mom. She was a tall, lanky, blonde beauty who looked exhausted. There were black smudge marks under her eyes.

"You have such a beautiful house. If you want any work done on the house, just to let you know, my husband Mark works in construction," Muna said, handing them Mark's business card, which she had designed herself.

Mark had built the house Mark and Muna lived in. The first thing Mark did after he proposed to Muna was to start building their future home. His parents had handed down the property to him. He had grown up in the old house that used to stand on the lot, which his parents had bought three decades ago when the neighborhood had been working class. Mark had demolished his childhood home and then designed and built a brand-new house for Muna. Mark owned a construction company, so it was no sweat for him. He loved the experience. For a whole year, he arrived at the site in the morning and stayed there all day, supervising the construction. The men were known to him, workers he had used for other projects. Often, he worked alongside the men on his house, singing with them to the Spanish songs blasting on the radio as he put in wiring or a piece of sheetrock. He had had to cut down a couple of trees to build the house, but he left the two crepe myrtles in the back standing. Mark's parents, who had retired and now lived on a ranch in Conroe, said the trees were their good wishes for the young couple.

While the house was being built, Muna accompanied Mark to the construction site at night after work (they had lived separately before they were married, she in a studio apartment in the Heights and he in an apartment on Shepherd, as she was a good Muslim girl). Each time she visited the site, covered with cement and dust, her eyes misted with hope for their new life together. When the house was finally finished, it stood two stories tall, painted in a lavender-purplish color, Muna's choice, with lots of glass and chrome inside, and all-white counter tops and sinks and commodes. She liked bright, simple colors and straight lines.

Muna was an optimistic, cheerful person. She was the kind of person that people describe as having a sunny disposition, someone who puts a smile on everyone's face. Certainly, for Mark, she had been that person during his bout of depression after he had fallen through the roof of a house he was fixing and broken his back. He had lain in a hospital bed for three months, and she had gone to visit him every day.

Muna was big and busty and liked to wear strapless sundresses with matching sandals. She loved shoes and handbags. Her favorite pastime was to go shopping at the mall and buy herself something every week. She wore her naturally curly, dark hair in moussed ringlets held back by a headband. She owned and managed a nail and hair salon called Henna. She offered henna treatment for nails, hair, and face, whole-body henna treatment, and henna products for sale. Her secret twist was to use ingredients she knew from her Bangladeshi heritage.

For example, she offered her customers turmeric smoothies, clove and cardamom tea, and black seed oil for their hair. Sometimes, she held workshops in which she showed women how to make and apply turmeric face masks. Her own face was immaculate, smooth, and shiny from the constant application of face masks and framed by thin, plucked eyebrows and kohl-lined eyes. Her lips were Mark's favorite, always painted a scarlet red. She laughed loudly and ate well, and she hugged and kissed everyone she met.

Muna's absolute favorite person in the neighborhood was her neighbor on her left side Mrs. Smithers. Mrs. Smithers and Muna hit it off instantly the moment they met. Muna called her Miss Mary Ellen.

"How you doin', Miss Mary Ellen?" Muna asked over the fence every morning as Mrs. Smithers watered her plants.

The old lady straightened with a startled look on her pink, round face. Seeing Muna, she smiled. "I'm doing well, Muna. It makes me so happy to see you. Talking to you always makes my heart glad."

Muna thought Mary Ellen was just an adorable old lady, with fluffy, white hair and rosy cheeks, and clear, sharp, blue eyes that warmed Muna's heart.

"I can tell you were a beauty once, Miss Mary Ellen," Muna said with a laugh. "You're always fluffing that lovely hair of yours. It's perfect. You know how to keep a good figure too."

It was Mary Ellen Smithers who first told Muna about the Nextdoor app. One morning in the fall, they were standing in their yards talking across the low, barbed-wire fence as the crepe myrtle tree in Muna's backyard rained ochre leaves on both their heads.

"Now, Muna. I don't have the app myself, but my friend Sally tells me all about it every day when we talk. She gets all the neighborhood news on it. Muna, if you get *on it*, you can advertise your business."

"Oh, thank you, Miss Mary Ellen. That's an *excellent* idea." Muna gushed, scratching her upper lip with a painted nail. "I'll do that as soon as I get home from work!"

In fact, Muna got on it at work, finding the app and filling in her information while sitting at the nail salon. There weren't many customers that day. She didn't worry about the low days because then there were days when there was a wedding shower or a birthday party, and, oh, boy, she was in business. Twenty young women would skip in sometimes, laughing and holding on to one another. After she sent her information to the app, Muna sat at her desk in the purple-lit room set up with swivel chairs and tall mirrors, refreshing her cell phone to see if she was in the group.

That evening, when she got home, the crepe myrtle tree in the front was still raining red and orange leaves. Mark had chili going on the stove. He cooked chili every few weeks with five different kinds of peppers, lots of garlic, and chocolate.

"Oh, darling! Thanks. I'm pooped." Muna laughed, shaking her hair out of her eye and shrugging off her high heels. Today, she was wearing a yellow, capped-sleeve A-line dress and matching yellow heels. She had painted her nails yellow sitting at the salon.

"It's our anniversary," Mark said. He was a tall, handsome lad, black bearded and broad shouldered, with bushy eyebrows and a square jaw, laid back, with a lazy smile always playing on his lips.

"Oh, darling! Really? I forgot!" Muna made a moue of disappointment with her painted lips.

"Yeah." Mark smiled.

Muna entered the kitchen and embraced him. He handed her a small box. Muna struggled with the red and blue polka dot wrapping. Inside, there was a hand-written note, *to my girl next door*, and a dog tag.

"What's this?" Muna asked.

Mark laughed shyly. "Come out!" Holding her wrist, he led her to the backyard, where a Golden Doodle pup crouched, wagging its tail. "I just rescued her from a shelter," Mark drawled. "She's all neutered and vaccinated and everythin'."

"Oh, my darling. I couldn't be happier," shrieked Muna, gathering up the little creature in her arms. "Ooh, she's nervous. It's okay, baby." She rubbed the pup's soft fur with her fingers.

"We wouldn't be a perfect family without a dog," Mark said.

When they retired to bed that night, with Goldie the pup between them, Muna checked her phone again, to see if she had been admitted to the Nextdoor group for their neighborhood.

"Yes!" she cried.

"What is it?" Mark asked.

"Nothing. Just a perfect end to the night."

Within another month, Muna had two dogs, Goldie, the Golden Doodle pup, and an elderly Labrador named George, a big, lumbering, friendly fellow with half a tail whom Muna had rescued. He had been abandoned in the middle of a thicket by the 610 exit off I-45 with a bowl of yellow water. Nowadays, Muna could be seen walking the two dogs around the neighborhood on sunny afternoons, wearing a pink hoodie. Whenever she passed someone, she waved and called out *hello* in an upbeat voice. People waved back to her—old women working in their gardens; kids playing basketball in their driveway, with a mom on watch; an old man who walked his German schnauzer at the same time.

"It's a good neighborhood," Muna said to Mark. "It's a good group of people."

She had successfully logged into the Nextdoor app by now and was one of the most avid participants on the site. She read every post greedily, interested in finding out about local dentists, restaurants, and businesses. There was something so intimate about these posts from her neighborhood. She didn't usually like to read newspaper articles and books bored her, but she had become a constant reader on the app whenever she was bored, at the salon, on her couch at home, or even while walking the dogs around the block. The response was enthusiastic when she posted about Mark's construction business and her salon. Of course, people were always looking for someone in construction, and everyone needed a hair salon. Whenever Muna found out about a neighborhood event on the app, like a barbecue or a crawfish cookout at a local restaurant or the local farmer's market on Saturday, she showed up with a smile, dragging Mark along, their two dogs in tow, eager to make friends.

"Look, Mark," Muna said one day, from the grey Ikea couch where she was snuggling with her dogs and a glass of red wine. "Someone posted, *Is this your dog?* Oh, poor pup. Looks like someone found him on the bayou trail."

"You could get involved with that kind of work," Mark said, coming in from the kitchen. "Rescuing dogs. Alerting neighbors if someone lost a dog or sheltering them till someone offers to adopt."

"That's an excellent idea. I'll do that," Muna said, stroking her dogs' bellies.

Soon, Muna was posting on Nextdoor about rescues regularly. *Is this your dog?* She had an online army of friends, dog lovers like her, who would find dogs on the street, bring them in, give the poor, shivering animals some food, and post to the site, asking if anyone would adopt them. *A cute husky. A friendly guy. Seems nervous, but very loving, giving me lots of licks!* Muna would type with her long nails. Soon, she was regularly dropping off a dog she had rescued off the street at BARC. Then she would keep posting, asking for donations, pleading with people to adopt the animal. It was Muna's favorite pastime to come home at the end of a hard day of work and sit on the grey couch overlooking the backyard with the crepe myrtle trees, nestle against her dogs, their furs fondling her skin and hair, and check the news on Nextdoor. There was so much gossip on the app! Someone had posted that their little free library was emptied out overnight.

"People are so sick!" Muna said. She read the posts aloud to Mark.

Someone wanted to give away free boxes. Then there were the urgent posts. *Please help us find our missing son.* Some posts were lifesaving. One day, when it had rained hard and there was high water on the roads, neighbors were posting flash flood warnings on the app long before any news sites. Mark had a truck with big wheels, but Muna depended on her neighbors on NextDoor to get home safely that night.

Within a year of their marriage, Muna was pregnant. Only a year ago, Mark had driven her to Big Bend and proposed to her. He'd had to reserve the campsite a year before that, jumping on the site at the first possible chance to book it. They had packed a small picnic and hiked up to a mountain from where they could see the sunset. She was nibbling on a biscuit and sipping some wine in a plastic cup when he had proposed to her. It was the most romantic thing. Although they had been dating for almost six years—since their senior year in high school—Muna hadn't always been sure that Mark would marry her. She supposed their relationship had gotten serious when he had got into that accident and broken his back, and she had looked after him.

Sitting on top of the mountain at Big Bend, Mark said to Muna, "I knew then, at the lowest point of my life, that you would be there for me. You know what they say? In sickness and in health. You had already proved to me what that vow meant because you were right beside me in my sickness."

"Oh, Mark." Muna buried her head in Mark's breast, asking softly, "Do you really like me?"

"Yup," Mark said. "You're the image I've always had in my head of the girl I would marry. The girl next door."

Muna's parents had come to the United States two decades ago from Bangladesh, when she had been a baby of four, with cute curls and a snotty nose. Her parents ran a gas station together. The gas station had bullet-proof windows and grills on the doors, but apart from this precaution in guarding their business against the bad elements of the neighborhood, her parents were open, friendly, and curious about all the people they met. Her mother's best friend had been an auntie from El

Salvador who taught her how to make pupusa, tamale for Christmas, and tres leches cakes for birthday parties.

The school Muna attended had been rough, though. People were always being hauled off to the principal's room, or worse, the police station. Once, the police came on a suspicion of drugs at the school and banged up students against the lockers to do a strip search. Some of the boys came from broken homes. They had missing parents and broken teeth. Sometimes, a girl would cry in the bathroom because her uncle had been deported that day. Another girl would leave early to pick up her younger brother from school. Her friends got pregnant all the time. That was all Muna's parents ever asked of her–don't get pregnant. And Muna didn't, but she sure did try make up and nail polish and cigarettes. She started drinking in high school and she flirted with boys who liked her, but she saved herself for Mark till they were out of high school, both starting out in their businesses, proper adults.

I'm pregnant. Muna wrote on the app. *Does anyone have maternity clothes I can borrow?* A basket of replies poured in, women offering clothes in a variety of sizes and styles. Muna pressed her hand to her heart, filled with emotion. Her dark eyes in her bronze skin shone brightly. She moved her dogs on the couch, making herself comfortable, pulling up her tired legs. She had applied henna on her palms in the salon that day, and her hands smelled of it, a dark, musty smell that reminded her of her parents and her childhood. She typed, tapping out a string of heart emojis.

Thank you! You guys are all so nice! My neighbor said if I get too big, she'll go to the grocery store and buy things for me. And if it comes to it, she will cook for me and look after the baby, too! More comments poured in. *You're lucky to have such a sweet neighbor! That's what neighbors are for.*

"We live in such a good neighborhood, darling. Look at these people," Muna called to Mark.

"Coming!" Mark yelled.

Muna's eye fell on a post about thieves. *Thieves stealing packages from porch.* People had posted videos from different cameras of a pair of young men going from porch to porch stealing Amazon packages. She told Mark about it, shouting in the direction of the kitchen, remarking how sad that was.

"Well, that's what the app is for. Just neighborhood crime watch," Mark shouted back. "That's why I don't get on it."

"Ha ha." Muna laughed, although to her, it was about community, neighbors offering free toys, someone asking for a last-minute nanny, a couple of people joking about the long line at the neighborhood doughnut shop. It was like standing with neighbors at a corner street and chatting together.

"Wait," she said, sitting up and leaning into her screen. "Mark! Come here!" She wiped her dank, thick hair with both hands.

Mark entered the room and pushed Goldie and George off the couch, onto the hardwood floor. They left with loud yelps.

"Mark. Who's that?" she asked, pointing to her cellphone screen.

"Why, it's you. In your pink hoodie," he said in his simple, quiet way, peering at the image, bending over her dark head.

"It looks like that," she said. "Oh!"

"What's wrong? What are they saying?"

"They think I was trying to steal a package from a house! *Thief in pink. Appears to be a lady or boy from build. Two dogs. Tried to take package but then decided against it.* Now I remember that day. I saw a package getting wet on the steps and moved it further up the porch, next to the front door!"

"Well, just comment and explain!" said Mark.

"All right. I'll do that," Muna said. She had a big tear in her eye. She didn't like to be misunderstood.

"What? Don't stew in it. Go for a walk. It's good for you. You're pregnant," Mark said.

"Okay."

Muna pulled on her pink hoodie over her white dress and a pair of squeaky-clean, white sneakers and gathered her dogs, putting the pink leash on Goldie and the blue leash on George. On the way, she passed sweet Miss Mary Ellen, who grinned and shouted that Muna was getting very big. Muna and the dogs continued their jaunt, Muna whistling happily. Goldie was just old enough to be able to walk on the road without hurting herself. At the traffic light on Golf, on a whim, she crossed to the other side of the road, into another part of the neighborhood, taking a different route from her usual walk.

"Why not? Right?" she said cutely to Goldie and George.

The dogs really liked their walk in the sun, in the mild fall, among the oak trees. She imagined the years rolling out in front of her, strolling along these paths with her child in a stroller and her two dogs, Mark, by her side. It would be idyllic to raise their children in Mark's old neighborhood, where he had grown up. The funny thing was that the neighborhood had been deed restricted before. The original deed that Mark had showed Muna stipulated that no people of color were allowed, except as help. That language in the deed had been so funny that Mark and Muna had had a big laugh about it. A lot of new families had moved in recently on their side of the street, young people starting out just like Mark and Muna, Asian, Hispanic, Black, and White.

Muna strode down the street lined with mature oak trees, admiring the big custom-built houses in this part of the neighborhood—upstairs balconies with chairs arranged in a circle, cute garage apartments at the back, circular driveways, curved trees, and manicured gardens, classic southern-style architecture and modern builds, and oh, a lovely old brick house with three ducks in front basking in a sunlit puddle.

"No, no, Goldie. George." Muna strained the dogs' leashes, laughing as their backs arched.

Walking past the house with the ducks, they crossed Alba. Here the sidewalk ended, so they stepped onto the road. Muna walked at a brisk pace, her mind wandering. Her dogs kept pace with her, angling their bodies as they moved in unison. A car approached from the front. She could hear another car coming from behind. Quickly, she stepped onto the grass, tugging the leash on both dogs to take them off the road. Just in time, too! A Toyota truck sped by them at highway speed.

"Whew, that was a narrow call!" Muna said to Goldie and George, blowing air through her hair.

"It would help if you walked in the right direction," a voice called from behind her.

Muna looked up to see a lean man with a thin face, approaching her from the opposite direction. He wore a football jacket with maroon and white stripes. A baseball hat covered loose strands of long blonde hair that draped his neck, and a mousy strip of blonde mustache quivered above his lips.

"Thank you," she said, being polite.

Nearing them, the man stopped. "You need to get off that grass!" he snarled.

"What? This is city property," Muna said.

The guy rolled his eyes and walked on, shaking his head. "If you don't know how to walk, maybe you, uh, you don't belong here," he said over his shoulder.

"What?" Muna frowned, her blood roiling now.

After a moment, she started walking again. Did she imagine it, or were Goldie and George alert and hesitant? American flags flew on all the houses, which had well-kept lawns and painted fences. On the road she would have to take to head back, a few moms stood outside with their babies, chatting and laughing. Toddler bikes lay strewn on their sides in the middle of the road. The moms wore bright T-shirts and jogging pants, and baseball hats, their golden hair in ponytails, coffee mugs in hand. The moms and the bikes took up the entire road. Muna didn't feel comfortable walking between the women, with all the bikes and scooters lying on their sides.

She kept walking past that intersection, deciding to turn at the next block. But that street was a dead end, so they turned left.

She didn't feel so great about the walk anymore. It was getting cold, and her nose felt stuffed up. She wanted to go home and get inside, sit safely on her couch. Turning two corners, she realized that she had landed on the same street that she had seen before, the one she had wanted to avoid. The moms were still standing on the road, chatting in loud, relaxed voices. Muna hesitated. On the one hand, she really wanted to get home fast. She was lost and she didn't want to risk walking into another dead end. But she really did not want to walk into those moms. Something about them made her pause. Something about everything here, which she could not name, but her dogs sensed too.

Goldie and George growled when Muna started to walk forward.

"What is it?" she said. "It's fine. Come on. Don't you want to get home?"

Muna grinned widely as she passed the moms. "Hiya!" she said, raising her hand high. "Nice day for the kids to be out, huh?" She walked with her stomach out, bulging under the velour dress, so that they could see she was one of them, soon to have a little one of her own.

The moms turned to her, then turned inward and went on talking. From the opposite direction, the man in the baseball hat that she had run into earlier came back up the street, walking toward her. One of the little girls, with lovely, long hair, a red dress, and cowboy boots, ran up to the man and cried, *Daddy!* He picked her up, laughing. The women laughed as well.

Muna was now neck and neck with the man.

"You still here?" he snarled.

"It's my neighborhood," she muttered.

"I don't think so, by the way you look," he shot back at her,.

"Oh, yeah? I'll see about that." Muna started to walk past the guy.

He yelled at her behind her back, "Hey, aren't you the thief in the hoodie they're writing about on Nextdoor?"

Muna kept walking. Her heart was pumping furiously. She had half a mind to fetch Mark and come back to confront the heckler. She crossed the road and walked past the houses she had passed before, having to tug on Goldie and George. A group of middle-aged people, tall, with greying brown hair, dressed in sweaters and jackets, huddled together, one couple on their driveway and another standing in the street, talking languidly, hands stuffed in jacket pockets. They stared at Muna with big eyes. The air became chilly, and a slight wind froze her extremities and her nose and lips. Even the windows of the houses seemed to stare down at Muna and her dogs. She picked up her pace, out of a need to get home safely. Goldie and George began to bark loudly and sharply, tugging at their leashes, making her task difficult.

"Stop it, you two!" she cried. "Let's work together so we can get home. Cooperate. All right?"

The dogs looked at her. She halted and bent her head, trying to get some oxygen. When she straightened, a bare-chested black man was jogging toward them, wearing neon running shorts, with headphones in his ears. He ran with his eyes half closed, so he didn't see Muna or the dogs as he ran past them. But at the sight of him, George and Goldie yapped, wagging their tails. Muna's head cleared.

"It's all right, guys," she called to the dogs. "Come on. Let's go home and have a nice dinner."

They walked the length of the block and reached the main road. They still had to cross the busy road, where the cars buzzed past recklessly, at highway speeds. They would keep walking at a fast pace till they reached home, and once they got inside, Muna would lock the door. Then she would sit on the couch, with her puppies beside her, and delete the Nextdoor app. From now on, she would only walk in the neighborhood on her side of the road, near home, perhaps to the next block, and the next, but no farther.

Urgency

Polly's father died in Bangladesh. Her mother had died a year before that. Polly, an only child, unmarried, had been living by herself in Houston, far from her parents. She had left home two decades ago for a master's degree in the US and never returned. Now she was surprised to receive an outpouring of love from her father's friends in Bangladesh. Her way of grieving was to not receive any calls—no tears, no ceremony, just silence—but these were international calls, coming from Bangladesh, in the middle of the night, so she had to answer.

"Come back and settle your property," Bashir Uncle advised Polly over the crackling phone one night.

Another night, she woke up to fierce, urgent ringing, *crriiing, crriiing, criiing.* "Hello, this is your Rahim Uncle. We are all meeting to discuss how to help you."

Yet another friend of her father, Musa Uncle, cried on the line for several minutes, then asked in a clogged, emotional voice, "Tell me, child, what can I do for you?

Polly called them all uncle, but she was not related to them by blood, and she did not know them well, knew them only by name or remembered them only dimly from the past, separated by many long years of absence. Her real uncle, her father's younger brother in Dhaka, had given her the news of her father's death (her father had been ill for months, suffering from lung cancer, and she had been meaning to visit in December). She had been frightened by the news.

"Should I fly home now?" she had asked her uncle with a child's cry of alarm.

"It is up to you."

In the end, Polly did not attend her father's burial. They would not have waited for her in any case. Her uncle had explained that according to the rules of Islam, the body had to be buried as quickly as possible. But he told her to come soon, to settle her affairs while he was alive. Her parents had been university teachers at Dhaka University, but they had still managed to build a house in Dhaka, and her father had some agricultural land in his village. Her uncle wanted her to come home and complete the paperwork to take possession of these properties.

This frightened her as well, that she was suddenly an adult expected to take care of her affairs. She was afraid to open the bowels of her parents' accounts, their lands, legal documents, and the annals of their home, bulging with their personal belongings and the dark tunnels of their memories. Polly's parents had never taught her about money matters, never involved her in their affairs, leaving her to study and earn degrees, relegating the twists of legalities and money to the grownups. She still did not consider herself up to the task of taking stock of her inheritance.

In December, Polly finally flew to Dhaka, scraping together Christmas holidays and three days of grief leave with her paid vacation days from work in the finance section of an oil company. On the plane, her chest felt heavy. She couldn't breathe. For the duration of the flight, she sat in her seat with a stricken expression around her mouth, her eyes frozen on the personal TV screen in front of her, watching one episode after another of a funny sitcom on the flight's entertainment offering.

Her uncle was supposed to receive her at the airport. When Polly emerged from customs, dragging only a carry-on roller suitcase, there was no one waiting for her inside the airport building. She was to go outside and find her uncle. When her parents had been alive, they had a trick of meeting her in the domestic terminal, which was deserted and calm compared to the crammed, crowded anxiety of the international arrivals. Polly pushed herself through the crowd, thick with the odor of her countrymen. This was her first time visiting in December. The fares were usually higher in the winter months, so she had preferred the off-season opportunities, a week in February or March. Before that, in the ancient past, when she had been a master's student, she used to go home for the whole hot, sticky summer.

At first, she could not find her uncle and had to wander farther out on the dusty balcony outside the brick building, and then onto the dust-swept parking lot, where she was thronged by coolies wanting to carry her luggage.

A thin, short man in a tan shirt emerged out of the mass of faces and said, "Apa, this way. Sir is waiting inside the car."

Her uncle sat inside his blue refurbished Toyota, a car she still remembered, a family icon, his fingers stuffing a cigarette into his mouth. He was a retired diplomat and a big smoker like her father.

"Hello, Polly," he greeted from the backseat, through smoke. His eyes were squeezed, and his forehead was furrowed. He looked thin and dark, and shrunken.

Polly climbed into the back beside her uncle while the driver rolled her carrier bag around behind the car and lifted it into the trunk. On the ride home, her uncle spoke slowly, sounding garbled and frail, laboriously going over her father's burial details (her father had been buried in their village home, outside Dhaka), while Polly listened dumbly.

Her uncle lived on the north side of town, in a respectable, ancient house with a garden and tall trees, one of the last remaining houses in a rapidly developing city where houses were being torn down to erect high-rise buildings to accommodate a growing urban population, or perhaps to make money off rising real estate values. The furniture in the spacious drawing room was old, heavy tables and ornate sofas brought over from Turkey, China, and India, relics of all the places where her uncle had been posted as a diplomat. Frumpy curtains kept the room dark and heavy, covered with dusty upholstery. Polly had to sit on the sofa and chat with her uncle without washing or taking a bath from a bucket, things she would have normally done had she gone to her parents' home.

"You have to go to your parents' flat tomorrow, to decide what you will keep and what you will throw away," her uncle said.

A manservant dressed in a khaki suit rolled a dinner trolley into the room bearing cucumber sandwiches and chicken patties on the upper tier, and little quarter plates painted with a floral design on the corner and triangular, folded napkins on the lower tier.

Her aunt entered the dark room and greeted her in a somnolent voice. "How are you, Polly?" She was an emaciated woman with black lines under her eyes. She still wore a gold bracelet on each sticky wrist. She asked what Polly planned to do with her dead mother's saris. "You should give them away to poor women," her aunt advised.

Polly nodded. She ate five of the mini sandwiches and felt her throat run dry. A wave rose in her chest. She thought of all the things she must do, and how little time she had.

"Tomorrow, you must go with me to obtain a death certificate," her uncle said, picking out a fresh cigarette from his packet.

"Doesn't she need a national ID?" her aunt asked.

"We will get that done. Is your passport current?" her uncle asked, turning to her.

Polly nodded with chicken flesh in her mouth.

"Don't forget her parents' bank accounts," her aunt said.

"We must go to court after that. The court is in Sadar Ghat, near the Buriganga River…"

"Are you sure she has to go to court? She'll get sick traveling to Sadar Ghat. There is so much dust, and you have to sit in the traffic for hours on those narrow roads."

Polly' parents had lived in a flat on the university campus, provided to them for the duration of their teaching jobs. The court was even farther south. Dhaka traffic meant that it might take the whole day just to get one thing done.

"I have to meet my father's friends tomorrow?" Polly spoke up timidly. "They've set up a meeting tomorrow morning to figure out how to help me."

"Is the car available to take her where she wants to go?" her uncle asked her aunt.

"No. The driver agreed to take his vacation tomorrow–"

Polly's eyes became heavy. She leaned back against the dusty upholstery of the sofa, rested her bare feet on the Persian carpet, and closed her eyes, comforted by her uncle's and aunt's voices buzzing around her head as she drifted off into her childhood.

The next morning, Polly's father's friend Bashir Uncle sent a car to Uttara to Polly's Uncle's house to bring Polly down to Dhanmondi. The Pajero arrived at ten in the morning. Polly climbed in happily, resting her plump body in the backseat, panting for breath. But the sleek Pajero soon became stuck in traffic with buses and trucks and other cars honking and hooting in the clogged air. The landscape of Dhaka had changed while she had been away. There were new bridges and buildings, but also the sheer number of cars had increased.

Bashir Uncle lived on the eighth floor of an apartment building, accessible by elevator, on top of a tight parking space crammed with cars that had to back into their spaces with precise movements. The lobby was crisp and modern, with a marble floor and tiled walls. The building her parents had lived in, from an earlier era, had had stained inner walls and blackened stairs. Inside Bashir Uncle's flat, there was more marble. The mirror-polished floors threw off a blinding light. Every room was on a split level, multiple rooms spinning off into their own universes, painted walls, high ceilings, and murals on all sides, a world apart from the brick and plaster of her parents' flat on the university campus.

"How was your journey?" Bashir Uncle asked Polly.

Polly could not place him in her memory. He was a thin man sporting a thin, grey mustache and close-cropped, immaculate silver hair. He looked elegant, well preserved in a sleeveless blue sweater and collared white shirt, unlike her smoker father, who had exploded in a dust of decay and rot. Polly stared at her father's friend with jealous eyes.

"The traffic was very bad. It took me three hours to travel, what, a few miles?"

Bashir Uncle laughed. "You're telling me about Dhaka traffic as if I don't know? I meant the trip from the US to Bangladesh."

A slight boy with matchstick brown legs sticking out of shorts wheeled a two-tier dinner trolley laden with food into the room. He parked the trolley and handed Polly a porcelain quarter plate with a stern, serious expression on his brown face. He had a high forehead, and large eyes narrowed in acute observation. Polly checked out the familiar wares of *nashta*, offered midmorning and then again at high tea, a relic from her childhood—samosa, chotpoti, and little fried vegetable fritters. She rose from the sofa and helped herself, clattering silver utensils. The bell rang rapidly a few times in succession. Each time, another uncle walked in. The uncles greeted one another in loud, cheery voices, alive and hearty.

"This is your Rahim Uncle." Bashir Uncle introduced Polly to a tall, big man with jet black hair and a red face. "He just flew in from Rajshahi today to meet with you."

"I'm honored, Uncle," Polly said, setting her plate down and rising to meet the tall man. "What do you do in Rajshahi?"

"Oh, I retired and settled in my ancestral home. My father used to have a small house there and some agricultural land. I'm not rich like your other uncles here." Rahim Uncle laughed vigorously, showing strong lung capacity. "But it's enough for me to live off. I get everything I need from the land. Rice. Vegetables. We have a few mango orchards."

"Your uncle goes fishing," Bashir Uncle said to Polly. "He is living the life."

Polly looked from one face to the other, the uncles with their able bodies and rosy, youthful faces, and recalled her shrunken parents in their last days, their skins grey from lack of sunlight, cooped in their flat, eating processed noodles because they had stopped going to the market to buy fresh food. Their lives had shrunk to just existing to pay bills and taxes.

The meeting began after Musa Uncle arrived. The other uncles evidently thought him the most capable among them about property matters. Polly remembered him as the uncle who had taken a share in the cow her father slaughtered for Eid. He used to come to their university flat to discuss club activities, and he played bridge with her father at the club.

The little boy returned carrying a heavy porcelain tray of teacups and stood perfectly still while the uncles helped themselves, one black tea, one tea with ginger and sugar, and one milk tea with no sugar. Polly took the tea with milk and sugar, helping herself to two spoons of sugar, then sat back down.

"You all look very well," she said to her father's friends sitting on sofas and chairs around her.

"We meet frequently," Bashir Uncle said, crossing his foot over the opposite knee and stroking his chin with a ringed finger. "We meet to play cards and badminton. You know what they say. Good feelings flow when old friends meet." Bashir Uncle was the host, although she kept getting the uncles mixed up. She stared at each uncle, trying to burn their faces and their identities into memory.

"Now, Polly," Musa Uncle began, "you know that I helped your parents build their house in Gulshan. You have to hand it to a developer now—"

"Musa knows everything. He will help you with your property," Rahim Uncle said to her confidently, closing his eyelids and stretching his lower lip.

"Can't I just sell the house?" Polly asked, a hot samosa crumbling in her mouth.

"No, no," Musa Uncle objected, "no one will buy a whole house now. You have to build an apartment building, and the only way to do that, since you don't have any liquid money, is to hand the property over to a developer."

"But my father did not believe in apartment buildings. He believed there was overbuilding in Dhaka. He would not have wanted to turn his house into a flat building," Polly said, retrieving this memory of him out of dust.

Even as she objected, she knew that his friends knew this about her father, they knew her father and loved him. And that was why they had gathered to help her, his daughter. Dressed in stylish jackets and sweaters, throwing off the scent of roses and jasmine, they surrounded her in the warm enclosure of the drawing room, the winter sun trickling in through the glass windowpanes, falling on the familiar glass showcase in the corner holding curios, resembling the showcase in her parents' old flat that she had not yet entered, and on an old glass-paned bookshelf pushed against the wall, the spines of Bengali novels visible, standing upright next to dark volumes of the *Encyclopedia Britannica*.

"We know that your father was opposed to apartment buildings, but times have changed. For you, that is the best solution," Rahim Uncle, the country gentleman idling his retired years in Rajshahi, said confidently. Polly remembered that her father, too, had wanted to retire one day and move to his village, but he had died before his time. She tried to swallow her disappointment. "Musa Uncle is right. He knows everything. Sell it to the developer, they give you an advance, and they handle everything. Otherwise, it's impossible for you to deal with so much from so far–. Trust your uncle."

"I'm selling my own house to a developer," Musa Uncle said. "We can approach them together, get a good deal on the advance and turnaround time. You will get a lot of money as advance."

"The amount of money your parents have left you…you will never have to work a day in your life." Rahim Uncle guffawed (he was the one who had called the others to Polly's aid).

"The developer could even sell the flats for you once they have been built," Musa Uncle said.

"Don't worry about a thing," Bashir Uncle said. "Your uncles are here to protect you."

At these words, Polly's eyes glittered. She began to imagine a new level of financial comfort, a gift from her parents and the country she had left behind.

Polly spent the next two weeks following her father's brother, her real uncle, to government offices, getting her passport renewed, a national ID card, a death certificate, and a letter from her uncle to show that he had no right to her father's property. Her uncle used devious means to get these documents, which normally took months to procure.

One day, accompanied by Musa Uncle, Polly met with the developer in a high-rise office building in Gulshan. They showed her a sample contract, pages and pages of it, which Musa Uncle promised his lawyer would look over. As they looked over the brochure of what their future building would look like, high rises soaring above the city, the wind blowing over a rooftop swimming pool, the developer sweet talked them and served them milk tea, which Polly and Musa Uncle drank in companionable silence.

There was one thing Polly had to do on her own. She still had to clean out her childhood home, her parents' flat on the university campus. After her uncle's chauffeur Ali returned from his village home in nearby Tangail, where he had gone to see his ailing mother who was on her deathbed, the newly bearded Ali, gaunt and squinty eyed, accompanied Polly to her parents' flat in the university quarters, which the authorities had left empty for her to sort through out of respect for her father. When Polly and Ali entered the flat, the dust engulfed them. Polly held up the orna of her shalwar kameez to her mouth, and Ali raised the collar of his shirt to shield his lips and nostrils.

"Get out of here quickly, Apa," Ali cried, addressing her respectfully as an elder sister from behind the material of his shirt. "You will get a fever otherwise."

While Ali leaned against the front door, shielding himself aloofly against the dust, Polly stepped through the dank rooms. Dust balls entered through her nose, ears, and eyes and settled in the corners of her mouth. Glancing from the old television with knobs in its cabinet to the showcases laden with glass figures and the armoires packed with tumbling saris, she called Ali to pack up the saris, her aunt's advice ringing in her ears. Then she fled, taking nothing else, directing Ali to throw away or sell everything. Later, after she had left the premises, after a good night's sleep, she realized that those rooms had held, at the least, her parents' diplomas, PhD dissertations, her own degree certificates, family albums, and everything belonging to her that her parents had carefully preserved over decades.

At the end of two weeks, Polly returned to America. At first, she called her uncles for every question she had. Whenever the real estate developer asked for this document, or proposed an advance of this amount, Polly called her uncles in a panic. Perhaps her questions were exceptionally needy, or perhaps she called them too much, or her voice screeched, but slowly, the connections began to weaken. The very capable Musa Uncle had a heart attack and could no longer answer her questions about the developer. She called him a few times after he returned from the hospital. After a preamble about his health, she proceeded to ask about how the developer was processing the contracts. She couldn't help it. Panic gripped her. She wanted to get everything she could out of the country, to her present life in America, where she could use it. Bashir Uncle visited Australia for six months to be with his daughter, so he was out of communication during this time, and Rahim Uncle's phone connection in Rajshahi was particularly bad. The little web they had built around her slowly disintegrated. She got the message and stopped calling eventually.

A decade later, Bashir Uncle called Polly out of the blue. His wife had died, and his daughter had moved from Australia to Austin, Texas, where he was visiting her. He wanted to see if he could come visit Polly, his old friend's daughter, in Houston. Bashi Uncle's daughter had agreed to drive him to Houston so that he could see Polly.

When they met, at a Starbucks Polly had named in Katy, she stared at him out of shock. Bashir Uncle's daughter had dropped him at the store and left, and he was sitting alone at a table sipping coffee out of a paper cup. He was missing two front teeth, and his mouth had caved in, as if he were missing more teeth at the back. The skin on his face and neck were loose, and his eyes were glassy. He spoke in a soft, barely audible voice, taking a long time to form each sentence. After they had chitchatted for half an hour, he said he was tired. He called his daughter on his cellphone to come fetch him. Even sitting down, his movements appeared sluggish and depressed. A part of Polly was satisfied to see her father's friend looking as bad as he had a decade ago.

During those thirty minutes of visit, Bashir Uncle asked Polly, out of the blue, "What is the status of your parents' house in Gulshan?" As if it mattered.

"I don't know. It's still there…nothing has been done about it." She stared at him, bitterness on her lips. There had been no one to help her navigate the process of turning it into anything.

Bashir Uncle nodded. "Musa's sons signed with the developer. They got ten flats, but Musa was never able to move into his own home. The flats were complete, but Musa died two weeks before he could move in."

"Oh, I'm sorry."

"How is your father's brother?" Bashir Uncle asked, sitting up with energy.

"He died last year. Of lung cancer," Polly said. She had ordered a grande latte with extra sugar, and she slurped it now, burning her mouth. She had gained another twenty pounds in the last ten years. She was breathing hard nowadays, and she thought she ought to see a doctor, given her family history.

"Your Rahim Uncle is not doing well," Bashir Uncle continued, his eyes looking over her shoulder at the wall behind her. "You remember him. He retired to Rajshahi, to his ancestral home."

"Of course, I remember him! He was very healthy when I saw him."

"He has dementia now. He doesn't recognize anyone. He can't make out words when his friends call."

Polly nodded. It occurred to her why she had agreed to meet him. She had had a faint hope that he had come to help her, that he would do something about that house that sat like a dead weight. But now she saw that he was too unfocused, too weak for that. Then why had he come to see her? Why had he asked about the house? As he went on talking, and she went on nodding, his words not quite penetrating, she realized that this meeting wasn't about her at all. Bashir Uncle had wanted to see her simply because she was her father's daughter, for whatever memory she held for him.

Bashir Uncle's daughter arrived and picked him up. Driving away, Polly felt bad that she had not asked Bashir Uncle about his wife's death or about his own health. At one time, she had been so jealous of all her father's friends who had lived past him. She remembered that day after her father had died. Those uncles had sat in a circle around her, focused on her, sorting out her affairs. On that day, when they had looked so healthy, and she had been so distraught that her parents were dead and they were still alive and hearty, at least she had still had *them*. She had been surrounded by them. Now, she drove home in the falling light of day to her apartment in Katy, where she lived alone.

The English Teacher

i am a student from bangladesh.

Julia Smith circled the "i" and the "b" with her red-ink ballpoint pen, her purple glasses hanging low over her nose. She was sitting in her office marking papers. This particular one had been written by Asma, a student from Bangladesh. The ESL students at the two-year college adored Julia. They called her Mrs. Smith and brought her presents as offerings from their cultures–knickknacks from their home countries and delicacies in their cuisines that they wanted her to taste. Julia adored them back.

"My students are so sweet and respectful," Julia had said to her friends at dinner at an outdoor icehouse the past weekend. They had been sitting on a bench under the night sky, under a cool breeze. "And from such interesting places. Pakistan, Nigeria, Bangladesh, Colombia. El Salvador." She strummed the table for each country. It seemed that every year she met a student from a new country.

Julia had traveled far and wide in her youth. When she and her husband Mark had first got married, young kids fresh out of college at UT, Austin, they had traveled throughout Southeast Asia and logged their experiences on a travel blog, accompanied by delectable, high-resolution images–pretty beaches and gaudy palaces in Thailand and Ha Long Bay in Vietnam with its dreamy water sounds. She had loved Laos best–its French colonial buildings traversed by the Mekong River. That had been a long time ago, before Mark had landed a job with an oil company in Houston and they had returned to Texas, and Julia had enrolled in a master's program in teaching.

Julia had always been interested in international cultures, so she felt that she was well suited to teach these students. She only wished that she could teach them to write better. They really struggled with their English. No matter how much grammar and sentence mechanics Julia taught them, no matter how many times she marked their mistakes in red ink, they didn't improve much.

"Miss." A young woman ducked her head at the office door.

"Yes, Maria?" Julia jerked her head up and opened her lips in a wide smile.

Maria was a shy, soft-spoken young woman from Colombia. It wasn't Julia's office hours, listed in bold on her syllabus. The students rarely checked the syllabus. The faculty were always complaining about this, shaking their heads at these students who did not know a professor's office hours, or even remember their professors' names.

"Miss. I can't come to class today." Maria stood with her hands clasped in front of her, her glossy pink backpack swinging from one shoulder. Her throat trembled.

"Okay." Julia spoke in the sweet, patient tone she reserved for her students. "Is everything all right?"

The girl hesitated. Black paint dripped from her eyelashes. Her eyebrows, too, were heavily painted. "Miss. My brother is sick. My mother called and asked me to pick him up from school."

"All right, Maria. I understand. But tell your mother that you have school too. Just because you're a girl doesn't mean your education is not important. You have to be in class too. Okay?"

Maria nodded shyly, said thank you, and left. Julia knew that Maria appreciated her harsh comments. The student had complained many times about how she had to be a mother to her younger siblings and cook and clean for her elder brothers. Julia's students' home lives often stood as an obstacle to their studies. The boys helped their fathers with construction work and the girls cooked, did household chores, and looked after younger siblings.

One young woman, Juanita, was always late to Julia's morning class because she had to drop off her younger sister at school. Julia had marked Juanita tardy a few times. One day, Juanita had turned up to class sweating, her face red.

"Juanita! I'm marking you absent today. As a lesson. You can't be half an hour late to class every day!"

Juanita looked at her. Her eyes jerked open, and her face ballooned up. She clutched at her chest and shrieked, "You're giving me a panic attack!"

The next moment, she crumpled to the floor in front of the whole class. Other students fished out their cellphones and called the police while Julia stood and watched with her mouth agape, clutching the beaded necklace she had bought at a beach in Cambodia. After that incident, Julia had given up on marking Juanita tardy, opting instead to make eye contact with her when she entered the room and smile, taking care not to make any quick movements so as not to upset her.

Julia picked up the marked papers and headed to her next class, the one Maria would be missing.

"Hello, Mrs. Smith!"

"Hi, Miss!"

Cheerful voices called out as Julia entered the room, heels clicking, her tall frame encased in a long, fashionable pin-striped skirt with a slit at the back, holding a small terracotta mug containing a shot of espresso in one hand. She took care with her appearance for class, her lips brushed with scarlet lipstick, her blonde hair arranged neatly over her shoulders. She had learned early from graduate school friends at UH, when they had been teaching fellows, to dress up for class– a figure of calm in the face of storms.

"Hello, everyone! Najma, that is a beautiful headscarf! Juan, are you feeling better today? You were out sick?"

Placing the mug on the desk, Julia walked in the narrow space between the rows of tightly arranged desks, passing out the papers she had just graded.

"Now, don't panic when you see your grade. Remember, you're allowed to revise. I made comments showing you some of your errors, so you can edit. This is all about learning, remember? I'm teaching you how to write better."

The students nodded meekly. The room was silent, as papers rustled. Jeremy, a curly-haired boy from Nigeria who sat in the first row, his tall, ample frame spilling out of the small desk, glanced at his paper and groaned, clutching his head.

Julia laughed. "What's wrong, Jeremy?"

"Professor! I don't like the color red. This…this here…it's all *bathed* in red!"

"Look past the color, Jeremy. Look at what I wrote." Julia returned to her desk at the front of the room and clapped her hands. "All right, we're going to spend some minutes going over the most common errors I noticed. Okay?"

The students nodded.

Julia lifted a fat red marker from her leather pouch, bought at a market in Thailand, and began to write on the whiteboard in small, neat letters. Her smooth hand with its thin bracelet and red, polished fingernails moved across the immaculate white surface.

"You are all wonderful writers," she began. "But when I look at your papers, I see all the comma splices and dangling modifiers and run-on sentences. And that's what another reader will see, too. Someone would have to get past all those errors to be able to read your thoughts. Do you understand?" She spoke gently, slowly, enunciating every word.

On days Julia had to grade a stack of twenty papers from each of her sections– she taught five sections–she was overwhelmed by the grammar and spelling errors.

"I need twenty coffees to get through twenty papers," she had joked with her colleague Aimee when she had been grading in her office an hour ago.

"I need to stand up and exercise every ten minutes," Aimee had confided, standing at Julia's door. "In fact, this is exactly what I'm doing at the moment," she said, flicking her gold hair back from her eyes and swigging coffee from her giant mug with the words *their there they're* painted in glossy black letters. "Do you know what a student said to me the other day? I told her that she needed to go to the library to do research, and she said she didn't know where the li-berry was. My mouth fell open. Can you believe that she doesn't know how to pronounce library? Not only did she not know where the library was, but she didn't even know the word for library!" Aimee had raised her eyes to heaven and opened her mouth wide.

"The students are *sweet*," Julia had said carefully. "I only wish they were better prepared. We have to be patient with them. We have to give them time." She thought of her students' hesitant writing as an extension of their shyness in life. Their eyes grew big when they tried to understand all the things they encountered in America. She had seen some of the young women startle at the automatic toilet flush or the hand drier in the women's bathroom.

"All right," Julia said now, putting down the marker on the teacher's desk. "I want you to go through your papers carefully and see if you understand my comments. If there is a word you don't understand, ask me what it means."

"Miss, you look lovely today. I love your hair." This from Asma, the Bangladeshi student with the capitalization problem. She was a lovely young woman herself. Dark, cascading hair reached her hips.

"Yes, you look lovely, Professor," several other women murmured.

"Your face is so smooth. What kind of cream do you use?" Asma asked.

Their minds had a way of wandering off like that. Julia didn't blame them–they'd been raised in homes where family members turned on the television when they tried to do homework.

"I'll tell you all my skincare secrets at the end of class," Julia promised the girls. "But now, I want you to spend the next twenty minutes reading through my comments and taking notes about how you will revise your paper."

The students worked quietly at their desks, poring over their own writing in the papers that Julia had just handed back to them. The hum of the computer console on the lectern filled the air. As she waited for the students to finish, Julia stood behind the lectern and read a *New York Times* article on ancient eastern cultures on the computer and planned what to cook for her husband for dinner. At one time, fresh out of graduate school, Julia had wanted to be a tenured professor, write books, and say intelligent things, but life had happened. Because of her husband Mark's work in Houston, good income that brought in the money and turned on the lights in their home, she hadn't applied to jobs outside of Houston. She had settled for working at a local two-year college, teaching students from low-income backgrounds, international students, and first-generation students whose parents spoke little to no English.

"Mrs. Smith."

Julia smiled at Asma standing at her desk. The fashion conscious, pretty, petite young woman wore a flowery purple shirt, loose and long (for modesty, Julia suspected) over matching purple pants and high-heeled sandals. The class had ended, and the other students had filed out, calling out "Bye, Mrs. Smith" in cheerful voices.

"You want the info on my skincare, don't you?" Julia teased her.

"Mrs. Smith, your skin is beautiful. What do you use?" Asma smiled shyly.

"Makeup. Lots of powder and foundation."

"Oh." Asma's face shrank. She clasped her arms in front of her body, as if barricading herself.

The students often didn't understand humor, or teasing. Communication was a problem.

"I use aloe vera," Julia said kindly.

"Oh!" Asma opened her eyes wide. "How do you use it, Mrs. Smith?"

"I just peel off a bit and rub it on my face."

"You look so young, Miss." Asma touched her hands to her own face. She was a little awkward, enormously pretty, with a frank, earnest face.

"Thank you." The forty-year-old Julia blushed.

"Miss, I have something to tell you." Asma hesitated, rocking awkwardly on her feet, her large, white eyes regarding Julia out of a dusky, triangular face. Putting her fingers in her hair, she tucked her thick, dark tresses behind her ears.

"What is it, Asma?" Julia asked kindly as she packed up her markers in the leather pouch.

"Miss!" Asma's face twisted. Her eyes filled with tears.

"Oh, what's wrong?" Julia stopped packing. "What is it?" she asked again, in a gentle voice.

"Miss, my parents got picked up by the police. They…they…" Asma began to sob, her shoulders trembling.

Julia handed Asma a ply of baby-pink tissue paper. She carried a box of tissues for just these occasions. These students transformed so quickly from laughter to tears that Julia hardly knew what to believe. Was this Asma's ploy to cover for not turning in an assignment, or a future absence?

"Miss, my parents don't have documents," Asma said, rubbing her eyes with the proffered tissue. "They came to the US with me on a visit visa from Bangladesh many years ago. I was only ten years old. Then they just stayed back."

"Oh, dear."

Julia remembered reading something about it in Asma's essay that she had just been grading. *my father works very hard for my family. he works 3 jobs. he loves us very much.* At the time, she'd just been busy marking all the lower-case letters that should have been capitalized. It was difficult to read for content sometimes, to derive any meaning out of these sentences, really. Julia worried about what would happen to these students. How would they ever get out of working-class jobs into middle-class professions without a basic grasp of standard English?

"Is there anyone to take care of you? You have no other guardian in the US?" Julia asked.

"Our uncle said he's…going to provide for us," Asma managed through sobs. "Me and my two younger sisters."

"Well, that's good…"

"But he's not in Houston, Miss. My uncle lives in Dallas. So I have to look after my younger sisters. *I* am their guardian now. They're only eight and ten, Miss!"

"I'm so sorry." Julia placed her hand over her chest in a gesture of compassion. "Give me your contact information. I'm going to make a few calls to get you in touch with campus resources. And keep me posted, okay?"

Julia jotted down the student's information expertly in a neat hand, already making a mental note about the people she would notify, the funds and counselors she could tap into. This wasn't the first time a student had come to Julia. Other students had come to her, confiding about being kicked out of home, living in a shelter, or losing a family member. Julia and Aimee had talked before about the unimaginable plight of the students' lives, the massive gap between their realities and the expectations of school, and the tenuous line that held them in their classes. She was glad that she could offer some help to Asma.

Mark had cooked crusted salmon and stirred up a big kale and spinach salad studded with bits of cherry tomatoes. Julia ate dinner silently (they were sitting in the garden, on their new deck that Mark had built). Mark asked her what was wrong, and she told him.

"It's not your problem, babe," Mark soothed her. His big face was ruddy from the heat and the wine. His neck pooled with sweat.

She loved him. He had done all this for her. The deck; the dinner; even earning money at his boring job so that she could have an intellectual life.

"You do enough. You're an awesome teacher!"

"Oh, come on!" Julia blushed.

"No, really. You're my favorite teacher. I wish I had a teacher like you in college. Then I would have marr–"

"Stop it. Stop it," Julia shrieked, stabbing the air at him with her fork.

Mark was right that she couldn't worry about everybody. She couldn't fix every problem in the world, could she? She was grateful to have the life she did, the cute little house in the recently gentrified historic First Ward with its industrial sink in the kitchen and double-height ceiling living room peeking into the upstairs balcony and bedrooms, money to hire landscapers, gardeners, and housekeepers, time to go to nail salons and hang out at coffee houses with friends.

Once, meeting friends for coffee at a coffeehouse in Montrose, Julia had said, ironically, it was her lowly job exposing her to these young people with hard lives and gentle hearts that gave meaning and angularity to her life. She had learned a great deal about Houston in the ten years she had lived in the city, about neighborhoods and lives she would have known nothing about if not for her students—the railway line in Historic Fifth Ward and chickens that wandered the roads in Aldine, fufu and khichuri and other foods from around the world, and family farms in Mexico and El Salvador.

"I do this great thing with my students," Julia told her friends. "I have them journal. It's a powerful tool for writing practice and English proficiency. But it's more than that. When I read these little confessionals, they do something for me," Julia had said, placing a hand over her heart.

In their journals, the students told Julia about their lives. They told her about crossing the border, about coyotes, about police stops and construction jobs and neighborhood gangs. One of her students, Juan, had cut off three of his fingers when he had put his hand in the wrong place while fixing a lawnmower. He had been lucky enough to have them stitched back on. Edwin stood on stilts to paint houses. He worked with his father, his uncle, and his cousins, a family business. Maria's father had left her mother, and since then her mother had been depressed and angry. Her students told her everything. They brought all their problems to her, entrusting her with their care.

For her part, Julia spoke protectively about her students, addressing them as *my* students, thinking of them, really, as her children (although a few of them were in their thirties). She did everything in her power to shield them, offer them comfort, and help them find their way through the American system, filling in where their families (out of a lack of education, money, or knowledge) had failed them. Unfortunately, because of their family situations, her students often did not complete the course. They dropped out in the middle of the semester, driven out of home by a stepmom or an abusive boyfriend, or because their kids and their jobs and cooking for their husbands stood in the way of their education.

On Tuesday, Julia wondered about Asma. Asma was in her Monday-Wednesday section, but often on Tuesdays, Julia passed Asma in the hallway heading to her other classes. She didn't see Asma that Tuesday. After her first class, Julia returned to her office, determined to finish grading the next batch of papers. She read an essay by a student describing what it was like to work as a waitress, getting ill-treated by male customers, and another one about Hispanic Christmas traditions. Then she rubbed her sore fingers, stood up for a moment to stretch, and sat down again, reaching for the next essay. The name at the top said Georgia Martinez. Georgia had big, dark eyes and a wide mouth, voluptuous brown hair that curled over her back. She dressed to compliment her figure, in crop tops and low-waist pants with slim legs. In contrast to her elaborate dress, Georgia's face was fresh, without a trace of makeup, innocent as a young child's. Georgia liked to joke in class and Julia had to tell her to stop whispering and to stop looking at her cellphone, which she had a nervous way of checking every few minutes. Julia's lips curled in a smile as she lifted the paper out of the pile.

I am a table dancer by night I am so ashamed this is what I have to do to support my family I have two sons I am a single mother.

Julia's eyes blurred. She sat transfixed with the words she had just read.

"Julia, do you want the last of this coffee?" the staff assistant Ginny called.

Julia stood up with her terracotta cup, stretched, and moved to the suite kitchen.

"There you go. I wanted to tell you before Aimee grabbed it," Ginny said, pouring the coffee for her from the plastic carafe.

"Ooh, thanks. I needed it."

Julia gulped down the delicious, acidic liquid, then walked back to her office, to the paper that awaited her teaching, and the twenty more that she hadn't even looked at yet. Sighing, Julia picked up her red pen and held it between her fingers tipped with red varnish. "This is a powerful story, Georgia. But you need to work on your sentences. Run on sentences. Use periods! Short sentences. Can you think of combining these to form more complex sentences?"

Done. She needed to stretch again.

"Ginny!" Julia called, reemerging from her office, standing tall on stiletto heels, a ruffled, frilly olive blouse she had just bought, and slim, tapered dress pants. "I just remembered!"

Ginny turned obligingly in her swivel chair, wheeling herself closer. "What is it?"

"Can you put a few calls through for me? To the emergency fund and to the...?"

On Wednesday, Asma didn't show up in class. Julia wrote her a short email.

Hope everything is okay.

She was genuinely concerned. Would Asma be allowed to stay in the country? Would her siblings be okay?

On Saturday, Julia and Mark rode their bikes along the bayou. They enjoyed the same activities—bike rides, hikes through state parks, and taking vacations to interesting places.

Neither of them wanted children. Julia was always reading, alternating between the classics and new releases, never missing anything on the *New York Times* bestseller list. In her guilty moments, she confided to Mark that such writing appeared exquisite to her after an arduous day of checking papers without periods or commas.

On Monday, Asma appeared in class again. She sat at the back, her head bowed, her long hair covering her face, not talking. Julia's class involved a lot of participation. She asked questions, had students act out dialogue in plays to practice their English, or arranged debates between opposing teams. But she let Asma off the hook that day.

At the end of class, Asma appeared at Julia's desk again.

"Asma," Julia said, in a rush to tell her the news. "I have some good news! I spoke to the international students' office, and the emergency fund, all the resources we have on campus. It seems that they'll be able to give you a hundred dollars…you just have to fill out some paperwork."

Asma stared at her, the whites of her eyes milky with alarm.

"Will that help?" Julia asked, smiling sweetly. Her lips unfurled. "Just a little?" She waited for the words of gratitude from the student's mouth.

"My parents will be deported, Miss," Asma said quietly. "My uncle is taking us away to Dallas so he can look after us. I have to stop coming to class, Miss." She spoke flatly, with no trace of tears or sobs this time. She stood perfectly still, with her hands by her sides, the fingers spread out, pointing downward.

Julia's face crushed. She brought her palms to her cheeks, crying, "Oh, no! Asma! Are you serious?"

Asma nodded. Julia moved forward to put her arms around the girl's thin shoulders and hold her tight. The girl's body felt insubstantial like smoke. Asma pushed her away.

Julia sprang back and looked at the girl with surprise. "Asma, are you all right?"

There was a mixture of revulsion and anger in the student's eyes. Her face was hard, without a trace of her customary admiration and sweetness.

"Miss, I don't need your hundred dollars! It won't help." Asma shrieked. "It won't make any difference at all!"

"Asma, I'm hurt. I've tried to help you…"

Asma shook her head, her lips curled. She walked out of the classroom.

At home that night, Julia was too distressed to do any housework. Mark cooked dinner again— a pasta and arugula salad with pink radishes.

"Babe, forget about it," Mark said, wiping the crease from her eyebrows with a finger.

"I'm trying," she said.

"Her parents are illegal. What did she expect?"

"Mark!" Julia cried. "Don't say that!"

"Sorry. You look so disturbed, darling. I hate to see you this way. They're getting to you, these students. You should quit this job."

"Mark, please," Julia said, putting a hand over her eyes. "I don't want to quit."

Mark had said to her many times that she could retire early, since he earned enough. She had explained to him that as hard as the work was, she didn't work for the money. She labored out of love. Her students looked up to her and expected her to protect them.

"All right, truce," Mark said, engulfing her in his strong arms and kissing her forehead.

After dinner, they sat together on their couch, Mark with a popular economics book and Julia with her last stack of papers to grade.

"Need a glass of wine with that?" Mark asked after a few minutes, gesturing at her stack and laughing.

"Yes, please."

Mark walked to the kitchen. Left alone, Julia remembered the cold, hard look on Asma's face again and shuddered slightly. Shaking her head to clear it, she scooped up the batch of stapled papers in her arms. She had to get through them, no matter what. She started reading the essay on top of the pile, then stopped, looking around on the couch for her red pen. Then, laboriously, she started marking the verb tense errors and missing apostrophes, the proper nouns that hadn't been capitalized, and the spelling mistakes, all the things that stared at her out of the page, clouding the words around, so that she could see nothing but errors, and her own markings in red ink. Red lines everywhere.

Cigarette

When they were first married, Shumi's husband Pavel went out for a smoke on the roof after sex, standing in the dark leaning over the parapet. They lived on the roof in a single room on top of Pavel's parents' house. She watched him from the back, the red glow of his cigarette a lone light against the black sky. Sometimes, she went out to join him, hastily dressed in a cotton kameez and shalwar, a shawl wrapped around her shoulders. He turned around and gave her a smile with his stained yellow teeth, then turned back to gaze at the street below, his large, almond-shaped eyes widened in awe, draped by long, black, curled lashes.

What was it about young eyes? Why did they appear different from older eyes, innocent and joyful? Was it simply because the muscles that held them up at the corners were tighter? A doctor might know, but Pavel was a terrible doctor. He did the bare minimum, only fulfilling his hours at the P.G. hospital, whereas his friends studied day and night for their FCPS exams and earned extra money by putting in hours at various private clinics around Dhaka, shirking their duties at the government hospital to do so. Pavel, on the other hand, returned home by five or six at the latest, slicing through the traffic on Mirpur Road in a three-wheeler baby taxi, parting buses and trucks in front of him. Paying the baby taxi driver with wrinkled cash from his pant pocket, he raced up the stairs, his sandals slapping the cement steps, stopping on the first floor to say hello to his parents. A few minutes later, he bounded in the front door of their home (the young girl who worked for them unbolted the double-panel, painted doors and stood aside hastily), tore out of his office clothes, shed shirt, socks, and shoes, down to a sleeveless, white, ribbed undershirt, and sat down at his desk to write.

The desk and the bed were the only furniture in the room. An attached square kitchen to the side doubled as the maid's sleeping area. There was a small bathroom outside (consisting of a toilet standing next to a shower that rained on the commode seat). The mahogany writing desk was too heavy to lift or move even an inch. Ages ago, it had been pushed against the window of the bedroom, with a view of the evening sunset, and there it remained. It had belonged to Pavel's grandfather, and when Pavel had been a medical student, it had served as his study desk.

It was Pavel's habit to break out a fresh packet of local cigarettes, lift out one fresh, crisp stick, insert it in his mouth, and inhale, then open up his nostrils and inhale again, before picking up a ballpoint pen and a stack of newsprint paper and applying the pen to the mottled grey sheet, sighing with pleasure as the nib scratched the cheap, rough surface. Pavel wrote plays for his theater group as well as for Bangladesh radio, and he acted on stage as well. Before they were married, he had boasted to Shumi that he was an A-list artist at Bangladeshi radio, enlisted by audition, but that was not why Shumi had married him. She had been attracted to him because he was brilliant, a good student, a young, bright doctor, a young man with promise, on his way to big things, surely.

Pavel's writing drove Shumi to distraction. It dragged her down, along with all the other things about him that she had discovered only after marriage, namely his lack of ambition and direction. She had been a young bride—an M.A. student at Dhaka University in the English Department when Pavel's parents had picked her out for their son—with small, pretty features, soft and pliant, as young faces are before they harden into their natural character.

She complained repeatedly to her university friends about his writing, smoking, and lack of ambition. They advised her to speak to him directly, to let him know her true feelings, and make her intentions clear, her *niyat*.

"What are you planning to do with your life?" Shumi asked Pavel one night, when they were in bed, the lights turned off and the maid tucked in her bedding on the floor of the dark kitchen, separated by a thin wall. "Don't you care that you have to rise in your career? Without a higher degree, what will you be? How will you feel when all your friends are big doctors, and you are nothing?" She had begun sweetly, in a soft voice, but now her voice had risen and thinned out. She might have shouted these words. Her cheeks were red. Her nose was inflamed and her pretty, dark eyes swollen with the injustice of life.

Pavel rose angrily from the bed, slipped his feet into plastic slippers, and went out to stand on the roof, dressed in an undershirt and a cotton lungi tied at his navel. The breeze played with his hair as he blew smoke. Shumi was still conscious, when she heard him come back inside and scrape past the bed to the writing table. She heard the wooden chair being dragged, and the scratchy sound of newsprint paper. She lay still, her chest heaving, her eyelids shut from exhaustion.

Luckily for Shumi, one day, Pavel's senior professor gave him a lecture about his career.

"Give up this play-acting business!" the professor shouted at his favorite student. "The radio is standing in the way of your becoming a great doctor. How will you pass your medical exams like this, giving so much time to your play-acting?"

Shortly after receiving this lecture, Pavel gave up theater. Within months, he passed the FCPS exam and went on to become a respectable doctor at P.G. Hospital, with a private side practice at a small clinic in Gulshan. Shumi congratulated herself, thinking that it was perhaps her recent change in tactic that had done the trick.

From the day Shumi had discovered Pavel with a cigarette, she had been bothered by his smoking habit. They had gone to New Market together, sitting together on a rickshaw with the hood down, a light breeze playing in their hairs, to buy the latest Bengali novel that had just come out. Pavel wanted to read the book so badly that he had put in an order for it with his favorite bookseller, at the narrow shop that stored its books in boxes upstairs. As they waited on the footpath outside the shop for the doors to open, Pavel wrestled a cigarette packet out of his pants' back pocket and pulled out a slim, white cigarette, a local brand-named Boss, with tobacco-stained fingers. The sight of the yellow tips of his fingers and his bared, mud-orange speckled teeth turned Shumi's heart cold.

She began to cry, standing in the open public market beside the drain, the stench of the stagnant water accosting her. "I never imagined that I would be married to a smoker, someone who would smoke himself to death day by day!"

He threw back his head and laughed loudly at this as if she had said something very funny, then started to hack, his lungs rasping.

Since this incident, taking the advice of her friends, Shumi had gone hard after Pavel's smoking habit, crying about it at dinner at his parents' house, where they ended up eating on several days of the week, in front of Pavel's doctor friends and childhood friends and cousins, and in front of her own friends, who were in on the plan to make him quit smoking. At the slightest cough or clearing of Pavel's throat, Shumi cried about his health. She convinced his doctor friends to force him to get a chest X-ray, which showed dark smudges on his lungs. To help him quit, she bought him peanuts, sunflower seeds, and dried chickpeas roasted in sand and packed in newspaper packets, until one day he stopped smoking.

Soon after passing his FCPS exam and getting promoted, Pavel completely changed his appearance, again thanks to Shumi. Now he was clean shaven. He did not hack to clear his throat and chest like he used to do. Nor did he gaze at the world with wide eyes, laughing idiotically. Shumi bought him Western shirts and pants from the new export shops in Gulshan, paired with imported ribbed dress socks and pointed black shoes. She was still not satisfied. What were they doing in Bangladesh when all their friends were moving to England, America, and Australia, buying BMWs and yachts with the money they earned? Under Shumi's expert navigation, Pavel applied to American schools and gained admission to a master's degree program in public health.

Shumi and Pavel moved to Texas, where some of Pavel's doctor friends from his medical college lived. Borrowing their books and notes, Pavel took his US Medical License Exam to practice as a doctor in the US, passing quickly with high marks. He completed his residency with ease and went on to become a surgeon at a big hospital in Houston within a few fast-moving years. It was remarkable how disciplined he could be now that he was focused on the serious business of life, after he quit smoking. Often, in group chats with friends or with his parents on WhatsApp, Pavel credited Shumi for this improvement in his life.

One day, Shumi was clearing out their old suitcases in the attic of the new house they had just bought in the Woodlands. They had hauled the suitcases from their first apartment in Houston to two successive houses, filled with forgotten things that they had never bothered to throw away. She was determined to get rid of the last of their unnecessary belongings. Throwing back the hard cover of one of the suitcases on the floor, she leaned into the cavernous hole. Her eyes narrowed as they fell on a tube of newsprint paper, bound with a yellowed elastic band. The exposed top page was crowded with neat little rows of small, upright handwriting in Bengali.

"Do you want to keep these?" Shumi confronted Pavel when he returned from the office, at eight in the evening, crisp in a laundered shirt and blue blazer, his eyes small and glittering with success. She had been standing upright in the kitchen, brushing her hands on her apron, as she waited for him to make his way from the front door to the interior of the capacious house.

He looked intently at the bundle in her raised hand, then shook his head. "No."

"Do you want to look through the pages first?" she asked.

"No," he said, closing his eyes.

"All right," Shumi said, smiling, and threw the papers in the kitchen trash can.

Late at night, she thought that the old papers might be infested with silver fish, so she rose from bed, pulled out the trash bag from the kitchen trash can and dumped it in the tall black city trashcan parked outside the kitchen door. The night fog touched her skin, and an owl made a terrible crying sound.

Shumi and Pavel had achieved everything in life, in all spheres. They had two strapping boys and a big house in the posh suburb of the Woodlands, with two staircases, five bedrooms, and a backyard that backed up to the woods. They had a landscape gardener, a housekeeper, and a nanny to help them maintain their lives, but Shumi often felt impatient, pacing the shiny floors of her house, looking in mirrors, searching for meaning. She wasn't young anymore. Her face had settled into thick lines. She had spent her life pushing Pavel and the boys to success, but what had she done for herself? She was driven to distraction by these questions, which pestered her even at night, making her get out of bed in a hot sweat to go stand outside on the second-floor balcony and stare out at their manicured lawn shrouded with dark shapes. A small moth floated near her on the floor of the balcony. It hopped randomly, trying to get off the ground, and moved around in circles, as if it was lost, or trapped, with no sense of direction. She watched it for a long time, with tears in her eyes, then she stepped on it and crushed it.

She pulled out her cellphone from the pocket of her silk house coat in the dark. The light from the phone lit up the dust particles in the air, the old parts of her floating about her. Although they were separated by great distances, Shumi kept up a regular correspondence with her university friends, who were now spread out over several continents. One of their chief ways of keeping in touch was on Whatsapp.

"I used to read *Shakespeare*," she typed out with her long nails on the WhatsApp group chat that included all her university friends. Words appeared on the screen like a long wail, the bright light hurting her eyes and making them tear. "Remember, one semester Hamid Sir taught us *Beowulf* for three weeks, covering it in detail from every angle? And remember when we read the *Love Song of J. Alfred Prufrock*? Oh, how much I loved listening to English songs, how I used to listen to the songs of Jon Bon Jovi, playing the same cassette again and again!"

Within minutes, her friends responded. Words appeared below hers, because someone was always awake, somewhere, and they were all addicted to their cellphones and their little chat group.

"How can we forget?"

"I thought you would marry Jon Bon Jovi!"

"No, she wanted to marry Beowulf!"

One day, while out shopping for groceries at Costco, Shumi felt faint. The shelves and the boxes of food around her appeared as if at a great distance, floating away from her, out of reach. She clutched the shelf nearest her and slowly slid down to the floor so that she would not fall. A worker called the store manager, and soon there was a crowd around her, asking what was wrong, and insisting that they should call an ambulance to send her to the hospital. At last, an ambulance arrived and carried her to the hospital in the Woodlands, where they checked all her vitals and released her after several hours. She told them to drop her at the store, so that she could fetch her car. When she returned home, hours later, the house was still silent. Nobody even knew what had happened to her.

That evening, she waited in the kitchen with the lights turned out for Pavel to return from the office. The children played upstairs with the hired nanny, who picked them up from school, drove them to after-school activities and a café for dinner, then brought them back home and stayed with them till bedtime.

The minute Pavel walked through the front door, she faced him with folded arms. "I want a divorce," she said.

They parted ways easily and smoothly, splitting time with the kids so that Shumi would have them on the weekends only, because the schools in the Woodlands were better than the city schools. Shumi moved into a small garage apartment at the back of someone's house in the city, where she took a poetry class at a community college, signed up for a Groupon group to take photographs in Central Park, and joined a small writing group of ragtag, middle-aged people in their forties and fifties, men with greying hair and expanding foreheads and women with bulging bellies and sunken faces. Her new writer friends came over to her apartment sometimes after work, bearing a bottle of chilled red wine and a pack of cigarettes. They hung out on the narrow balcony outside the garage apartment at the top of a flight of a stairs, leaning over the railing and staring down into the houses below.

One day, a man from her workshop handed a cigarette to Shumi.

"I never smoked in my life," Shumi said, taking the cigarette between two nervous fingers. "For fifty years I never smoked, and now here I am–"

She held the cigarette in her mouth. A woman lit it with a hot pink lighter, and told her to inhale, then inhale again.

"Life is too short!" Shumi said. She took a long drag and blew smoke. "I'm fifty now! Everything I've been told, everything I believed, is a lie! I'm going to die soon! If I don't live now, then when?" She let out a cry, her eyes red with smoke, a cough rising in her throat.

"Exactly," her friends said, lighting up their cigarettes, too.

Together, they stared into the night sky, little bobs of light in a vast, dark universe. And for a moment, the world was still.

The Wheels of Progress

Bakher Khan bought a shell key chain on Cox's Bazar beach from one of those bare-chested girls who sell trinkets in the dark and had the name "Mohua" carved on the shell. He showed it to Mr. Vincent when Mr. Vincent climbed in the Jeep the next morning.

"Very nice," Mr. Vincent said. "Your wife?"

"No, my daughter," replied Bakher Khan, placing his pudgy hand on top of his heart.

The Bangladeshi engineer Siddiqi, who had also climbed into Mr. Vincent's car, said, "You have a daughter? In that case there is no question of writing your wife's name."

Mr. Vincent's car was full today. Bakher Khan was pleased that he was driving more people than Robiul, the driver of the other car. Mrs. Ann was coming with them. She had left her daughter behind in Dhaka. Mr. Vincent, Mrs. Ann, Mr. John, and Mr. Frans had flown in the night before to Chittagong Airport. Bakher Khan and Robiul had driven down from Dhaka ahead of time to wait for their arrival. Bakher Khan thought they could have made the trip to Sitakunda on the way from the airport to the hotel in Cox's Bazar–Sitakunda was only 37 kilometers away from Chittagong–but the foreigners had been tired. *Geological tour by the exploration department!* Bakher Khan had memorized the words. He was good at learning and improving himself.

Bakher Khan felt happy to be in Chittagong, his hometown. He drove in a trance-like state, thinking about his three-year-old daughter Mohua. She ran about the small flat in Mohammedpur in circles, her bangles tinkling all the time, even when she slept in the dark between Bakher Khan and his wife. He remembered her feet, so tiny and fat that they made him think this moment with her would pass, she would grow, the feet would get bigger, and she would no longer run about his little home.

Mrs. Ann and Mr. Vincent also had babies. Mrs. Ann's was just four months, although she had come back to work after her maternity leave all slim, her tummy flat, wearing narrow slacks and long sweaters as before, her nose hooked in her thin face, stealing outside where the drivers huddled to blow smoke through her nostrils. After some moments of eavesdropping, Bakher Khan gathered that they were discussing what Mr. Vincent and his wife and Mrs. Ann and her husband did when their babies cried at night. He felt immense satisfaction in gleaning this from their soft tones. His English had improved vastly since he had become Mr. Vincent's driver.

"So Mary says you get up, and I say, it's your baby," Mr. Vincent was saying, "and we both lie there groaning. Then it's always me . . . Mary just can't do it at night."

Mrs. Ann chuckled, saying her Bill was quite good at handling little Cara, but she just couldn't let them be. There was more laughter from the back seat, a warmth in the car. Siddiqi, sitting in the front passenger seat, also laughed.

Mr. Vincent asked Siddiqi, "Do Bangladeshi fathers ever take care of their children?"

Siddiqi stopped laughing and said he didn't know; he was not a father yet. Something about Siddiqi's manner and his long face soured the atmosphere in the car. Bakher Khan did not know what was wrong with him. Siddiqi had seemed cheerful enough when they had driven down together. Siddiqi had traveled ahead with the drivers to settle on the hotel, buy the supplies, and choose locations for the tour. Bakher Khan had driven him in Mr. Vincent's car. They had laughed a lot then and sat in circles singing popular film songs, but now Bakher Khan felt that Siddiqi had ruined the sense of camaraderie in the car. His scowls, his silences, and his short replies to the foreigner experts disturbed Bakher Khan greatly.

They were stuck in traffic. Mr. Vincent gave Bakher Khan smart directions from the back. "Can you believe that?" he cried out. "Look at those trucks blocking the shoulders and coming the opposite way. Sure, go ahead, make it worse. I've never seen more idiotic behavior in my life!"

Bakher Khan watched with a sinking heart as the trucks coming from the opposite direction took up the road space that would have allowed the cars to pass by. After a year of driving Mr. Vincent, Bakher Khan had become increasingly aware of Bangladesh's shortcomings: drivers who did not follow rules and blocked the roads and police sergeants who did not know their own duties, not to mention the corruption, the greed, the lack of law and order, and the dirt everywhere. He now looked at his country, which he had always regarded with a lazy warmth, through new eyes. When he drove Mr. Vincent home at night—Mr. Vincent worked late at the office, after everyone else at the gas company had left—they would have philosophical conversations about Bangladesh.

"I don't know, Ba-ker," Mr. Vincent would say, pronouncing his name like the English word baker meaning one who bakes cakes, rather than Baaa-kay-r like sound of a sheep and kay rhyming with hay like the cows eat and then an r, and Bakher Khan would wonder if he should teach Mr. Vincent one day how to say his name, if that would please his boss. "I get depressed every night," Mr. Vincent would continue, loosening his tie and leaning back his tired shoulders in Bakher Khan's car. "This place is so corrupt; I wonder if we can make any progress at all. This country could have been so much. You have so much gas, Ba-ker, if only the officials weren't so pig-headed and corrupt. If you could develop this gas, there would not be one hungry man in your country."

Bakher Khan honked his horn and Mr. Vincent said not to; it wouldn't do any good. Bakher Khan immediately recognized the wisdom of this advice. He was very proud to be working for the gas company. When his old gas company sold out to this one, he had become an employee instead of a mere contractor. The foreigners at the company were so intelligent, they had so much to teach. When he was waiting in the car for Mr. Vincent while he attended a meeting, Bakher Khan often dreamt that his country would change; there would be superhighways, electricity in every village, and high-rise buildings for everyone to live in.

At last, the traffic cleared, and they began to move. Mr. Vincent asked Siddiqi if he had remembered to load all the food for their trip to Sitakunda, and Siddiqi sullenly answered yes. Mrs. Ann coughed in the sudden gust of exhaust and roadside tar work (which had probably been the cause of the traffic jam). She told Mr. Vincent that her little Cara had been ill with breathing problems at least three times since she had been born—the doctors thought it was the pollution of Dhaka. Mr. Vincent had the same problem; his son had developed asthma. Bakher Khan felt disappointed that his country was so backward, and that Mr. Vincent and Mrs. Ann were having to making such grave sacrifices to help it progress.

The road was clear now and he sped on, the wind flying against the outside glass, the air inside cool from the AC. He had to brake only occasionally, when he passed a slow rickshaw or van, or a fool of a man walking his cow by the roadside. Bakher Khan thought that perhaps one day his daughter Mohua would attend the local university and become an engineer, too, like Mrs. Ann: a…reservoir engineer. He loved Mohua so much: her long cotton dresses that reached her ankles, the bell that tinkled around her waist, the drop of *kajal* on her forehead that protected her against evil.

Mr. Vincent's firm was so good to the local workers that when the managers met to decide the company's mission and vision, even the drivers were invited to give their input. It was a long, drawn-out process, with every department making several proposals. In the end, there was a big meeting with lunch—sandwiches from Coopers. In the meeting, the most popular slogan was 'Circles of Progress'. But the exploration manager, who was Mr. Vincent's boss, pointed out that progress was linear. Someone joked that circular was a good slogan for their partner company in Bangladesh because all the Bangladeshi officials talked only in circles. Everyone thought hard, and so did Bakher

Khan, and finally, when they chose a slogan—something that would appear underneath the company's title—it was 'Wheels of Progress'. Bakher Khan really liked this slogan because wheels had something to do with driving and his own role in the company.

At last, they were approaching Sitakunda. They began to climb uphill. The other car, with Mr. John and Mr. Frans, followed behind.

"Go slow," said Mr. Vincent. "Ease up on the brake."

Mr. Vincent always gave Bakher Khan tips on driving, how to handle the Jeep on dunes and uphill, in mud and through water. There were signs announcing that Sitakunda would soon become an eco-tourism park. For now, it was green and quiet, terraced agricultural fields cut along the steps of the hill. Little boys walked carrying harvest on their heads, or herding goats up the hill. Up ahead, they saw the bare walls of hills that had been cut for quarries. Mr. Vincent explained that a quarry was a good place for a geological exploration. Mr. Vincent was too good, always explaining things and educating Bakher Khan, even though he was a mere driver.

"Vincent, I think we should park here," Siddiqi said, sitting up straight.

"No, let's go further up," Mr. Vincent said.

They continued driving until the stalks of the paddy pushed up against the car windows. The boys who walked along the narrow path had to jump into the ditches.

"All right, let's get out here," Mr. Vincent said. "Siddiqi, bring the equipment. Leave the lunch in the car."

Mr. John and Mr. Frans, both geologists, stepped out of the other car, laughing and making jokes. Mr. John was the leader of the geological tour. He was a plump man with a red beard, dressed in khaki shorts and boots. The group walked along at a leisurely pace, their shirts out of loose pants, sandal shoes slapping on the earth. Frequently, they would stop at a site, measure, look, discuss. The drivers followed behind, but Mr.

John did not ignore them. "Siddiqi, come here," Mr. John would say, showing him something.

Robiul said to Bakher Khan, wasn't it nice to see their Bangladeshi engineer walking alongside the foreigner experts? But Siddiqi looked so dark and shriveled that it was impossible to be proud of him. Mr. Vincent, strutting up ahead, wore a stylish white hat to keep off the sun. He carried a small camera in the pocket of his slim white pants. Bakher Khan hovered close to him, anxious to act as his personal attendant, catering to any sudden need. From time to time, Mr. Vincent drew his attention to interesting features in the landscape, pointing with his slender white finger. Bakher Khan repeated the words to himself: shale, sandstone, dislocation, faults, formations. He had once worked for an NGO, where he had picked up some words that he still remembered: sustainable, participatory, development. This vocabulary continued to serve him well.

As they climbed, Mrs. Ann and Mr. Vincent discussed the importance of their work, saying that the development of gas was the means of sustainable development for Bangladesh.

"Think," Mr. Vincent was saying to Mrs. Ann. "Now Bangladesh only survives on aid, on other people feeding its people. It's eternal, this giving. But with gas, Bangladesh could feed its own people."

Bakher Khan was hopeful. He imagined his country making linear progress, his Mohua in a slim skirt like Mrs. Ann's one day, wearing long boots, pushing up her glasses to study a quarry.

The local people crowded around the group and the drivers had to shoo them away, saying, "Go, go. There is nothing to see here." Sometimes a man would ask what the foreigners were doing, and the two drivers would explain that these were great technical experts come to get gas out of the ground.

"Is there any gas here?" the boys asked. "Under the ground? Really?" But mostly, they just stared at Mrs. Ann and Mr. Vincent, or at their contraptions, the hat, the shiny metal compass, the camera.

Mrs. Ann smiled sweetly at them, although Bakher Khan could see that the staring made her uncomfortable. They stood right behind her when she stopped, followed her when she walked, breathed the shampoo in her hair. As soon as one group of boys chewing on sugar cane disappeared, another group appeared.

"Are they bothering you?" Mr. Vincent asked, and Mrs. Ann smiled: *no*.

Mr. Vincent explained to Bakher Khan that the sandstone held the gas, and the shale acted like a cap to hold in the gas. He pointed with his finger at the lines of sand and shale. Bakher Khan memorized the phrase 'trapped gas'. At last, when he thought there was no end to the information that he could swallow and keep within—as if by being able to keep it all in he could apply his knowledge to help his country move forward on the path of progress in the energy sector—they reached the top of the hill. The temple of Sitakunda appeared as they rounded the corner.

They stood at the edge of a cliff that fell to the valleys of cultivated fields below. Steps led up to the temple where pilgrims had climbed to pay their respects for hundreds of years. For hundreds of years, the temple had stood unchanged and unchanging. Bakher Khan wondered what would happen once the eco-park opened. Mr. Vincent and Mrs. Ann were discussing the options if they discovered gas or oil under the temple. They joked that they could put a rig there and make it resemble a temple.

The survey was over now. Mr. John lowered his bulky body to the sandstone and sat by the edge of the cliff. Mr. Vincent sent Siddiqi back to the car with the other driver Robiul to gather the lunch supplies. Perhaps Siddiqi was sullen because he was an engineer, but he was having to do all this menial work. Although Bakher Khan found Siddiqi's twin roles slightly confusing as well, he disapproved of his attitude; he thought Siddiqi shouldn't look down upon any work as menial. Siddiqi was the foreigners' guide on the tour. Without him, how would the foreign experts know which hotel to stay at, how to negotiate with boats and ferries for the next day's trip to Maheshkhali? This was the trouble with the Bangladeshis: they thought work was beneath them.

Mrs. Ann and Mr. Vincent stood by the cliff's edge looking down below and admiring the scenery. They compared the landscape to Scotland. Bakher Khan felt proud. Mr. Vincent had once said Dhaka was all concrete and bewilderingly depressing. Bakher Khan had been depressed by Dhaka ever since—the alleys that got clogged up with plastic bags, the children who got wet in the rain, and the dirty buses with their black exhaust which choked the lungs of infants.

Mr. Vincent had once visited Bakher Khan's home when Mohua was very sick. She had pneumonia, but Bakher Khan hadn't realized. She would have died if Mr. Vincent and his wife had not admitted her to PG Hospital. Bakher Khan felt indebted to Mr. Vincent for his kindness. He felt sure that in the same way Mr. Vincent had helped his daughter, the company would bring progress to his country, which he had begun to feel was a very sad place to live in. But here, in Sitakunda, Bakher Khan felt happy. Here was something he could be proud of, the open air, the temple overhead, the children who walked with their goats. This was the Bangladesh Bakher Khan had grown up in, the essence of his soul, and he was happy that Mr. Vincent and Mrs. Ann also appreciated these surroundings.

The night before, Mr. Vincent had asked the two drivers to join them for dinner at a local restaurant in Cox's Bazar, to which Siddiqi had directed the party. Mr. Vincent said he had been happy in his job, until he arrived in Bangladesh. He had had such high hopes at first, but now he had begun to despair. If only he could change things, if only all his efforts resulted even in the most infinitesimal change. But this country was unchanging and unchangeable, solid in its decrepitude.

"Can you even hear birds in the morning in this place?" he had asked.

The party had been silent for a long time, considering this question. Mr. Vincent had not been pleased with Siddiqi's choice of a restaurant, either. Even though it was a five-star restaurant, they had seen a mouse run over the carpet.

There was a cry. Bakher Khan turned to look, his pulse accelerating. Mr. Vincent had a protective arm about Mrs. Ann's shoulder and was leading her away. Bakher moved closer to Mr. Vincent and Mrs. Ann to ask, what happened, what happened?

A group of boys who had been standing by them, teenagers wearing Sando shirts and lungis, had been staring at Mrs. Ann. They had formed a circle around her, and someone had touched her golden hair. Mr. John had stood up from where he was resting on the grass and moved swiftly to her side. Mr. Frans had been studying the sand and the shale a little distance away, and even he answered her call of distress. Mrs. Ann was very shaken. They all surrounded Mrs. Ann to comfort her.

Bakher Khan said to the boys, "Go, go! Don't you have anything better to do? Go!"

He wanted to explain to Mrs. Ann that they had meant no harm. They simply wanted to touch her golden hair, which seemed as unreal to them as dreams of gas and wealth would seem to any Bangladeshi now. But he knew he could not explain this to Mrs. Ann, that he did not possess the English to do so. It was more than just the lack of language—it was something he couldn't put into words. He hovered, feeling sorry for everything.

Mr. Vincent said to Bakher Khan, "Bakher, come here. Just ask them what they're doing for their country, standing around with nothing to do, the silly fools!"

Bakher Khan stood like a statue, unable to move. His chest throbbed with pain. Siddiqi and Robiul were back with the food in ice boxes. From where Bakher Khan stood, he could see the mossy steps that led to the derelict temple, and out of the corner of his eye, under the cover of his eyelashes, he could also see the boys, their checked collars and faces and eyes that reminded him of his own youth, and he felt very downcast about them. He felt that he was a silly fool himself. What had he done with his life after all, what good was he, what good was anybody in his country? Even the professors at the engineering university where Bakher Khan wanted to send Mohua were never trusted to do work on the samples that the exploration team collected; the company had to send everything for analysis abroad. He felt disgusted with the boys, with all the worthless youth of Bangladesh, and with himself, because he saw how they all appeared to Mr. Vincent–absolutely useless.

"Let's eat," said Mr. Vincent. "Siddiqi, fetch the food."

Siddiqi had forgotten to bring a bottle opener. He stood awkwardly with two Coca Cola bottles in each hand, apologizing. But even when he apologized, he did it resentfully, as if he might explode. Bakher Khan looked away. Robiul tried to help by fumbling inside the bags.

"Not to worry," said Mr. Vincent. "We shall make do. We can eat our sandwiches dry and swallow our saliva."

"I can do something," said Siddiqi. "I can open."

Bakher Khan didn't look to see how Siddiqi would manage this, but he heard a smash. Siddiqi had broken a bottle trying to open it against a rock.

"Good job, Siddiqi," said Mr. Vincent.

Bakher Khan could feel Mr. Vincent's anger. He sank further within himself. He wanted to sit down. Mr. John held out a sandwich to him and his fingers closed around it weakly. He didn't trust his grip.

Then Siddiqi, dark and sulky in a dirty white shirt, threw the bottle to the ground. Bakher Khan was astonished to see him standing with his hands at his waist, shaking like a stalk of paddy in the wind.

"Mr. Vincent!" Siddiqi cried in a shrill voice. "Mr. Vincent, I want to quit. I . . .I have been very unhappy in this company. I am get no respect."

Bakher Khan folded his arms around his chest and watched Siddiqi.

"What kind of respect do you want?" Mr. Vincent asked quietly.

"I get ordered, I don't get a promotion, and you talk to me in that tone."

"What tone?" asked Mr. Vincent. Then enunciating his words slowly, carefully: "Really, Siddiqi, I have been very patient with you. Your performance in the company has been dismal, but I have waited. The trouble with you people is that you want to climb fast to the top by any means other than hard work and competence. So cut your bullshit about tone and respect."

Siddiqi began to cry like a woman, the way Bakher Khan's wife cried when he scolded her for burning the rice or making the daal too thin. Siddiqi's body shook as he sniffled. Bakher Khan half expected someone to walk over to Siddiqi and put an arm around him, but no one moved. Then Siddiqi turned around and walked away down the hill. The rest of them stood finishing their sandwiches in silence.

Mr. Vincent said, "Well, I guess we had better pack up. Baker and Ray-bial, can you manage?"

"Yes, Mr. Vincent," Bakher Khan assured him.

He busied himself packing up the trash and lifting the ice boxes. He waited for Mr. Frans and Mr. John, Mrs. Ann, and Mr. Vincent to lead the way. As he did so, he stared again fondly at the temple, now radiant in the sunlight. The pounding in his chest had stopped. The boys began to go on their way, waving their sticks gaily, returning to their work in the fields that would be harvested the same way year after year. Mr. John had been explaining last night over dinner the cyclical nature of tides and their importance for geologists, but Bakher Khan could no longer remember that lecture. He watched the children and hoped that their lives wouldn't change too soon.

Siddiqi refused to return with the party. He would find his own transport to Dhaka and hand in his resignation at the office in Dhaka.

"You simply cannot do that, my good fellow," said Mr. Vincent in a quiet voice. "There are procedures. You need to give notice."

But Siddiqi walked away childishly. Robiul and Bakher Khan assured the foreigner experts that they knew the way back to the hotel. Bakher Khan climbed into the driver's seat and let Mr. Vincent advise him down the hill. He drove back on the highway to Cox's Bazar, taking his time, no longer in a hurry, no longer even listening to the hushed conversation, about Siddiqi no doubt, in the back seat. Instead, he admired the scenery around him. Mohua would be home now, playing by the drains, dropping beads down them, or perhaps she would have gone down to the river in Mohammedpur with her mother to watch the fishermen and the boats. He thought of Chittagong's great harbors and its container ships, the hundreds of years of naval history, and the ocean. He thought of Ram and Sita and the beautiful stories that he had heard in his childhood, stories that never led anywhere but started where they had stopped the night before.

When they reached Cox's Bazar, it was getting dark. Mrs. Ann and Mr. Vincent sat in the shadows. The two cars pulled up side by side in front of the hotel and Mr. John rolled down his window to confer with Mr. Vincent. They decided to shower and go on to dinner. The foreign experts went to their rooms, telling the drivers when to meet them again in front of the hotel. Robiul and Bakher Khan did not shower or wash. They sat together in silence thinking of Siddiqi, whose duty it would have been to act as guide for the evening, and to organize the next day's trip. Presently, the four experts came out and Mr. Vincent and Mrs. Ann, both dressed in clean starched shirts and cotton pants, climbed into Bakher Khan's car.

Mr. Vincent said, "Ba-ker, you have the great honor of choosing where we should eat tonight. Lead us. Onward!"

Bakher Khan was from Chittagong. He grew up in Chittagong. He had visited Cox's Bazar many times. Although he had never eaten in the best restaurants himself, he could have led the foreigners to any number of good ones, efficiently and expertly, in a straight line. But to his own surprise, he took no initiative. When he had reached the busy town center, where all the restaurants were, he just drove around aimlessly.

Mr. Vincent tapped him on the shoulder. "Ba-ker, you're on the same street we just passed," he said. "We're hungry, my man."

Bakher Khan nodded at Mr. Vincent's clean-shaven reflection in the mirror. He thought again of Siddiqi, who would be hungry now, walking still or on some dusty bus, and he thought that he cared nothing for the hunger of these foreign experts. Let them tell him where they wanted to eat, when they wanted him to stop. He just kept driving. His shell keyring jangled, reminding him of his musical Mohua, and he forgot everything else.

Two Mothers

The rain pooled outside the house in Katy as Simi poured the food into warmers for the party. This was the problem with Katy that she had discovered when they moved to Houston. If it rained, floods became an immediate concern. All their Bengali friends had recommended buying a house in Katy, the suburb to the west of the city, which had become home to the never-ending flow of fossil fuel engineers to Houston. The subdivision had expanded past Cincho Ranch to new territories, over prairie lands and rice paddies where field mice had once roamed. Simi and Sumon had bought a modest house in Cinco Ranch, three bedrooms, one extra to accommodate an occasional guest. Sumon thought they could have bought something grander. The houses in the new subdivisions were much larger, six bedrooms, three garages, two stairways, Roman Columns, and Mediterranean balconies reaching out to the sky. Whenever he drove past these new mansions, Sumon stared at them with awe. They seemed to him to be death defying, as if the massiveness of the houses and the sheer number of rooms could secure one from the world outside.

Sumon poked his head in the kitchen. "Everything ready?"

Simi nodded. She was used to working quietly and steadily, like a squirrel. Everything was planned and neatly done. She had bought a dozen warmers for parties just like these when they had lived in Louisiana. She had brought the warmers with her to Houston when they had moved.

"Don't mention to anyone that it's Maria's birthday," she reminded Sumon as she set candles under the warmers and lit them with a stove lighter.

Had she been around, Maria, who had just turned eight, would have protested and made a fuss at hearing this, and Simi would have had to turn on her and scold her. Thankfully, the child had settled down to play on the computer in her room. Usually, Maria refused to do anything quiet, like watch TV. She liked to prance about the house and make a mess, pulling flour out of the pantry for her chemistry experiments or cutting up paper in odd shapes and spilling them all over the floor. Her anticipation of the birthday party and her friends arriving had helped to buy her cooperation for a few hours.

The sky darkened, and the rain drummed more loudly, sounding ominously in the dark. The wind whistled, lashing the saplings in the yard. The crepe myrtle, the only mature tree on the lot, creaked dangerously. Just a few weeks ago, acting on advice from her neighbors, Simi had made Sumon call a tree service company to cut down the two oak trees, lest they fall on the house during a storm. She was glad of it now.

As it grew closer to eight, Simi began to worry that the rain would upset everything. No one would be able to drive through the heavy downpour, and the party would be canceled. But the first guests began to arrive on time, right on cue, at eight, running from their cars with umbrellas, shaking off wet saris and squishy shoes, the men carrying the children, one in each arm. There were umbrellas everywhere. Sumon hurried to get these off the wood floor and find a place for them, because Simi was particular about such things. He dragged a big plastic sheet for the wet shoes and dripping umbrellas. It was a mess, and most of the guests were flustered and out of temper.

"It was impossible to see on the road. So dangerous!"

"Almost got into an accident!"

Simi and Sumon stood at the door, receiving their guests, commiserating and soothing.

"Maria, your friends are here!" Simi called. "Take them to your room."

It was the custom for the children to disappear upstairs to the den or into various rooms, separated by age and gender, where they would pose no trouble.

Maria, a stout and pretty girl, came out of her room now wearing a heavy brocade party dress and scratching her neck from the itchy fabric, her mouth downturned, her thick eyebrows raised, and her little brown hands poised on her hips in an extreme expression of suffering. She was under orders not to reveal that this was her birthday party. Her bright black eyes pooled with intelligence, expressing–everything, if only someone would ask.

Simi's closest friend in Houston was Bithi. Bithi's two daughters, twins, were Maria's age and her best friends. The other children had arrived with tablets and chargers and were already demanding the password, which Sumon had presciently taped onto the back of the front door so that he only had to point. But Bithi's two children liked to play without technology, like Maria. The three got along well.

Bithi entered the house complaining of a sore throat. "Sorry we're late. I had to take a Tylenol to lie down first." She was dressed in a heavy blue sari and blouse, with a silver choker at her throat, her hair pulled back from her round face in a ponytail.

"You look very nice," Simi said, taking her by the hand to ease her inside her home.

Bithi paused near the shoes and umbrellas to talk more. "Oof. It was so difficult getting the twins ready. One ran this way and the other said I have to play first. One said, I have to finish my dolls' birthday party! I had to lock them both up in a room in the end and dress them by force while they were screaming!"

Simi laughed. Bithi was always telling funny stories about her travails with her children. But Bithi was blocking the door to other guests, so Simi nudged her gently toward the kitchen.

Soon, the inner quarters of the house pooled with women in silk saris, three-piece satin outfits, and dangling fashion jewelry, crying out in mutual admiration until no one could hear the rain anymore.

"Appetizers are served," Simi said, bringing down plastic bowls and spoons from the high cupboards, standing on a metal ladder.

"Need any help?" one of the women asked.

"No. Everything is ready. Being tall, I'm able to reach the high cupboards easily, and being thin, I can bend down to the low cupboards," Simi joked. She was overly skinny, so she wasn't bragging.

"How is the gym going?" someone asked.

"Good. I go every day to build muscles, so I can carry you all in case of a flood," she said, working as she talked. She was dressed efficiently, in a no-nonsense kameez and shalwar and house slippers that would allow her to work fast without obstruction.

"Ooh, it's warm in here. Come, let's sit down for a little." Bithi withdrew from the heat of the kitchen, where the other women were still serving themselves fried spicy things and tomato chutney. She walked to the adjacent dining area and sank into one of the tall chairs arranged around the high round table. "Sit, sit." She waved some women to her, who hesitated before sitting down at the table.

She poured herself lemonade from the jug into a blue plastic cup placed on the table. Her hands shook. "No one knows how difficult it is to raise two kids. It's very hard on me."

"Are you all right?" a young woman asked as Bithi raised her trembling hand with the cup to beaded lips. "Your hands are trembling."

"I have had hypertension since the twins were born. It was so difficult when they were newborns. I had tremendous heartburn, so I could not lie down at night. I would walk around all night with one of them in my arms. Oh, those days…what shall I say? They were terrible. I cannot describe them to you."

"Are those real glass bangles?" the young woman interrupted her.

Someone snickered and moved away. Bithi was fond of talking about her difficult pregnancy and childbirth. It was a constant refrain with her. Her face was swollen, and her body heavy and round. She had difficulty breathing in the heavy silk sari and blouse and panted to get her breath back. Simi's other friends often gossiped about her, that she should just exercise instead of reveling in her bad health. Others joked and said, "She acts like she's the only one raising kids. Haven't we raised kids ourselves?"

When she had laid out the dinner, fanned out on the kitchen counter in a mixture of colors and steam, topped by cilantro, vertically positioned red and green chili peppers, and chocolate-brown caramelized onions, Simi asked Sumon to call the men first. Sumon's mother had just passed away two months ago after suffering for years from kidney failure, so Simi checked his face to see if he was holding up okay. He had flown back to Bangladesh in June when she had been taken ill and turned right back after the funeral. He had never spoken a word about it after returning to Houston. She hadn't seen him shed a tear. They were throwing Maria's birthday party two weeks after her actual birthday, as soon as they could manage after he returned from his mother's funeral.

The women had served the children the pizza from boxes flayed open on the island. Now they took plates of rice and meat for themselves, slipping into the living room next to the open-plan kitchen carrying foaming Coca Cola in red plastic cups. As they ate, they watched a Bengali serial on satellite TV and talked idly. But they could hear the conversation in the men's drawing room near the front door, loud and heated. It often happened this way at parties, the women exchanging pleasantries, trying their hardest to talk about nothing, while the men exploded into conflict immediately. The women considered it unseemly to let politics invade their drawing rooms, or to even consider what was going on in the world outside. If someone surfing through channels accidentally crossed a news channel, with scenes of war and mayhem, people looked away quickly. Someone might remark, I don't understand politics. Others would nod.

"No! A coal plant *cannot* be clean. A coal plant in the Sundarbans Forest would destroy the habitat!" Someone was shouting, arguing about a project plan in Bangladesh to build a clean coal plant to export power to India.

The women recognized the voice as belonging to Mr. Haidar Khan, an elderly graduate of their engineering university in Bangladesh. The men were all engineers and had all graduated from the same university in Bangladesh. Then they had all come to America to get their master's degrees before getting jobs in oil and gas. Mr. Haidar, a thin man in his fifties who wore glasses held together with Scotch tape, was always creating conflict. He would get agitated debating some point that went over everyone else's head, causing unpleasantness. Whenever he expressed one of his explosive opinions, the other men looked away and started talking about something else.

Once, Sumon had explained to Simi that Mr. Haidar's frustrations sprung from the fact that he was an unsuccessful scientist at the university, earning very little money, compared to the younger men, who worked at various oil and gas companies. Even in appearance, Mr. Haidar stood apart from the others. While the younger men had assimilated into American society, eating chips and drinking Coca Cola, rounding out, their receding hairlines and their rice bellies announcing their newly acquired American wealth and prosperity, Mr. Haidar had held onto his indecent, famine-like figure from Bangladesh. His sunken eyes, stretched taut skin over his forehead and cheeks, and skeletal, stick like arms and legs appeared almost indecent.

"Why is it bad? It's called clean coal, after all." Someone laughed.

"You think technology can solve everything?" Mr. Haidar shouted, getting more excited.

This objection was so laughable that the other men could only guffaw in response. Everyone who lived in Katy had a deep faith that technology could solve everything. Sumon had often explained to Simi that to ignore the man was the best thing. Any response got him only more excited.

"Is the food okay? Is it edible?" Simi asked the women in the living room, to drown out the men's voices.

"First class."

"It's raining much harder than before!" Bithi exclaimed. She stood up from the round table where she had been sitting and walked to the window by the table to look out into the dark yard. "Oh, my God. I can't see anything! That crepe myrtle tree is rolling around dangerously. Its branch could break," she cried, turning her head. "Simi, look!"

Mr. Haidar Khan's wife Pansy joined Bithi at the window. She stood looking out through the glass, burying her face in the darkness. Her cool bare arm under her sleeveless blouse brushed Bithi's hot arms.

To the other women, Pansy was an embarrassment like her husband. She wore long, dangling earrings and green nail polish, and frosted pink lipstick, at her age! She pulled her hair up high on her head, drawing down tendrils at either side of her face. And when she talked, she mentioned smoking and drinking and old boyfriends and wild parties in her youth. Of her two sons, both grown, one had married an older woman with a child, and another was living together with a woman, according to rumors. Whenever Pansy spoke of her youth or her sons, the younger women at the parties clad in modest blouses with sleeves covering their upper arms and saris covering their navels, who had higher aims for their own children, would stand up, their ears burning, and walk away before they heard too much. It was clear to the other women that Pansy wanted to talk. She had a lot to say, and she didn't mind spilling her scandalous secrets. In fact, she might have no idea that these were scandalous things to say.

The two women stood together in companionable silence, staring into the darkness outside, witnessing the horrifying theater of nature. The crepe myrtle swayed dangerously toward the house, as if lending evidence to their constant fears about trees and all things in nature. They feared snakes in gardens, the infestation of squirrels and mice.

"Once, I saw a bright, leaf-green lizard on the pine tree," Bithi said to Pansy. As she had stared at it, through a glass window, from inside the house, the lizard unfurled its disgusting red dewlap. Bithi said she had screamed and had her husband Ali cut down the tree within the week.

"Oh, my God!" Pansy put her hands to her lips. "These things can be poisonous."

"Do you know what happened a few weeks ago?" Bithi continued, staying away from the subject of coal and Pansy's offensive husband (Bithi was an engineer herself and excited about clean coal). "I came home with my two children and parked in the garage, and my twins said, "Something is moving, Mummy!" I scolded them and said, overactive imagination! But later I saw that they were right. There was a snake in the garage! Like a ribbon. It was caught in the trap I had set out for the rats. Our house is built on what used to be rice fields, so we are always getting rats."

"Oh, my god. What did you do?" Pansy balled her eyes into black beads and made her mouth into an O, touching Bithi's sleeve.

"I ran inside, locked the house, and called animal control. They took hours to come. And when they came, would you believe it, they scolded me, saying it was a rare snake, blah blah, and I shouldn't have set the mousetraps in my garage because they were a danger to snakes."

"Good for you that you trapped it. Oh my, I don't like snakes at all."

The men's raised voices burst over the air again, Haidar Khan's shouting voice piercing above all others. "What do you think all you young men are doing here? Do you think you are helping this society? Hmm? Do you know how many poor people sleep on the streets of Houston? Do you know how often we have a h...h...hurr...hurricane or flood, because of you guys and the work that you do?" The older man was stuttering, his words coming out in angry, guttural barks.

There were coughs, a clearing of throats.

"Oh, Haidar Bhai, calm down!" someone said in a honeyed voice.

"Noooo! I will not stop! You think you can stop the world outside, the c–c–climate change, by carrying on, going to your f–f–fancy jobs in your suits and living in these massive houses?" Haidar Khan stood up and started gesticulating with his arms, loosening the top buttons of his shirt.

Still the responses were polite. "Calm down. You don't have to insult people. We can be civil to one another," someone said.

"Do you know a reservoir was supposed to be built here in Katy to hold the flood water? But the city abandoned those plans and sold the land to developers to accommodate you guys. This is prairie land. It's supposed to be barren to let the water flood it! Now where will that water go, huh? You're scientists, for God's sakes!"

The children ran out of a side room to see what the fight was about, their eyes wide and mouths open.

"What's going on?" Maria clapped her hands and jumped up and down, the heavy party dress bobbing with her. The plastic band Simi had placed on her hair had come off, and her curls fell over her face in wild disarray.

"Nothing. Go and play," Sumon said.

Maria skipped to him and put her plump arms about his neck, rubbing her soft cheeks against his rough skin. "Are you sure?" she said tenderly, reminding him through this caress that his mother had died.

"Yes." Sumon smiled and sent the children back.

In the kitchen, Simi froze. She had been serving the dessert quietly. Now, at the sounds of Mr. Haidar Khan's yelling, she stood with her two hands raised and clasped in front of her chest. She had invited all these people to serve them, to make sure that everyone had enough to eat and a good time. Sumon entered the kitchen, smiling brightly at his wife, and went up to her, standing close till his perfume, fresh like the ocean breeze, hit her nostrils and persuaded her to lower her arms. Sumon had a round, fair face, handsome, with long eyelashes, pink lips, and even teeth. Everything about him was pleasing, his manners matching his pretty features, his words with her as gentle as the face he presented to the world.

"Is the dessert ready?"

"Yes. I'll get it right out," Simi said. She started to move again, with purpose.

Pulling open the fridge doors, she lifted out an orange caramel custard she had made, yogurt and pink custard with little bits of colorful fruit. Sumon started the percolator, expertly getting out teabags, sugar, and condensed milk from the cabinet for the evening tea that would complement the dessert.

Slowly, the raised voices faded away into murmurs. When the men filed into the kitchen to serve themselves sweets and tea, the waft of sugar and warm milk in the air, talking about salaries, work, and the share market in low voices, the rain could be heard again.

As usual, Bithi and Ali and the twins stayed behind long after the other guests had left. Their children liked to play with Sumon and Simi's daughter, and the men were classmates. The adults got along as well as the children. Besides, the other guests lived nearby in Katy, whereas Ali and Bithi would have to drive further off, an hour's drive down to Clear Lake, so it was worth their while to stay longer and make most of the trip.

"Sit, sit," Simi said, settling down herself on the sofa that had been occupied all evening. She had just said good-bye to Mr. Haidar and his wife Pansy, who had both shuffled out into the wet night in an embarrassed and angry way, without any umbrellas. She felt easier now, having got rid of the trouble.

Bithi, who had been hot under her silk sari after eating and from the overcrowding of guests (she often became overheated and breathless after eating), wiped her forehead with the back of her hand and breathed more easily. "Oof, it feels much cooler now."

The children had been huddled together all night in one room watching TV and playing on their devices, but now Maria and the twins, freed from the party decorum, rushed upstairs and started to jump up and down noisily, banging the pool sticks on Sumon's pool table.

"Never mind, let them play," Simi said, suppressing a yawn with her hand and raising the same hand to stop Bithi, who was about to get up. "Do you want another cup of tea?"

"The other children don't play with real things," Bithi agreed. "This is why your house is the only place I feel comfortable. Here they can be normal and run around and be naughty."

"Yes, children need to play," Simi agreed, her eyes heavy with sleep.

"I have grown so fat. I need to exercise. Do you work out, Simi?"

"Yes. I go to the gym. You look very nice. The lipstick is very nice."

"You always look like you are going to work out," Bithi said. "That's what I like about you. You never dress to impress, as if looks don't matter. Don't take it the wrong way. I really admire it, that you're not overdressed like the other women."

Simi laughed. When she went to work, as a pharmacist, she dressed in efficient clothes, blouse and slacks. When at home, she donned an apron and got down to cook in her tidy, clean kitchen. She swept the floor and mopped it with wet water from an automatic swirling bucket, at the end of every day. Her only purpose in life was to raise her daughter, to work, to keep in good health and keep her family in good health.

"But of course, you look good because you are slim. I was skinny myself before my marriage," Bithi said. "I should say before having the twins. It's hard raising two children."

Simi nodded sympathetically. She spoke little, but she was a good listener. The rainwater guttered down the drainpipes.

There was a drumming on the ventilator and on the glass of the narrow skylight upstairs. A large window upstairs, beside the pool table, led to the roof. Sumon had walked out onto the narrow ledge from this window to rake the leaves on the roof before the guests arrived.

Bithi was telling a story. "When I was a young girl, my parents lived in Iraq. My father was working there in oil. They were employing a lot of foreigners all over the world. I remember going to the hospital with my mother when my little sister was born. It was during the Iraq-Iran war. These soldiers had gone off to fight, and their young brides were having babies. These poor girls. One of them had given birth to two premature babies. The hospital didn't know what to do with the babies, so the young mother placed them in cotton under the bed on the floor. They were like little mice, smaller than my palm." She held out her swollen, pink palm. "I don't know what happened to the babies. I was too scared of the whole thing. I still remember that pale young girl giving birth to those little creatures mewling under the bed."

Simi nodded.

"Maybe they died…" Bithi continued to muse.

Sumon came inside the house with Ali. They had been standing outside having a smoke, checking out the weather. "Just this morning, I went out on the roof through the open window in the den upstairs and cleaned out the leaves on the roof. Now the roof is covered with fallen leaves again!" Sumon was saying to his friend.

When the two men entered the living room, Sumon said to Simi, "Turn on the news. My phone just went off with a flashflood warning."

"I remember when the twins were born. That night, too, it was raining like this. Do you remember, Ali?" Bithi asked her husband. Her voice rose, searching for sympathy.

Ali, a tall, silent man, was as stoic as his wife was talkative, willing to bear the burden the world had given him on his wide shoulders. He nodded slightly, giving his head a shake to the side.

Bithi shivered and closed her eyes while recounting the horrors of that night. "I can never forget it. The long labor, the emergency C-section. My parents had both passed away, and there was no one to help us. It was just the two of us. It is too cruel being alone in a new country, with no family around to help."

Sumon rolled through the cable channels until he found a local channel with weather news. His pretty face crumpled into a frown. All the highways were underwater. Bithi shrieked at an image on the screen: The water on I-10 in one place had reached the highway sign on the bridge!

"In this situation, we cannot go home!" Bithi cried.

"You must stay," Simi insisted at once. "We'll have a party."

"An after-party party," Sumon joked. "More tea? Simi, put some tea on."

"Yes, I'll put on a proper kettle on the stove now," Simi said, standing up. She was tired and needed some strong tea with milk and sugar to stay up with her guests.

The children could be heard jumping on the pool table. There were thumping and scratching sounds.

"Ei!" Sumon called them halfheartedly. "No jumping on the pool table. Also, too much jumping will make you cough again, Maria."

Once, a kid had dropped a pool ball from upstairs in the middle of a party at Simi and Sumon's house. The ball had crashed into a glass table directly in its path, and the table had shattered, spewing glass among the women sitting with their handbags around the table. Luckily, no one had been hurt. But since then, Sumon always confiscated the pool balls before a party.

"I didn't think they would think to jump on the table," he said, shaking his head.

"These children!" Bithi said. "They are not human. Monkeys, I say." She said it proudly.

They heard Maria coughing again upstairs.

Sumon said, "Her allergies are acting up again. We are worried about her. The doctor said to put her back on steroids."

"Steroids!" cried Bithi. "They are very bad for you. I was on steroids. Don't you see, my body is all swollen up? Steroids save you, only to kill you. Never put her on steroids."

"She's been on them on and off, her whole life. There were complications when she was born…"

Sumon began to tell the story, but Bithi, who had been feeling hot again, stood up to go to the kitchen, where Simi had put a silver kettle on the stove.

"Do you have a cotton nightie or something?" Bithi whispered to Simi. "I have hypertension, so I can't wear these rich clothes for too long, you see." She laughed.

"Wait, I'll give you a whole selection to choose from. A whole wardrobe. You can have your pick!" Simi joked and took Bithi into her bedroom.

"What kind of complications does Maria have?" Ali asked Sumon politely in the living room. He had been sitting with his legs crossed, hands on his knees, watching the news of the worsening weather on TV.

Other than the sound of the TV, the room had fallen silent. Sumon had stopped talking. He was thinking of his parents. If he turned his head around to face the back windows of the living room, he would be looking at the crepe myrtle tree in the backyard. After his mother's burial and some legal work that he had to take care of, he had flown back immediately, as soon as he could. Then he went right back to work. He would sit in his den on the second floor, working at his desk all day and night. He even carried work home from the office, determined to bury himself in work. One day, he found himself staring at the crepe myrtle full of pink flower, bursting with life. The tree had not been in bloom the day before. The flowers had appeared out of nowhere. Staring out the window, he had felt the tree to be a startling reaffirmation of life. Life had crawled back after the violence of what had happened to his mother– the frightened hospital run, being stuck in traffic in the ambulance, the cold, sallow skin of his mother after her death.

When Simi had been pregnant, they had discovered that she was going to have twins. But she had developed pre-eclampsia. There were complications, so the doctors decided to get the babies out early. During the surgery, the doctor came out to Sumon and told him that his team didn't know if they could save both the babies and the mother. Both babies survived in the end, but the doctors said that they were in poor health. The doctors had to deliver them two months early. They were tiny, two pounds each, in the NICU.

Sumon had been startled by the terrible news. And his mother had come to the rescue for him. In the old days, they used to speak of raising such babies in cotton balls. They stayed in the hospital for months, it seemed. Up to that experience, Sumon had been a sheltered boy, raised by two loving parents. Like Bithi's father, his father had worked in oil in Iraq during the seventies and made his money there. They were upper middle class, well to do. Sumon could not recall a moment's sorrow in his life.

The worst memory of his entire childhood was from a time before the family had lived abroad in the Middle East, when they used to live in a tiny flat in Dhaka. The building had a flat roof on top, like the roofs in Dhaka were in those days, lined by flowerpots, red peppers and mango laid out on mats on the ground to dry in the sun, and clothes lines overhead, and no guard railings. One day, a child who had accompanied his parents, visiting someone at the building, had escaped to the roof and had been walking around the edge of the roof and had fallen off. It had happened in the afternoon, a little before the time they used to call *bikel*, before the children woke from their naps and went down to play, before the descent of the sun, before the decent time that guests could arrive for tea and fried snacks. He had been sleeping in the enormous, solid wood bed he shared with his parents. He awoke to his mother screaming. She ran into the bedroom, picked him up from the bed, and clutched him to her bosom, crying, "Sumon, Sumon! You are alive!" She had been young then, perhaps younger than he was today, her cheeks soft against his, damp with tears, the wetness transferring to his skin, her sari bright green and soft cotton, warm against his chest and neck.

Later his mother said that death had been calling to that child that day. His mother's relief that Sumon had escaped death, that it was not he who had died, was the only concept Sumon had of death until his wife gave birth to two premature babies. It was too much for him. They used to live in New Orleans then. He was a graduate student. He would walk by the levee, smoking one cigarette after another. Simi was at home. Two creatures he could not fathom were waiting for him at NICU.

Sumon and Simi went to the hospital every day to touch the babies. The nurses said contact was good for the babies.

"The babies need to be touched, comforted, listened to, understood," the nurses said. "It's a human need."

But that human need of his babies took everything from him. Then, one baby died in NICU. Only Maria came home. The doctors said they didn't know if she would live.

At the time, his parents were comfortably ensconced in their retired home in Gulshan. They took daily walks on a lane lined with krishnachura flowers, with other retired people, who had also made their money in the Middle East, whose children were also comfortably settled in America. Their proud greeting to one other was about their offspring settled abroad.

"How is your son?"

"My daughter bought a big second house in California!"

"My son just got his Ph.D."

A nod of the head, canes raised in the air, the smile of parents whose children had made it. Sumon always chose the brief period when the krishnachura bloomed blood red to visit Dhaka. His parents called him early in the morning to walk with him and their retired friends under the krishnachura (Sumon was up

anyway from jetlag), showing him off proudly to their friends–
their American son.

Hearing news of Maria's illness, his parents decided to come
out of retirement. They offered to fly to America to take care of
their son's child for him. Simi, too sick to stand, got up in the
morning and went to work, while his mother took care of the
baby all day. His mother taught Simi how to feed Maria, how to
hold her, and how to give her a bath. His mother stayed up all
night holding the vomiting baby, listening to its mouse-like
wails, forcing herself to stare back at those large eyes staring out
of that horrifying bony face, with no flesh on it. There was no
flesh anywhere on that body, so that they had to be careful not
to break her bones. It was his mother who had saved Maria, had
given her last strength to her granddaughter. No one had asked
anything of Simi. She had been dumb, mute.

Sumon missed his dead mother. The last time he went home,
to attend her funeral, he had walked on that path under the
krishnachura trees again, but they were not in bloom.

"I'm sorry for your loss," Ali said. He did not have many
words, so these words were meant sincerely.

Sumon nodded. His black eyes shone like jewels. They went
on quickly to talk about his job. Sumon had just been promoted.
He was ambitious and was rising rapidly through the ranks.

"I have five engineers working under me."

"Wow. That must be a lot of responsibility."

"I have to work till at least eight every night and on
weekends. But Simi manages at home…"

The men talked, with the women gone. Sumon grabbed the
remote control and turned up the volume on the TV. There were
loud noises upstairs: dragging, scratching, and jumping.

"Stop it! No naughtiness," Sumon shouted.

There was a thud. Even this invasion of their tranquility the
adults would have ignored, had it not been followed by screams.
The twins ran downstairs to them in a fright of limbs, scurrying
across the carpet like squirrels.

They burrowed their heads in their father's chest, crying. "She fell! She fell down!"

The men rushed upstairs. Simi and Bithi had not heard the screams because of the heavy insulation of the master bedroom. But upstairs was the wrong way to run. The child had fallen out the window that Sumon had unlocked earlier in the day to go out on the roof and clean it out for Maria's birthday party. The men ran downstairs again. Maria had fallen by slipping on the wet roof and cracked her head on the concrete road and broken her neck. She lay under the water, a foot deep on their road, until they found her. Sumon called 911 and could barely answer the barrage of questions. His friend Ali had to seize the phone from him and speak calmly, walking up and down, pants soaked in dirty water up to his knees.

"Sir. Sir? We can't get there soon. There is high water on all the roads. A lot of people are stranded and looking for help. Meanwhile, what you do is…"

"Oh god, oh god!" Sumon kept crying, standing on the road in the rain and holding Maria in his arms. Her neck and limbs were twisted at an impossible angle to her torso. He tried to check her breath the way he used to when she was an infant, when he had to check every night if she was alive. He couldn't hear anything.

Simi came out of the house, screaming, "What happened? What happened?"

They carried Maria inside and set her wet body on the carpeted floor of the formal drawing room where all the men at the party had sat a few hours earlier arguing about the disaster of climate change and overbuilding in Katy, where Haidar Khan had been shouting, taking up space ungenerously at the house where he had been invited and breaking every decorum. Simi had been trained as a pharmacist in lifesaving. She bent down to take the child's pulse and her heartbeat.

"Give her mouth-to-mouth resuscitation!" Sumon shouted.

Simi nodded and worked hard, blowing into the child's blackened mouth again and again. She pounded on her chest and started again. And then again. But the child was already dead.

The fire truck didn't come till the next day. Simi had been pounding Maria's chest and blowing into her mouth all night. She had refused to give Maria cake and candles to blow out at the party, so she thought it a little painful that now she was doing all this blowing of air. The next day, there was still water on the road. Sumon and Ali had moved their cars into the garage earlier. Other cars lay submerged in the water. Water had crept into neighbors' yards. The firefighters came to their house first. They said they had orders to do so. They checked with their instruments and confirmed that the child was dead.

Simi and Sumon didn't miss a day's work. They had a funeral at the mosque, a burial, all as should be done. After forty days passed, and people stopped bringing food, they cooked as normal people do. They ate facing each other at the high kitchen table, looking out at the crepe myrtle tree in the backyard.

Once, Simi said, "The next time there is a storm or rain like that, that tree could fall on the house. You better cut it down."

Sumon nodded.

Simi had a sister in New York and another in New Jersey. But she never called them to cry or tell little anecdotes about Maria. She found the candles and balloons Maria had insisted on buying for her birthday, which had never gotten used, and threw them away in the trash can without tears. Only sometimes, when she returned home from her job before Sumon, after she had worked herself to the bones washing the kitchen floors and all the bathrooms of the house, Simi sat down with a steaming cup of milk tea and stared out through the double-glass window at the backyard, where the rain had dried up, and the sun shone in the new and bright suburb of Katy, covering up all the things that had passed a month ago.

Marker

Four weeks after their father had been buried, Salma and Asif finally drove up to the cemetery office in Forest Lawn to choose a tombstone. The woman at the desk, close-cropped dark hair, dressed in a neat green suit, asked them if they could wait, please. Mr. Munoz was meeting with another family. Panic gripped Salma. She had called ahead to make sure that they would be served on time, that it wouldn't be a wasted trip. All official business seemed to her a looming task.

Both brother and sister smiled politely. Salma sat down on the wooden church bench in the front office while Asif excused himself to use the restroom. Salma could see the family inside with Mr. Munoz and hear them speaking in muted voices. Soon, it would be their turn, and she would have to make decisions. She wanted a stone headstone, something old, like a grave in an English churchyard, natural and close to the earth, what her father would have liked. The kind of grave that would reflect his personality best. She already knew there would be disappointments. Compromises would have to be made. The question of money would enter into it. Already, the decorations hanging in the front office—large plastic sculptures of cherubic angels and vases with plastic flowers—did not give her high hopes about the options that would be on offer.

The time passed quickly enough. While Asif was in the bathroom, the woman at the reception was on the phone, and Mr. Munoz kept on talking with the other family. But everything happened at once. As soon as Asif returned, Mr. Munoz walked the other family out, and the woman in the front office said something, smiled, and led Salma and Asif inside to the small sales room at the back.

"Please have a seat. He'll be with you shortly."

Salma and Asif kept standing. The room was small and cold, crammed with samples of gravestones hung on the walls and displayed on small tables shoved in corners. Four upholstered chairs were drawn up around a large center table. Various blocks, bricks, and tiles were laid out on this table, as well as on a long side table pushed against one of the walls. All kinds of plaques hung on the walls, large rectangular plaques and small ones, with wreath-like decorations on frames, presenting pictures of angels and different letterings.

"I think Abba would have liked something plain," Salma said, turning away from a plastic-looking brownish rectangle. "These are really ugly."

She had majored in Art History and English in college. Now she was an English teacher who wore long, flowing skirts paired with artistic earrings. She felt particularly burdened by their task. She felt that there had to be aesthetics and meaning in the choice of a gravestone.

"I was looking for stone, you know?"

"This is interesting!" Asif said, reading a tomb marker on the wall. "This plaque says Linda Grissell. 1974. That's younger than you."

Salma turned. For several minutes, they read the names and dates on the plaques and commented on the different designs (flowers and petals and leaves), precious details that family members had eked out of the unnatural materials they had to work with.

Mr. Munoz entered the room, smiling, his face round and cherubic, wearing a pale summer suit. He shook their hands warmly. Salma was slight and thin. She often felt cold in rooms. Now she felt the warmth return to her skin with Mr. Munoz's handshake, as if she had been abandoned in the room before and now Mr. Munoz had come to take care of everything.

"Do you have stone gravestones? Is that what they're called, gravestones?"

"Unfortunately, we don't have stone in our cemetery. What we have is a granite base. Like this."

Salma frowned at the sample Mr. Munoz held up. She had to be rational about the choices offered to her. Mortality itself was a reality she had come to acknowledge in the last days of her father's life. She had had to witness this man who had once seemed so powerful and full of life unable to stand, or feed himself, or go to the bathroom.

"Touch it. So smooth and supple." Mr. Munoz handed the tile to Asif when Salma looked away.

"Ah, so this is granite," Asif said amiably.

Salma was glad of her brother's presence. Through the burial and afterward, he had been friendly and calm. Everything about him was pleasing: his average height, thick hair, dark, flashing eyes, and even the way he dressed, laid-back khaki pants paired with a collared T-shirt.

"I'm sorry for your loss," Mr. Munoz said, putting his hands together and smiling sincerely. He had a nice mouth and even white teeth.

Salma and Asif nodded quickly, yes. They didn't want to talk about it. They had avoided everything having to do with their father's death so far. Salma's husband, Kamal, had taken care of all the official business, checking out the gravesite and paying for the plot. Since the burial, the cemetery office had been calling Salma's husband Kamal to make arrangements for a permanent marker. They had sent a bunch of letters along the same lines.

Sorry for your loss—your loved one's courtesy temporary marker will be kept for one month—please make arrangements to pay for a permanent marker.

But this was one decision that Kamal couldn't make. He had been insisting for several days that Salma and Asif visit the cemetery office and choose a permanent marker.

"Please. Have a seat." Mr. Munoz was a salesman, yes, with the expected clean-shaven look and slicked back hair, dressed in a sky-blue suit, but not quite so pushy. He was easy to get along with in spite of his gaudy granite wall plaques.

They had been standing so far. Now Salma slid into an overly soft, yellow chair. "So, everything is granite. We just have one choice."

"Yes, let me show you." Mr. Munoz took blocks and piled them on top of each other. "The base is granite and on top of it you have a bronze marker. All our graves are bronze on granite."

"Oh! My father had never liked gaudy things."

He had been a deeply philosophical man. He would not have liked a gravestone at all, perhaps. Or perhaps he would have cared very much. He had been a sentimental man as well.

After he had died in Salma's home in Houston, there had been a lot of confusion about where he ought to be buried. Salma had always assumed that when her father died, he would be buried in his village home in Bangladesh. It seemed wrong, pointless, all of these decisions involved with burying him in a foreign land, where no one knew him.

When their mother had died a year ago in Bangladesh, she had been buried in a hurry in her family graveyard in Dhaka. Salma and Asif had both flown to Bangladesh, taking advantage of summer vacations from their respective schools. They had known even then that there was no space for their father's body in that graveyard. Their parents could never be buried next to each other.

A few days after their mother was buried, Mukul Bhai, a cousin on their father's side, invited Salma, Asif, and their newly widowed father to his house for dinner. Mukul Bhai told Salma and Asif that he had had a nightmare the night before. In the middle of the night, Mukul Bhai was awakened by a deep restlessness. Salma's dead mother's spirit had come to him, distraught. She had walked around his room in a lost and sad way, begging him for something wordlessly. Her mouth was stretched in a painful scream. In his dream, Mukul Bhai had realized what she was trying to say: that it had been wrong to bury her in Dhaka. She should have been buried in her husband's family graveyard in his village in Jessore.

This story had alarmed Salma. She had just wanted to think of her mother as being at peace. But after hearing her cousin's story, it felt as if the burial itself had been a wrong that could never be righted, a choice that would lead to other difficult choices in the future.

After her mother's death, Salma had brought her father to America to live with her. He had declined rapidly. Salma couldn't remember a single happy day since he had arrived at her home in Houston. He had been a well-known scientist in Bangladesh. He had published important papers on the topic of fluid mechanics in international journals and received a few awards from the government. He had always seemed larger than life to her, dressed in his baggy slacks and ink-stained shirts, gliding above the dust and noise and quarrels of everyday life in Dhaka in his own intellectual plane. But after arriving in Houston, he had rapidly lost control of his brain and his body. His last days had been tainted with all the baseness he had seemed to escape all his life.

The night he died, Salma's husband Kamal called the Islamic Society in Houston because he and Salma had no idea about the traditions of burial. What did someone do with a dead body? Salma's cousin—the same cousin who had claimed to have seen her mother's ghost—called from Bangladesh saying that his uncle's body should be flown home to Jessore to be buried in his family graveyard in his village.

"Please, I beg you, Salma!" Mukul Bhai cried over the crackling phone line. "After his death, my uncle's body belongs alongside his parents. Both his parents were buried in the graveyard in his village. It is so beautiful. It is in the middle of the family orchard of mango trees and guava trees, many of which had been planted by your father himself! As a child, he played among these trees, climbed them, and ate their fruits. Think about it. It's the right thing to do."

"But how will I move the body?" Salma asked. She clutched the cellphone to her head, her ears buzzing.

"You don't have to do anything. I'll do it all. I'll get permission from the embassy. I'll fly there myself right away."

While she spoke on the phone with her cousin, four men from the Islamic Society in Houston sat in Kamal's office. They had arrived at their house within an hour after the firefighters had pronounced Salma's father dead. When she put down the phone on the kitchen counter and went to see them, they told her sternly that the custom according to their religion was that 'a body should be buried immediately, wherever a person died'. A person should be buried where he had come to die, not where he had been born, they said.

Salma's father's body lay on the cold hardwood floor of his room in Salma's house. Kamal had lowered him from his bed and placed the body on the floor to practice CPR with instructions from the 911 operator. Then the firefighters arrived and pronounced him dead. After the firefighters left, a police officer arrived and cleared the death as being from natural causes. Now while the police officer waited outside the house in his patrol car for someone from the Islamic funeral home to take away the body, Salma and Kamal negotiated with the men from the Islamic society. The four men didn't even want to wait for Asif to fly in from California—he was frantically calling for flights to Houston at that very moment. Kamal had to put up a fight. At last, the men said that they would wait until Thursday, two days, to bury the body.

Over the next two days, the battle over where to bury Salma's father continued. Her cousin called several times a day to plead to bring the body home where it belonged, so that Salma's father could be given his due respects and lie in peace. Other relatives and her father's friends called with counter arguments. Putting a body on a plane would mean that it would have to sit in a freezer for weeks while Salma would have to apply for a permit from the embassy in Washington, D.C. to fly the body. The body would have to be embalmed—an intrusion that seemed violent when described by various passionate voices on the phone.

In the end, Asif decided the matter for Salma when he called her via Skype from the airport before boarding his flight.

"Listen, Sis," he said, "I want my father buried where his children can visit his grave, in Houston. Yeah?"

"I didn't have a strong opinion myself," Salma explained apologetically to her cousin later that night. "I see your point. I know you are hurt. But this is what Asif wants. He's arriving tomorrow. We will bury the body in Houston then."

"You are his children, so of course, you have first right over his body," her cousin said tightly.

"It's not that," Salma said. "I agree with you that he should be buried where he was born. I'm sorry. But it's what Asif wants."

Secretly, she was convinced that her father, who practiced no religion, would not have liked the hassle of being embalmed and flown on a plane. She was sure he would have abhorred such a fuss being made of his body.

She, with whom he had lived in his final days, felt most strongly how futile it was to fight over his dead body when she had not been able to care for him while he had been alive. Only Salma knew the ugly truth about how her father's life had ended, in so much neglect. On many nights, he had called to her, waking her in the middle of the night. Salma had run down from her upstairs bedroom to his room, her heart stopped from being jerked awake, her head ballooned from being sleep deprived from his chronic nighttime calls and moaning.

"Please stay with me!" he had begged from his bed. "I am scared. I see something in the dark."

"I can't stay up!" Salma shouted. "Do you know what time it is? Go to sleep. You'll make us all mad."

Everything had been exhausting for Salma and humiliating for her father—feeding him, which involved sometimes forcing things down his throat because he could not swallow, and taking him to the bathroom, which involved him slipping and sliding.

Now Mr. Munoz coaxed Salma and Asif into taking at least some pleasure in their decisions. He had a salesman's art of convincing. Or perhaps all three wanted to get it over with, helping one another toward their common goal, moving through the laborious steps of making choices. Mr. Munoz explained that there were several colors available in the granite base. They could choose black or brown granite. The bronze plates had various textures as well. On top of those combinations—he pulled a brochure in front of their eyes (they had been trying to choose from the samples on the walls and tables, but apparently the right way to go about it was to look at the brochure)—they could have different designs for the marker. They could even have a slab that covered the entire grave, like a mausoleum, or they could dedicate a bench to their father!

"How much is a bench?"

"Starts at two thousand."

"Ah."

They stopped moving in the direction of the mausoleum or the bench. Their father would not have liked to spend thousands of dollars on such a thing as a mausoleum. Still, every dollar withheld felt like a curtailment of their love.

Mr. Munoz left the room for a few minutes to consult the lady in the front office about the prices for the different sizes of bases (it turned out that she was his boss rather than his secretary), and Salma and Asif quickly made their decision in his absence. They chose the simplest design, the one that would best describe their father's personality, a man of high thought who had a low regard for show and recognition.

When Mr. Munoz returned, Asif quickly pointed out the plain rectangular design they had chosen to Mr. Munoz. With Mr. Munoz's help, Asif decided quickly on the size of the base and marker, spelling out his choices while Mr. Munoz wrote rapidly with a ballpoint pen on a yellow notepad. In a few minutes, it was over.

"There, all done," Asif said happily, leaning back in his chair with his feet planted on the ground.

"And now for the words you want on the marker," Mr. Munoz said.

Salma gasped. She had forgotten that a tombstone required words. Mr. Munoz smiled apologetically. There were more discussions about fonts and sizes, more back and forth about prices. Salma pushed through the decisions mechanically, always choosing the simplest and cheapest option.

"Now are we done?"

Mr. Munoz smiled. "We're done."

Asif asked, "Can we have a poem? There is a poem that best describes my father, a poem that my father used to recite."

"Yes, of course!" Mr. Munoz said, his face lighting up.

More words meant more money, Salma thought.

"Can we have the poem written in Bengali letters?" Asif asked.

"Yes, yes, definitely," Mr. Munoz said. "People have asked for writing in different scripts. We had some people request writing in Arabic, for example."

Painstakingly, Salma wrote down the Bengali words on a piece of paper, words that meant nothing in English. Someone could easily make a mistake writing the characters.

Mr. Munoz said he would send them the proofs first for their approval. "What do the words mean?" he asked with childlike curiosity.

"They mean: When will there be born in our land a boy, who speaks little and is big in deed?" Asif chatted easily with Mr. Munoz, telling him what kind of man his father was.

Mr. Munoz seemed interested in hearing about their father. He had an open face and a sweet, kind smile. His manner was mild and his voice slow and gentle.

"All done now?" Salma smiled brightly, standing up.

A man in jeans walked into the room and spoke in Spanish with Mr. Munoz. He had been hired to cut down the tree in the parking lot, and he needed Salma and Mr. Munoz to move their cars. When they came back inside, Mr. Munoz finally finished calculating the price from the quotations list and writing down the design details on his notepad. At last, it was over, and they were joking, talking about the World Cup Football games taking place. Mr. Munoz was Colombian, and they discovered that they were all three supporters of the South American countries. Then Salma and Asif were free to leave.

They shook hands with Mr. Munoz and walked out, spilling out into the beautiful sunny day at the end of summer. As they hurried down the steps, they passed a mother and daughter entering the cemetery office. The mother and her daughter, about twelve or thirteen, smiled weakly at Salma and Asif. Their eyes were red, and they looked uncertain whether to behave normally or to show their grief.

Back in her car, Salma said, "I'm glad we did it now. You know? Instead of just immediately afterward, like them. We would have been like them, just paralyzed. It would have been painful. At least this way we were able to enjoy it. You know what I mean?"

"Yeah," said Asif, pulling his seatbelt on. "Can we visit the grave before we go?"

"Of course. I was thinking the same thing!"

The car followed the narrow road crowded with cars parked along the side, to Garden nine, where the Muslims were buried. They walked on the soft, damp lawn, stepping over other graves, trying to find their father's. Had Kamal been with them, he would surely have told them that it was disrespectful to walk over graves.

Salma felt lighter, a world away from the day they had buried her father four weeks ago. Everything had seemed still and foreign on that day. They had stood around watching, unbelieving, as a crane had lowered a slab of concrete and then piled dirt on the grave. A few people had come to pay their respects, but the words of condolence had sounded faint, miles away. There had been so few people at his burial, for a man who had had so many friends.

Salma and Asif had just wanted to get away, climb into the car and drive back home, where a warm meal awaited them, and television, and the World Cup games.

"Strange," Salma said now in the sunlit day, after they had walked for a few minutes. "His grave was at the end of the cemetery that day. Where is it?"

They both realized at the same time what had happened. Their father's grave was no longer at the edge because other people had been buried since they had been there last. They walked on, continuing to step over other graves, trying to find an unmarked grave with a temporary bronze vase filled with plastic flowers, a small paper marker with their father's name and date of birth pasted on.

In the distance, Salma could see a cantilever tent that had been set up by the roadside for the spectators of a new burial to take place on that day. A crane stood ready to dig. As they plodded on, Salma and Asif began to idly read the markers on the other graves. They became really interested.

"Look, Salma. This one says it expires a month from now," Asif said, "so this is a completely new grave, since a temporary marker is supposed to expire in a month."

"1954. You can tell their ages from the markers."

They passed an infant's grave, so tiny that it took up no space. "It's comforting, in a way, to see that so many people have died in the last two weeks. It's almost as if death is natural," Asif commented.

Salma let his words fall around her, comforting and natural. She walked nimbly now, her steps light in the warm day. They kept walking, reading the markers and letting themselves be surrounded by the commonness of death.

"Look!" Salma said, stopping at three graves with the same last name. "What could have happened?"

"Car accident?" Asif guessed.

"You're right."

By the dates of birth on the graves, they calculated, the three dead had been a twenty-year-old, an eighteen-year-old, and a fifteen-year-old of the same family, all buried at the same time. Salma and Asif tried to guess the relationships among the three dead people. Salma read their names: Miriam, Sara, and Haider—two girls and a boy. Their deaths could only have been tragic. Their last name was unusual, Muquddum. Salma memorized it, interested, determining to Google it once she returned home. At last, they found their father's grave, surrounded by fresh mounds of earth. They sat beside it, touching the mound of earth, and wondered aloud what was happening to his body now.

When their mother had died, suddenly, from cancer, Salma had felt an acute urge to steal her back from her grave in Azimpur graveyard. She had wanted to raise her from the grave when no one was looking. She had felt that urge for a long time after her mother's death, every time they visited her grave during their month-long stay in Bangladesh. But now Salma felt no such longing to pull her father back from his grave. She felt removed from her father's body.

"He was so far gone," Asif said when she confided in him. "When I looked at his dead body, when I was washing him, he didn't feel like my father to me. His body was emaciated and changed."

"You know, he starved to death," Salma said. She was sitting with her knees on the earth, pulling grass at her feet. "He was thirsty, but he couldn't drink water. He couldn't swallow. I kept trying to push him to get better. If only I'd realized he was dying, I could have been kinder to him."

"Don't be hard on yourself," Asif said. He was looking away, squinting into the sun.

After they returned home, Salma Googled the name Muquddum on her iPad. At first, it didn't seem a particularly deliberate act, just an idle way of browsing the Web. She did so many things just to pass the time, to distract herself. For most of Asif's visit, they had been watching the World Cup games, cooking elaborate snacks together, eating, taking walks, and dining out at restaurants. They discussed football, and read about football, and Googled various statistics on football. So, from researching the World Cup, it was an easy stretch to Google other things as well. Marvelously, with a few strokes of the key, the keywords Muquddum and Houston thrown in, she pulled up the news about the family. It hadn't been a car accident, after all. Thrilled, Salma lay in bed that evening reading all the articles she could find on them on her iPad. She could hear Asif and Kamal downstairs, talking together in a soothing, distant drone. She kept searching for the name in different browsers and different search engines, with different combinations of keywords, and the story emerged.

The Muquddums had been siblings. It was a murder suicide. Salma kept reading. For the first time in weeks, she was focused on something outside of herself. According to all the news articles, no one knew what exactly had happened to the three siblings. It was a mystery. All the children were polite and nice, according to friends and neighbors. There had been nothing out of the ordinary about them. The twenty-year-old sister had dropped out of school and was working as a nurse's assistant. The fifteen-year-old sister was a sophomore in high school. The police suspected that their teenaged brother had shot them both and then turned the gun on himself.

No one called Salma for hours. At last, when it got dark outside her window and she realized her room light wasn't on, she put away the iPad and came downstairs. Kamal and Asif were watching a detective show on TV.

"Do you remember that family of the three siblings who died?" Salma said, standing in front of the TV. "I just Googled them. It was a murder suicide."

"Wow. Really?" Asif sat up and slapped his knees, exclaiming.

"No one knows what happened exactly. But they think the brother probably killed his two sisters and then shot himself."

"That's really sad," Kamal said.

Asif and Kamal returned to watching the show. Salma sat on the sofa and patiently waited for them to finish, but after the show ended and she switched off the TV, they moved on to other topics. When Salma brought up the story of the murder-suicide again at dinner, Kamal and Asif seemed suitably touched. They talked about it, but no one else bothered to Google the story. The three ate dinner, talked some more, went outside to stand on the front steps drinking coffee under a full moon, came inside, and went to sleep, never once mentioning the Muquddums again.

In the middle of the night, Salma crept out of bed, moved to the window seat, and turned on the iPad, hoping its light would not spread to the bed and wake up Kamal.

More of the story had built over time. People were referring to the victims' Twitter accounts and Facebook pages that hadn't been taken down yet. The boy, Haider, had a Facebook post looking forward to the World Cup games. Friends of the victims were now writing their own accounts on their blogs. Also, by going back to the original news stories, Salma discovered a growing thread of comments underneath. A friend of the younger girl Miriam wrote that Miriam had been "the sweetest person on earth, not just on the outside, but also on the inside." Several people speculated about how the parents must be feeling.

Now it seemed to Salma that her father had lived a normal life and died a quiet death. The more Salma read, the more comforted she felt about his death. After Salma's father had died, friends had dropped by and said nice things about him, but none of those visits had offered Salma as much comfort as this story about the murder suicide of the three Muquddum siblings. She stayed on the iPad until the first markings of daylight. Then she crawled back into bed beside Kamal, exhausted.

For the next several days, Salma Googled the name repeatedly on her iPad. Muquddum. It was an obsession. She regained an interest in talking on the phone with people who had called to console her before, whose calls she had not received. What would she have said to them then? The only way to truly understand her father's death was to avoid it, to do anything but focus directly on it. Given space, understanding came in brief flashes, after a good TV show or in the middle of tea with her brother and husband. But now Salma called those friends back to tell them about the tragedy of the Muquddum family. She wondered about every detail, what the mother must have felt on her first discovery of her babies lying dead in her home, or how the sisters must have been scared in the moment when their brother had attacked them. She could have gone on for hours talking about the Muquddums.

They had spent most of Asif's visit lounging around at home, just resting from the world. Being academics, they were both off for the summer. One day, toward the end of Asif's visit, Salma suggested to Kamal that they should all drive to the cemetery again to visit her father's grave.

"Yeah, let's go," Kamal agreed. "Let's go today."

The cemetery was an hour away. The motion of the car was soothing. They played music. At Garden Nine, Salma looked around furtively for other visitors. On the way to her father's grave, Salma led Kamal and Asif back to the three Muquddum siblings' graves. Someone had stuffed fresh flowers in the bronze vases, Salma noted, as Kamal and Asif started to walk away. They seemed uninterested.

As on the previous occasion, they had trouble finding Salma's father's grave. At last when they reached it, the area seemed even more full of new dead bodies all around. Salma felt curiously detached from her father's grave. Her father's living self was still alive in her memory. She remembered his every discomfort and suffering. At home, she felt a shiver when she passed his empty room. But his grave had no effect on her.

"Hey, someone left flowers," Asif cried happily.

Perhaps another visitor had come. Some of her father's friends and students lived in Houston. Salma studied the flowers, tall irises and lilies bent and spilling over the vase. She and Asif wondered aloud who it might have been, a welcome distraction. The day was beautiful, clear blue, with a light breeze that slanted the grass near the grave. There was a small apple tree nearby in the otherwise characterless land and an embankment with pine trees in the distance, possibly planted to cut off the view and sound of the highway. Asif said the tree could serve as a marker for their father's grave in the future.

Their mother's body lay in the Azimpur graveyard in Bangladesh, where she lay next to her parents and two of her sisters. That graveyard had character, planted with trees by the family members of those buried there, mango trees and guava trees and flowering plants that filled the air with a heavy scent. In the evenings, crows came to sit on the trees and a nearby mosque belted out its call to prayers, making the atmosphere gloomy and somber.

But here, in a foreign land, in a commercial cemetery, there was just a body under the earth, fast disappearing. Salma sat down near her father's grave. Asif sat down, too. The breeze lifted Salma's hair. There was a drone of cars on the highway as they sat together silently, searching for meaning.

Salma realized that she had been hoping to run into the Muquddum siblings' mother come to visit their graves and discover more of their story. She had found out a lot more about the family. The father had moved out only a few days before the murder. The boy, Haider, had hated his father. The father and son had gotten into fist fights several times. The more Salma found out, the more she wanted to know. Why had the brother killed his sisters? Why did the father move out? And how did the father feel now?

For the next few days, Salma suggested to Asif and Kamal that they visit the cemetery again, but Asif had caught a cold and said he was too sick to go, and he was flying home in only four more days. Kamal had to work on a paper he was writing. In the end, Salma drove to the cemetery herself. She stayed for a long time, sometimes sitting by her father's grave and sometimes walking around reading the markers on other graves. She still did not feel any connection to her father's grave. Her proximity to his body did not yield any special thoughts, except to make her wonder how much more his body had decomposed since she had last visited.

She had posed such questions to Asif, as well as questions about life after death. Their father had been an atheist, so the question about what had happened to his body after his death was interesting to them. He must have found out at last what happens after death.

Salma kept looking to see if other visitors would arrive. Other graves held more interest for her, distracting her. She kept wondering about a grave where the person had been born in 2000 and died in 2013. That would make the person a mere child. Then she would wonder how the child had died. She was also impressed by how many old people were buried in the cemetery. Her father was not the only one, after all, to be buried far away in another country. There was some romance in starting one's life in one place and ending it in another, as if life were an adventure and one could never know where it would end. Her parents could not have known how things would look for them in the end, the sudden death of one leading to the other's journey to another country and his humiliating, lonely death far from home.

Squinting in the sunlight, staring ahead, Salma saw a middle-aged woman in a shapeless shalwar kameez with her head loosely encircled by a dupatta and an elderly man wearing a dirty, collared shirt, and baggy slacks climb out of an old Toyota Corolla. The elderly couple walked slowly to the three graves of the Muquddum siblings. Then they stood side by side offering prayer. Salma stared open mouthed at the couple in the sun, shading her eyes and squinting, facing them nakedly. They did not look in her direction or pay her any heed, so she had an open view. Salma drank them in greedily. She could not be sure, but they could only be the father and mother of the three dead siblings. They appeared to her as abject, tragic figures. Their gaits were slow, and their facial features were vague, washed out by their sorrow. They held their hands at their breasts, their heads bent low in prayer. Several times, they knelt, stood up, and knelt again. Then they rose and left.

Salma watched their departing backs as they walked slowly to the Toyota Corolla and climbed inside. She stared straight at them as the car reversed, made a K turn, and drove off.

There had been no encounter, no contact. They, presumably the Muquddum parents, had told her nothing of their story or their feelings. Nevertheless, Salma was satisfied with just seeing them. She wondered why. Perhaps they had just been entertainment for her. A distraction. She had so many questions for them. Why did the boy not wait to watch the World Cup games before taking his life? And what was he thinking at the moment he killed his sisters, one by one, or earlier in the morning when he probably had no intention of killing anyone? Or later, if he had had a later, what regrets would he have felt?

When she returned home that day, Salma didn't tell Kamal or Asif about her sighting. They seemed to have forgotten the Muquddum family. After four days, Asif left for California, still sniffling from his cold. Kamal drove him to the airport. It was too much for Salma to accompany them, to face another difficult parting.

After Asif left, Salma settled into bed, trying to get as much rest as possible before the end of summer and the start of classes and students and syllabi. The World Cup games ended a few days after the semester started. Salma started pulling novels from the shelves downstairs and carrying them up to her bed. She would read them lying down, skipping meals, depending on Kamal to take pity on her and bring her a jam and butter sandwich.

She would go up to her bed and start reading as soon as she returned home from campus. This went on for days, weeks. She was late on grading, distracted during office hours, slovenly about most things she did. By then, Palestine was being bombed and children were dying, but death was entirely natural to Salma. She had discovered an antidote to life's stubborn miseries: the distraction of fiction, the made-up world of what happened next.

In October, when the few maple trees on campus had begun to shed their leaves, Salma walked to her car parked in the faculty lot at the end of the day, checking her cellphone. There was a voicemail from the cemetery, leaving a courtesy message that the permanent marker 'for her loved one's grave' was ready.

Salma had fretted about the gravestone before, wondering why it wasn't ready yet, but now she felt only relief that the business had been completed. She felt no desire to actually see the cheap tombstone. However it looked, it was an inadequate marker for her father's life. Even if Salma had erected a marble mausoleum in her father's honor, it could not have taken away the disappointments and the guilt and the sadness. Those feelings could only be squashed under other things. In the light of the setting sun, Salma walked across the parking lot and climbed into her car, tossing the phone in her bag, and started the engine. Then she turned on an audio recording of a new novel, a long one.

The Limits of Speech

Joya grunted as she climbed out of the tiny Volkswagen. The car's size wasn't the problem. Joya had put on a lot of weight recently. She was meeting her friend Meg for a walk on White Oak Bayou after dropping her younger daughter at the R-Elementary school, and she just remembered now that Meg was always late.

As she stood in the parking lot, breathing in the early morning air, looking out onto the trail along the bayou at the line of trees and scattered houses on the other side, she stretched and raised her arms and cried out in pain. Her muscles ached all the time, but they weren't always the same muscles. The pain was often in her joints, knees, or fingers, or on the soles of her feet. She clutched her lower back, rubbing the tissue tenderly.

"Hey there!"

Seeing her friend, Joya grinned. "Hi, Meg. You look nice!"

"Oh!" Meg drew out the long o and pulled down the corners of her mouth in appreciation.

"I'm so fat!" Joya touched her palms to puffy cheeks, rubbery to the touch.

"You look nice, too!" Meg wore a faded blue T-shirt that brought out the blue in her eyes. She was a big boned, tall woman. Her face still showed the signs of a once beautiful woman, sharp, blue eyes, pale blonde hair, an angular shape. She gave Joya a quick hug, then drew in her chin and considered Joya, gazing down at the diminutive figure of her friend. "You look *very* nice! I'm so sorry I kept you waiting. I was driving here when I realized I had no gas. *Then* I had to go back to let the dog out…"

Meg had a way of drawing out her story, pausing at random words, and Joya waited impatiently, raising her ankles to start her exercise. "Shall we walk?" she asked. She would have to be at work in an hour at the hospital.

"Oh, yes. I'm sorry to be annoying you!" Meg fell into line behind her obediently, stamping her sneakers, following Joya across the parking lot and past the dumpster onto the wet green grass.

Joya felt bad for feeling impatient. Meg was her oldest friend, and always so kind. Joya had gone to her house so many times over the years and poured out her life while drinking Meg's microwaved tea (tap water with a teabag) and cookies. Meg had given her many presents– a handknit blanket for Shima, Joya's second daughter when she had been born, and a large Christmas-themed mug painted with multicolored maple leaves that Joya used exclusively as her cup to drink water. They started to walk on the trail, dumpy in their ordinary T-shirts, elastic pants, and scuffed tennis shoes damp from the grass. Two tall, young women dressed in spandex running shorts and bright blue nylon tank tops zipped past them.

"How did your doctor's appointment go?" Meg asked, twisting her head toward Joya as she tied back her heather-colored strands in a ponytail with a black hair tie.

"Oh, it was horrible!"

"Horrible? Why?"

"The doctor didn't even look at me for two minutes! She wanted to know why I hadn't taken the steroids she had prescribed me and, when I asked for a bone density test, she said my insurance wouldn't pay for it."

"Was she a *young* woman?" Meg asked with a knowing look.

"Yes!"

"I *know*!" Meg said sympathetically, drawing out the *o*. "They always treat me like that *too*. I was reading an article about it, how older women, middle aged women, get treated badly by younger doctors. It's ageism."

A smiling, short, elderly gentleman ambled past them, walking his aged German Schnauzer. Joya and Meg waved at him, and he waved back, bowing his head in the gesture of taking off an imaginary hat.

"How's Rob?" Joya asked.

"Oh, you know, plodding along. He doesn't like school." Meg sighed, pushing her hair back from her forehead.

Joya noticed some graying strands.

Rob was Meg's youngest, of three sons. Rob and Joya's elder daughter Prothoma had been classmates through elementary school, middle school, and high school in Houston. Meg and Joya had met when Rob and Prothoma were in kindergarten. The children used to play in the school park after dismissal while the moms stood together in groups by the swings or around the pine trees, gossiping about their day.

"Rob's not happy at school. He seems depressed. I worry that he's not eating right," Meg said.

Joya nodded solemnly. Rob was studying engineering at Texas A&M. According to Meg, he had been complaining about the large classes and the workload ever since the semester started.

"You're so lucky. Your Pro has been on the honor roll all her life," Meg said. "Teachers at R-Elementary still remember her. Right?"

"Oh, yes!" Joya's face lit up at the mention of her elder daughter Prothoma. "I was up at R– the other day, and Miss B said Prothoma was her all-time favorite student of her entire teaching career!"

"That's amazing. How does Pro like Harvard?" Meg asked.

"She's acing all her courses. She loves it! She made lots of friends." As she spoke, Meg was transported to the past. Prothoma had been a serious little girl in elementary school and middle school, shorter than her classmates, with tight braids, thick glasses, and an impish smile.

"And how are things at R-Elementary? You're glad to get Shima in there, I bet," Meg said, referring to Joya's younger daughter. "I heard the lottery was tough this year."

"Oh yes, Shima was waitlisted at 40. I don't know how we made it in!" Joya said brightly. "But you know, the school's changed."

"Oh? How so?"

"It's just a wealthier community. The old houses have been torn down and now the school's surrounded by million-dollar homes. All the kids who lived in apartment complexes are gone. All the Hispanic kids are gone. Now it's just us magnet families and wealthy families, mostly white families. We feel like scholarship kids."

"So, it's not diverse?"

"They say it is, but you can literally see the few families like ours strung out in an ocean of white, like we should be grateful to be there. Like, somehow, we don't belong."

"Oh!" Meg made a sympathetic face. Wrinkles stood out on her forehead and in the dimples of her cheeks. "That's too bad."

"The first semester, in the fall, we were hanging out with all the other kindergarten parents after school at the park, and we were invited to all the birthday parties. But the other families must have invited each other to their homes and chosen their friends by now, because this semester Shima doesn't even get birthday invites," Joya confided.

"Oh. Poor thing."

"Even if I make eye contact with a parent in Shima's class, they don't acknowledge me. Once, I was talking to another parent. A mom whose kid is in Shima's class came up to us and said hi to her, to the other mom, and she didn't even look at me! Shima is in her child's class! I introduced myself and she just nodded and turned back to the other mom!"

"That's terrible," Meg said. "But you don't need them. You have us!"

Joya nodded, but in her mind she saw Shima's tiny face and big eyes, the little dangling gold earrings and two tight braids, and felt sorry for her. Shima was quiet and soft spoken. Joya had observed Shima quietly looking on as her classmates walked together ahead of her. Prothoma had always been on the go—sleepovers, birthday parties, then robotics friends, debate friends, and piano friends. It was all Joya and Prothoma's father could do to keep up; in all their years with Prothoma, they had felt as if they were on a thrilling roller coaster ride, holding on to their hats.

The two women walked south on the bayou, taking the dirt path beside the main trial to avoid the fast bikers on the asphalt road. Looking down below, Joya could see the dirty water snaking through the bayou. A little ahead of them, a manmade clearing led down a slope of grass covered with an explosion of wildflowers.

"*Oh*, look at those lovely bluebonnets!" Meg said. "Remember when we used to dress up the kids and go out on I-10 to see the wildflowers?"

Joya nodded. Wildflowers brought back the past, when Prothoma had been little and Joya's husband had been alive, when they had been surrounded by friends and parties, when they had possessed an earnestness that drove them hours away to find the best wildflower lookouts.

"Do you want to walk down that beautiful path?" Joya asked. "I feel infected by the cheerful bloom."

"Yes, let's do it."

They were two young women again, giggling, their eyes bright with excitement as they descended the hill cautiously.

Meg's phone burst into life. "Sorry," she said, zipping it out of her purse (yes, they were unfashionable women who carried purses on their walk). "Oh, it's Rob." She stopped. "Hi, I'm out here walking, getting my exercise in! With Pro's mom. You want me to call you back? Everything okay? Okay!"

Joya's phone rang next. She fished it out of her pant pocket and laughed. "It's Prothoma. They seem to be on the same wavelength."

"Go ahead. Answer it," Meg said kindly, waving her hand. She clutched her left side in her palm and rested her weight on her right leg.

"Okay." As soon as Joya put the phone to her ear, her heart jumped.

Prothoma was sobbing uncontrollably.

"What's…what's wrong, baby?"

"Ma, I'm so sad."

"Hold on. I'm walking with Meg. I'll just stop." Joya looked around wildly.

Meg nodded.

"Oh, you're with somebody?" Prothoma wailed.

"With…with Meg, baby."

"I'll call you back later then." Prothoma hung up abruptly.

Joya rang her back. No answer. She tried again.

"What's the matter? She's not answering?" Joya heard Meg ask in the distance, her voice coming from far off, over Joya's right shoulder.

The spring air was crisp and clear, on a rare day in Houston before the heat of the summer descended. Joya stared at the explosion of red and blue wildflowers, Indian paintbrush and bluebonnet, as she rang Prothoma again and again. A text popped on her screen. *Stop calling me.*

"I'd better go." Joya said faintly. Her back had started to ache again. It was a strange sensation. The muscles above her hip had flared up, as if on fire. It could also be described as a cold sensation, as if all her muscles had been transformed into jelly. With one part of her mind, Joya tried to describe her symptoms.

"Are you sure?" Meg said uncertainly.

They had only completed half their walk, just over twenty minutes.

"I'm late for work anyway, since we started late," Joya said.

"Oh, I'm sorry. It's my fault. I'll try to be on time next time." Meg spoke rapidly in an apologetic tone, casting her eyes downward.

"No, no, it's okay," Joya said. "You keep walking. I've to get back in time to get changed in the office. I'll just hurry ahead." She left Meg behind and huffed up the slope to the main trail, where bicycles zipped past her.

When she reached her car, the side mirror of the Volkswagen showed a plump, middle-aged woman with a pregnant tummy. Belly fat. Joya studied the sallow skin, thinning hair, and puffed face that told her that her liver was going bad. Her heart was beating rapidly. She wouldn't feel normal until she heard back from Prothoma.

Joya struggled to consciousness, fumbling for the phone on the bed beside her, to turn off the alarm. It was time to pick up Shima from school. Joya had called in sick from work again and slept in the whole morning. She had been so focused on her backache that she had forgotten to describe the migraines to Meg the other day. Like hammers going off in the front of her head, she would have said. Struggling to sit up, she remembered the sarcastic look on the young Dr. Jamieson's face at her last visit.

The painted chocolate lips had sneered at Joya. "I can give you a referral to mental health. It's hard to accept, but your ailments might just be in your head," Dr. Jamieson had suggested.

Joya had shaken her head mutely and left, dressing quickly and picking up her sagging handbag from the doctor's chair. She should have told Dr. Jamieson that she had been trained as a doctor in Bangladesh. Joya and her husband Bipu had graduated top of their class from the premier Dhaka Medical College in Bangladesh. After finishing their internship, they had been posted to village positions in two different villages outside Dhaka. Then they saw that their friends were busy passing their MRCP exams, getting promoted in their government jobs, moving to private hospitals for higher pay, or settling abroad. They began to assess their own careers. They were happy, but they felt that they had to take the next step. That was when Bipu had the idea of applying to the United States for higher studies. They had come to America together, Bipu on a master's degree visa and Joya on a spouse visa. The plan was that Bipu would finish his studies first, and then it would be Joya's turn.

At first, everything seemed to go well. Bipu passed his master's degree in epidemiology, passed his US Medical License Exam, and started his residency, while Joya gave birth to Prothoma, cooked, and kept house. Bipu had been a brilliant student, so he had sailed through school, the exam, and the residency like a ship on a bright, sunny day. For a time, it had been a great adventure. They lived in a small apartment by the bayou, and their home was always filled with other Bengali graduate students and postdocs–bachelors and young families. There were parties with quickly cooked khichuri and egg curry and lots of laughter. Joya and Bipu rode the bus wherever they had to go; they wheeled Prothoma in a rickety, plastic stroller to city parks and the beach in Galveston, living the life. Then Shima was born (Prothoma had just turned thirteen) and they bought a house–a modest cottage with a rectangle of yard at the back, at the edge of the Heights. That was the final marker of their success. They had made it in America.

One night, Bipu was ill with a high fever, chills, his body shaking. The next morning, he started behaving abnormally. The doctors said there was a biochemical imbalance in his brain. They diagnosed him with schizophrenia, but they couldn't help him. Joya and Bipu had many doctor friends across the US. Their friends started to fly in, giving Bipu off-label prescriptions, treating him themselves. But nothing made Bipu better. He grew fat and thick-necked, and violent. He threw dishes at the wall and shouted and raged while their daughters hid in the corner. Then he had heart damage. Was it from all the medications they were trying? Joya would never know. Within a year, he was dead.

People thought that Joya was a widow, but, actually, Joya had divorced Bipu before he had died, in the hope that the kids wouldn't catch his mental illness, living in that atmosphere of stress, if she cut him off quickly enough. She had made the decision when Bipu lost his power of speech. He sat in a corner, rocking and making guttural noises in his throat. Both the children had been frightened by his behavior. She could tell by their wide eyes and how they wandered around the apartment, not even coming close to her.

Joya had put her husband on a plane and sent him to his family in Bangladesh, where, hopefully, they could treat him and take care of him. He died there within the year. In another year, Joya's parents had died too, one after another, in quick succession, of heart disease and kidney failure. A few relatives called Joya long distance to suggest that her parents had died from the grief Joya had caused them by doing such a scandalous thing as sending her husband back home to die.

Joya sat up in bed and pulled her fingers one by one to relieve the joint pain, checking her phone for any call or text from Prothoma. Nothing. There was an email from her boss at the radiology department where she worked, hoping Joya was well. Joya felt guilty. Was she ill, or was this her normal, everyday state of malaise? She couldn't tell the difference anymore. As it was, she was sick of her work. Every day, she peered at ultrasounds and wrote reports, but she wasn't authorized to diagnose the patients herself. When the patients asked her in hushed voices what she saw, she had to say, "I'm sorry, ma'am, I'm not qualified to say."

There was an email from the PTA at school. Joya quickly deleted it. She had tried to get involved at the school initially, but the teachers hadn't taken her up on her offers to volunteer. When she had attended PTA meetings, she had felt shoved, unheard, invisible. So now she just played the role of the bad kid, kicking a stone around, not contributing. Her younger daughter Shima had applied to the health club. The kindergarten teacher Mrs. Jones was obsessed with health, so she had opened a club where students would research how the body functions. There were only ten spots open, so students who were interested had to fill out an elaborate application.

"You have to apply!" Joya had cried to Shima in a shrill voice that betrayed her desire that her children, at least, should become doctors in America, where both their parents had failed.

Joya had stood behind Shima at the dining table as the child filled out the forms with her tiny hands, in neat, upright block letters. They had used the best pen in the house, Bipu's fountain pen, which Joya kept tucked away in a kitchen drawer.

"Think! Think about what you are going to write first!" Joya cried, pulling out an old notebook of Pro's. "Here. Write a draft."

In the end, after four days of work, the completed form was so good that Joya felt tears in her eyes. She envisioned Shima in a white lab coat one day, an oncologist perhaps, talking to patients in a calm, intelligent voice.

"It's very good, Ma!" Joya had gushed, holding Shima's squirming shoulders close to her chest. The last time she had experienced such joy had been when Pro had received the email about her admission to Harvard. Joya had cried then, too, thinking that Bipu was gone, Joya's parents were dead, and now she was alone with two children, but the admission email was an affirmation of who they were as a family and what they had come to achieve in America.

Now Joya swung her legs and leaped out of bed, dashing to the bathroom before the heavy weight of depression pulled her back to bed. Prothoma hadn't called in two days. They had texted back and forth, each message a screech in the darkness.

"What is it, baby?"

"I don't like it here."

"Is the work hard?"

"No! Don't you listen? I don't like it here. I don't like the people. I don't like the weather. I don't like the dorm. I want to come home."

"Baby, can I call you?"

"No."

Standing in the shower, in the house that Bipu and she had bought together, Joya felt cold and alone. It was a shotgun house, Bipu had explained when they had bought it, showing Joya the layout—the drawing room and dining room in a straight line, leading to the backdoor. Now not only was Bipu gone, but their old friends in Houston had also moved away, to the suburbs, where they had bought big houses, and disappeared from Joya's life. She had lost contact with their medical friends from back home as well. The few times she had called a friend from medical college, she had felt ashamed that they were practicing doctors while she was a mere technician.

R-Elementary had a beautiful garden, with plots for different classes that the students planted with vegetables and herbs that bloomed into strange flowers. Joya had never beheld an avocado flower before, or an okra flower. Parents and children stopped and gaped at these. The school had planted orange trees and apple trees around the perimeter of the garden. One of Joya's mom friends, Dani, used to maintain the garden at the school back when Prothoma used to attend R-Elementary. Dani was at school every day, tall and broad shouldered, dressed in baggy overalls with a wide hat over her eyes, planting a butterfly garden. Dani died the same year as Bipu. Both their kids had moved on to middle school by then, and they had lost touch.

There was a bench in Dani's honor in the middle of the garden now, donated by Dani's husband. Every day, when Joya walked through the garden to pick up Shima or walked back after dropping her off in the morning, she sat down for a moment on this bench and remembered how things used to be. She wondered where Dani's son was now. She would ask Prothoma about him some time. Thinking of Prothoma, Joya fished out her phone from her pant pocket, holding it with her fat fingers, checking to see if Prothoma had written anything. No.

Joya stood with the other parents on the raised porch, waiting for the kindergarten classes to be let out. Up ahead, Crispin's mom stood talking to a friend. Crispin's mom was young, in her twenties perhaps, pretty, a face carefully caked in makeup. She wore a yellow sundress in a buttercup print, and she had put up her blonde hair in a golden bun, exposing the nape of her neck, and tiny golden hairs. Joya stood close to the two women, but Crispin's mom didn't acknowledge her.

"My Crispin just loves Kombucha. Just laps it up," she was saying to her friend.

"Oh, my God, Ginny, that is so brave of her!" Her friend, dressed in a romper, clasped her breast with a spread hand, flashing two giant rings on two fingers.

Joya looked around hopefully for some eye contact or a smile, from anyone, then fished out her cellphone, settling into a scowl as she scrolled through her texts. A few kindergartners had been released by the teachers from the other classrooms. They emerged wearing jackets and sweaters–it was a cold day in March. Several students held grey envelopes in their hands. Joya stared at the envelopes quizzically as she waited for Shima.

A musical voice floated from somewhere behind her back. Joya turned around to look. A tall, young Indian woman stood in a group of moms, laughing. She had the undulating, curly hair common in the subcontinent, the same curls that Shima and Prothoma had, tight sine curves, black, oily, and thick. The Indian mother's hair was tied in a thick braid at the back with an elastic band. She wore a batik-print, cotton top paired with cotton pants and Indian leather sandals with low heels and a loop for the toe. Her face was heart-shaped, with a mole at the side of her mouth. Thick, black eyebrows met at the center of her forehead. The diamond stud on her nose quivered as she laughed.

"We are arriving just six months ago, so everything is still very new to us." She spoke musically, placing an accent on a word here, a syllable there, so that there was a beautiful tension in the flow of the words. "Before we came to Houston, my husband only came to America. He was attending graduate school in New Jersey for his PhD. Then he got a job offer in Houston and he went home and married me and now he has brought me here."

"How did you and your husband meet and get married?" one of the other moms asked her. "Did you know him before he left for the US?"

"No, I was married by arranged marriage."

"Oh, my Gosh! Arranged marriage. Are you serious?" the three white mothers standing with her screamed with various gestures. One held her hand to her lips. Another widened her eyes. The third was laughing soundlessly with her mouth open.

"Yes, I had an arranged marriage," the Indian mom repeated, laughing with them.

Joya stared at the group.

"I am serious!"

"Well, you're a beautiful couple!"

Joya studied the women greedily. There seemed to be no wall between the Indian mom and her three white mom friends. They stood close together, speaking conspiratorially.

"Oh, there you are!" A group of four kids ran up to their moms. The moms lifted the kids and swung them in the air. There were whooping cries of joy from the children.

Joya was surprised when Shima gripped her from behind. She turned, slowly coming to the surface. It took her some time to concentrate on her own daughter. Shima was tugging on the long sleeve of Joya's button-down shirt. She wore her hair parted in the middle, with two neat ponytails tied with elastic bands with strawberry beads. The two gold earrings Joya's mom had bought for her when she had been born hung from her little ears. Shima's backpack, heavy and slightly too large, hung from her shoulders to her hips. Her round face was clouded, eyebrows drawn together, her large eyes anguished.

"Ma!"

"What?" Joya barked in an irritated voice.

"I didn't get in!" Shima, who was usually quiet and well-mannered, started to wail.

"Didn't get into what?" Joya's head hurt and her confusion grew. Her back arched in anxiety.

"I didn't get into health club!" Shima cried loudly.

Crispin, tall and slender, walked up to Joya and Shima and said, "They told us today who got in and who didn't. Here are the letters. I got in!" She held up her grey envelope to show Joya.

"I see," Joya said, tight lipped. "Let's go," she said to Shima.

But Shima stood rooted, crying loudly. Dirty tears rolled down her round cheeks. Several children and their moms walked around Shima, shooting her glances as they passed to show their irritation.

"Come on," Joya said softly. "Let's go."

Crispin passed them with her mom in tow. Crispin's mom looked down at Shima, staring with wide eyes at the crying child, avoiding Joya's eyes as she passed. Joya had to pull Shima off the porch. They descended the four steps and entered the garden path. Joya held on to Shima's tiny hands, tugging a little so that Shima would not stop again.

"Oops, excuse me." A dad and his son sidestepped them as Shima planted her foot in the grass again.

"Come on." Joya pulled Shima.

They weaved on the path to avoid colliding with other parents coming to pick up their child and departing groups just ahead of them. As Joya and Shima passed the bench dedicated to Dani, Shima grabbed the metal arm and plopped down on the bench.

"Shima!" Joya cried. "What are you doing? We have to go home."

The fifth-grade garden plot had been dug up, the dark soil turned over with rakes and spades, everything upside down. Up ahead, the Indian mom and her friends stood together with lunch bags and backpacks slung over their shoulders as their kids played in the garden.

"Do you know any of them?" Joya asked Shima, standing beside the bench.

Shima frowned and squinted her eyes.

"Well?" Joya asked impatiently, but Shima seemed to have lost her power of speech.

The Indian mom and her friends began to gather their kids to leave. "Bye-bye. Have a good weekend. Got any plans? Bye, Randy. Bye, Amy," the Indian mom called out happily.

"Come on, please," Joya pleaded with Shima, rubbing her lower back in the lumber region, stretching out the muscles.

At last, Shima stood up and followed Joya quietly out of the school grounds.

When Prothoma called her back finally, Joya's heart leaped with relief. She hurried outside to the backyard to talk on the phone. Shima had cried herself to sleep. She had not touched her dinner. Joya had punished her by sending her to bed early. It was a moonlit night with a clear sky, slightly cold. Joya stood under the pine tree with the phone, facing a line of jasmine trees Bipu had planted beside the back fence (they gave off their fragrance only at night, a burst of surprise). He had also prepared raised beds for a vegetable garden that now stood dry and overrun with thorny weeds.

"Ma, I bought my ticket. I already got a leave of absence. I'm coming home."

"What? Why?"

"Ma! I've been trying to tell you. I'm depressed! I cry all day. I can't get out of bed. I don't go to my classes."

The blood drained from Joya's head. Her vision melted into black and yellow lines. "You can wait till spring break, no? That's only weeks away, in March."

"Ma! I'm sick. I'm *dying*, and you want me to still stay here?"

"So, so you'll take a leave of absence for a semester?"

"Maybe. Whatever. I don't know. Or I may drop out of college."

"You can go to Rice, maybe. or UH. Just finish out the year and apply for a transfer…"

"You don't care about me. All you care about is that I get good grades, and that I become a doctor to please you. I'm trying to tell you that I'm so unhappy I want to kill myself and you don't even care!" Prothoma started sobbing again. But this time, she didn't hang up.

Joya wanted to get off the phone. Her head tried to wrap around what Prothoma had said. She wanted to lie down and absorb it.

"What? Say something, Ma."

Joya couldn't think of anything to say. At last, Prothoma said goodbye and hung up, crying. In the dark, Bipu's vegetable beds appeared as one continuous shape. In Joya's muddled mind, she thought the shape was his grave, tucked neatly in their backyard.

When she reentered the dark house, she could hear the soft sounds of Shima snoring. She sat down at the dining table and called Meg, letting the phone ring till it went to voicemail. Wildly, she thought of a number of old friends in Houston whom she could call, after all these years, anyone, to keep her company and fill the void. But what would she tell them? At last, she rang a friend from Dhaka Medical College who was now an oncologist at Boston Hospital. They chatted for a few minutes, then the friend said she had to go to bed early as she had to get ready for work the next day.

Joya walked to the girls' room and stood at the door, watching Shima sleeping on the double bed that she had once shared with Prothoma, the child's body twisted at an odd angle on top of the pillow. Then she returned to her own bed and lay down, snatching her phone. Lying alone in the king-sized bed, Joya missed Shima's warm body. There was an email from Shima's teacher Mrs. Jones congratulating all the students who had been accepted into the kindergarten health club.

We thank all the students for applying. It was a tough competition, and ultimately we chose students based on the quality of their application and their passion for science.

Copied in the email list were all the parents of all the kindergarten students, including a Chinese family who had left early in January. Joya had said hello to the mother, Jessica, a few times at the school park in the fall, and Shima had played a few times with their daughter Joy. They had laughed together about how Joya and Joy were such similar sounding names, nodding and gesturing because Jessica and her husband John, both doctors, spoke halting English. Those had been their only interactions. But Jessica and John must have felt that Joya was their closest connection at the school, from just these few conversations, because one day, at the start of the spring semester they had found her at school and taken their goodbyes from her— they were moving to Katy. They had just bought a house there, near other Chinese friends. They felt that Joy would be happier there because all her Chinese friends went to the school in Katy. Now Joya thought that Jessica and John must have felt as alienated as she did at R-Elementary.

In a fit of rage, Joya hit reply all. Then she began to compose an email. Compose was the wrong word. She tapped it out at furious speed.

My daughter was not accepted into the talent show. Also, her art did not get selected for the school magazine. Finally, she did not get selected to compete in chess at the interscholastic league. Now you are telling me that she does not even have a passion for science. I am beginning to think that the same students are chosen again and again for all activities. Their moms run the show, and their children are chosen..."

Joya didn't limit herself to the subject of the health club because she realized as she typed with fluidity, it was much more than that.

There are only a few non-white students left at the school, and instead of being cherished for the diversity they bring, they are pushed to the sidelines. White parents treat us like guests, as if we don't belong and this is their space, and we should be grateful to be even allowed to be in the same space...

Joya finished her composition with a flourish (her fingers didn't even hurt to type) and hit send. Rubbing her temple, she refreshed her email expectantly. She did this aimlessly on most nights, for hours, checking her email, Skype, Whatsapp, Facebook, and texts on a loop, till she was able to fall sleep.

There was a reply to her email, under the same subject line, "Health Club Applications." Someone had written, *Tut tut. Will people stop at nothing? Turning an innocent kindergarten club into race baiting? Give me a break!*

Joya sat up, pulling her pillow higher behind her for support. She was about to tap out another furious reply, leaning into the screen, when she saw a bolded subject line. Another email appeared.

There is no racism. I've lived in Houston for fifteen years, and I've only seen good people and generous interactions. My husband and I belong to a church charity organization, and we help so many Mexican families. There were several other emails in this vein. *Frankly, I'm tired of people who see racism everywhere. You and your family should be grateful to be attending this school.*

Another dad wrote that he was sorry Mrs. Jones had received such a nasty email. Joya wondered if she should pen a reply to all four of the responses in one email. Then the email thread showed up bolded again. There were several emails nestled in the same thread. Greedily, Joya read every single one. Every time she refreshed her inbox, more replies poured in.

Someone had written that they were a Hispanic family, and their son had never been invited to a birthday party. No family had ever expressed the desire to befriend them. No one had invited them over to their house. Once, when the whole class had been invited to a birthday party and her son had been the only one who had not been invited, she had bought a card at Walmart and driven to school to hand her son the card, saying, "Here is your card. Let no one tell you that you did not receive a card!" Another mom wrote that she had heard of many racist incidents at the school, and it was high time these issues were addressed. A black mom wrote Joya a private email.

I'm so sorry, Momma. My heart breaks for you and your little one. Hang in there.

More and more parents joined in the conversation. After two hours of reading emails, Joya fell back onto her pillow from good exhaustion, feeling less alone for the first time in years. She had finally made a connection, aroused a response!

At work the next day, the hours passed quickly. Joya spoke cheerfully with each patient, informing them in a soothing voice about each step of the procedure. One patient said she liked it when Joya gave her a warm towel. She liked the feeling of the warm jelly Joya pressed onto her skin. Joya chatted with the patient as she worked, asking questions about her family, talking about her own.

"Oh, your daughter's at Harvard, eh? Bet you're a proud mama!" the woman said.

By the time Joya turned up at school to pick up Shima, she was not feeling so unwell. Still, she planted a ferocious frown on her forehead as she stood on the balcony outside the school doors to ward off any potential attacks from other parents. People were looking at her, whispering. They had all seen her email to Mrs. Jones about the health club. She fished out her phone from her pant pockets (she wore maternity shirts from Target, topped by a long cardigan that covered her hips) and started to read her emails. Several more responses had come in the morning. Joya hadn't heard from Prothoma again. Something in her wanted things to be that way, just for a while longer, till Prothoma realized her mistake.

"Hello, Preeti!" one of the Indian mom's white friends greeted her.

"Hello, Amy! Do you have any plans this weekend?" the Indian mom asked her friend.

The Indian mom was wearing a handknit pink sweater over blue jeans. Her hair was tied back in a thick braid with a pink bow at the end. Two globes of gold dangled from her ears, much like the earrings Prothoma and Shima wore. At the thought of Prothoma, Joya closed her eyes. A stab of pain hit her in a place she could not name, even as a trained doctor.

Out of the corner of her eye, Joya saw a figure approaching her. She tensed and dug her head deeper into her cellphone screen.

The woman reached Joya and planted herself beside her. "Hello! I've been meaning to say hi for a while." She had a pleasant face, tight curls cropped close to her head, and a thin nose. She was tall and slender, standing a foot above Joya, dressed in a prairie skirt and T-shirt, with a manly cardigan on top, striped knee-high socks, and bright yellow sloggers.

"We met, I think, once or twice on the street," Joya said shyly.

"Yes, I think I remember. I'm Hannah, by the way." The woman smiled and dropped her voice.

Joya's heart quickened, dreading what was coming.

"Listen, I read your email. A couple of us were talking about it. We'd like to get to know you better."

"Oh, thanks." Joya tried to smile, but it came out as a terrified sneer. She looked to her side, trying to escape.

"Really, we'd love to get to know you and your little girl. What's her name?"

"Shima."

"Shima." Hannah smiled again, showing big, even teeth. "We play at Donovan Park after school, if you'd like to join us. Tomorrow?"

At last, Joya met Hannah's eyes and smiled. "Thank you," she said, not quite trusting the invitation. It had been so long since anyone had approached her. "I'll think about it."

"Well, here's my number," Hannah said, pulling a card out of a tote bag pasted with the applique figure of a black cat.

When Shima's teacher Mrs. Jones, a pale woman with freckles, saw Joya, she walked out, holding Shima by her wrist. Mrs. Jones said she had spoken to Shima already, but she wanted to apologize to Joya personally for the pain she had caused Shima and Joya. She spoke gently, pushing back her ginger hair with her fingers. Joya nodded sheepishly, not quite sure now if she had been right in her accusation of unfairness.

At least, Shima seemed happier today, skipping through the garden as she chatted with Joya about her day, as if nothing had happened. When they reached the car, Joya's phone rang. Meg was calling. Joya smiled at Shima and gestured for her to get in the car. Then she answered the phone hungrily, standing under the warm sun.

Meg arrived late, after Shima had fallen asleep, covered in a blue jacket and carrying an umbrella, standing on the porch. The weather had changed again to wind and rain.

"It's Houston weather!" Meg laughed as she shook off her jacket at the door. "It's mild in December and January and you think you're done with winter, and then it's freezing from February."

"Is that so?" said Joya. She hadn't realized, even though she had lived in Houston for so many years.

As she made coffee from a Folgers tin, heating up water in a saucepan, Meg sat at the dining table talking to her. She apologized to Joya for not picking up her calls earlier. Her three sons had come home for a surprise visit (Meg's sons lived in Austin, San Antonio, and College Station).

"It was my birthday," Meg said. "They wanted to celebrate. They brought me a giant tres leches cake."

"Oh, my God, Meg, I'm so sorry I didn't remember your birthday."

"Here, I brought you some. Shall we have some now?" Meg's eyes glinted with excitement. She bent down to slide out a packet wrapped in tinfoil from a canvas shopping bag.

"Sure," Joya said.

When they sat down with their tea and their plates of cake, Joya told Meg about the email she had sent and the controversy it had generated.

"Look!" Joya showed Meg her phone, forking the fluffy, soft cake into her mouth. It felt good to be eating cake late at night, two middle-aged women who didn't care about their figures.

Meg listened like a good friend. She read the emails, creasing her forehead. It was exciting to look at the emails together and gossip.

"Oh, my God. This is so upsetting. Is this what you wanted to tell me about last night?

Joya nodded. She didn't mention Prothoma. She even convinced herself that if Prothoma was dropping out of college, that was Prothoma's news to tell, and Joya had no business discussing it with anyone else.

"Do you know what's really strange?" Joya said, waving her fork in the air.

"What?"

"There's this Indian mom who's obviously just moved to the US. She speaks with an accent. I even heard her telling some other moms that she was married by arranged marriage. But they seem to adore her. Isn't that strange? Here I am, accusing everyone of being prejudiced. Yet, here *she* is, she arrived more recently than me, yet she seems to have none of my difficulties making friends with the moms at the school!"

"Ah! But here's the thing," Meg said. "Do you realize that she's probably at least thirteen years younger than us, if that's her first child in school?"

"That's true!" Joya said, her eyes widening. She bobbed her head. "Do you think that's it? They like her because she's young and pretty?"

"No, that's not what I meant," Meg said, shaking her head. "I meant, you were probably like her thirteen years ago, open and friendly, and approachable. Now you probably can pick up a lot of things about these moms that make you not as friendly with them now. You're giving them those vibes, probably. You're probably not making as much of an effort as she does."

"What do you mean?" Joya frowned.

"Perhaps she's more submissive, more eager to please, perhaps she knows too little for things to bother her."

Joya sat mutely digesting what her friend had just fed her.

On Tuesday, when Joya collected Shima from school, Hannah, the mom with the tight brown curls and dangling artist's earrings, approached her again.

"Meet us at the park? We're going over there now on our bikes."

"Sure," Joya nodded shyly. "I'll drive my car."

When Joya and Shima arrived at the park, the other children were already there, playing inside the castle. Their moms gathered them and brought them over to meet Shima. They said hello shyly while their moms held their wrists. Shima looked at the other children with clear eyes and said hello back.

"Do you want to come play?" A little boy asked shyly.

"Yes!" Shima leaped to join them.

"Come, let's sit on the hill," one of the moms said to Joya. "My name is Maddie, by the way." Maddie looked a lot like Hannah, the sweater top, the prairie skirt, and dangling earrings— blue topaz teardrops.

Joya followed Maddie and the other moms to the hill, where they all introduced themselves to her. Besides Hannah and Maddie, there were three other moms. Joya forgot their names as soon as they told her, and she kept having to ask.

"Sorry, I know that's a lot to remember at once," Maddie apologized.

They all fell over giggling, including Joya, who had not felt this way, this light, since Prothoma had been at elementary school. She sat cross legged on the grass, the same as everyone else, folding her legs. Her body felt lighter and nimbler. Hannah opened a bamboo hamper and lifted out juice boxes and Tupperware filled with cut apples, grapes, and clementines, laying the offerings on a checkered, red-and-black flannel blanket. Joya gazed at Shima playing with the other children. Prothoma used to run around this same castle when she had been little, up and down the stairs and across the bridge, as fast as the wind.

"So, Joya, what do you do?" Hannah asked.

"I'm a radiology technician," Joya explained, smiling widely. She liked Hannah and her friends. They talked about picture books, their children's favorite toys, and the trips they had taken abroad.

"Do you know, Joya, I went to India once, after I graduated from college," Maddie said.

"I'm from Bangladesh," Joya mumbled, but when Maddie didn't hear her, she was glad. She listened with interest as Maddie described the Taj Mahal, Mughal architecture in the north, and all the good street food she had eaten, whose names Maddie could not remember anymore. Maddie was gracious and eager to please—Joya felt herself warming to the younger woman.

"Shima's earrings are so cute," Hannah gushed, leaning forward as she chewed on a slice of apple. "Where did you get them?"

"They're a gift from my mother," Joya said. "They're a traditional thing, the bells. Called *jhumka*."

Hannah nodded and passed Joya a clementine. Joya opened it and sucked the sections with relish, getting juice on her fingers. She could hardly believe that she had so much to say, that she could laugh so hard. The moms called the children to eat. They ran down the hill, skirts and shirts flying. Hannah passed the fruits to the children, and they devoured them, holding the slices of fruits in their tiny hands.

"Isn't it an idyllic day?" Maddie, the mom who had traveled to India, mused. "So beautiful."

"Well, the grass is a little wet." Hannah laughed, wiping the bottom of her skirt.

"We come here at least two or three times a week," another mom confided in Joya. "You must join us."

Joya nodded greedily. "Yes, it'll be nice for Shima."

Maddie watched the kids, who ran away to play hide and seek under the tunnels. "See? They get along famously," she said. "You must come," she said again to Joya.

"Yes, we will," Joya agreed, smiling.

"Does Shima like henna tattoos? We love henna!" Hannah said. "My little Hattie likes to put it on the backs of her hands and all the way up her arms." Hannah pointed at her own arms, laughing. "Most of the time, she's covered in tattoo. Luckily, it's temporary."

"Is the dye safe?" Maddie asked Hannah.

"Probably not," Hannah said. "We buy one that's made in India, China, wherever. I'm sure they're not great ingredients."

"Actually, traditional henna is very safe. It's made from a plant," Joya explained.

"I'm sure it's not good to put it on kids, though, is it?" Another mom, Julia probably her name was, asked in a tentative voice. She was quieter than the others. She had freckles on her nose and cheeks. Her eyes were keen and small, with a scientist's discerning gaze.

"Oh, Julia would know!" Maddie laughed. She turned to Joya to explain. "Julia's a scientist. She's a PhD student in mechanical engineering at UH."

"Oh," Joya said, and stopped arguing.

"I mean, imagine putting dye on skin. That's not good," the scientific Julia continued.

"No," Maddie agreed, nodding uncertainly. She cast her eyes on the juice boxes. "Oops. We forgot to offer the kids juice. Never mind. They'll be back soon enough when they're thirsty."

"Yep," Hannah said.

"Henna comes from the henna plant. Many people in Bangladesh have a henna plant growing in their yard. The henna plant has healing properties," Joya went on.

"Really?" Maddie said, picking up a grape between her forefinger and thumb.

"It's an antioxidant with anti-aging properties." Joya spoke more loudly.

"That's amazing!" Maddie said, smiling.

The other women turned back to face her. They were looking at her with slightly stunned expressions. Their faces were young and supple, with none of the puffiness that Joya had acquired with age. They could hardly be above thirty.

"It can heal wounds, clear infections, cure a fever, and stop diarrhea," Joya continued, leaning forward to pick up Julia the PhD student's hands. "Your nails will be stronger if you paint them with henna."

"Paint them with henna!" Julia laughed as if Joya had said something absurd. She yanked back her hand. "For a tattoo, it sure has a long legend."

"It's not a legend!" Joya cried. "And it's not a tattoo!" She studied Julia more closely. "I'm a doctor," Joya said huffily. "I should know."

"I thought you said you're a radiologist technician," Maddie said. "I had no idea you're a doctor!"

"Why are you not practicing medicine anymore?" Hannah asked. "Tell us the story."

Joya's eyes welled up. She had a lot to tell. About Prothoma dropping out of college, and how her husband had died, and how she was afraid that Shima, too, would change and become sad in time. She turned her face away before they could see that it had crumpled up.

Sensing that she didn't want to answer their question, the other mothers continued to talk among themselves. What camps were they thinking of for spring break? What was the best lunch to pack? Were they sending candy to class for Valentine's Day? They went on talking in low, soothing voices, sitting on the grass, with their knees bent, arms locked across knees.

Joya stood up from the grass slowly. Her lower back had started to ache again. Joya kept standing near the group, not participating in their conversation. She could not speak. She pressed her face with her palms, trying not to cause a scene by leaving abruptly. Her hands on her cheeks were cold. Her face was burning. The sky rumbled and the wind picked up a piece of paper lying on the grass. Far away, the children played on top of the long train by the gate.

She was remembering how she used to talk to her mom friends when Prothoma was little. Silence was the key. If someone called her Indian, she didn't correct them. If someone spoke about how the rest of the world was miserable and America was the only place to live, she only smiled. She had taught her daughters to be agreeable too. What good did it do?

"Shima!" Joya called with all the force of her lungs. She started to trudge down the hill toward the train, stepping carefully so as not to slip, dragging heavy legs. When she had taken a few steps, she turned around to face the young moms. "I'm sorry, I just remembered I have to be somewhere."

They nodded mutely. Joya turned back and hurried down the slope, calling for Shima. Soon, they would be out of the park and home. Tomorrow, she would call Meg again and ask if she wanted to go for a walk. They would walk around the school where their children used to go when they were young. Around and around the block they would walk, talking about the old days. That was something to look forward to.

Three Sisters

When I was a child, Kanta Apa was always turning down marriage proposals. She was my mother's eldest sister Boro Khala's daughter, the eldest among my cousins. My aunt's house was in Dhanmondi, on Road number 27. Scarlet bougainvillea draped the metal gate. An orchard at the back was visible from the street–lush with mature trees laden with fruit, guava, jamun, mango, and lychee trees. A long, screened verandah led to the interior. The house was ancient and mysterious, with long, dark rooms where the sunlight never entered, wood frame windows, and black-wood furniture. Cobwebs swung from the ceiling. These houses have been torn down now to build apartment complexes and commercial buildings. It is impossible to find these old neighborhoods in Dhaka nowadays, the old way of life with the sprawling houses and orchards full of fruits. One can only find that Dhaka outside of Dhaka, a sudden glimpse in another city. Sometimes, walking around a neighborhood in Houston, I come across a screened porch, and I am reminded of that house in Dhanmondi.

Boro Khala had three daughters– Kanta, Shanta, and Renu. I went to my aunt's house on many occasions with my parents bearing a marriage proposal for Kanta Apa. When I was very young, ten or eleven, I had no opinion of Kanta Apa. She was pretty, dusky, plump in an acceptable way in a young woman, freshly graduated from university with some obscure degree that she had no interest in pursuing, geography, history, or Bengali. Even in my earliest memories, she wore saris, the end of the sari wrapped modestly around her shoulders, although her sisters Shanta Apa and Renu Apa were allowed to wear shalwar kameez and trousers and shirts at this time. You might argue that this difference in dress code stemmed from a difference in age, because Kanta Apa was older than her sisters, but the sisters were less than two years apart each.

I remember a lot more about Shanta Apa and Renu Apa. They were very pretty and wore a lot of makeup. In their shared room stood a dressing table full of jewelry and creams that I liked to run through my hands, till one or the other scolded me. Renu Apa rode around the neighborhood on an oversized man's bike belonging to one of the men servants. My aunt Boro Khala shouted at Shanta Apa and Renu Apa to put on a dupatta ("*orna gaye dao!*")–a scarf to cover their bosoms– whenever they headed out of the house, but her remonstrations slid off their shoulders like air. Shanta Apa and Renu Apa's shared room was a bright spot in the dark house, with a long line of windows facing the backyard letting in a healthy dose of sunshine. Shanta Apa and Renu Apa introduced me to Hindi movies and to *Stardust*, the magazine about Bollywood movie stars. They taught me how to style my hair, do my makeup, and take off my glasses to look pretty for a party.

Later in life, when she couldn't get married, the eldest sister Kanta Apa hated everyone. She was always fighting, griping, and making life hell for her mother. But when she was young, in her twenties, Kanta Apa imbibed her mother's every opinion. Once, I accompanied my parents to Boro Khala's house with a proposal for Kanta Apa, a biodata and photograph of a young man who had graduated from Rajshahi College. Kanta Apa, perhaps twenty-five then, was apoplectic. She stood in the middle of the drawing room, placing her hands on her waist sometimes, gesticulating at other times, all the while shouting at my parents for bringing such an audacious proposal.

"How dare you think I would stoop to marry such a man?"

She felt insulted by the proposal because the man in question was not living in America or Canada, and, moreover, had not even graduated from the engineering university in Dhaka but from another engineering college in another district.

Boro Khala's drawing room was long and rectangular. It received little sun. Windows along the boundaries let in draft in the winter. My father wore a V-necked sweater and woolen pants. My plump mother, dressed in a Georgette sari reserved for winter days, wrapped in a thick shawl, sat with her mouth downturned in distress, her expression in any situation in which she dared not speak. My aunt and uncle, Boro Khala and Boro Khalu, declared that they too were "disgusted by the proposal". My uncle and aunt were a decade apart in age, and they did not have a good marriage. My uncle was lean and short, with a white stubble on his chin and no hair on his head. My aunt was always clad in a wrinkled cotton sari, with premature lines on her face and forehead and a grey mousetail for hair. Each bore a look of self-loathing induced by the hatred of their life partner. If they ever came face to face in the course of the day in that big house, they shouted insults and shook their fists at each other.

"How could you even think to bring a suitor who isn't from America? Do you think so little of my daughter?" my aunt challenged my parents, her gravelly voice emerging out of the box in her narrow throat.

As a sign of their disapproval that day, we were offered no refreshments, which I looked forward to usually, snacks wheeled in on a trolley, milky sweets and tiny glasses of orange juice, with folded napkins on quarter plates. It was all rejection, rejection, rejection! My parents were driven out of the house in shame.

Over the years, many of our other relatives also tried to get Kanta Apa married, with similar lack of success. In those days, it was the duty of the family to get all the younger people married. Marriage was a serious business. I believe Kanta Apa also wanted to get married, but the conflict lay in whom she deemed good enough for her. My uncle and aunt demanded tall, handsome men, of good families, with good salaries and respectable jobs (in those days, what profession would an eligible bachelor have? Engineers working in roads and highways or at one of the tea companies, medical doctors, professors, bankers perhaps, or lawyers).

Kanta Apa's sisters Shanta Apa and Renu Apa shot down all of Kanta Apa's suitors with aplomb, effortlessly listing the qualities of an eligible bachelor for Kanta Apa. "He has to be an expat, a US or UK or Canadian citizen, a PhD, a wealthy man, a young, handsome man."

Whenever a photograph accompanied a biodata, Shanta Apa and Renu Apa seized the photo and laughed at the prospective groom's snub nose or receding hairline. Once, they picked out a stray curtain in the background, pointing out that the shiny satin material of the curtain and the gaudy blue color were in bad taste, showing that that family were not high class. Their merry, tinkling laughs broke like waves over Kanta Apa's head, making the business of rejection a rollicking ride filled with hilarity.

This was in the eighties. Within a few years, a marriage proposal came for the second sister, Shanta Apa. She was studying in the final year of her master's degree in psychology at Dhaka University, months away from taking the final exam. One day, one of my other aunts, Shejo Khala, carted Shanta Apa off to a Chinese restaurant to see a man who had come to visit Bangladesh, on leave from his job in America for seven days, during which time he hoped to find a bride and get married.

Every member of our family arrived at Boro Khala's house for this event. All our aunts were involved in the important decisions of our lives. We young children sat and looked on, keen, hawk-eyed witnesses, as our aunts prepared Shanta Apa for the occasion. Shanta Apa was dressed against her wishes in a satin pink sari that hugged her too-thin hips. Her hair was piled in a bun for the first time in her life. Her pale face and liquid lips, usually full of mirth, were trembling. We children milled around Shanta Apa, staring at her reflection in the dusty dressing-table mirror as Shejo Khala dressed her, panting and huffing from her exertions, her round, plump body wrapped in a Georgette sari. Shanta Apa looked transformed, like an elegant and beautiful Indian actress out of *Stardust*. She had fair, soft skin, made brighter by her pimples, which acted like blush-on. Her eyes were large and dark, and her eyebrows were arched and painted.

When Shanta Apa returned to the house from the restaurant, we were still sitting around Boro Khala's long, rectangular table in the dark room lit up with four tube lights, chatting and chewing crisp, red guavas still warm from the tree, waiting to hear what had happened.

Shanta Apa dashed past us like the wind and locked herself in her room. We could hear her throwing herself on top of her bed, crying and crying. Later, she agreed with this account, that she "cried and cried, cried her heart out". We managed to unlock the door and gape at her heartbroken body. She complained that the suitor was very short and plain and too dark. He wore glasses. He wasn't at all like the heroes in the Hindi movies she watched on the VCR, the ones she read about in her magazines. But within days, she was married to this man, by the magical workings of Shejo Khala, who had used all the powers known to her to threaten and coax Shanta Apa.

Soon, Shanta Apa sat for her final exam at the university and left on a plane to join her husband in North Dakota. On the day of her flight, my mother and I accompanied her to May Fair beauty parlor to get her hair done with masses of glue and bobby pins. She was dressed in a heavy, embroidered wedding sari, her hair done up with glue and her face made up with heavy makeup at the parlor and put on the flight to meet her husband.

After Shanta Apa left, Renu Apa and Kanta Apa were the only ones left at home. They spent their days locked up in two different rooms. There was minimal communication between the two sisters. Shanta Apa wrote us romantic letters from America, bubbling about her "hubby", who told her a hundred times a day that he loved her, with whom she had toured Rome and Vienna for a honeymoon, who made her breakfast in bed. "Do you know?" she wrote, in small, neat handwriting, "I never imagined that I would be so happy. Always listen to your elders. They know what's best."

Within a year, Renu Apa was married as well. She studied English at Dhaka University. At home, she wore trousers. She still stole any bike lying around to ride on the streets of Dhanmondi. She returned from the university full of energy, her thin ribs cracking with laughter, large eyes flashing in a skinny face. Whereas Shanta Apa was striking, Renu Apa had a cute button-nose, stylishly bobbed hair, and tiny freckles on her nose.

I would often go stay with my aunt, being an only girl at home and craving the company of my female cousins. Nowadays, I followed Renu Apa around the house as she watered the potted flowers she was growing (chrysanthemum, marigold, and gardenia placed in red-painted pots on the steps of the front verandah), plucked ripe, pinkish guavas from the tree, cut them, salted them, and ate them, or entered the stained, smelly kitchen to cook with the staff, asking one to cut up onions, and another to supply her turmeric paste, as she put on a pot of spicy beef on the stove.

One corner of Renu Apa's room was stacked with her schoolbooks, running the gamut of British literature from Anglo-Saxon literature to modernism. At random moments, she would recite to me from Shakespeare and Beowulf, and the poetry of J.B. Prufrock, but her main reading, for pleasure, were her glossy film magazines and the paperback Mills & Boon romances you could buy at New Market. She was not classically beautiful. Yet, men fell heavily for her. At night, when we got in bed, she would regale me with delicious stories of the many suitors who pursued her. We hung the mosquito net like a canopy around the bed and turned the fan on at full speed to get air through the barrier. Beads of sweat formed on our lips as we lay in bed in our cotton shalwar kameez, a light cotton sheet covering us both. "You understand, Dolly," she said to me, "I can pull men by their nose rings, like pulling a bull by its ring."

I laughed with tears in my eyes. "Pull their noses by a ring!" I could not stop laughing.

"Listen," she said, propping her head on an elbow. "There is this guy, senior to me. He graduated with a first class first M.A. last year in English. He came to see me and asked me to have tea with him at the canteen. He said he had been in love with me for years, and he asked me if I would marry him."

I squealed. "What does he look like?"

"Tall. Chiseled face and thin lips," she said. "He has large eyes that crinkle when he smiles."

"Will you marry him?" I cried, sitting up in excitement and accosting her.

"Nah," she said.

"Why not? What don't you like about him?"

I don't know if it was the laughter or if I had drunk too much Coca-Cola, but I could not sleep from a tummy ache the whole night.

Like Kanta Apa and Shanta Apa, Renu Apa received a steady string of proposals, biodata and photos. Like her sisters before her, Renu Apa turned down all these men, shuddering at the prospects lined up in front of her–the possibilities of her life, parallel universes stretching out to their ends. My mother said Renu Apa was arrogant to turn down so many good men. I remember many tea sessions when my mother and her sisters talked about how vain my pretty cousin was, how foolish to turn down these perfectly decent, ordinary men.

By and by I realized what it was that made Renu Apa reject one suitor after another. She looked down on anyone graduating from a local university, trying to make it in Bangladesh. The world in her imagination was larger than the world that she was forced to live in. In life, she was constrained by rules and barriers–the mandate to wear an *orna* to cover her bosom, the warning not to go out alone at night on a rickshaw, or the scolding she received when she rode a bike and wandered out onto the dark, open, tree-lined streets of Dhanmondi. I don't think any of us understood how desperate Renu Apa was to escape Bangladesh until she married.

Whom did Renu Apa marry in the end? Who was deserving of her hand after all the discards? My mother woke me one Friday morning (we had school off on Fridays), saying, "Come on, we have to go to your aunt's house. Renu is getting married. Boro Khala has asked us to go right now."

I jumped up and got ready in ten minutes. We lived in Kalabagan, near Dhanmondi but on the less posh side of Mirpur Road. We all piled up on a rickshaw, my mother, father, and I. We arrived at Boro Khala's house for the *aqd*, the legal marriage ceremony in which Renu Apa would sign the papers. We had not been part of any of the deliberations leading to the marriage. We had no idea how the marriage had been arranged or who the groom was. Everything had been kept a secret from us. All the relatives gathered in Boro Khala's drawing room grumbled about this secrecy.

"Why have they not consulted us before this? We're just invited like guests?" one of my uncles hissed, crossing his arms across his chest.

"Just sit quietly," my mother advised her brother in a whisper. "All we want is for Renu to get married." She sat decked in a heavy silk sari for the wedding, powder on her face and gold at her throat, hunched forward on a sofa, her mouth tense with anticipation.

Distant relatives, Renu Apa's relatives on her father's side and the relatives of my aunts' and uncles' in-laws, were whispering, sitting in Boro Khala's drawing room. It was a large room, with big, square windows with shutters that opened out, wooden frames and glass panes, and thick cream curtains that could be drawn to make the room dark or pulled apart to let the air in, a cool mosaic floor under our feet, and two sets of ceiling fans rotating gently overhead, pampering us with a light breeze.

"You don't know whom she's marrying?" Boro Khala's sister-in-law jabbed my mother in the shoulder. "I'll tell you! The guy is related to me. A distant cousin! He used to live downstairs from us when we were growing up. Do you know what?" The woman was tall and lithe like a giraffe, her silk sari wrapped callously around her long, shapeless body without a hip. She lowered her head conspiratorially and brought it close to my mother's left ear. I leaned in to hear. "He's a bit slow in the head."

"What?" After this initial involuntary cry, my mother turned her head away resolutely and clamped her lips, refusing to hear or respond.

"He didn't even graduate from high school!" the woman announced loudly, shaking her head triumphantly. Her gold earrings jingled.

As if changing her mind, my mother whipped around to face the loud guest. "He has an MBA!" she retorted, her jaws tight, her throat bobbing up and down.

"Is *that* what they told you?" The woman laughed. "That's a lie! I've brought so many proposals for Renu myself. When I heard that this marriage might take place–and I heard from the boy's family, not our family, mind you–I ran here yesterday, and I begged them. Please, let me bring you another suitor, right now, I said. But they wouldn't listen. Do you want to know why I think Renu is marrying this guy? The guy's father is filthy rich, a doctor in Texas. Just filthy, filthy rich."

My mother kept shaking her head. She didn't want to hear.

When Shanta Apa and Renu Apa both got married, people lost interest in Kanta Apa. The great conspiracy to get Kanta Apa married had always been predicated on the threat that her sisters couldn't be married before their elder sister was married. As soon as Shanta Apa and Renu Apa were married, Kanta Apa's marriage became a moot concern for the family. Kanta Apa faded into the background as the already proscribed lonely spinster.

So began Kanta Apa's life as a recluse. My next memories of her are all negative. I began to dislike her very much. For the most part, she hid out in her dark corner room, among her books and diaries. She squirreled food into this room and often left plates of half-finished rice lying around on tables and chairs or on the floor under her bed. On rare occasions, she would hurtle out of this dark hole to hurl insults at people who had angered her, shaking them with her accusations. Her once pretty, sharp features and large eyes in a thin, dusky face had faded into a bloated mass. If she had been young once, that young self was lost in a plump body shrouded in the layers of garments with which she covered herself, the end of her sari pulled tightly over her head.

One day, when I was at their house for Renu Apa's wedding, I got into a big fight with Kanta Apa. She had asked me to get her some books from the British Council Library on my library card, one of the books that was going around at the time, perhaps *Murder Most Royal* by Jean Plaidy. Now the book was overdue. As an anxious fifteen-year-old, I harangued her. I needed to return it. I asked her timidly at first, going up to her heavy, black painted door and knocking softly. I may have badgered her too many times about it. She accosted me in front of all the guests gathered for the wedding, shouting at me about how rude I was. I hung my head under my long hair, feeling powerless and enraged that my library record would be ruined because of Kanta Apa. I believe I hated her because of these kinds of behavior. I began to avoid her after that incident.

After the wedding, all the young cousins gathered at Boro Khala's house to go out to eat at a Chinese restaurant with pretty Renu Apa and her handsome husband. We younger girl cousins were decked out in our silk shalwar kameez with rouge painted on our faces. Renu Apa was dressed up elaborately in a pinned sari (pins all over the place!). Her hair had been done up at May Fair beauty parlor.

As we were about to leave for the Chinese Restaurant, Boro Khala told Kanta Apa that she could not go with us because she was an unmarried elder sister. "It looks indecent if you go with the couple, being an unmarried elder sister," my aunt said.

Kanta Apa whipped around and retreated inside her room without a word. But before she disappeared inside the dark cave, she hissed at my mother from the door, curling her finger to indicate that my mother should enter her room. I went with her. Inside, the air was dark and musty.

"Why didn't you get me married?" she growled at my mother. Her eyes were red with fury and shame.

"But I did try–," my mother protested. Her plump face melted in consternation.

Kanta Apa let out a blood-curdling scream. Boro Khala rushed into the room, dragged my mother and me out, and shut the door on the lunatic.

Later, my mother and my other aunts gossiped about what a shame it was the way Kanta Apa's mother and sisters had conspired to ruin her life, by filling her head with ideas of false grandeur and bringing ridiculous objections to the perfectly decent, ordinary men who had wanted to marry her. And now they were trying to lock her up in her dark dungeon precisely because she was an old maid.

My father was an engineer, a graduate of the engineering university in Dhaka. Like the men my three cousins had rejected, he had worked his entire life at the water development board. We rented a tiny house deep inside Kalabagan, and my father never owned a car or made a house for himself. To go anywhere, we had to pile on top of a rickshaw and ply ribbons and ribbons of smelly alleys, past open dustbins and pecking crows, scraping by little shops selling eggs and bananas. When my time came to get married, after I graduated from Dhaka University, I didn't make any objections. I went to all the restaurants to meet all the young men who wanted to see me, and I let my guardians choose my groom. If I didn't like one man's receding hairline or another man's jutting front tooth, my mother told me that those things didn't matter in life because everyone's hair and teeth fall out, eventually. I had to have priorities, she said. In the end, I was married to a man my cousins would have approved of, an engineer working in America.

My husband and I lived in many states in America. After we had moved around for many years, we relocated to Houston, intending to settle down here, as the weather is similar to Bangladesh, mild winters with the same fruits and vegetables available in Bangladesh. We bought a large house in Fulshear, but I lived in it mostly alone. My husband was often away on assignment to different countries for his oil company. He would turn up in Houston for a month, we would throw parties for all his engineer friends, people would admire our house, and then in the blink of an eye he would pack his suitcase and leave again, for another assignment, in Nigeria or Scotland or somewhere else.

The wonderful surprise about moving to Houston was that I met up with my three cousins Kanta Apa, Shanta Apa, and Renu Apa after nearly four decades. I was fifty then, but I felt as giddy about it as when I used to go to their house in Dhanmondi as a child. I called them up immediately. They already knew from our other relatives that I had moved to Houston. We made plans to meet, but for one reason or another, we kept putting it off.

I hadn't really kept in touch with my cousins in the intervening years. It's difficult to say why. Laziness, perhaps, or drifting apart from not seeing one another for so many years, our lives separating and going different ways. But it may also have been my feelings of bitterness about the past, surfacing at last. I resented, for example, how my parents were always responsible for Boro Khala's family problems, how they had to turn up to help and were shouted at when things didn't pan out as Boro Khala wished.

Finally, after six months of calling one another back and forth, I invited my three cousins to my house. Kanta Apa snatched the phone to scream in my ear, asking if I had thought about how they would arrive at my house without a transport.

"If you invite someone, you have to also think about how they will reach your house," she lectured me, the familiar booming voice ringing in my ears.

"I am very sorry," I said. "I didn't know that transport was a problem."

Putting down the phone, I resolved to have nothing more to do with them, no matter how exciting it was to have cousins living in the same city.

I might never have seen my cousins again, except that about six months later still, in the middle of my first summer in the hottest city I had ever lived in, Renu Apa gave me a call.

"Doll, why don't you come over one day?" she asked sweetly over the phone.

I kept trying to make excuses, still smarting from the unpleasant exchanges in the past. But Renu Apa kept insisting. Her familiar voice, with the soft, lilting tones, touched me. I was genuinely moved. We all had difficult lives, I thought. Renu Apa's husband, the high school dropout, worked at an oil rig offshore. He lived out on the rig six months at a time, while Renu Apa went back to school to study nursing, raised three kids on her own, and now worked as a nurse at the Memorial Hermann Hospital.

"Please come, Doll. I haven't seen you in such a long time. My heart is crying to see you."

My heart melted at her familiar voice and the tenderness she still showed me. It was agreed that I would visit the following Saturday. Since I owned a car and I could drive, there was no question about how I would transport myself. When Renu Apa gave me their address, I was shocked. They lived in an apartment building in Sharpstown, near Bellaire, Chinatown, an area known for crime and poverty, filled with new immigrants lumped in crowded buildings, waiting for a turn in their fortune.

From Bellaire Boulevard, I turned the Mercedes into a dreary apartment complex and waited for the creaking gate to part. I found myself staring at a row of yellow-stained buildings with broken windows and overfilled dumpsters. I found my cousins' building with difficulty, as the numbering system didn't make sense. A set of metal stairs led upstairs to a breezeway reeking of rodents and cooking spices, with a row of flats. My cousins had planted gardenia and chrysanthemum flowers in pots outside their door. I knocked on the cracked red door. The doorbell was broken.

"Hello, hello!" Renu Apa greeted me at the door, throwing her arms about me. She smelled of talcum powder and glycerin soap. Her face was lean and drawn, and she was still skinny, dressed in a long-sleeved T-shirt and sweatpants.

"Hi," I said tenderly. "You look just the same, Renu Apa!"

"So good to see you, Dolly. Look at the beautiful flowers we planted. Isn't this just a cute apartment? Look at the red door. Cute as a button."

Shanta Apa, appeared behind Renu Apa, a little gray and shriveled, resembling her mother.

"Hello, hello, Dolly." She kissed me, pulling me inside.

"I'm so sorry about not sending a car that time I invited you, Shanta Apa," I said self-consciously, standing in a cheerful hallway packed with tall plastic flowers in vases and a rubber mat to deposit shoes, several women's shoes arranged in a row.

Shanta Apa bobbed her head cheerfully as I shook off my heels. "Don't be."

Shanta Apa's husband had died from cancer a few years back, and Renu Apa had asked her to move from South Dakota, to come live with her in Texas. From what I had heard, Shanta Apa had married off her two children from this home. The two sisters led me further down the hallway, until we reached a dining table covered with a plastic cloth. My eyes darted, looking for sudden danger emerging from a dark corner.

"Sit. Sit. So, Doll, we cooked khichuri for you. I hope you like khichuri," Renu Apa said, cupping her chin in her hands.

I nodded eagerly. "I love the highlights in your hair," I complimented her, whirling my head to admire her. "Your short hairstyle suits you," I said to Shanta Apa. In my cousins' presence, all my years melted away, and I turned into a young girl again.

"Thank you. The kids like it," Shanta Apa said with a snort. She had a habit of laughing like that, through her nose, I remembered now. "I teach at a daycare, you know. The kids love colorful things. I wear everything bright. Hair, jewelry, and the reddest lipstick I can find." She laughed maniacally, revealing all her teeth and pink tonsils.

I kept staring at her, the thick foundation and powder on her cheeks, false eyelashes, moussed hair, big, vermillion nails, and a fat, beaded blue imitation necklace at her throat.

"I love your caftan," I said.

"Thank you, Dolly. You didn't bring your husband?" she asked, even though my cousins had not, in fact, invited him.

"He's out of town," I explained.

"What does he do, again, your husband, Dolly?" Renu Apa asked. She was sitting across from me.

Shanta Apa sat down next to me. The three of us sat very close in a tight cocoon, looking back across years and years.

"He works in oil and gas," I said. Inspired, I added, "like your husband, Renu Apa."

Renu Apa's eyes narrowed. Shanta Apa shifted her gaze and adjusted her caftan sleeves.

"Actually, Dolly," Renu Apa said, "I divorced him two years ago."

"Oh," I said.

"He must be very handsome, your husband," Renu Apa said, cheerfully again. "Do you have a picture, Dolly? On your cellphone?"

"Yes," I simpered. I showed them some pictures. In reality, I looked on my marriage with confusion. Waking in the morning, I was faced with the sight of a stain on a kitchen counter or a dripping faucet, a car that had to be cleaned, or a yard that needed attention. If anybody had told me that marriage was simply the management of a household, I would not have believed them, but my mother had prepared me well for this life, and I fulfilled my duties.

We went on talking merrily. Renu Apa and Shanta Apa walked back and forth between the kitchen and the dining table, bringing down plates from a cupboard in the dining room, transferring the rice to a serving dish, carrying the egg curry in a bowl, scrambling for embroidered napkins, and clattering cutlery. They were as swift and hard-working as I remembered them in their youth. I asked about Shanta Apa's children and their spouses, where they were living now. And about Renu Apa's three children, now studying at different colleges in Texas. All the while we chatted, I trembled a little in anticipation of my third cousin.

"Dolly, I am so sorry about your parents passing. Your mother was my favorite aunt," Renu Apa said.

"Mine too," Shanta Apa said.

"Thank you. And I miss your parents," I said. "I am very sorry about their passing."

I asked if their house in Dhaka had already been developed into flats after my aunt and uncle had died, as they had been planning.

"Yes, there are six flats. We each inherited two flats," Shanta Apa said.

"Actually, Dolly…That's why I called you." Renu Apa sat down abruptly at the table. "It's about Kanta Apa."

Shanta Apa, too, dragged another chair out from under the table and sat down.

"Where is she?" I squeaked, looking behind them fearfully.

"She's coming, my darling," Renu Apa assured me. "It takes her a long time to get dressed."

I nodded.

"Dolly, you know that each of us inherited two flats from our parents," Shanta Apa said.

"We don't let her talk on the phone with anyone," Renu Apa said.

"Oh?" I said, turning to Renu Apa now, trying to follow two conversations.

"She had a cellphone, but we took it away because she calls up people and yells at them," Renu Apa went on.

"I see," I said, hands pressed on my lap, turning my head back and forth between Renu Apa and Shanta Apa, trying to follow the connection between the flats and the phone.

"She can only make local calls on the landline," Shanta Apa said.

"We brought Kanta Apa here on a Green Card when our parents died," Renu Apa said. "We had been processing it for years."

"So you can imagine, anyone would want to marry a Green Card holder," Shanta Apa said.

"Is Kanta Apa getting married?" I asked.

"We took her phone away, but our cousin Farooq Bhai calls her on Skype on her computer and talks to her for hours about religion. He convinced her that she could not go to heaven if she did not marry. So now she wants to get married so she can go to heaven! Any gold-digging man would want to marry her just for the Green Card and the flats. We might lose the flats because of her crazy behavior!"

A loud cry broke from the inner recesses of the flat. "Is Dolly here? Why didn't anyone tell me?" Kanta Apa entered the dining hall at great speed, following her booming, full voice. She seemed genuinely delighted to see me.

I stood up nervously. "Hello, Kanta Apa. It's nice to see you," I said, holding my hands in each other.

"Call me Halima," she said, coming closer. "Sit, sit."

A thick, musky scent of spices oozed from her. She had dropped wearing saris altogether, thinking them immodest perhaps. She was wrapped now in layers and layers of cloth over what looked like a maxi. I sat back down nervously.

"Doll, you know, it's very lonely not being married," were the first words out of her mouth.

I nodded nervously. Kanta Apa (who now called herself by the more modest name Halima) took over the conversation, asking me how I was doing, where my house was, what my husband did, and complimenting me on how good I looked, how I resembled my mother. Why didn't I have any children? Shanta Apa and Renu Apa moved around dumbly, serving the food. They laughed at her jokes and nodded at her remarks, humoring her. A few times, Kanta Apa (Halima) asked for my phone number, but each time Shanta Apa and Renu Apa interrupted her and changed the conversation, looking at each other furtively.

After leaving my three cousins' home, I immediately called my *other* cousins and gossiped about them. Imagine that Kanta Apa, who was more than sixty years old, wanted to get married now only because she wanted to go to heaven! What a bizarre turn of events, I said, drinking tea, my mouth filled with hot liquid and malice. One of my cousins defended Kanta Apa, saying that Kanta Apa had always wanted to get married, and it was Shanta Apa and Renu Apa's fault that she wasn't married. Another confirmed the edict about a woman having to marry to go to heaven—a woman could not go to heaven if she was not married—but if she couldn't get married after trying so hard, it was not in her destiny.

I began to remember Kanta Apa more sympathetically. There was a time when she had been sweet and childlike, full of curiosity when she would sit at the dining table and tell me about stories she had read in the *Reader's Digest*. There was one true story about an American woman whose husband had left her for an Asian woman and gone away to live in Asia. Years later, when the husband died, the American woman brought his wife and children to America to live with her. Kanta Apa really appreciated stories like that. *You see, that is what love is,* she would say to me.

My phone calls with Shanta Apa and Renu Apa intensified. They wanted me to intervene and persuade Kanta Apa not to marry.

"What will I say? I haven't talked to her for years," I protested.

"Just use your own arguments, darling," Renu Apa said, with that buttery, toasty affection in her voice. "We're trying to reason with her about the foolishness of marrying at this age, but she gets angry. Maybe you can give her a different perspective. Come to our home. Come often. She's lonely. She'll listen to you."

In the absence of my husband, this was a welcome distraction, a purpose to my monotonous life, so I jumped into their mission. I started dropping in on my cousins' flat at all times, nervously driving my new Mercedes through the rusty gates of their apartment complex before they closed in again, making my way up the smelly stairs and knocking on their red door, which soon became a familiar part of my life in Houston. I would sit in their living room stuffed with old furniture and have tea and samosas and chat late into the night, spying on Kanta Apa (Halima) and making guarded arguments designed to persuade her not to marry.

Shanta Apa, Renu Apa, and I laughed and hooted like old times. Kanta Apa only joined us to shout at us or accuse us of something or send one of us running on an errand for her—to replace a broken toothbrush or a lost nail clipper. From her hushed Skype conversations, we could gather that Kanta Apa (Halima) was getting introduced to one man after another, some of them decades younger than her, chatting with them, flirting with them, and sizing them up for marriage. All we could do was hush in the middle of our urgent plotting against her and eavesdrop on her when she talked with a guy on the computer in her room, her voice booming.

At this time, Renu Apa was getting her eldest daughter ready for marriage with help from her husband's family.

"It's so stressful getting a girl married," she confided in me one time. "The boy's family always acts superior to the girl's family."

In six months, Renu Apa fixed her daughter's marriage. The wedding would take place at an Indian restaurant in Hillcroft. Renu Apa sent me to the restaurant ahead of time to check that everything was in order. When I arrived at about eight in the evening and parked in the strip mall, out of place in my new Mercedes among all the dented, secondhand cars, I found that the owner, a lean man with a moustache that crossed the boundaries of his narrow, long face, had not opened the restaurant yet, had not put the chairs in order or turned on the air conditioning. Without air conditioning, the inside smelled of old food and burnt oils. At my words, the owner turned up the air conditioning and hit the lights, which fell on a small hall, packed with unruly tables, dim-lit, rundown, and mouse ridden. I supervised the preparations for two hours, until the restaurant came alive–through the laying of tablecloths and a simple decoration of a white plastic rose in a vase on top of each table.

Guests began to arrive decked in dark suits and glittering saris, and I was still the only one from our family to greet them. Renu Apa's ex-husband and in-laws entered the hall, and I introduced myself awkwardly. They didn't really pick up any responsibilities, just moved around like guests themselves. Then the groom's family arrived. A stage of two upholstered chairs had been set on a dais in one corner of the restaurant, lit up by garish yellow lights and a white cloth background. The groom ascended the steps and took his place on the stage alone, crossing his legs, which were encapsulated in narrow white shalwar and pointy shoes. There was still no sign of the bride or my cousins. The guests chatted, wandered around, served themselves appetizers, then fanned themselves with the table napkins, muttering under their breaths. I called my cousins on their cell phones again and again, but there was no answer.

The owner of the restaurant gestured to me a few times, took me aside to the kitchen area and said, "Madam, our restaurant will close soon. Shall we serve the food now?"

"Not yet," I said, "my cousins will arrive any minute now."

Three times he asked me, and three times I said, not yet. Finally, he found me. I was trying to hide from him by running to the bathroom. He stopped me outside the bathroom and said he was serving the food now. I nodded.

When I emerged from the bathroom, the bride had arrived. I had not seen her more than twice before. Renu Apa's daughter looked like her, although she was a quieter, less energetic version of her mother. The bride was seated demurely beside her husband, dressed in a bright red sari. Looking at the bride and groom, I remembered my cousin's weddings and mine, all the work of so many relatives that went into each arrangement, and the promise each marriage had held. As I stared at the young couple through emotional tears, I noticed Renu Apa and Shanta Apa pulling Kanta Apa (Halima) behind them. They were dressed rather untidily in Katan saris (woven silk saris of high quality) in different shades of blue, looking hot and bothered. Kanta Apa (Halima) had covered her entire sari with a big, bulky white shawl. They sat down together at a dark table, huddled together, looking out of place and lost at their own party.

I hurried to them. "Renu Apa! What happened?"

"Dolly! Isn't this a beautiful restaurant? The food is excellent," she said, with her penchant for painting everything with a rosy hue.

"Yes, what took you so long?" I pressed, still standing, hunched over in my own sari, which stuck to my body after so many hours of trying to push this wedding along, trying to make things work. I had not realized before how exhausted I was from the effort.

"Are you angry? You look very angry," Kanta Apa said. "You should sit down!"

I looked at her. She was scowling and scolding and negative as usual. I wanted to say to her that *she* looked angry, but then I realized how afraid I was of her.

"Doll, there is no need to spoil a beautiful event by fighting," Shanta Apa said, supporting her sister's accusation.

I was stunned. "What?" I said. "I've been here trying to handle everything, keep the wedding party going."

"Everybody is putting in an effort to get the wedding going, not just you," Kanta Apa said. "No need to get in such a huff."

I left them then. I was almost ready to leave the wedding, but I used the last of my affections to stay. Shanta Apa and Renu Apa's children were present. Shanta Apa's two married sons and Renu Apa's two sons, decked out in dark suits, milled around chatting with guests. The restaurant had to stay open an hour past their closing time. I planned to escape early, with the other guests, and never return.

At the end of the evening, I stepped out of the glass doors in my high heels and stood in the wind-swept parking lot, looking for my car keys in my purse, shivering in the cold wind. Renu Apa caught up with me, a dark silhouette in the night.

"Dolly, I'm sorry," Renu Apa called out, hobbling toward me in her high heels.

Seeing her, I felt my body tense. I felt cold and afraid of her.

"Kanta Apa was shouting at us, saying that we had ruined her life. She would not get dressed or let us leave the house. We had to sit with her for hours till we had coaxed her out. Please. Forgive me."

I looked at my cousin in the dark. We were close once, stuck under the canopy of a mosquito net, trying to breathe on a hot summer night. The years and events in between had taken that closeness away from us. Still, when I peered into Renu Apa's lined face, I realized how much of her effort went into taking care of Kanta Apa. People gossiped all the time about how Renu Apa and Shanta Apa had conspired to keep their elder sister from getting married, and yet, they were the ones stuck with her.

"Please, come back with us tonight. I feel so lonely and afraid. I just married off my eldest. It will be nice if you stay the night."

"All right," I muttered.

Back at their apartment, Renu Apa, Shanta Apa, and I made tea on an old stove, using a tiny saucepan, standing up in the tiny kitchen. It was near midnight when we finished our teas, dumped the cups in the white enamel sink, and said goodnight. Shanta Apa, whose wedding we had attended so many years ago, when she had been a bride once just like Renu Apa's daughter, retired to bed alone. Renu Apa, who had divorced her husband, lathered moisturizer on her face and rubbed oil on her arms. Then she, too, went inside her bedroom. They had made a bed for me on the sofa in the living room, with two pillows, a cotton sheet, and a light flannel blanket. I lay down on the sofa and turned out the lamp beside me. My husband was out of town, but what of it? Even when he was in town, we simply played our parts, talking only about the parties we would plan. We had nothing to say to each other beyond these niceties.

We had all shut our doors and turned off our lights, preparing to slip into the unconscious. What was the unconscious, but a surrender to our separateness, the fact that we were each alone? My mother used to say, everyone dies alone. And what if our dreams were shattered, the promise of marriage a lie for each of us? We could still dream at night. As I began to feel muddled with sleep, I heard the ringing of bells, and then a woman's passionate voice, followed by a man's response. A conversation had struck up somewhere out of sight, deep and intimate, full of interest and curiosity, with questions asked, and answers given, back and forth.

"What is your favorite food, *Jaan?*" A man's deep voice asked, using a term of endearment.

"Rice. And yours, *Jaan?*" Kanta Apa's voice boomed in the dark. "What is *your* favorite food?"

Camping

Jharna was excited to go camping with her daughter's kindergarten class. She had bought a tent and air mattress, a thick comforter, flannel throws to put on and sit around the fire, little metal plates, and camping utensils, packing the new items along with three plastic folding chairs and an electric griddle, jamming everything into her blue station wagon. By the time her husband Rob returned home from the University of Houston, where he taught as an art professor, she was ready to go.

They had never camped before. Jharna had heard from the other moms that R-Elementary was a big camping school. They were camping at Stephen F. Austin Park near Katy, an hour away from the city. Jharna had picked Lilli up early from school. The other parents had talked about starting out early, so that they could arrive at the campsite before dark.

"Pitching a tent in the dark is the devil's work!" Meredith, another mom with whom Jharna was getting friendly, had said when she picked up Lilli. They were standing outside the orange brick school building, their kids blinking in the bright sun. "It's a gorgeous day for camping. See you there, Jer!"

"See you, Mer!" Jharna had called back, full of excitement.

Jharna had shortened her name and dropped the *h* sound from it a long time ago. She'd been altering her name for years, since she had been in middle school, till she liked it. She'd altered her clothes, her hair, everything about herself that she'd inherited from her immigrant Bengali parents while growing up in Boston. Now her hair was reddish brown, cut short around the nape of her neck, her thick, bushy eyebrows plucked to a thin line. Her clothes were boyish—tops and shorts, rompers, backless, strapless, sleeveless outfits that would have given her parents a heart attack. Jharna still grimaced when she remembered her embarrassing childhood, when she had been different, thanks to her parents–the cringe henna she had to wear on her palms to school, bright orange and garish, and the lunch her mom used to pack, leftovers of bright yellow *khichuri* and smelly fish.

They arrived at the park while there was still daylight. Jharna was excited to put up the tent in proper light. She wanted to enjoy the experience. Lilli had fallen asleep on the ride, exhausted from school, her mouth open. Her curls, inherited from Jharna, were flung around her shoulders over the car seat. Lilli's classmates were walking in groups on the park road, carrying flashlights. Eyeing them, Jharna felt envious that Lilli couldn't join them. She left the door open so Lilli could get some air and hauled the long tent bag from the back seat. The site had a screened shelter with a lock. The flat, grassy clearing was large enough to set up two tents. Beyond the cleared area, the grass grew taller, disappearing into a forest of oak trees. In the distance, winking between trees, Jharna could see other campsites. All the sites around them had been booked by R-Elementary families.

Rob was leaning against a tree.

"Hey!" Jharna called. "Some help?"

Rob raised his head slowly and looked at her with a bored expression. "It's a tent in a bag. How hard can it be?"

"What, are you telling me you aren't excited about putting up a tent like every American boy? Have you never gone camping in your life?" Jharna asked in surprise. "Not even when you were a boy?"

"You could say I've camped too much. I was in Boy Scouts."

"Here. Let me get you a chair." Jharna pulled down one of the new electric blue chairs she had bought at REI, unraveling it triumphantly from its plastic tube. "There. Have a seat, Sir." She extended her arm, pointing with a flourish, after she had set it on its legs.

She considered asking Rob to light a fire, then reconsidered. Mer's family would arrive soon, and they could all build a fire together then. Instead, she walked off to the flat area with the bag, trying to decide which was the best spot. With a heavy feeling, she started to assemble the tent, making big sounds and a big show of it. It wasn't that she needed Rob's help. She just wanted him to show a little more enthusiasm.

"Sorry," he said, sighing guiltily, as if sensing her displeasure. "I had a long day at work." He sat down on the chair she had set up, planting his legs apart. He was still wearing dress pants and a pale blue shirt from work. His pale-yellow hair fell over his blue eyes.

"It's fine," Jharna grunted. She even gave a little laugh to let him know, no hard feelings. She couldn't understand why he wouldn't make more of an effort. These were their daughter's schoolmates' families. They needed to build a community.

The tent was surprisingly easy and fun to set up. Jharna walked around in boots and jeans and a checked shirt, her hair in a ponytail, hammering stakes into the ground, straightening hinges, pulling the canvas tight. As she worked, whistling, she noticed SUVs pulling up and families spilling out. Scraps of conversation floated in the air. She longed to join the others, talking easily, laughing together. The trees sparkled, bright green in the afternoon sun. A light breeze lifted her hair. At the campsite next to them, someone strummed a guitar, singing softly.

Mer finally arrived near dark in a black SUV, at about the same time Lilli stirred, hot and bothered, crying.

Jharna embraced Lilli to her chest as she pulled her down from the station wagon. ""Hush. You're a big girl now. All your friends are here." She brushed Lilli's hair away from her forehead and studied the pale skin, thin lips, and hooked nose Lilli had inherited from her father. "Drink some water, and then run play with your friends. Look, Johnny is here!"

Lilli skipped down from the station wagon, spotted another friend, and ran off, followed by Johnny. Jharna sighed with relief. The fun part was beginning.

"Hello, hello!" Mer greeted Jharna.

"I thought you said campers should always arrive before dark," Jharna teased her friend.

"Traffic was awful," Mer complained.

Mer and her husband Bobby were tall and broad-shouldered, with short-cropped brown hair. Working together, they lifted down crates, shopping bags, and boxes, filling the shelter with a household's worth of supplies. As they worked, they chatted lightly and laughed together.

"We have to get a fire going," Jharna said when the two emerged from the shelter.

"Yup," Bobby said, hauling a pile of logs to the pit. "You need to build a pyramid first. You know that?"

"No," Jharna said, interested, sitting down on her haunches on the grass to watch.

"Now remind me, Jer, did you use to go camping when you were a kid?" Mer asked.

"Never," Jharna said, chipper. "That's where my parents drew the line. They were too chicken to attempt to brave nature."

All through the activity of lighting the fire, Rob sat on his chair, scrolling through emails on his cellphone. When Jharna raised her eyebrows at him, he stared back at her, saying, "What? My students turned in their projects."

Bobby held out a purple stove lighter, eyeing his handiwork with pride, and lit the fire. A flame leapt up momentarily, but as they watched, it came down again.

"The wood may be wet, have to dry it out," Bobby explained to Jharna. "So, what do you do, Rob?"

Rob looked up slowly from his phone. "I make art, and I teach art."

"Oh, really? Cool. What kind of art?"

Rob looked like he was suffering. His eyelids were hooded, and his jaw was set in a tight line. "Concrete," he answered curtly, going back to his cell phone.

"God, talking to him is like pulling teeth sometimes," Jharna said. "What do *you* do?" she asked Bobby, turning to him chirpily.

"Here, throw some sticks in there," Bobby said, touching the back of Jharna's arm and handing her a fistful of kindling.

Jharna flung them. The sticks scattered and fell outside the pit. Still, some caught fire, and the flames licked the wood.

"There, see?" Bobby said, nudging her elbow. "It's catching slowly. I work in defense contracting. All the fighter planes, weapons, everything, we supply them."

Jharna nodded. Rob looked up from his phone and stared rudely at Bobby.

"It's beautiful," Jharna said, admiring the fire to make up for Rob's rudeness.

Rob frowned and stared harder at his phone.

"So, we're going to sit around the fire and talk all night, right?" Jharna said, turning to the others.

Mer laughed. "Right. I'm already tired." She turned to her husband. "We still have to put up our tent, Bobby."

Mer and Bobby walked off hand in hand to the place they had chosen, in the middle of the wood, a little distance away from the high, flat spot Jharna had grabbed first. Bobby dumped several bags on the ground.

"Is it okay if we put up our tent here?" Mer called.

"Yeah! Of course!" Jharna said.

Rob yawned.

"Rob, you have to cook the hot dogs," Jharna reminded him.

"Did you bring any?"

"Sure. I bought hot dogs and buns and skewers."

"Okay, I'll do that then."

Jharna watched the couples walking together around the loop, going to other people's fires and saying hi. A man and a woman wearing matching white T-shirts and carrying matching coffee cups sauntered to their campsite.

"He-llo!"

"Hi!" Jharna sprang from her camp chair, smiling, showing teeth.

"We're Leila's parents," the woman said. "I'm Ginny, and this is my husband Tom. I think our girls…"

"Our girls are mixed up a lot because of their names," Jharna finished.

"Yes!" Ginny laughed. She had straight brown hair hanging off her shoulders, the kind of hair Jharna had always wanted. "What's your name?" Ginny extended her hand.

Jharna took Ginny's slender, cool hands in hers. "I'm Jer. And this is my husband, Rob." Jharna gestured toward Rob, who had pulled up his chair near the fire.

He looked up coldly.

"Ooh. It's getting chilly, isn't it?" Tom said. He was dressed in only a light T-shirt and shorts and seemed fine in the cold.

"Isn't it strange how the weather changes so abruptly in Houston? Always takes me by surprise!" Jharna made her eyes big, making conversation.

"So, what do *you* do for a living?" Rob asked Ginny's husband Tom.

Jharna frowned at her husband's rudeness. She turned away from him to smile at Tom and Ginny.

"I'm a lawyer," Tom said. "I work in litigation. I represent corporations when their employees file suit against them."

Rob nodded, stood up, stretched, and walked away abruptly. Tom stared after Rob curiously. His eyes widened in surprise at Rob's rudeness. He brushed back his thick hair with both hands. "Ginny, I really need to go to the bathroom."

"Me too," Ginny said.

Since their relocation to Houston, Jharna had only moved in Rob's circle, socializing with other professors in his department, Rob's MFA students, and local artists. Among these friends, she had seen him smiling, laughing. Jharna couldn't understand why Rob wouldn't stand beside her and make an effort to be a family together so that they could make friends with the other families at Lilli's school. It would be so easy for them to blend in, an-all American family, the way her own parents had never been.

Rob only returned when Ginny and Tom had left. Lilli and Johnny came to say hello in the dark.

"Aren't you going to eat first?" Jharna wailed. "Rob, didn't I ask you to make the hot dogs?"

But Lilli had already eaten at someone else's campsite. Lilli and Johnny reported that there was a small park off the loop, with a playground, with swings, where all the kids were hanging out. It was pitch dark, away from the campfires and cabin shelter lights. According to Lilli and Johnny, ghosts had been sighted near the swings!

"Are you going to eat?" Rob asked Jharna when Lilli had run off again. He was sitting on the blue camp chair again. "I can make the hot dogs for you."

"Well, hot dogs aren't my favorite food. I brought them specifically for you and Lilli. I thought they were fun camping food."

"I'm sure she'll eat them tomorrow," Rob said.

"You can eat with us," Mer said. Mer and Bobby had thrown a grill on top of the fire and stacked coals on top. "We're making burgers, and we have salad."

"Sure!"

Bobby and Mer moved around busily, with paper plates and pots and pans, talking to each other, laughing softly.

"The fire's so beautiful," Jharna said to her new friends.

Sparks flew off the logs. The fire roared, red and orange at the bottom, exploding white sparks at the top. The flames jumped from log to log. Jharna gathered some kindling and threw it into the logs, stuffing them under the grate. Smoke hit her eyes, making tears come out. The night was calm and kind, clear of clouds. Jharna thought Mer was the nicest person she could imagine, always smiling, always making sure to say hi. She ate with Mer and Bobby, chatting with them. Rob said he had a headache. The skin on his face looked dull and pale in the light from the flames. His mouth was downturned, and his eyes drooped. Jharna suggested that he lie down.

"I don't know what's wrong with him," she said to the others when Rob had gone inside the tent.

"Camping's not for everyone," Bobby mumbled good naturedly.

They sat on camp chairs, legs crossed, paper plates on their laps, biting into the grilled burger buns and forking watercress with chickpeas and red onions into their mouths.

"Mmm. So good, Mer. The cheese is so soft, melting." Jharna said, crunching on the spicy onions. From a young age, she'd been used to eating at friend's homes, appreciating what their moms cooked, like a greedy outsider trying to get inside. "So, do you guys camp a lot?"

Bobby nodded. "Yeah, when I was a boy, I used to go fishing and hunting with my dad."

"So Jer, where did you grow up?" Mer asked.

"In Boston," Jharna said, "In Sommerville. I know every coffee shop there. I used to go into those on cold days and beg my mom for a piece of cake. In Boston, it's cold and rainy even in May, so I had cake the year around." She laughed loudly.

"I had no idea you grew up in America! Your parents live here?"

"They both passed," Jharna said, staring into the fire.

"I'm sorry to hear that."

"Oh, that's okay. I hadn't seen them for years by then. They left America when I was a teenager. My dad worked as a physics professor at a local college and my mom used to be a schoolteacher in Bangladesh, but here she was just a housewife. When I graduated from high school, suddenly one day they said that there was nothing for them here and they left. All their friends were moving on to big jobs and buying their second mansions by then, but they just left." Her voice dropped at the end. She stared ahead blankly. She had felt abandoned. She couldn't believe it then. They had just left her behind. Her father had refused to take a good job at an oil company, like a normal person, like all his friends, rather unscientifically saying things like *we shouldn't be drilling the oil, we should leave the oil in the ground,* ridiculous opinions that had driven her mad as a young girl.

"My dad died when I was eleven," Bobby said. "Just before he died, he and I went fishing. That's the last thing I remember about him. I was ten. I fell in the water and my dad had to dive in and save me. I think he already knew then that he had leukemia, and he was going to die."

"Oh, that's so sad." Jharna put a hand to her mouth.

"As a matter of fact, we came right here, to the Brazos River," Bobby said, his eyes alight with memories.

"Bobby brought fishing gear. We were going to go fishing in the dark. D'you wanna come with us?" Mer asked.

"Uh, I've never fished…," Jharna said.

Her father had loved to fish, but she hated it. Once, she had accompanied him to Castle Island when she was about twelve or thirteen. Her father had been lightly dressed in just a windbreaker, intent on his line, his thin face relaxed and happy, his eyes expectant under the dusty glasses. She was so bored standing on the boardwalk for hours, the roar of the water in her ears, bundled up in the cold, that she'd cried and screamed to go home. That was the last time he had taken her fishing.

"Bobby can teach you. We have three poles," Mer said.

"The children…Johnny and Lilli…won't they look for us?"

"Oh, they're with their friends. I'll tell Julie to keep an eye on them. We can pass them at the park and tell them to go to Julie."

"Yeah, she'll be more reliable than Rob," Jharna said. "I don't know what's wrong with him today."

The three of them stood up and brushed their pants, stuffing plates into the large plastic trash bag they had hung up on a pole, beneath a lantern, working together conspiratorially. Their campsite was suffused with light from the lantern on the pole and a bulb inside the shelter, but once they stepped onto the tarmac road, they were surrounded by darkness.

"Look!" Mer cried to Bobby, nudging his elbow. They were walking hand in hand, bare arms touching below the rolled-up cotton sleeves of their shirts.

Jharna looked up at the clear night sky, lit up with stars, the constellations bright and sharp in the complete darkness, away from city lights. The three of them pointed out the constellations to one another, crying out the names. They hooked a left on the road, walking toward the dark playground area that they had heard so much about from the kids, who had described it as a place of *"complete darkness, like, there is no light, no light at all."*

The park was at the edge of the road, where the road wound back to start another loop of sites for RV hookups. It was so dark that they couldn't see anyone. Only the air moved. Formless voices shrieked at one another.

"Johnny!"

"Lilli!"

No one answered, but when they drew nearer, they found the children. Someone had given all the kindergarten students glow-in-the-dark bracelets. The light from the bracelets shone in Jharna's eyes as she approached the swings.

"There you are, Lilli," Jharna said, seeing Lilli on a swing. The child's hair was plastered to her forehead, her face hot and sweaty. "Listen, I'm going to go with Johnny's parents to the river. You stay here, okay? When you and Johnny are done playing, go to Julie's campsite. Daddy's probably sleeping. D'you know the way back?"

Lilli nodded uninterestedly.

Jharna walked with Bobby and Mer, leaving the park to enter the loop of RV sites. Mer whispered in Bobby's ear and the two of them laughed. The fishing poles swung awkwardly from Bobby's arms, banging against his legs. The families who had brought RVs or campers of various models were parked here at the RV sites. People sat on camp chairs or stood around their fires, cooking, drinking, and chatting.

Some people waved to Mer when they passed. "Where are you going?"

"Goin' fishin'," Mer yelled back.

"Oh? We may join you soon!"

The three of them passed a bathroom building and finally reached the trailhead. The trail was dark, except for their flashlights. Their shoes made crunching noises as they stepped on the dirt. Pointing with the narrow beam of his flashlight, Bobby pointed out cottonwood, cedar elm, hickory, and green ash trees. Jharna's nostrils filled with the acrid scent of the earth. They spotted earthworms on the mud path, greyish, splotched frogs that tried to hop away, and bird droppings. When they had taken a few more steps, it became apparent that the droppings belonged to a group of silent black vultures perched high on the branches of a tall cottonwood tree in their path. Mer clutched Bobby's arm. Jharna picked up a stick.

Walking straight on the trail, they reached Brazos River. A mud bank dropped abruptly into the water. There was no proper pier. A sign, barely visible, proclaimed that it was a high erosion area. Bobby began to reel his pole, adjusting hook and line. Mer carefully lifted out bait from her bag. Jharna stood uselessly, watching the two of them. Near the water, the stars were bright and powerful, filling the sky like light bulbs.

"O–kay," Bobby said, handing Jharna a pole and line.

Jharna took it uncertainly, giggling a little.

"So, you just drop the line and reel it in. Yeah, like that. Just throw the line. Then. There. Slow. Slowly."

Jharna did as told, but without strategy or prowess. The three of them sat side by side on the bank on their haunches so their bottoms wouldn't touch the muddy ground.

Voices sounded in the dark, followed by footsteps.

"Hey!" The tall couple Ginny and Tom appeared out of the darkness, holding lidded coffee mugs.

"You came!" Mer cried with delight.

"Yeah. We brought more people. More people are coming."

"It's going to be a party!" Jharna shrieked. "Where's Leila?"

"Oh, playing by the swing…"

"Like everyone else," Jharna finished, laughing.

Soon, they were joined by more couples. A small, slender woman, her dark hair in a long braid, and her partner, a slender, white man with a thin, rectangular face and wireless glasses introduced themselves as Maria and Harrison. The organizer of the camping trip, a Hispanic woman with triplets in kindergarten, Amanda her name was, also joined, carrying alcohol in a paper cup. There was a jumble of faces, chattering, gurgling with laughter. Mer handed her fishing pole to a dad who professed to love to fish, and walked up to the trail, where she stood talking to Ginny, one hand on her cheek as she listened to the other woman.

"Yeah, yeah," she was saying.

Jharna placed her pole on the ground and stood up, climbing up the slope till she reached the trail where the other moms were gathered.

"Hey, Jer, I've been meaning to introduce you to Maria and Harrison," Mer said, turning to Jharna. "Maria is Asian, like you."

"Hi, I'm Korean American."

"Hi!" Jharna grinned at the handsome couple, baring her teeth.

Maria was short, Jharna's height, with the same black-hair-dyed red-brown and black eyes. Shadows from the moonlight and the waving flashlights dappled everyone's face in the dark.

"Maria is an English teacher. Maria's husband Harrison studied English literature in college, like *you*. He used to work for the *Houston Chronicle*. Jer here has a graduate degree in English literature. You two can talk poetry and stuff." Mer laughed.

The handsome Harrison had a long, conical face with blue eyes like little stones and even, white teeth. He sported an elegant goatee, a thin trickle of mustache and a minimalist beard on his chin. He was dressed in a Polo shirt with beige shorts, ankle length socks, and white tennis shoes. A light blue sweater was wrapped around his shoulders, tied in a loose knot below his chin.

Harrison extended his hand toward Jharna. "Nice to meet you." He stood over six feet tall, his wife Maria only coming up to his chest.

Jharna shook hands with the blue-eyed Harrison and his Asian wife, Maria. "Wow! *Houston Chronicle*, that's huge." Jharna made her eyes big and gulped dramatically.

"Oh, I don't work there anymore. I *used* to work there," Harrison said politely, his voice smooth like cream. "Do you read it?"

"Yes, I love it, especially the editorials. It has a…a sort of small-town feel to it. To read about places and things happening right around you is really wonderful. It's a great paper, actually."

"Ah," Harrison said happily.

"Do *you* read it?" Jharna asked him.

"Not as much as I read my Shakespeare," Harrison said softly. They both chuckled, a shared joke between two literature majors. "No, I'm afraid I don't get to, I'm so busy nowadays."

"Yes, life gets so busy." Maria nodded, affirming her husband's words. She had a soft, round face, a complexion like chocolate dropped in milk. Their daughter Gabriela was in the same section as Lilli. They had the same teacher. People often mistook them for each other at school.

"So where do you work now?" Jharna asked Harrison, with a friendly nod to Maria, her brain already churning. She and Rob needed to have them over, get to know them better.

"At –." Harrison named an oil company.

"Is that so? My husband works at the company too!" the camping organizer Amanda squealed. "Were you working there when the oil spill happened?"

Now the tall Harrison was surrounded by a group of women, all asking him questions.

"As a matter of fact, I was not working at the oil company at the time of the oil spill…I was still working at the *Chronicle* then."

"Harrison reported on the spill, as a matter of fact." Maria spoke proudly about her husband. "He worked night and day, doing investigative reporting for eighty-six days straight. We'd just gotten married then. I was already pregnant with Gabriela. We were supposed to go away on our honeymoon…"

Jharna suddenly remembered the oil spill in the Gulf of Mexico, news that had faded from her memory. It had been called the largest oil spill in the history of marine drilling at the time. She had been pregnant too, with Lilli. She and Rob had just bought their house in Houston, a tiny cottage at the edge of the Heights. She remembered the images on the news of marine animals that had died from respiratory failure, dead fish, sea turtles mired in oil, carcasses of birds, pelicans with crude oil stuck to their feathers, and of oil washed up on beaches in Louisiana.

"Oh, no! What did you do?" Amanda asked.

"We cancelled our honeymoon, naturally. I didn't see much of Harrison for the next three months."

"That's so heroic of him!" Amanda said in a sweet, low voice. She was dressed in a pretty printed dress with a ruffled blouse, a cardigan on top, and black slippers. "My husband was gone a lot, too, at the time. He was working at the oil company, and he was busy trying to solve the problem. I hadn't seen much of him for months. Like you, I was pregnant with triplets! His team was trying to contain the oil spill. He didn't sleep for nights. He got a room in a hotel next to his office and stayed there so he wouldn't wake me up when he came home. Imagine what would have been my state if I had had the triplets then!"

"Heroes, heroes, I tell you," Harrison spoke in a nasal tone. He had a strong, square jaw and perfect teeth. His mouth was open in a moon-shaped smile.

"Well, *you* were a hero, too, for sure, doing that fantastic reporting," Amanda congratulated Harrison. "So, when did you join –?"

"It's a long story. Ha, ha. When I was covering the story, I met a few good people at the company. They seemed to be trying to do the right thing. Their hearts seemed to be in the right place. So, uh, you know, they offered me a job. And…I took the offer."

Jharna listened as they talked, her mouth slightly open, twirling a leaf between her fingers. She had a faint memory of Rob saying recently that the oil was still leaking into the ocean, still killing animals. According to Rob, it had been one of the biggest crimes of recent times. The company had got away with murder.

"What do you do for the company?" Jharna asked Harrison.

"I manage their PR with the government, write press releases, and talk to the media when there's an incident…"

"That's so important," Amanda said, nodding her head appreciatively.

Jharna took a step back so that she was looking at the little group she'd just been standing with. They looked like earnest, decent people, white teeth shining in the dark, people who were convinced of their own decency.

"So basically, you do the opposite of what you did at the *Chronicle*?" Jharna said suddenly. "Instead of investigating the company that spilled the oil, you cover up for the company now?" Her lips wrinkled like Rob's. Her voice came out sharper than she had intended, high and wavering.

Harrison stared at her briefly. Then he said cheerfully, "Yes! I do the job well because of my prior experience working as a journalist. I feel that being able to explain yourself is so important. The writing part. You appreciate that, of course, as an English major."

"Thank God for us English majors, right?" Jharna laughed, trying to appear chipper and friendly again, but staring into Harrison's smooth face, she heard her father's voice after all these years. *Leave the oil in the ground.* Her eyes burned, and her head felt heavy. "It's getting dark!" she said.

"Yes," Mer agreed. "Bobby, are you done?"

Bobby had been sitting hunched, concentrating on his line. He had fixed the other two fishing poles on either side of him. He reminded Jharna of her father, sitting like that, looking out at the water. So still, he had blended with the dark water and sky and become almost invisible to the naked eye. Now he stirred slowly. "Coming," he said, abruptly pulling the line and reeling it in.

"Did you catch anything?" Harrison asked interestedly.

"Nah." Bobby wobbled a little as he climbed up the slope, unsteady on his feet.

"I wonder what the children are up to," Jharna said loudly. "I have to go. I should check on Lilli." She backed away and turned around, starting on the trail.

"We're coming, right behind you, Jer," Mer called warmly behind her.

Jharna walked with big steps, striding past the tall cottonwood trees, remembering that the dark path before her crawled with unknown creatures. She could hear the vultures overhead, a creaking sound, like a saw going back and forth, a couplet. A vulture flew high above, wings spread in the dark sky. She could hear the party behind her, talking, walking together, laughing.

When they reached the large clearing at the trailhead, Jharna said she had to use the bathroom and trotted ahead. The others stopped to chat, standing in a circle, saying they would wait for her. Perhaps because it had been in use all day, the bathroom was very dirty. Muddy water pooled on the floor. The countertop was wet. Jharna threw cold water on her face and stared at her reflection in the dirty mirror. She had her father's small, frightened eyes and her mother's too-pleasing smile. Thankfully, no one had followed her into the bathroom. She used the toilet quickly and stumbled outside into the night again. The others were still standing huddled at the trailhead, with cups and bottles in hand.

"Hey, Jer! Wait up!" Mer called.

"I have a splitting headache!" Jharna cried. "I'm just going to go ahead and have a lie down." She started stepping away, walking backwards.

Mer's face fell. "Oh, you poor thing," she said. "I hope you feel better soon, Jer."

"Yeah!" Jharna cried.

Jharna walked past the RV trailers, hands in pant pockets, staring at the explosion of stars overhead, longing to hear the call of the vultures again. The way back to the camp seemed a lot longer in the dark, now that she was walking alone. Jharna wound her way through the playground, away from all the campfires and lights. The playground was empty now. Finally, she reached the loop where all their campsites were located. People sat on chairs by fires in the dark, chatting, making food, their cars parked out front. Someone had found two trees and strung up a hammock in front of their campsite. A child walked out of a screened shelter wearing a glow stick around her neck. A man with a thick, masculine voice was singing a country song somewhere. Jharna walked fast. She just wanted to go back to the campsite and find Rob.

Rob was awake now and sitting on one of the blue chairs she had bought. She had imagined them sitting side by side on these chairs, staring into the fire, talking. As she neared, she saw that Lilli and Johnny were with him. He had grilled hot dogs for them over the fire. He had piled on more logs and the fire was going strong, orange and red flames leaping high with big plopping sounds.

"Hi," she said, coming upon him from behind.

"Hello." Rob turned and smiled at her, his eyes crinkling.

"Do you feel better?" she asked.

He nodded.

Mer and Bobby appeared minutes later.

"Hello, hello. The return of the prodigal son!" Bobby called good naturedly to Rob. "How are you feeling, my man?"

"Fine, thanks," Rob said quietly. "I just had a slight headache, that's all."

"I have a headache too now. Perhaps something to do with the air," Jharna said.

"Well, you missed the fun. We had a big fishing party," Bobby said, sitting down heavily.

More people arrived at their camp to talk to Bobby and Mer. Mer and Bobby stood around the roaring campfire, chitchatting with their friends.

Rob excused himself, saying he had to go to the bathroom. "I'll just brush my teeth and prepare for bed. Sorry, not feeling well."

Jharna nodded uncertainly. She didn't know if he really did have a headache, or if it was something else. She followed with Lilli, toothbrushes in hand, thinking she might as well turn in for the night.

Walking back from the bathroom, Jharna and Lilli spotted Rob a few feet ahead. Jharna started to walk faster to catch up with him when she caught a glimpse of one side of his face. His cheek was pulsing, and there was a hard, steely look in his eye. She drew back then, letting Rob walk ahead. He walked past their car and wandered down the road, melting into the darkness.

Mer, Bobby, and their friends were still standing around the fire, hands outstretched over crackling logs and the spitting, hissing flames that Rob had tended while they had been away. Amanda was there, and Ginny, and a few other people Jharna didn't know. A few hours ago, Jharna had longed for just such an ending to the night, standing up and laughing with other parents at R-Elementary school just like hers. She had imagined taking a nice, hot shower, changing into clean clothes, and then, finally, having abundant time to spend with people who were there to do just that. The children had gone to bed, and now the adults were relaxing, spending grown-up time together.

"Hey, we're going to go to bed. So tired," Jharna said, yawning.

"Okay," Mer said. "I hope your headache gets better."

Luckily, Lilli was exhausted from playing in the park and didn't make a fuss about turning in. Jharna pressed her body to Lilli's back, holding her close. Neither of them changed out of their clothes. Lying inside the tent, Jharna could hear scraps of conversation, the strum of a guitar, a few aberrant children still awake, screaming. She didn't know when Rob entered the tent or fell asleep, but at some point in the night she sensed him lying on the mattress, at the far end, pressed against the tent without a blanket, shivering in the cold.

Later, she awoke, needing to go to the bathroom. For some minutes, she lay in the relative warmth of the mattress, covered by a comforter and Lilli's body, trying to muster the courage to rise in the cold and walk on the dark, lonely path to the bathroom. There were no more sounds of chatter. Everyone had gone to sleep. Then she realized what had awoken her, a series of strange calls and responses, not like the hissing and sawing, hacking sounds of the vultures, but full throated. She lay there, drifting between sleep and waking, listening to the unearthly conversation. She had seen the signs about the barred owls at the park. Bobby had mentioned them. They sounded ominous, loud and human, like several people having a loud conversation. People were coughing in their tents. A child cried. Above them, dwarfing them, stunning them, engulfing them all, the owls chattered among themselves. Jharna had an overwhelming feeling that her parents were close by, hovering outside the tent. She lay still, trying to keep them close a little longer.

With a giant effort, Jharna shrugged free of the comforter and spread it on top of Rob and Lilli, tucking in the ends. Working laboriously, she unzipped the canvas and stepped outside the tent, pushing her feet into sandals. Even with a jacket on, it was cold. She walked uncertainly through the tall grass in the dark until she found the road (the weak beam of the flashlight didn't reach far). Once she was on the road, there was sufficient light from the stars and campsite lanterns to keep moving. When she passed under the oak trees, a shimmering mist like rain fell from the branches and soaked her. What was it? Could dew be so thick? In a daze, Jharna walked the long way to the bathroom and used the toilet, the bright lights glaring inside the building. On the way back, she felt more comfortable walking under the eerie cover of the stars, the hooting owls on trees, and the mist shower falling from the trees. Their campsite lay quiet and peaceful in the dark. Everything had been put away neatly. The fire had been put out, the logs soaked through. Bobby and Mer must have poured water on them. Instead of turning in, Jharna walked past the campsite and kept walking.

During the day, there had been cars coming and going on the road, people driving up to their campsites or driving to the nearby town of Sealy to buy forgotten supplies and pizza for dinner. But now the road was dark and empty. She walked by herself, like Rob had done, understanding now his urge to be alone and, also, the look on his face when she had seen him disappearing into the night. Her parents had left America abruptly, leaving all their friends with bright mansions, new cars, and brand-name jobs at big corporations. Her parents had wanted no part of any of this. They had dared to be loners and go their own way.

Turning at the bend, Jharna reached the ghost playground, distinguishable only as a pitch-black shroud. Feeling her way in the dark, she tried to find the swings. The wet grass clawed at her sandals. She held out her hands till she found the metal chains of a swing. Pulling the plastic, bendy seat toward her, she hauled her body on top of it. Then she sat on the swing, swinging gently back and forth in the dark, alone.

Borders

"Brother, please move your feet."

Faria glanced up from her seat on the Emirates Airline plane to stare at the scene a few seats ahead. A very pretty, petite young woman with a boy cut and large eyes was speaking to a laborer seated beside her.

"Madam, how much more you want me to move?" the man shouted. "Why don't *you* move?" His face was bearded, scruffy, his thin brown cheeks pockmarked by white and gray hairs. His eyes were small and shifty. He was one of the laborers traveling from Dhaka to Dubai.

Unfortunately, anyone flying from Bangladesh to the US had to share a flight with the laborers to the Middle East until the stopover in Dubai. That was the only drawback to traveling via the Atlantic route and using one of the Middle Eastern carriers, which were superior in every other aspect to the other flights.

Faria leaned forward with concern. Several other passengers looked up as well, turning toward the man and woman seated in Row 20. Faria recognized them both from Dhaka airport. The man was wearing a dark, smelly suit. His whole person was musty, his armpits, his breath all stinking. Faria had been standing in the line next to him and the other laborers at immigration at Dhaka airport. Her line had moved fast, while theirs, to the right of her, to counter number ten, had been held up by complications, shady goings on, tough interview questions in raised voices, and furtive demands for hard cash. Faria had watched with pity as the laborers had been shepherded by some sort of leader through the immigration line, obviously lost, with ugly looking bundles of luggage put together with rope and cheap black bags. Some wore tight jeans and T-shirts with random words like "I LOVE NEW YORK", bought at the garments surplus market. Others were suited like this man, reeking of men who did not take frequent baths, and cheap cologne. After the arduous, suspenseful theater at immigration, the laborers had hung out in the waiting area, sitting on orange plastic chairs, their faces taut with tension, chewing on blackened fingernails, with frightened eyes. But now, this man's face was twisted, his teeth bared at the young woman who had protested.

A pretty, young stewardess of some European country, with blonde hair tucked beneath the uniform headdress, leaned over the man's seat and spoke to him in English. "Sir, is there a problem? Please give her some room. Your arms are on her seat."

"I bought this seat!" The man shouted apoplectically, spurting spit from his meat-red lips, and standing up from his seat. He was not so tall, about five seven, and the stewardess was wearing heels, so the difference in their height was not great, but her bright blue eyes retreated in horror at his aggression. "I'm sorry, sir, but it's against the rule…"

"Shut up! Shut up! Shut up!"

The laborers sitting nearby laughed and shouted encouragements in Bengali to the shouting man. A couple of them clapped. The back rows were filled with laborers. The few families on the plane, America bound, were quite far, up in the front rows. Only Faria and the other female passenger had been left behind with the laborers. Faria shifted in her seat, wondering whether to intervene. This same man had tried to light up a cigarette a half hour ago and been scolded by a male steward.

"Sir, if you don't sit down, I'll have to…," the stewardess began again, pursing her frosted pink lips.

"What? What? What?" the man barked, jumping up.

The stewardess recoiled with horror, her eyes rocking, as if uncertain if he would strike her. Faria had half gotten out of her seat, when the British male steward, towering at above six feet, the same one who had confronted the man earlier, strode over to the scene.

"What's your name, sir?"

"Malik."

"Sit down, Mr. Malik!" The male steward shouted, his chin trembling with anger. "Sit down this minute. When the plane lands, we will report you to ground authority."

Mr. Malik sat back down demurely. Faria gathered her courage to stand up from her seat and approach the huddle around Row 20.

"Please, if it's possible, I'd like to exchange seats with–with this gentleman here and sit next to the young woman." She leaned toward the woman passenger and said in Bengali, "Is that okay? *Thik Ache?*"

The woman nodded gratefully, her eyes brightening in the thin, pretty face.

Faria turned back to the English male steward. "Sir?"

In a short while, Mr. Malik was shouted at and persuaded to move down two seats, where Faria had been sitting before. Faria brought over her large handbag and settled down, a little uneasily, in the rather warm chair Mr. Malik had vacated, still scented with his overpowering cologne.

She flashed a warm, friendly smile at the young woman sitting beside her. She had noticed her too at Dhaka airport. The pretty woman had arrived with a large family, a matronly looking woman wearing a wrinkled brown cotton sari wrapped all around her, across her shoulders and over her head, a thin elderly man who seemed to be her father, for he clutched her and cried every few minutes, a line of weeping women, and little children who hung on to her and cried and kissed her. The young woman had cried along with them, hugging a little boy who may have been her younger brother to her waist and weeping tears over his back, extracting such bizarre promises from her companions as "Please tell me you will write me a letter every day" and "Abba, promise to take your medicine and don't strain yourself." It was the most tender and surprising spectacle of farewell taking, compared to the dry, businesslike way in which a distant cousin connected to the airport had brought Faria in through the VIP gate. Faria had first left home at seventeen and she had been living by herself for over a decade now, so she had watched the emotional scene with a voyeur's interest.

Afterward, Faria had run into the other woman several times in the duty-free area at Dhaka Airport, where they had waited for five hours, as the flight had been delayed. Faria had noticed her particularly because she was the only other young woman traveling on her own, or perhaps because she was striking, wearing a pretty, black polka-dot shalwar kameez. She had a dramatic face, like a child's, a button nose, soft pink lips, smooth pale arms, and long, delicate fingers. She had sat on the orange plastic chair reading a magazine, turning over the pages carefully, looking uncertain and distracted, wandering by the various handicraft shops, and stopping at the sweet shop to buy a sweetmeat.

"Thank you," the young woman said now, showing even white teeth. She could scarcely be older than a teenager, Faria thought.

"Your name?" Faria asked in Bengali that had acquired a thick American accent.

"Polly."

"Listen. Apart from the two of us, the rest of the people on the plane are all men or families." Faria glanced around the plane meaningfully, bending toward her companion conspiratorially. "I'm glad to be sitting beside you."

Polly laughed loudly, as if Faria had pointed out something very funny. "Where are you going, Apa?" she asked. Her voice was surprisingly deep.

"New York. You?"

"New York."

"Well, then, we're even better buddies," Faria said.

They settled in their seats, relaxing their bodies, no longer worried about modesty. It was a relief to both the young women to be sitting together. The first flight would take them to Dubai. About half the passengers would get off there. The rest were traveling onward to America, or Canada. There was a gulf of difference between the two kinds of passengers, the laborers traveling to the Middle East and the shiny, polished passengers going onward to North America. It was a strange irony for the two worlds to have to share a journey together. Faria always found it surprising, and a little disconcerting, that she felt closer to the people from America. She identified with the other young college students and the families who looked like her and dressed like her, and even the few white Americans traveling to Bangladesh. The America-bound passengers always huddled together on the seats at the airport, laughing together and talking easily in English.

There was good reason to be wary of the male laborers bound for the Middle East. The young men pushed past the other passengers, including women and children, running to get the first seats on the bus. On the plane, they cleaned their noses with their fingers, smoked in the plane bathroom, stole the blankets by stuffing them into their cheap plastic bags, and called the stewardesses rudely as if they were lowly servants, crying one-word demands, like water, water, while gesturing rapidly with their hands.

On the plane to Dhaka, there had been several other young women traveling with Faria, wearing jeans and blouses in the latest fashion. They had hung out together, exchanging life stories and talking about their plans in Dhaka. Faria had been visiting family, but also doing research for her PhD on sex workers, meeting and interviewing sex workers in street settings. This flight back to the United States, in contrast, had no young women traveling by themselves, other than Polly and Faria.

"What do you do in New York?" Faria asked Polly.

"My husband lives there." Polly's face turned pink to her ears. "I'm going to visit him."

"How romantic," Faria said encouragingly. She noticed that Polly's boy-cut hair had been freshly styled, probably at a salon, and plastered with gel. Her palms had fresh red henna on them, and she wore a thick gold bracelet on each wrist.

"Are you newly married?" Faria asked.

"No! Eleven years."

"Eleven years!" Faria cried. "But you're so young."

"And you, Apa?"

"Call me Faria. I'm a student, a graduate student at a university in New York. I was just visiting Dhaka for the summer."

"Are you married?"

Faria shook her head. The two women looked away from each other, falling silent for a while, as tired passengers do on the plane after talking for a while, caught up in their own thoughts, in their own different worlds.

At the airport in Dubai, Faria and Polly both checked their tickets and found that they had a layover of eleven hours.

"We should spend the time together," Faria said. She had carried Polly's luggage for her, seeing the young woman struggling. Faria had carried her own heavy luggage since she had left for college at seventeen. She was tall, big-boned, wide-shouldered, loud mouthed, and brazen. She felt protective toward the younger woman.

"Yes, we could spend time together," Polly said, looking uncertain, biting her lower lip. "I was going to go shopping outside to the market."

"You're going to take the bus outside?" Faria exclaimed in surprise. She had never ventured outside the airport in Dubai, although she had passed through so many times over the years.

"Yes, Apa, I was planning to. If they give me a visa."

They were standing in a long line of people with foreign passports. The immigration officials at Dubai Airport asked tough questions with stern faces.

Did you pack your bag yourself?

What do you do in America?

For how long have you lived in America, Sir?

Why does your face look different in your passport?

I can't find your visa here. Where is your visa?

Several of the adults seemed near crying with frustration at the questions, while the children bearing Barbie dolls, matchbox cars, and Nintendo games fell to the carpeted floor in heaps from exhaustion. Faria glanced at the next line, which was shorter and faster, and realized with a shock that soon, *she* would be in that line, for green card holders and US citizens. At least, the huddle of laborers who had gotten off the plane with their baskets of smelly mangoes, bedding tied together with plastic rope, and synthetic black bags had disappeared into the city.

"Do you want to come, too, Apa?" Polly asked once they had finally made it through the immigration line. "I heard the market in Dubai is spectacular! They have the best gold in the world. I've always wanted to see it." Her pink lips were open with delight and her eyes were bright.

"No." Faria shook her head quickly. She had always regarded the airport as a stopover, to sleep, read, and recover from the previous leg. At most, she had wandered through the duty-free shops, looking at European shops with their different chocolates not available in America. "I'll meet you when you come back."

"All right," Polly said. "I will see you later."

Faria gazed after the young woman, unpolished in her clothes and manners, surprised at this first-time traveler's sense of adventure. She went away to find a coffee place to recharge her laptop.

When the two women met again, quite by accident, they were both wandering near the Harrods in the duty-free area. Polly was laden down with shopping bags. In addition to the brown heavy bag that pulled her right shoulder down below her left, pinching her dress, several yellow plastic bags hung from her wrists.

"Hey there!" Faria ran up to her.

"Hello," Polly said, looking around startled. For a moment, she regarded Faria with a blank expression. Then, recognizing her, she smiled and indicated her wrists, where the ropes of the shopping bags twisted and left angry marks. "Apa, I did a lot of shopping! I bought so much gold!"

"Call me Faria," Faria said. "You look miserable." She pointed at the heavy carry-on bag and offered to take it off the smaller woman's shoulders.

"No, it's okay."

But Faria insisted and took the bag. Polly said thank you many times, gratefully, her girlish voice breaking in bright waves.

"No problem," Faria said graciously, marching ahead. "Come on, slow poke, keep up." She looked behind affectionately at the weaker woman. "Shall we get lunch somewhere with the tickets they gave us?" She knew that without her, Polly would be lost at the huge airport.

"Sure," Polly said, using the polite form of you in Bengali.

"I was looking for you," Faria said. "I was worried for you."

"Oh, why, Apa?" Polly asked, walking a few steps behind her.

They found the Indian restaurant where they all had tickets for lunch. Faria helped Polly to find her ticket and showed Polly how to use her ticket (she had misplaced her ticket, as unseasoned travelers do, so Faria made her also check if she had her passport and boarding pass to America).

Once they sat down with their trays, Faria asked, "So why is it that you haven't visited your husband for eleven years?"

Polly was digging into the food with her fingers. Lunch was generous: Tandoori chicken, Naan, and various kinds of chutney.

"Long story," Polly said, looking away, but she didn't tell it. After some moments, she said brightly, pointing at her tray, "My husband really misses my cooking. He liked for me to cook for him. After we were married, every day, he asked me to cook this and that." She pointed to the chicken bone she was biting. "Apa, this chicken is easy to make." She took apart the flesh at the bones and showed Faria where the spices had been inserted and how to fry it so that the meat was cooked but not tough. "I make a good fried chicken that is his favorite. And various kinds of fried vegetables. He eats and eats. He says he misses his wife's cooking in New York, so I have to go and cook for him all his favorite dishes!" Polly laughed with pleasure. A miniscule diamond stud glinted in her nose.

"How long were you married before he left?"

"One month."

"So, he keeps in touch with you?" Faria asked. She had thought that perhaps the woman had been deserted after her marriage, as was too common among the women she researched.

"Yes, of course!" Polly laughed girlishly, using the back of her hand to wipe her nose, which was running from the spicy food. "He calls me on the phone every day to ask me how to cook this or that."

For no particular reason, Faria remembered the Bengali café she and Dan had once visited down in the Village. Of course, they hadn't known then that the owner was Bengali. The restaurant had an Indian name, and the menu touted itself as selling Indian food. But when the owner had come out, and started talking to them, he had turned out to be a Bangladeshi man.

Dan had asked for beer, and the owner had said that they did not have beer yet, but they had applied for a liquor license.

"Please, Apa, pray for us that we get it," he had said to Faria in Bengali.

Faria had been wearing a thin black tank top that hugged her body, and she and Dan, the Viking like giant Dan with his blonde hair and blonde eyelashes, had been holding hands. The Bangladeshi man had been wearing shorts and scratching his crotch. Yet, they did not judge each other, for the tank top, the American boyfriend, the shorts, or the liquor. Rather, they had felt a strong sense of camaraderie, speaking in their tongue in this foreign land, wishing each other mutual success in their different paths.

"Why did you open a restaurant?" Faria had asked the Bangladeshi man, as he had sat down at the table to talk to them.

"I used to be a taxi driver," he said. "And I really missed my wife's cooking. And I knew all these other Bangladeshi drivers who cried to me, Apa. Imagine. Grown men with tears in their eyes, because they missed their mother's cooking or their wife's cooking. At night, they dreamed of white rice and thick daal with onions and lemon. So, one day I decided to open a restaurant, for myself and for them. Now, this restaurant stays open twenty-four hours. And these taxi drivers, when they get off their shifts, sometimes in the middle of the night, at one or two in the morning, when the other restaurants are closed, they come in here to my restaurant and sit here like it is their wife's kitchen, eating beef curry and talking with other Bangladeshi drivers about back home. I created a home for them here in my restaurant."

"How long have you been living here?" Dan had asked affably, throwing his hands in the air to indicate the Village, New York, America. Even sitting down, he had towered over the shorter, darker man.

The man lowered his voice conspiratorially, leaned in, and whispered to Dan that he was ill-le-gal, still waiting for his papers. Then he drew back and grinned slyly, showing even white teeth. Like most immigrants who had started to do well, the man had acquired fat on his belly, face, and arms. He told them that he had come to New York on a visitor's visa, planning to stay behind. He had friends in the city who had written to him and promised to help him when he got to America. Once he had arrived on American soil, he had disappeared into the folds of New York. He used to live with a distant uncle first, up in Queens. Then, driving a taxi for a company day and night, he had saved enough to buy a taxi of his own on loan. For two years, he had driven sixteen hours a day (no, really) to pay off the loan. He earned eighty thousand dollars a year, all his own money, to keep. Dan and Faria had joked later, falling off their narrow bed laughing, that *he probably kept his money under the mattress in cash, hidden away from the IRS.*

"So, you still don't have papers?" Dan had asked with concern.

"No, still waiting. I go to court regularly. I have a lawyer working on my case. Please pray for me, brother."

The man spoke with dramatic flourish and self-importance, gesturing with his arms, winking, or nodding his head, where his vocabulary could not fill the gap, and Dan and Faria had thoroughly enjoyed the visit and the conversation. They had talked about it for days, months, imitating him and laughing. He was such an oddity. He wore shorts and a Polo shirt, a thin gold chain around his neck. Faria had wondered how much of his home he had left behind, how much he had abandoned of his culture and his religion, along with the modest trousers he should be wearing. They shared an odd intimacy, this man in his shorts and Faria with her American boyfriend. Had the café sold beer, they might even have shared one across a table.

Later, Faria and Dan had laughed at the irony: This Muslim man was going to sell liquor, and he was asking Faria to pray for him in their religion, in which alcohol was forbidden, so that he could sell alcohol. The two of them had thought this funny. It had become their private joke. They would tell it like a most amusing anecdote to friends. The story never got old. So odd, they would say after they had finished telling the story, wiping away tears, such an odd sort, so devout yet selling alcohol, so religious yet willing to do something illegal.

New York was full of such Bangladeshis, selling hot dogs on corners, emerging as a waiter in an Upper West Side restaurant, a taxi driver piping up in Bengali. Faria loved these encounters, but she felt a world of divide between herself and these men who lived in dark corners, probably without documents. Faria and Dan walked the streets of Manhattan, Faria's hand in Dan's wool jacket pocket, discussing these things. In a few months, Dan and she would get married, nothing big, just get their license in court, then celebrate with a few friends in his parents' backyard in their Long Island mansion.

Once, she had run into a pharmacist, who had turned out to be Bangladeshi, in a drugstore high up on the Upper West Side. He had asked her what she did and when she told him that she was graduating soon, the elderly man had asked, "What will you do after that?"

Faria shook her head, laughing, not wanting to say she would be marrying Dan, her American boyfriend. She would take some time off, taking advantage of her immigrant status to not have to work for the first time in her life. Then, when she had rested enough, she would apply for academic jobs.

"You should just stay," the elderly man had suggested, lowering his voice. "Just stay. Nobody will notice in this big city. So many of us here." He had smiled, showing a missing upper tooth in front.

Faria had smiled and got out of the store fast. She'd been so shocked by even the mention of such a possibility of doing something illegal. It was that line that the working-class Bangladeshi men in the city had crossed, that meant they belonged in two different worlds.

Now, at the airport restaurant, Faria stared dreamily at Polly, who was digging into the rice and yogurt with her greasy fingers.

"You must be happily married," she said.

"We have one boy, Apa. He is ten." Polly paused, her eyes becoming moist and dreamy.

"You have a child? A ten-year-old! You don't look it. I saw a boy with long eyelashes, about that age, hugging you around the waist at Dhaka Airport. Was that him?"

"Yes! When my husband married me, I got immediately pregnant, Apa."

"So why don't you move to the US? With your son?"

Polly hesitated. "My husband is illegal there. That is why. The American Consulate in Dhaka won't let the child visit. The consulate people made me keep my child in Bangladesh and get a visitor's visa so they can be sure I'll return. I left my son with my parents. This is the first time they gave me a visa. Every year before this, they refused. Too risky to let me go to America, they said. I might stay behind. For ten years, I applied for a visa, and I got denied. But this time I tried again because my husband cried on the phone. He said he missed having a wife. And this time I got it."

Faria squinted, narrowing her eyebrows, and studied the young wife's face. For the first time, she noticed the dark lines under Polly's eyes. She understood the tears at the airport now. They had not been tears out of fright at leaving home, but tears of loss about leaving her little child behind, his little brown hands grasping at her. Polly was making a journey into the unknown to meet her long-separated husband, choosing between her son and her husband. What strange, cold, world did her husband live in, separated from her sunny, warm home of familiar trees and balconies and markets and neighbors?

"How about you, Apa?" Polly asked, wiping up the last of her curry and looking at Faria with her mouth open. "Are you married?"

"No."

"You didn't find time to get married? You were too busy getting an education?"

"Ha, ha. That's funny." Faria turned away, feeling faintly offended.

She felt unable to explain who she was and her wide, expansive world to people whose lives were narrower and more straightforward than her own, as she imagined Polly's to be. She had even felt this alienation from her relatives and her parents' friends in Dhaka. Never when doing her work, though, when she went about the city on rickshaw, talking to the sex workers on the streets, or their clients, or their pimps in white shirts and jeans. But when she talked to relatives or her parents' friends, people would say things like, "Faria, get married before you become infertile." Or "time is ticking, you can't defy nature." She only laughed uproariously at the rude comments of such people and made some rude joke as rebuttal. Her parents had tried to introduce her to several young men, who dropped in very awkwardly at the house and gaped at her. They did not know about Dan.

"Shall we walk around and see what's on sale?" Faria dabbed her lips with a tissue and scraped back her chair, looming over the other woman. From her height, she noticed that Polly's hair was oiled and slicked back, smelling faintly.

"Oh, yes, Apa." Polly stood up, picking up her tray with a jaunty step that was new. "I saw some nice shops I can show you."

Faria took a step back, holding her tray, and almost fell. She felt that she couldn't trust Polly for the same reason she couldn't find common ground with her old friends and cousins in Bangladesh who wore shalwar kameez and got married according to their parents' wishes. She could not trust other Bengalis to respect her or understand her if she revealed herself to them.

Once, Faria's friends in Dhaka had taken her to drink local alcohol at a shady shop. They could have gone to a foreign party for liquor, the American embassy or one of the other foreign embassies, but they wanted to have an adventure. The local liquor shops were undercover so that there was no regulation at all. They could be drinking something that would kill them. She and her friends raised their glasses and cheered, drinking possibly to their deaths, laughing uproariously. They would sit and laugh about so many things that were beyond the pale, or illegal, in Dhaka, like driving as a woman late at night, walking on the streets alone late at night, which was perfectly legal in another country.

As Faria and Polly walked past the various duty-free shops displaying Lindt Chocolate and whiskey and matching luggage in front, the beautiful sight of the chocolates melted Faria's tension away. Her shoulders relaxed. She'd been striding two paces ahead of Polly, but she slowed down and turned around, offered to take Polly's bag again.

"Keeping up?" she said, smiling sweetly at Polly.

Polly smiled back. "I'd like to see the gold shops."

"I thought you already went to the gold market?" Faria teased. She had a dry sense of humor and was good at making jokes. She teased everyone, men older than her, taller than her, patriarchal men working at Bangladeshi NGOs, even her uncles and her father's friends who offended her.

"I bought some good bangles and earrings, but I'm looking for a necklace," Polly said.

"Sure. I'll come with you."

Polly didn't know where the gold shops were, so Faria looked at the map. They were standing in Terminal B. They would have to head back to Terminal A. They took a train, then walked the long airport past the shops selling nuts, candy, cigarettes, and liquor, to the gold shops. Polly studied the glittering displays under glass with big eyes, a hand under her chin. She asked for pieces to be brought out, pointing with a painted nail, then asked the storekeeper expertly about karats, and designs, and prices. Faria looked on, smiling politely and suppressing a yawn.

As she waited for Polly, looking at the gold, she felt her forehead tightening. She was getting married in a few months. She wasn't going to tell her parents about Dan till she was properly, legally, married, when they couldn't do anything about it. She wasn't afraid; she just didn't want any fuss from them. But had Faria told her mom, perhaps her mother would have brought out the gold she had saved for her daughter's wedding all her life. Looking at the matching sets of necklaces, earrings, and rings, Faria's eyes shone with this daydream, of her mother adorning her with her mother's necklaces, bestowing on her generations of tradition. She shook her head to get out of the temptation that must be in her Bengali DNA to be attracted to gold like other Bengali girls and laughed aloud.

Polly turned around with a confused look. "Apa, are you okay?"

"Sure. Sure. Go ahead. Keep looking." Faria checked her watch.

Dan's parents had no concept of gold. Their house was sparkling white—every room, including the kitchen. Everything was flat with the surface, which was marble white. Even the bathroom, as big as two large parlors, was white, with mirrors on every wall and on the ceiling, and a large famous painting that Dan's mother had bought in a gallery in Newberry. Dan's mother had bought the painting from a struggling artist, an old boyfriend of hers, she claimed, but now he was famous; he had made a name. With each object came a story: the large Indian mask placed precariously on a coffee table in the dining room, from the Incas, the African drums in the long, white living room, the shard of glass by the pool, another piece of art, bought and shipped from Paris. Even the coffee cups had stories attached to them. They had taken her to old restaurants, where even the sauce of the pasta tasted deep and complicated, sophisticated, cooked by a famous chef. They had a private plane, so they could fly off whenever they wanted to have their next adventure. Dan's mom said that sometimes, on a warm evening in New York, they would think, why don't we eat in Alaska? And they would drive out to the hangar to get the plane and book a table at a restaurant in Anchorage, and there they would be, in a few hours, stealing out for a date, like two naughty kids.

Once, Dan had flown Faria in his small, single-engine plane. High in the air, he had teased, his voice rising in feigned alarm, "Oh, we're flying over Canada now! If there's engine trouble, I'll have to make an emergency landing."

Faria didn't find this funny. Her face became plastic. "No, no, please, I can't be in Canada. I have an F-1 visa!" she had cried out, her eyes big with fear. All her sense of humor had vanished then. The loud, funny girl, the no-nonsense foreign student who gave everyone else in class a hard time. Now she was crying for him to turn around. How naïve, how gauche she had been. She liked to tell that story now to friends, of that old, unsophisticated Faria, as if that were some other person in the past.

On another vacation, Dan and his parents had invited Faria to Texas with them, where they had a private ranch. After a few days at the ranch in Dallas, they had kept driving west, all the way to Laredo. They walked to the Rio Grande River. Standing in a park right on the border, they looked across the narrow river, and they could see across to Mexico, where people stood by the water like them, some strolling, some fishing. Border patrol marched along the park with guns slung lazily across their shoulders.

"This is where people cross over." Dan's mom had pointed with her long, slender ring finger with the single diamond ring. Then she suggested that they walk across the bridge into Nuevo Laredo and check it out.

"No!" Faria had cried, her eyes darting, pupils large with fear, like a frightened wild animal. "I can't. I don't have my passport." She began gesticulating wildly with her hands, like a person who does not have full command of English. Again, that time, she had lost all her acquired sophistication.

Her passport was always the first thing she seized during a fire drill. Once, there had been an actual fire with real smoke in the university dorm, and she had spent about ten minutes going around trying to find her passport while the smoke built in the air around her. This paranoia about carrying her documents with her all the time to prove her legal status was something she would joke about and tell as an anecdote to make her friends laugh. But at the border, shaking without her passport, she had become the joke to Dan's family.

Dan's parents had laughed at her affectionately.

"Come on," Dan's mother Cheryl had said smoothly, fingering the pearls at her neck. "Come with me. Nothing will happen."

In contrast to the gaudy gold and heavy brocade saris that her mother and aunties wore to dress up for parties, Dan's very wealthy mother Cherly wore a simple T-shirt and shorts, her hair cut short to her nape. Her nails were clean and short. Faria looked up to her and had learned so much from her. Cheryl had lent Faria books on gardening in New York, a book on the American West before their vacation.

As they had approached the stern immigration officer, Cheryl had pulled Faria close to her, the two women the same height, walking shoulder to shoulder.

"Nothing will happen. When they ask, I'll say you're a US citizen. You're with us. You're practically my daughter."

And Cheryl had been right. The border had been crowded. The immigration officers were exhausted trying to get through the long line.

"She's my daughter," Cheryl had said. "We're US citizens."

"Welcome home, Ma'am. God bless."

No one even asked to see their passports [they were not carrying any]. Dan's parents had laughed and laughed at Faria later on. They would not let her forget. On the other side of the border in Nuevo Laredo, in one of the plazas, Faria had seen a sight she could not shed from her eyes. There had been little fat children in pink frocks playing, boys with their sandals off, chasing each other. One plump family, a father, mother, and their two little children, sat with ice cream popsicles on the steps of a statue and ate, a family outing. A little girl in an embroidered, white cotton Mexican dress flung her arms out, shut her eyes, and whirled round and round, as if, with those eyes closed, her world was large and endless. By contrast, when they had headed back, the border security guards huddled on the bridge were all suspicion, checking people's bags, looking savagely at their faces, accusing them of trying to cross over illegally, as if Mexico was barren, as if no one lived there or they only lived there to one day cross over to America.

Finally, Polly made a choice at the gold shop. She held a fat necklace around her throat and checked herself in the mirror, turning her face sideways and plumping her mouth, raising an eyebrow, then turning the other way.

"Do you like it?"

"It's nice," Faria said in a plastic voice. She was no authority on gold. She wondered if she would ever fit in as a woman in Bangladesh; if she would even be accepted in that society as a woman if she didn't have any expertise in gold.

"My mother keeps all her gold at home," Polly chattered happily, holding the piece against her neck and staring at the mirror, fixing her pink lips. "Once, when there was load shedding and we had no power—we live in Azimpur where the power always goes out, every evening almost for one hour–, one day my mom brought out all her gold and started to sort them out, for lack of something to do."

In the end, Polly decided that she didn't want anything at the shop and moved on. Faria followed her. With half her mind, she was beginning to wonder if she should leave Polly and go back to the book she had to read for school, or perhaps sort her notes from her research, but she followed along, for want of company, partly, and partly out of wanting to protect the young woman.

Polly talked about her mom who chewed betel leaves till her tongue had grown red and about her son who played football with the other boys in the field in front of their house, and about how she and her sister would steal green mangoes from her mom's pantry in the middle of the night and eat them with red chili and salt.

"Have you never shopped for gold, Apa?"

"Nope," Faria said.

"Oh. It was our favorite excursion. Even as teenagers, when we had no money, we would go to gold shops." Polly giggled.

They passed several gold shops where Polly only took a cursory look and grimaced. "My cousins and I would go and make the shopkeeper take out gold bangles and we would put them on our wrists. They were too fat for our wrists, and the bangles would go *jhum jhum jhum.* Such a sound! Like rain shower. The shopkeepers would think we were real customers, and they would treat us with Coca Cola. Then they would wise up and get very rude, and we would run out, laughing, our bellies hurting. We would double down laughing as soon as we got out the door. Oh, how we loved to go to New Market. We went to our favorite bookshops and bought the latest novel by Humayun Ahmed, and then we ate that spicy chotpoti and that's it, our money was gone! Otherwise, we would go to Gawsia Market across the street and spend hours shopping for fabric and then telling the tailor how to make our dresses."

They came to another shop, this one with more intricate designs in their gold, more Indian classical. Polly stopped, her eyes widening. Again, Polly made the shopkeepers get out several sets of glinting yellow gold.

"These are more sophisticated designs," Polly said, turning to Faria. She explained to Faria how the gold in Dubai was pure yellow, whereas in Bangladesh it was softer, more fragile. She gave Faria a whole lecture on gold. "My sister would like this design," she said, smiling. "I will buy her one for her wedding."

It seemed that Polly's husband sent a lot of money home, allowing her to hoard gold not only for herself but also her sibling.

"I love gold." Polly closed her eyes and stroked the necklace the shopkeeper had put around her neck. "This one is called a *Sita Har*. It falls to the navel, see?"

"Why do you like gold so much?" Faria asked, her lips curling.

"It's the rule for all girls to love gold," Polly said, "It's the rule of the world. Don't you love gold, Apa?"

At last, Polly had bought two necklaces and Faria had helped her calculate the conversion. They walked back with their possessions, taking the train back to Terminal B. They had only two hours left before their flight. Polly kept talking about her mother and her younger sisters. Finally, they were seated at their gate. For once, Polly stopped talking. She rummaged about her many carry-on bags, trying to sort her things. Faria sat on the cold, sterile seat, remembering her time with her parents in Dhaka. Things had been hostile, to say the least. Once, when Faria had been heading out late at night, taking a taxi to meet friends, her mother had burst into her room.

"What are you doing?"

"Going out," Faria had answered rudely. "Why do you look at me like that? You look like you disapprove?" She had been standing at her dressing table, in front of the long mirror, powdering her nose.

"I'm not looking at you like that. But society is," her mother had answered crossly, frowning. "It's not all right for women to go out at all hours of the night in our society."

The frowns looked like judgment to Faria, so she turned away proudly, pouting in the mirror. "We need to take back the night then. I'm pushing back, so we have more space…"

"Everything you do, it's not acceptable here. A woman your age should be married. You should be going out with your husband in your husband's car. Not out at two in the morning. Not going to foreign embassies. Smoking, drinking."

"Oh, I can't breathe. You make me sick. Give me some space!" Faria had cried, pushing roughly past her mother and rushing out of her room, out of the tiny, suffocating flat.

That was how the entire summer had played out. She had felt sick, pressed in, as if her own childhood home wasn't home to her anymore.

Apparently satisfied with her packing, Polly sat back in her seat and asked, "So when will you marry?"

"Why do I have to marry?" Faria smiled coolly at the other woman.

"Do you have someone you want to marry, Apa? A boyfriend?"

Faria decided not to answer. Polly mentioned that she missed her son. Faria wondered idly if that restaurant owner in the Village whom she and Dan had met could be Polly's taxi driver husband. The two women fell into exhausted boredom.

A stewardess walked up to Polly and told her that she could not carry so many bags on the plane. Polly was in tears, begging, gesturing. Faria tried to translate for Polly.

"I'm afraid those are the rules." The stewardess's lips tightened, the way they did when speaking to laborers on the plane. She folded her hands in front of her skirt and spoke very slowly. "One bag. Yeah? One bag. Not many."

When she walked away, Polly turned to Faria. "Apa, can you not take one of my bags? The heavy one? After all, you've been carrying it all along for me."

Faria gawked at the audacity of the demand. She hesitated a moment before replying, just to gather how to reply to such a question. "The rules say that you can't carry someone else's bag," she said finally, enunciating her words, speaking firmly like the stewardess. "They'll ask me if I am carrying someone else's bags. I'm supposed to know everything that is in my bags."

This was exactly the kind of thing those other Bangladeshis in New York did, crossing this invisible line. Faria had never done anything the least bit in doubt–never carried a package for someone without checking it first, never carried food like other passengers did. She became sure now that Polly's black bag was loaded with food for the absent husband.

"Please. It will help me a lot. I can't leave any of this behind," Polly went on, as if Faria had not spoken.

"Well." Faria grimaced, extremely uncomfortable. "Can't you wear some of the things you bought? Like the gold, for instance. And–what else did you buy?"

"I'm going to see my husband after so long. He misses rice puffs from his village. And I'm bringing molasses. His books. I had to carry it all. Please, Apa. You're carrying nothing on you. Look. Is that purse all you are carrying? You are allowed to carry one handbag and one carry-on bag, Apa." Her face had become twisted and young again, her eyes red and moist.

Faria frowned. The incivility of the demand rattled her. She felt uncomfortable even sitting next to Polly, who seemed as if she would go on trying to persuade Faria. Now she felt that she should really be getting back to her book, which she had intended to finish on the journey back. Faria stood up. "I have some work to catch up on. I'll just go sit a few rows down for a bit…"

She regretted wasting so much time with Polly. She really could have used the extra time on the plane to catch up on work. Or nap. She would definitely sleep on the flight to New York.

"See you in a bit." She smiled politely.

They were interrupted by a man's voice at their elbows. "Sisters, didn't you both come from Bangladesh? Imagine seeing you again!"

Faria and Polly both looked in surprise at the man. He was the same pockmarked man in his musty suit who had been seated next to Polly on the plane from Bangladesh to Dubai.

At last, Polly spoke to the man. "Bhai, I thought you were traveling to Dubai?"

"I worked in Dubai for many years," the man said amiably, "but this time I got a visitor's visa to USA. I have a cousin there. He will set me up in taxi business." He sat down in the seat vacated by Faria and fluffed his jacket. "Apa, sit down?" he said to Faria, as if expecting to settle down to a nice, long conversation with the two women. "You don't have to go to the bathroom, do you? Then go and come back. My name is Malik. What are your names?"

He was all friendliness. He seemed to have forgotten their encounter on the plane. His thin, pinched face and the sunken eyes of malnourishment had all broken into a bright smile.

"I really have to do some work," Faria said coldly. She moved away near the gathering passengers at the gate: families with kids dressed in shorts and GAP T-shirts, and women who had been in shalwar kameez before but had changed into pants, people whose skin and bags and clothes all reflected an American polish.

Sitting far from the other two, she pulled out her laptop and spread out her book and papers to do some last-minute work. She noticed that Polly had not moved away from the man. The two had their heads together, talking conspiratorially.

When the airline started to board passengers, Faria heard an altercation at the gate. They had just called for passengers who needed assistance, followed by families with small children and first-class passengers. Faria usually waited patiently till the last zone was called, as she had no bags to stow away, and she didn't enjoy the rush to get to the gate only to stand in a long line. She spotted the troublesome man Mr. Malik from the plane, in trouble again.

"Sir, it's not your turn yet to board the plane," the same stewardess spoke slowly to him, pointing at him with a finger. "Please go back to your seat till your row is called."

Faria shook her head and went back to her book. When she finally stood up to join the line, she saw Polly, with all her duty-free bags piled into one duty-free bag, standing in line next to Mr. Malik, who was, horror of horrors, carrying Polly's heavy, black bag.

When they reached the gate, there was another altercation. It was astounding, really quite an achievement, how Mr. Malik seemed able to break the rules and get in trouble in every possible way. He seemed all right with inserting himself in these situations too, immune to the insults hurled his way.

"Sir, this is two bags. Not one. This one on your shoulder. And this one. Yeah? Two. You need to make one bag."

Mr. Malik said, "Handbag. Handbag."

"No, Sir. Handbag is for ladies. This is too big for a handbag. This is two carry-ons. Yeah?"

This went on for five minutes, till the stewardess's eyes rolled back and Faria's ears turned crimson. Her face burned with embarrassment for this man, on his behalf, for the insults he had to endure from the stewardess, who kept raising her voice, jabbing at him, snarling.

Mr. Malik kept standing grandly in front of the stewardess, as if he didn't understand English, or any of the insults; her words simply slid off his slippery suit. In front of Faria's eyes, he transformed into the hundreds of Bengali men she had encountered on the streets of New York, selling hot dogs in the cold, selling newspapers in the subway station, bravely navigating the city's grid system, its snow and cold and spiraling rent; selling Bengali CDs in Jackson Heights, songs she longed to listen to, opening shops, cafés, and restaurants where she ran when she felt homesick, for samosas, paratha, chicken curry, or milk tea. Brave men with taut faces, smiling at the unknown. Mr.

Malik's gray stubble, musty suit, and torn garments all appeared to define a man ready to take on the weight of the world. His old nemesis Poppy stood next to him smiling with the same stupid, plastic expression as him, as if they both did not speak English. Faria almost smiled at their daring.

On the plane, when Faria reached her seat, Mr. Malik was already seated there. He stood up as soon as he saw her.

"Sorry, Apa. Was just chatting."

"Well, no. You seem comfortable. I'll just–"

"Did you want to talk?" Mr. Malik gestured at the space between Polly and Faria.

Polly looked at her expectantly.

"Well, I have a lot of work…and I'm exhausted, so if you two want to talk, I'm sure…"

They exchanged seats (Mr. Malik had a great window seat a few rows down), and Faria settled in next to a young man with blonde curls who said he worked in the Middle East in oil and was traveling back to see his parents for a week, in Florida. They chatted for a while, and Faria took a nap for the rest of the flight.

Faria hated the long lines at immigration at JFK Airport. Inside America, she wandered freely, as if the land belonged to her, the fresh air, the mountains, the freeways. But at borders, she waited in line like a beggar asking for entry. She did not enjoy the unpleasant exchanges at immigration, the suspense, the rude, snide comments of the immigration officers. On the way to Bangladesh, when she had shown her ticket at the counter, she kept asking, "Do you need to see my passport?" The man had been nice, pleasant, chatting with her, and he kept saying, no, no need. Then he realized she was not a US citizen.

"Bring out your passport, Ma'am," he had barked at her, his cheeks hardening.

"Well, I've been asking you if I needed to show you my passport," Faria had said coldly, lifting out her passport from her cavernous handbag with slow dignity.

The long line for people entering the US on visas wound round and round. Tired families with children inched forward a few steps at a time. Faria saw a lot of people from the plane, a glimpse here, and then there again as the line shifted forward. She saw Polly a few times, lovely in the same polka-dot dress, cool and fresh as a bride, and Mr. Malik, still in his dark suit, looking solemn.

At last, Faria was up front at the immigration counter. She waited, holding her breath, remembering that in a few months she would be married to Dan, and she would have a green card. The next time she traveled, things would be different.

The elderly man checked her passport and glanced up at her face, matching the two pictures. Faria laughed to herself, thinking how that faded, ugly photo was woeful in describing her, all the spaces she had been in, the women whose stories she had listened to, all the things she knew about what they did for money, in the dark, all the fights she had had with her mother, all the philosophical conversations with friends. The officer asked her to pose for a photo and took her fingerprints. Then he stamped her passport.

"Welcome to the US." He flashed her a smile.

"Thank you."

Faria crossed the immigration line into America, feeling a great sense of relief. Now for her luggage, customs, a taxi home. Then she spotted Polly. The young, frightened woman was standing a few rows up, at another immigration counter. The immigration officer was speaking to her roughly. She was answering in faltering English. Her heart-shaped face looked pinched and sallow in the dim light. Her eyes were small and darting. The immigration officer became sterner in his manner. Faria stopped, initially thinking she would wait to exchange phone numbers with Polly when she came out, just so the young woman would have another contact in New York, and then, with alarm as she watched the scene. She listened with growing horror to the hostile interrogation. The immigration officer asked Polly where she was going, what her husband did, if he had papers.

Faria heard scraps of their exchange; she saw the sharp head nods, the jerks, the frowns, and the tense silences.

Faria remembered the stories Polly had told her, of going to New Market on a rickshaw with her cousins, piled three on top of one another, to buy materials for curtains or dresses, in the back alley of the market, where a shopkeeper would pull a stool and say, "Sit, Apa, drink tea while I get this done." The shopkeeper's young son would bring around a tray of rattling teacups, filled with sweet milk tea. There would be happiness in the confines of the musty, airless shop. How could Polly's frightened face at immigration, her halting English, or her awkward passport photo speak of these worlds? Faria stood, her heart beating fast, her handbag weighing heavily on her shoulder. She even forgot what she was waiting for. Dan would be out of town at his parents' house party in Long Island, but he would be expecting a phone call from her. And Dan's parents had made her promise to call them as soon as she reached New York. She would have to switch on her cellphone, see if it was charged.

She saw Polly pass in front of her with two immigration officials. Faria ran up to the group.

"Where are you going?" she barked in panic.

"Apa, they are taking me to a second immigration room."

Faria wanted to ask the immigration officials what was going on, but she didn't know if that would count as obstruction of their work. She gaped at the other woman.

"It's okay, Apa. My husband warned me about it." Polly's face was grey, young and lost like a child's face again.

In a flash, the group was gone, headed toward a closed room. Faria stared after them. They disappeared inside the room, and Faria could see them through the glass. She stood irresolutely for some moments, circled around, and then finally headed down toward baggage claims, along with the train of passengers hurtling forward. She felt bad. What would happen to Polly? Would she be okay? She kept walking with the crowd, down long corridors, down escalators, up again, weighed down with worry.

At baggage claim, the belt went around and around, empty, creaking. Their plane's baggage had not arrived yet. Faria had just one small red suitcase. Others had pulled trolleys up, stationed themselves in advantageous positions. Children sat on the floor reading comic books. A young mother stood with her infant, trying to rock her to sleep. Faria stood daydreaming. Then the suitcases came cascading down. Faria was lucky enough that somehow, the red suitcase was one of the first. She hauled it expertly from the belt, landed it smoothly on the floor, and headed out the door to her home, the city in which she breathed comfortably, the city that flowed in her veins. Once she was outside, breathing the air, it was impossible not to be happy. Oh, how wonderful to be alive! Faria walked up the curb jauntily to where the yellow cabs were waiting and called a taxi home.

Acknowledgments

I want to thank all the editors of all the magazines in which these stories were first published. Without their encouragement and edits, the stories would not be as good. I want to thank my editor Juan Martinez for choosing this collection and for working tirelessly on it, making it better. Without him, there would be no book. Short stories are my first love. I started writing stories when I was a child of seven or eight, so this book means a whole life of dreams to me. Thank you to my publisher Jen Harris for publishing me. And to my husband Arif for reading and rereading stories and helping me find out what I wanted to say, when we were stuck at home during a pandemic. Thank you to my brothers Zahed and Zaki, who wrote stories with me when we were children, when we had nothing to read but one another's stories. And to my brother Zaki for giving me a diary when I could not write. That diary brought me back! And to my friend Becky Tuch, for suggesting literary magazines, for her newsletter about literary magazines, and for helping me revise a story. Without literary magazines and writers like Becky Tuch who read them and form communities around them, short stories would not exist. I want to thank my daughter Maha, who can read any text and say what needs to be done, for helping me to edit some of these stories. Lastly, I want to thank the writers who read the collection and gave blurbs. I admire their writing, and I really wanted their validation.

The following literary magazines published these select stories.

Allium, "The Frame"
Arkansas Review, "Nature"
Change Seven, "Meghalaya"
Chattahoochee Review, "Marker"

Chicago Quarterly Review, "Katy Family"
Cleaver, "Urgency"
Concho River Review, "American Cousin"
Eunoia Review, "The Limits of Speech"
Granta, "Wheels of Progress"
Hypertext, "Dreams and Memories"
Last Syllable, "Two Mothers"
Pleiades, "Three Sisters"
Prime Number Magazine, Press 53, "The Lady Doctor"
River Styx, "Patent" as "The Patent Guy"
Scoundrel Time, "The English Teacher"
Superpresent, "Confetti"
Terrain, "Camping"
The Brooklyn Review, "Cigarette"
Third Coast, "Gracious"
Valley Voices, "Next Door"

V. Joshua Adams * Mark Baumgartner * Scott Shibuya
Brown * Michael Chin * Chloe Clark * Rivka Clifton *
Brittney Corrigan * Jessica Cuello * Barbara Cully * Allison
Cundiff * Curious Theatre Branch * Neil de la Flor *
Genevieve DeGuzman * Suzanne Frischkorn * Victoria Garza
* Reginald Gibbons * Joachim Glage * Caroline Goodwin *
Brett Hanley * Kathryn Kruse * Brigitte Lewis * Jenny
Magnus * DK McCutchen * Jean McGarry * Rita Mookerjee
* Mamie Morgan * Alexis Orgera * Zach Powers * Karen
Rigby * Jo Salas * Maureen Seaton * Kristine Snodgrass *
Cornelia Spelman * Peter Stenson * Melissa Studdard *
Gemini Wahhaj * Megan Weiler * David Welch * Cassandra
Whitaker * David Wesley Williams

jacklegpress.org